FRANK YERBY:
A VICTIM'S GUILT

FRANK YERBY:
A VICTIM'S GUILT

A TRANSFORMATIVE NOVEL

BY EUGENE STOVALL

REGENT PRESS
OAKLAND, CALIFORNIA

ISBN 13: 978-1-58790-124-9
ISBN 10: 1-58790-124-2
Library of Congress Control Number: 2005930828

design: roz abraham
cover design: Raymond Holbert

REGENT PRESS
6020-A Adeline Street
Oakland, California 94608
www.regentpress.net

THIS BOOK IS A
TRANSFORMATIVE LITERARY WORK ...

formative literary work in that it furthers the basic copyright goal of promoting human knowledge. It uses materials from out-of-print works that are unavailable through normal channels to provide new insights and understandings about Frank Yerby and his books. Many of Frank Yerby's books are unavailable to some of the specific markets about which he writes. These markets heretofore have been generally unaware of his literary contributions as well as his philosophical inclinations. In addition, *Frank Yerby: A Victim's Guilt* parodies Yerby's works in order to make literary comments and criticisms which otherwise could not be understood or appreciated by markets that were not originally penetrated. In many of his books, Yerby maintained a negative opinion regarding those he characterized as being guilty of becoming victims. Fair use of his materials allows for this negative opinion to be challenged. It is the author's purpose that *Frank Yerby: A Victim's Guilt* dramatize a response to Yerby's stated opinion that an entire category of American citizens deserve to be deprived of the benefits of citizenship because they are guilty of being victims.

A WORD TO THE READER...

FRANK YERBY adopted the writing style of novelists he greatly admired: novelists of the Victorian Age. Thackeray and Dumas were two of his favorites for obvious reasons. William Thackeray was born in Calcutta of Anglo-Indian parents and Alexandre Dumas was born outside Paris, the grandson of a black slave from Santo Domingo. Other Victorian Age writers, Hawthorne, Melville, the Brontes, Dickens, Byron, Fielding, Balzac, Hugo, and Maupassant, greatly influenced Yerby as well. Yerby found that his favorite Victorian Age novelists wrote of life's realities. They dramatized realities that they had personally experienced or researched and presented these realities in novel form for the enjoyment of their readers. Yerby called his retelling of these realities his costume novel. The fun that one gets from reading Yerby's costume novels is in unraveling the mystery the costume seeks to cloak. These Victorians whether by *fate* or *free will* lived and died as they wrote. The characters and the plots were believable because the reader believed in the writer. What reader of *Don Juan* could not bond with William Lord Byron after coming to know that Byron died in the freezing mountains with a band of resistance fighters trying to secure Greek independence from Turkey? Yerby patterned his writing after Victorian Age writers who excited their readers with characters drawn from a composite of real life people who had participated in real life events that had historical significance.

Yerby says, in his introduction to *The Girl from Storyville*, that the Victorian novelist enjoyed freedom from pretense. The Victorians wrote about actual trials and triumphs, infamy and sheer horror. The latter brings Edgar Allen Poe to mind. These writers told a straightforward tale. They did not pretend that they did not know all about the events that they described. They did not contrive plots so as to motivate their characters, feeding their readers clues so that in the final chapter the author could pander to the reader's own deeply held beliefs. Yerby believed that these writers produced *The Scarlet Letter, Moby Dick, Wuthering Heights, Vanity Fair, A Christmas Carol, Moll Flanders, Don Juan, The Count of Monte Cristo,* and *A Tale of Two Cities* because they chose to speak out in their own authentic voice, explaining, clarifying, predicting and commenting, keeping the reader fully informed of everything associated with the plot. Going along for the ride, the reader shares the adventure. Yerby saves readers from having to plod through the layers of subtly plotted scenes contrived around some simple point. Yerby's novels are interesting because he invites his readers to listen in on mysterious discussions, witness strange events and learn of evil motives. He entertained his readers with different experiences and delighted them with new ideas. Frank Yerby's *An Odor of Sanctity, Floodtide, A Darkness at Ingraham's Crest, Pride's Castle* and his other twenty-nine novels leave an impression with his readers for some time afterwards. In this book, I will entertain you with three Frank Yerby tales of mystery and intrigue. These tales speak of victims with restless souls. The tales are written in the same Victorian Age style that Yerby himself uses.

Much of this book is concerned with the interests, intrigues and plights of women. Such concerns have been raised by other writers of the Victorian Age and other periods including Wollenstonecraft, Shelly, Wolff and Stein. Aphra Behn deserves special mention because the title character of her seminal work, *Oronokoo* bears a striking resemblance to Yerby's Nyasanu Hwesu Kesu, also known as Wesley Parks. But to me, the Victorian Age writer whose heart-rending stories *Family Happiness* and *The Kreutzer Sonata* truly express the victimization that women have suffered over the ages is the great Russian novelist, Leo Tolstoy. So being guided by those whose interests run parallel to mine, I will give you, dear reader, the guide you need to attempt to penetrate these mysteries and find the essential truths contained in the mind and genius of Frank Yerby.

In this book, Yerby's characters and their realities merge together. All of Yerby's original characters are playing the roles Yerby wrote for them. There is, however, one difference; *Yerby is there with them and he, too, has a role to play.* And play it he must if he is to survive and accomplish his mission. Pulled into a reality of his own making, yet having absolutely no control over it, Yerby finds himself facing the same fate he gave his characters. The goal is immortality: *the only value Yerby and his characters share in common.* Yerby will either be remembered as one of the greatest writers of the twentieth century or be relegated to relative obscurity. Yerby did not ask for all of this. He did not call to be placed in this fictional reality. Given a choice, Yerby would have preferred to remain in his Madrid hospital room where Pride Dawson found him. Yerby's own characters caused him to be sucked into this fictional reality. *They summoned him* to live in their reality, know their pressures, know their fears. When Yerby realizes what is happening, Yerby is unnerved. After all, an author suddenly waking up and finding himself in ninth-century Spain sharing the same reality as someone *who happened to be born a slave* would unnerve anyone. This is not the normal situation between the creator and the created. Once they summon him, Yerby's characters tell him that he is responsible for becoming one of the immortals. And once

Yerby is immortal he will confer immortality on them as well. How or when or whether this will happen, Yerby does not know…neither does he know he cannot control his characters, they have a significant control over him. And one of his characters, Grand Vizier Abu L'Fath Nasr, plans to kill him.

So, dear reader, if you are not already familiar with these people, at the end of this book, I have provided you with a list of all of Yerby's characters appearing in this novel. There is a list of actual historical personages and a list of minor characters that I added…characters who do not appear in any of Yerby's novels, as well.

Not having read any of Frank Yerby's novels is no barrier to fully enjoying this one. All that is required is that you bring a mind willing to be entertained. Yerby's characters wish to speak to you in a way that has exceeded even their creator's own expectations and in a way that he cannot. Yerby's own seeming lack of involvement results not from a lack of will, but a lack of control…He has no power. It's tough to know how to behave when you are no longer God. Without god-like powers over the lives of his characters, Yerby now must face danger, intrigue and drama with only his own intelligence, his own values and his own courage.

Some might judge this book by the rather glaring breakdowns in the various spy networks that play such a part in the stories you are about to read. Some secrets seemed just too commonly known to be called secrets. To the twenty-first century mind, spy craft is the ultimate level in human intelligence. So, a modern reader might well react to my descriptions of less sophisticated intelligence gathering and spy craft as not being credible. In a world of James Bond-type secret agents who seduce, bribe, lie and murder with impunity…where entire government agencies fund eavesdropping technologies, launch satellite video surveillance apparatus and compile DNA histories on total populations…and where legions of agents, counteragents, double-agents and "snitches" armed with baskets filled with money can buy and sell anyone anywhere in the world, topple governments and bankrupt economies…and where the sophisticated intelligence gathering resources provide streams of data into computer profiles on every citizen in the United States as well as the upper two-thirds of the people of the rest of the world, it might be difficult to see a bunch of household servants and slaves as a spy network. But in the ninth century there was more reliance upon cooperation than upon compulsion.

No suspension of disbelief is required here. All that is needed is the realization that the techniques of spy craft have improved significantly over the centuries. And since these earlier spy networks were unwieldy, lacking in security and often ineffective, the ruling authority might often have been aware of these *so-called* secret plots, all along. The most securely kept secret still was delivered by *word of mouth*. Writing was just beginning to be developed as a cipher. Mostly used by the Christians, written messages were effective when the information was not required right away. So dear reader, you along with the author might well enjoy knowing all the secrets. But remember, even after you know all the facts, the mysteries remain. In some cases, *the facts make them even more mysterious.*

PROLOGUE

The drawn, gaunt patient lay alone in his steel, mechanized bed crowded into a small room. The white walls boasted a solitary black crucifix as the room's only decoration. The rich, fragrant aroma of a myriad of plants and flowers almost recreated the drab hospital room into a Garden of Eden, appropriately signifying both the beginning as well as the ending of life. When he had first arrived, the patient could escape the narrow confines of his room by sitting outside in the patio attached to his room. The patio marked the patient's wealth and rank. Now all he could do was gaze eastward in the direction of the Mediterranean Sea, the coast of his adopted land that ancient African desert dwellers had called Iberia. And Frank Yerby knew he would never again see his beloved Spain, the land of Iberia that he and his wife… Blanca…called home.

The door opened and into the room strode a young woman dressed in white with a funny little starched hat perched on top of her curly, brown hair.

"And how are we feeling today, Señor Yerby?" Yerby was close to death and he knew it. All he could do in reply was to turn slightly, nod his head at the nurse and manage a little smile. Though his body was weak, Yerby's mind seethed with many unsettling thoughts. *After all that I have done, is this all there is?* he wondered with sadness. *I have examined everything life has to offer: love and glory, debauchery and heresy, kindness and courage, faith and cruelty, valor and suffering, goodness and treachery, beauty and evil. I did not submit to convention, nor yield to standards or rules, I wrote about life. And now that it is over...is there truly nothing left for me?*

These thoughts dragged from Yerby not only his deepest fears, but also his profoundest sense of guilt. *What have I done to merit such a fate? What wrong have I committed to be punished so? How can my examination of human nature,* he wondered, *with all its frailties and weaknesses have been wrong?* Yerby lay in his bed desiring his reward, his honors, his recognition. He was troubled more by the lack of recognition at the end then by the end itself. *This is a lonely unmerited end,* he thought to himself.

Yerby's prodigious outflow of literary gems could only be exceeded by Yerby's own inestimable belief in his own worth. Yerby had always believed that the world was divided between gods and men. Though he might not be a god, he certainly was no ordinary man. Yet even as he ridiculed ordinary men's creation of the gods in a feeble attempt to ward off death, Yerby now found that he was no more immune to this particular fear than any other mortal. His works, Yerby thought to himself, somehow were supposed to proceed him down that dark road, lighting his way. When he faced his own mortality, Yerby thought the praises and honors bestowed upon him for his creative genius would be ringing in his ears. But alas, there were no honors and no recognition. It was as if this work did not even exist. Deep in his mind, a little voice spoke out, "Possibly you should seek forgiveness."

"Is there some reason I must seek forgiveness?" Yerby roared at the little voice. "Forgiveness? Forgiveness for what? For leaving wife, children, country even race, to follow my own will, my own mind?

FRANK YERBY:

That's the price mediocrity must pay to greatness." Yerby thought. *But look what I accomplished. I wrote thirty-three novels…every one of them a moving, passionate, engaging, irresistible, brilliant, lucid, entertaining description of Life…. Why should I feel guilty?*

"Why shouldn't you feel guilty?" a husky voice spoke out. "You damned your own soul to hell, didn't you!" Dimly, a trail of tobacco smoke lazily rose from behind a potted fern. Following it with his mind's eye, Yerby spied a large gentleman, lounging indifferently in a straight-back chair, staring back at him. As he gazed at his visitor, Yerby could see icy contempt clearly expressed on his visitor's face. The gentleman was dressed in a Prince Albert frock coat in the fashion set by his Royal Highness, consort to Queen Victoria, in the late nineteenth century. A white shirt with wing collars starched into knifeblade sharpness with puffed up Ascot scarf held in place by a glittering stick pin gave the visitor a look of distinction. Instantly the visitor's identity exploded into Yerby's consciousness. "Dawson! Pride Dawson!" Yerby blurted, thinking how strange it was to be visited by the central character from *Pride's Castle*, one of his better known books. As a matter of fact, *Pride's Castle* had become a television movie.

"Right you are, Frank," the American Yankee said.

"But how did you get here?" Yerby asked.

"They sent me to bring you back."

"Bring me back…where? why? Who sent you?"

"You've gotta set things right….Come along, now."

"You mean my time…"

"Oh no, no, you're not going to die…not yet. You've still got time to set things right….But you must accompany me, now."

. . .

Yerby felt a not altogether unpleasant sensation, as though his body was pulling inward upon itself. The room dissolved into a blur of disintegrating images until nothing remained of the shapes and all the colors began merging into one another, accompanied by harmonies sounding like a chorus of angels welcoming him back to his past as well as into his future.

Then Yerby found himself outside a familiar, fortress-like building squatting upon a broad expanse of swamp land. He knew that they were no longer in Spain, but in New York City's late nineteenth-century urban sprawl, where Yerby could hear the murky Hudson River gurgling off to the right. The fortress rose up into a great monument of soaring towers, fantastic spires and heavy battlements, like a medieval castle built to withstand attacks from rebellious serfs or feuding nobles.

"Welcome to my home," Pride said to Frank Yerby, who was now restored to complete physical and mental health. The two of them crossed over a ridiculous little drawbridge spanning a small ditch which ran around only one side of Pride's Castle. As they approached the entrance, massive wooden doors opened and a liveried butler escorted the master and his guest through the entrance and into a great hall. The interior design of the castle was overwhelming in its garish ostentation. Gilt fretwork and bas-relief covered the walls, enormous crystal chandeliers clung to the red plush high ceilings. Great oaken furniture in a Moorish design like something out of the Arabian Nights sank into thick carpeting. It was the décor found in Hattie Hamilton's sporting establishment in New Orleans' Storyville district.

Crossing into the hall, Pride Dawson motioned his guest over to two massive easy chairs positioned in front of a great stone fireplace.

"Frank, have you ever thought about what would happen to us when you are no longer around?"

"Who are you talking about?" Yerby asked, marveling at his renewed vitality and strength.

"All of us…your characters," replied Dawson. "Don't you realize that once you damned your own soul to hell, you damned us to oblivion. They will forget all about us...it will be like we never existed." Dawson gave Yerby an icy look indicating his contempt not only for Yerby, but for all coloreds. "We don't want that, Frank; we want to continue to live and be remembered. No one has forgotten Candide or Don Quixote or Lear or D'Artagnan or Edmond Dantes or any of the other famous creations of the literary world. Neither does Stephen Fox, Duncan Childers, Murielle Duclos, Ariston nor my own sweet Sharon O'Neill wish to be forgotten either. We want our share of that same immortality these others enjoy. We don't want to be consigned to the dark world of forgetfulness. We will not let this happen, Frank. We intend that you do something about it." With that, Pride rose from his seat and abruptly left the room.

· · ·

Yerby was not alone for long. He found himself seated at an immense dining table in a great banquet hall. At a number of smaller tables sat a multitude of persons of every color, shape and size. The diners were dressed in every conceivable costume. Some men wore ruffled white shirts, starched until they stood out rigidly from the dark cutaway coats with mother of pearl buttons and tight, form-fitting trousers with boots polished to a sheen reflecting every light in the room. Some women dressed in brocaded gowns of ancient French lace cut in extreme decollete, their hair falling luxuriantly about their shoulders. There were exotic enchantresses, wearing half veils as transparent as spring water extending from just below the eyes to a little beyond their chins and wearing short jackets, embroidered with gold and jewels, opening over their breasts and exposing the flimsiest of silken gauze above a bare midriff. There were men as well as women wearing white powdered wigs and silk stockings. Others wore short tunics covered by rich red togas, and still others appeared in army fatigues and combat boots. All the guests seemed happy, pleased that

Frank Yerby had joined the banquet. Many of them looked up to Yerby with genuine affection. These people were his own. They were the characters of his costume novels.

All around the hall, an army of servants continually served platters piled high with chicken, lamb, and beef garnished with every imaginable vegetable. Tureens of soups and bowls of salads and breads found their way to the tables of the happy diners. Afterwards, tbe servants tempted the diners with serving trays filled with pastries, cakes, candied fruit and cold and hot puddings. At the center of each table, a sculpted swan with vintage champagne arcing from its beak kept the banquet guests in a lively mood.

"You see how happy they are to see you, Frank," Pride said, leaning over to the guest of honor. "We don't want to lose you. So we're here to help you resolve some issues. We want to help you rescue your own soul and, in the process, rescue ours as well."

"How can you help me rescue my soul?" Yerby asked, bemused by the suggestion. "I don't even have a soul." Yerby had been telling his readers for years that he, himself, did not believe in an afterlife nor did he believe that he had a soul to enjoy it. Everything that could be experienced and enjoyed was in this life alone. "If you don't get it now," Yerby believed, "you'd never get it."

"You believe that in the beginning came the *Word*, don't you?" Pride's comment was an assertion rather than a question…an assertion Yerby could hardly deny.

"Yes, I suppose I do," Yerby said carefully, not wanting to fall into any logical trap.

"So you admit," Pride continued, "that words give life."

"Yes," Yerby agreed reluctantly, "since I am having this discussion with Pride Dawson, a character from one of my novels, I must agree that the word can become life."

"Then why would you write as you did in *The Voyage Unplanned* that your soul, while residing in hell, will retain the absolute arrogance that you possessed in your present life? Why would you say that, Frank?"

Yerby felt a chill passing over the soul that he didn't know he had and he shuddered. The idea continued to creep into his mind until he grasped the full realization of his disbelief. He had condemned his own soul. Why had he made such a statement? What fiendish urge motivated this curse that he had laid on himself?

Yerby had always been a healthy skeptic about Christianity. He admitted to agnostic and even atheist views. But this condemnation of his own soul, now that he fully understood his act, was one of those foolhardy aspects of Yerby's nature that had always caused him problems. Years earlier, Yerby had been warned not to blaspheme the gods or he would suffer a terrible death. But in his arrogance, Yerby believed he had protected himself. Yerby thought that his escape to Spain and initiation into the international clique of the rich and famous would give him the recognition he desired. Apparently, his initiation was a hoax and Frank Yerby was no more accepted as an equal among white Europeans than he was among white Americans.

"So you remember, Frank?" Pride smiled as his guest squirmed uncomfortably.

"It wasn't enough that you damned your own soul," a voice shouted out from among the diners, "you criticized the Church for destroying those thirteenth-century heretics, the Cathars, in the Albigensian Crusade. And finally you had the unmitigated gall to write that abomination about our precious Lord, Himself...." The voice came from one of the diners, Father Shannon, a Catholic priest and pastor of New York's Trinity Cathedral.

"I think Father Shannon takes a dim view of your book, *Judas, My Brother*, Frank," Pride said, recognizing and enjoying Yerby's discomfiture.

"Enough of that!" Nathan ben Yehudah shouted out. "Frank told the truth, priest, whether you like it or not. I'm here, I'm a

Jew and Christ was a Jew. Christ followed the religion of Abraham and Moses no matter what you say. It was the Romans, and those Jews who, betraying their own people to serve Rome, who crucified Him…not the Jews who followed and respected Him. I'm here to support you, Frank." So saying, the *thirteenth apostle* from Yerby's *Judas, My Brother* raised his fist defiantly.

"But you don't like to follow the rules, do you, Frank?" hooted Pride Dawson. "So now you feel like the 'golden ass'!"

"Well I think he's got a guilty conscience because he just doesn't like women!" a female voice shouted from another part of the banquet hall.

Yerby turned to see where the voice came from. Scanning the crowd, he saw her.

She was slim enough to be a professional model. Her face was El Greco, even including his distortions which her many admirers in *The Old Gods Laugh* claimed enhanced her beauty. Her mouth was wide, full-lipped, tender. Her face contorted mystically into the tribal fetish of some long forgotten Indian god. Nine men out of ten would have found her ugly, but Muneca embodied the bewitching beauty that inspired the gods who ruled over Central America's ancient Mayan civilization. Muneca sat there, drawing him closer with those enormous, long-lashed, slanting eyes.

"In your books, Frank," Muneca continued, "women are tortured. They must face an unending series of threats and torments. You give us more sorrow than we can bear. You take away our sons, our husbands, and you leave us emptiness. If we fail in virtue, we fall to the depths of your hell without any redemption available to us. When we love, our love is rejected and distorted. Never is our love sufficient for the men whose love is but a reflection of their own inflated egos. Nobles are chivalrous…they protect women. There is no nobility in your soul, Frank. You are not Cervantes; you hate women. Is it, Frank, that those fair, handsome boys that you always write about appeal far more to you than women?"

"Is that true, Frank?" cackled Gbochi, the little homosexual from Yerby's *The Dahomean* who sold his own brother into slavery, his little pig eyes darting from Muneca to Yerby. "Do you really prefer men…If so, I can make your trip to hell very delightful."

Pride barely contained his laughter. Yerby remained quiet but his face burned.

"Of course it's true," Muneca whispered. "Look at that poor vegetable, Fanny Turner, over there." She indicated a thin, drabbly dressed women staring vacantly into space, never moving, completely unaware of her surroundings. In *The Girl From Storyville*, Fanny had been driven into a despair that resulted in a complete mental breakdown and the loss of her sanity. "And just think of that savage beating that Iolanthe suffered at the hands of her own husband…Enzio Siniscola, just because she was in love with another man. As I think of all the other women that you have turned into prostitutes, cheats and faithless wives, Frank, it becomes clear that all women have suffered at your hands. You are a beast. I wish to see you suffer hell's torments at the hands of the avenging gods of the old."

"I do not hate women!" Yerby cried out to the amusement of the gathering, many of whom filled their glasses and offered Yerby a mock toast. And for several minutes, the banquet hall became quite raucous with shouts of condemnation and praise raining down on the author's head from every table.

"I do not hate women!" Yerby cried out again. "If I hated women, I could not have told the story about Giselle whom I met at a party in Paris."

The crowd quieted and Yerby continued. "…she was all alone… Her social climbing mother had tormented her and practically disowned her." He looked out over the diners as his mind drifted back to Paris, 1954, to a party given by some friends of friends in a huge and mostly empty apartment on the Left Bank the way he described it in *Speak Now.* "Giselle sat on a rumpled sofa all alone like a motherless child, tears slowly flowing down her taffy colored cheeks. She was a cute little Afro-French girl. She wore the first Afro I had ever seen. But I'm certain that Giselle didn't know it was an Afro. She simply didn't know where, nor did she have the money, to get her hair straightened."

"What is wrong?" Yerby remembered asking the forlorn figure as he stepped across the room and slid down onto the sofa next to her.

"Parle pas l'anglais" Giselle responded, pausing just long enough from her own personal sorrows to display the linguistic pride that is so typical of the French.

So he asked her again in his halting, crippled and childlike French, "What is it that arrives to you, my little cabbage?" Yerby thought his French was passable; the young woman found Yerby's French hilarious. The American was just funny enough for Giselle to trust. She told him that, in her youth, her mother was engaged to a handsome black from the Ivory Coast and she, Giselle, was the result. Now her mother was married to a member of *la haute bourgeoisie français.* And, yesterday, having to host a social function for her husband, Giselle's mother had given Giselle a maid's uniform. Her mother demanded that Giselle wear the outfit for the evening. Her mother wanted to avoid explaining the presence of the thick-lipped, kinky haired miss in her household. Refusing, Giselle left home with a broken heart.

Giselle was so charming, so sweet and innocent, Yerby remembered, that he had entertained the appealing idea of taking her to his home by the Vincennes Gate. She did not have a *sou,* nor anywhere to go.

"How is it possible that your mind can turn your pickup plan into some proof that you like women?" asked Muneca, as if she were lecturing a spoiled child.

"A tall, blond, exceedingly handsome young man with whom

she was in love showed up," Yerby completed the story out loud. "And that was that!" Then he thought to himself, *But it had the makings of a great novel. How a French woman who, in her youth had been a flaming liberal, retreated—or, better still, was beaten down over the years—into such a bone-marrow mean reactionary. And, in order to conceal her own guilt and shame, she had sunk to degrading her own daughter. Man, all that guilt.*

"And the fact that you once considered having a 'one night stand' with a dark-skinned woman is supposed to convince us that you like women!" spat Muneca. "Bah!"

"I have a question." The quiet voice spoke an impeccable French with a slight Southern drawl. Yerby had remained in Europe for thirty-seven years after this incident with Giselle. Now Yerby's French was as good as his Spanish and his Spanish was better than his English because he could make himself understood in Barcelona as well as Madrid. Yerby recognized the speaker as his old friend and brother, Harry Forbes. Good ole Harry, Yerby thought, if anyone can understand my situation, it will be Harry Forbes. Wounded in Vietnam, Harry played with a jazz band at a French night spot operated by North Africans in Paris. He, too, had been raised below the Mason-Dixon line but had emigrated from the United States to take up permanent residence in France. But unlike Yerby, Harry Forbes was so black that, in Yerby's words in *Speak Now*, his skin shone with the hue of blue velvet.

"I wanna know, Frank," Harry continued, "why you object so strenuously to the use of the word 'black' when it refers to the race of black people or black Americans, yet you use the word profusely when describing individuals like me?"

"What do you mean?" Yerby reeled from this unexpected attack. Yerby believed that race was a part of everything and had little to do with anything. He usually avoided the subject like the plague when dealing with white folks. But like so many other black Americans with an acute identity crisis, Yerby seemed to believe that he was better than most other blacks. Maybe it had to do with his light-colored skin. "I've far more Irish blood than Negro," Yerby often said, leaving the impression with whites and blacks alike that he harbored a great deal of contempt for his own people. But, in this situation, like so many other talented blacks, Yerby had no real defense from Harry Forbes' attack. Yerby believed, or rather hoped, that other black men, especially someone like Harry Forbes, were supposed to comfort and support him. Didn't they both suffer from a prejudicial white world? But Harry was in no mood to give Frank Yerby any support.

"You've got no problem calling me black," Forbes retorted. "You characterize all of the Moors as blacks, as well as calling Africans blacks. You even refer to the slaves on the plantations as blacks. Anytime you want to be derogatory or negative you use the term 'black'. But when you were asked—rather begged—to use the term 'black' in a positive way of describing the race, you absolutely refused. Why is that Frank? Do you hate black people who have black skin?"

Yerby reacted as if he had been slapped. *What if it were true?* Yerby asked himself. *I cannot abide the term, 'black.' To use 'black' to describe a racially mixed, multihued minority is an abuse of language. To call the young Georgia legislator, Julian Bond, Congressman Adam Clayton Powell... Senator Edward Brooke, 'blacks' is quite simply to reduce a descriptive adjective to meaninglessness.* Yerby identified with the extremely light-skinned Negroes who held political office and were considered political leaders. Furthermore, Yerby considered the controversy over the use of "black" in English, as against Negro, which means "black" in Spanish, an exercise in a semantic irrelevancy. Yet at the same time, Yerby seemed bothered not at all by the use of the descriptive adjective "white" to describe dark-skinned Arabs, brown-skinned Spaniards, or pink-skinned Scandinavians.

Stung by what he considered Harry Forbes' betrayal, Yerby blurted out: "I am not a racist; I'm a writer! I write novels that people will read and enjoy. I do not write to change their minds or to win them over to a cause. I write to bring to my readers' otherwise uneventful, boring lives, a sense of adventure and excitement. They want to read about courage; they want a glimpse of those wretched souls tortured and tormented by fears and desires. My readers appreciate how goodness and valor banishes evil and cruelty. They want to see Divine Providence in action and they want to know that Justice prevails, that their fate is malleable and that their soul lives forever."

But Harry Forbes was merciless. "Sounds awfully noble," he smirked, "particularly since you don't even believe in your own soul. Is that why your statement on the condition of blacks in America is that Africans sold themselves into slavery and that colored women negotiated with slave masters so that the white men would have willing mistresses?—or are these just additional, as you put it, semantic irrelevancies?"

"You want me to be a Negro writer and take on the black man's burden, but I am just a writer…." Yerby's voice trailed off and Harry Forbes was no longer listening.

"No, by God," Victor Drury thundered, "you are not just a writer, you betrayed your working class background by declaring Marxism and Marxists evil in *Pride's Castle* and now you make your home in Spain, a land that has become the symbol of fascist treachery, deceit and contempt for democracy all over the world."

Yerby closed his eyes and wondered how he could have caused such controversy, such bitterness. "Frank," Pride Dawson whispered softly, "you must go and learn about yourself. Go…."

PART I

CHAPTER ONE

Staring at her reflection in the mirror, Lady Sumayla considered how everything still reminded her of him, her Goth, Alaric, the father of her only son, Prince al-Kamil ibn Karim. She was pleased that she had lost none of her enchanting, if subtle, charm. *The more intelligent a woman is,* she thought to herself, *the more charming she should be.* Certainly Sumayla's charm as much as her intelligence, not to mention pure, dumb luck, all were responsible for her rise from one of the thousands of slaves in Córdoba to the mother of a prince of the realm. And her son was not just any prince, Kamil was the prince who could possibly become the next Emir. And if Kamil did become Emir of Córdoba, it would be Sumayla's crowning achievement. To make this impossible dream a reality, Sumayla was willing to sacrifice anything…everything. As Emir of Córdoba, Kamil would rule not only over the entire land known in the romantic Latin dialect as España, Spain, but also over all of North Africa, including Egypt, as well.

Centuries earlier, the Moors had exploded across the African sands and up into the Iberian Peninsula, wresting control of Spain from the Goths. But neither the Goths' Arian pretensions to racial superiority nor their faith in Christianity prevented the establishment of an Islamic rule stretching from the Pyrenees across the Mediterranean Sea, now an Islamic lake, all the way to the Tigris and Euphrates rivers and into India. With Córdoba as their capital, subject only to the Caliphate of Damascus, the Emirs ruled over all inhabitants of the Islamic empire from Spain to Egypt, imposing an Islamic world order in strict accordance with the laws of the Holy Koran.

Yet, even as the Emir ruled over all of Spain, the Goths, descendants of savage Germanic barbarians, remained secure within their feudal castles and lands that dotted the entire Iberian peninsula. The Goths dutifully paid the Emir's taxes and in return, the Emir allowed the Goths to worship their Christian God and recognized their hereditary rights to Spanish properties and chattels. In addition, the Emir's own police, the al-Khurs, protected the Goths' daughters and wives from molestation and assault…a protection only the Moorish nobility enjoyed. Al-Rahman II, the reigning Emir, prided himself on his moderate and peaceful reign. In keeping with the highest principles of Islam, al-Rahman II bestowed civil liberties on all his citizens. He maintained fair and impartial courts, administered by judges, known as *cadis*, chosen especially for their knowledge of the law. Christians, Jews and Muslims alike enjoyed the blessings of civilized society under the moderate rule of al-Rahman II, Emir of Córdoba.

Not that the Moors abolished slavery, brutality or violence. The lives of the lower classes, not to mention the slaves, were a living hell. But for the noble classes, the Emir established expectations of civilized behavior that made life pleasurable for Christian, Jewish and Muslim elites. The manners of his court were the measure by which Emir al-Rahman II wished to be judged. But even while the Moors fancied themselves the culture bearers of an advanced civilization, the Goths watched, waited and prepared for their opportunity to reclaim control of the land. Christianity, which maintained its claim to being the only true religion, watched for its opportunity to attack and destroy Islam. *Has fate deemed that I play some role in the re-emergence of Christian rule in Spain?* Lady Sumayla asked herself wryly, still staring at herself in the mirror. *But fate is always complicated. Yet complications are where the opportunities lie.* Then her thoughts turned once again to her son, Prince Kamil, and how upset she was with him. Impatiently, the Lady Sumayla rang a bell, summoning her personal house servant. Immediately, Yazmin, whose face had seen more than sixty seasons, appeared. "Has he arrived yet?" the princess asked the servant sternly without even turning her head.

"No, milady," came the ready answer, ready even before the question had been posed, with just the barest hint of impatience...or was it impertinence? Whichever it was, as long as Yazmin had been a slave, she knew better than to allow her mask of humility to slip. Beatings and even beheadings were the punishments for slaves who did not remember their place. There was nothing or no one so replaceable in the entire empire as a slave. Even though she had been a slave, the Lady Sumayla imitated the behavior of all Moorish nobility in the ninth century A.D. She tolerated absolutely no disrespect from her slaves. Especially since she had been a slave, she knew that behavior must coincide with the established order which exerts complete domination over the mind and body of a slave. If it did not, the slave soon might become master.

"There's no reason for Prince Kamil not to have come by now," Lady Sumayla observed, petulantly.

The servant held her tongue; she knew her mistress expected no reply. Anything said now might result in a beating that her ancient body might have a difficult time surviving.

"Was my message delivered to him as I instructed?" the Lady Sumayla asked.

"Yes, milady...I will bring Prince Kamil to your chambers as soon as he appears," the old crone replied.

I must be patient..., Sumayla thought to herself, *if it is Allah's will that we succeed, when Kamil is Emir, we will control these scheming Christians. I will put Alaric over all the Christians in Spain and end their scheming, once and for all.* But politics was not the only interest the black princess had in Alaric Teudisson, whom the Moors called Aizun. Lady Sumayla still loved him. Nasr and Sumayla planned to seize power through a military coup and the extermination of the present Emir and his entire family. But the plan rested upon their absolute control over Kamil. As a matter of fact, one of the subtle power struggles between Nasr and Sumayla was based upon who had more control over Kamil. Sumayla was so confident in the control she had over Kamil, she was already developing her schemes to reduce Alaric to a similar state of dependence. After all she had tricked him once before when he got her pregnant with Kamil. Once Kamil was the Emir, she could give Alaric complete control over the Christian power. And then Sumayla would have more control over him than either his wife or his daughters. Alaric would become hers.

The thought of having Alaric completely in her power made Lady Sumayla tingle with pleasure. But she quickly stirred from her daydream. How was she going to control Alaric when she could not even control her own son. She had not seen him in over a week now. Kamil ignored all her efforts to reach him. The terrible rumors about Kamil and the Emir's harem continued to reach her through her spy network. If these rumors were true, it could mean not only his life...but hers as well was in danger. "My son, my son, where are you?" she sighed, giving in to the worries of a mother that should never concern a princess. "Please come home to me."

As Lady Sumayla continued to gaze at herself in her mirror, she realized what a precarious situation her ambitions had taken her to. This was a dangerous game she played. *Are these dreams and ambitions really mine?* she asked herself. *...or are they the goals and ambitions of my creator's?* And putting her face into her hands, she whispered to herself, *They are not my ambitions, bah! They are my fate. What choice have I had?* She had no choice, she realized. She had been born a black slave! She was a victim of the fate that her creator, Frank Yerby, gave her.

Lady Sumayla knew better than any that as a writer, Yerby had neither pity nor piety. So she didn't know whether to hate him for creating her a black slave, or to love him for giving her a superior intelligence and incredible memory. *But soon I will call this Frank Yerby to task here in Córdoba,* she smiled to herself. *Hadn't Abulafia promised her and hadn't she promised Nasr?* In actuality, it was Nasr who demanded that Sumayla produce Frank Yerby. In an unguarded moment, she had let it slip to Nasr that the Jewish mystic, Abulafia, believed that Sumayla had the powers of the *Shekhinah* who could exploit the link between creator and created. "Bring that writer to me!" Nasr had commanded.

Nasr's demands had become familiar to Sumayla by now. She possessed a great storehouse of knowledge. Blessed with superior intelligence and a prodigious memory, she learned all she knew as a reader in the copy house of her master, the bookseller Horeth ibn al-Jatib. Under Horeth's strict tutelage, Sumayla learned Romance, Latin and Greek in addition to her native Arabic. At fifteen years of age, she could recite the Koran from memory. Yet, with all this talent and knowledge, Sumayla was only a slave…a valuable slave, but a slave nonetheless. It was only through her fortuitous relationship with Nasr that she was able to obtain her freedom…or more accurately, to exchange one master for another, for truly she had never tasted freedom. For even after achieving the exalted status of princess of the realm, Sumayla was not free. In ninth-century Spain, women were set upon, beaten, tortured, starved and killed with impunity by any man at all. Even with all her wealth and influence, she dared not venture outside her palace without a large armed guard and covered from head to foot. Not only was she a woman, she was a black woman, a she-thing, despised even by other women not of her race. What she shared with other women was the need to feel safe, to be secure, to be rid of that mind-numbing, overpowering, hysterical fear that haunted all women, no matter their station, no matter their religion, no matter their husband. No matter the Peace of the Prophet or any other kind of peace for that matter. So she conspired and plotted for the ultimate power...control of the throne itself. She lived to see the day when her son, Prince al-Kamil ibn Abd al-Karim, would become Emir of Córdoba.

Breaking into Sumayla's reveries, Yazmin once more appeared. "Yes, Yazmin," the black princess asked. "What is it?"

"There is a strange person in the reception hall, milady!"

"Well, how did he get there...who let him in? Why are you troubling me?"

"He is a foreigner, by the looks of him, milady. The guards are watching him. His dress is... peculiar. No one saw him enter, but he has no weapons. He just stands there, speaking a strange tongue. But he seems to understand when I speak to him. Should I have him thrown out?"

"No," Sumayla replied, anticipation in her voice. "Leave him there undisturbed, I will attend him shortly."

Entering her reception hall, Lady Sumayla found the strange visitor gaping about. His clothing did not depict nobility, his head was bare and his hair close-cropped. His open faced shirt, leather jacket and Italian-cut trousers displayed a simplicity and functionality in clothing that would only become commonplace among the nobility in the last decades of the twentieth century. By the touch of grey around his temples and sprinkled in the goatee that gave Yerby a somewhat dashing look, Sumayla judged Yerby to be in his forties. He wore a strange device across his face, with a transparent covering over each of his eyes. Yes, she thought to herself, he is the one. And in a low, husky voice, she said, "Welcome, Frank Yerby. I was told to expect you."

"Where am I?" Frank wondered out loud. His eyes wandered about the hall, with its immense marble pillars supporting a high vaulted ceiling. Intricate designs, arabesques and carvings decorated the walls. In the middle of the hall, a fountain sprayed a fine stream of water into the air from cleverly designed fish leaping from the fountain's center. Cushions, ottomans, tables and chairs were arranged throughout. Platters of fruit and sweetmeats sat upon sideboards on either side. *This is a palace, of that I am certain*, Frank thought to himself. "Where am I? Who are you?" he repeated once more in Spanish.

"You are in my home," Lady Sumalya replied. "This is the palace of the late Prince Abd al-Karim ibn al-Hixim, uncle to Abd al-Rahman II, Emir of Córdoba, Royal Seneschal of the Cailph of Bagdad and Ruler of all the land from the Pyrenees Mountains in the north across the Mediterranean Sea to the mouth of the Nile and the lands of Egypt in the South." Ordinarily, Frank would not have given Sumayla a second look. Yet, he felt himself irresistibly drawn to this Moorish princess whose dusky skin color could disguise neither her stately presence nor her subtle beauty. "I am the Lady Sumayla, widow of Prince al-Karim, Mr. Yerby" she continued, "...or shall I call you Frank? It seems so awkward to be speaking face to face with one's creator."

"Ah, you are Lady Sumayla, of *An Odor of Sanctity*."

"Very good, Frank," the princess continued, getting right to the point, "do you know why we sent for you?"

Recalling his discussion with Pride Dawson and the others, Yerby replied, "It has something to do with some of you characters from my books wanting to continue living."

"Not just wanting to live…wanting to achieve…wanting to excel. I want my son to become Emir…and I need your help."

Yerby tried to imagine the circumstances that could produce this reality, but it was beyond his ability to comprehend. He wanted to dismiss the Lady Sumayla, this palace and this reality out of hand. What was happening was not possible. But here he was. So Yerby did what he had so often called upon his own readers to do: suspended his disbelief and followed the Lady Sumayla to a small audience chamber.

In reality, Lady Sumayla appeared not so much as a Moorish princess as a high priestess of the Eleusian Mysteries directing him, as one of her hierophants, to do her bidding. And despite everything, it was eerie how comfortable and natural this all felt, as if this experience were a natural event. Yerby felt no anxieties or disorientation. "Wasn't it Sophocles who said that 'Thrice happy are they of men who looked upon these rites 'ere they go to Hades house, for they alone have true life'?" Yerby asked himself out loud.

"Are you referring to the Eleusian Mysteries, Frank?" Lady Sumayla asked.

"Yes," replied Yerby.

"I thought so," she observed. "That's a rather apt way to put it."

"Put what?" Yerby asked.

"To put the reason you are here. To put the task you must perform for yourself as well as the task we have for you," Sumayla replied.

"And what task do you have for me?" Yerby asked.

"We want you to tell us the future," she said demurely. "We want to know whether our plans for Kamil will be successful."

"If I may say so, Your Ladyship," Yerby began, shifting uncomfortably on his pillowed ottoman, "this seems to be a rather strange request, especially considering it comes from one of my own creations. I have a difficult time believing in immortality. So I don't see how I can give you something I don't have."

"I am not asking for immortality, Frank," she said to him. "I'm offering it."

"How can you offer me immortality?" Yerby scoffed.

"The same way I summoned you here," Sumayla replied keeping her attention focused on him. "You wouldn't have been the first writer forced to bend to the superior will of his creation."

"What!" Yerby snorted. "Superior will. How can a fictional character in one of my books have a will superior to mine? How are you going to force me to act against my own will?"

Sumayla gazed at him and a flood of memories poured into Yerby's mind. Then he had a vision of Sherlock Holmes forcing Arthur Conan Doyle to resurrect the master detective from his watery grave at Reichenbach Falls.

Lady Sumayla smiled at Yerby's discomfiture. "Did anything come to mind?" she asked with feigned distraction.

"Yes...," Yerby said somewhat confused. "You must be referring to Arthur Conan Doyle who killed off his literary creation, Sherlock Holmes. Doyle wanted to rid himself of Holmes forever. Yet three years later, Doyle was forced to bring him back to life once again. But, how do you know about this?"

"I don't," Sumalya responded, "you do. Tell me more."

"As I recall, Doyle was interested in all kinds of practices," Yerby observed, "including spiritualism and reincarnation."

"Ah hah," Lady Sumayla laughed. "So you are aware of characters who have been able to influence their creators?"

"Arthur Conan Doyle had delved into all matters of awareness. He continually sought answers to questions others were too frightened to ask, such as: What happens after death?" Yerby began to realize that he was involved in a battle of wits with this black woman; and he was losing.

"I'm the wrong person to ask about these matters," Yerby quickly continued. "I don't believe in such things. I don't believe that anyone who is emotionally dependent upon myth, legend or dogma knows anything at all."

"You believe you've had a successful career, don't you, Frank?" Sumayla knew how vain Yerby was about his work.

Yerby nodded.

"How do you judge your success?"

"By my work, of course," Yerby answered.

"Then what's the matter with you, Frank? You've written some great stuff. Are you so lacking in pride and ambition that you would allow your life's work to be ignored and consigned to the dustbin of obscurity so that even your own children will have forgotten you ever existed!" Yerby winced. "So you want to return to that hospital room in Madrid and die, not be heard of again? Are you afraid to die, Frank?"

Sumayla exposed Yerby's secret fear. And even though her touch was light, Yerby became completely unmanned. Later in his life, Yerby had begun to take risks. He drove racing cars, jumped out of airplanes, all to prove his manhood or to savor a life that would be all too short.

"Oh, I know you think you're facing your death bravely. But weren't you lying in your hospital bed wondering if this was all there was? Trying to be brave, but no closer to the truth than those same church-going 'believers' you seem to despise? Aren't you here with us now, despite your monumental arrogance, Mr. Frank Yerby, to see whether or not your creation can give you what you have denied to yourself: immortality?"

Yerby sat there, undone. Sumayla set his mind warring against itself. His doubts, fears and just plain ignorance were battling his own superstitions, beliefs and lost religious faith. Yerby often mimicked Socrates by stating that he knew that he knew nothing. But Yerby really believed that he was quite intelligent. He thought it was everyone else who knew nothing, But this experience with Lady Sumayla had stripped Yerby of that particular piece of arrogance. She had exposed Yerby's illusions and shocked him out of his smugness. Now he knew, in fact, that he really didn't know anything. Furthermore, there were others who actually had superior knowledge. And these others included some of his own characters.

"You are not compelled to give up your disbelief in God," Lady Sumayla continued as tactfully as possible, "you can continue as before, keeping an open mind and learning from your experiences. We need you because you open up possibilities that cannot exist for us without you. But we open up possibilities for you, as well. Continue with us, not as the arrogant fool you were, but as a person believing in his own abilities. Allow your own intelligence to give you the strength to face your own death."

Yerby sat listening; it was the only wise thing he could do… actually he had no other alternative.

"Your belief in your own intelligence ultimately is the only faith there is. Don't give it up. Not yet…we need you to believe in yourself so that the world will believe in us, in our struggles, in our voices, in our truth. Penetrate the dark with the light of your own intelligence…the power of your awareness."

"What would you have me do?" Yerby asked, quietly.

Lady Sumayla quickly answered, "I need your help. You can see the future and guide me in my great task."

Just at that moment, a stir among the servants began and a tall, muscular Negro strode into the antechamber where Sumayla had led Frank to be away from unsafe ears and whispering lips.

"Kamil!" Lady Sumayla shouted as she raced over to her handsome son. "Where have you been? I have been so very worried."

"Hello, Mother," the handsome prince said, approaching his mother after giving her a short bow of respect and fidelity. Yerby noticed that Kamil's coppery skin fairly glowed with color, a combination of his Gothic and African lineage. Kamil's emerald green eyes made the contrast with his skin all the more striking.

Many maidens, high-born as well as common, would do whatever they could to attract this young man's attention, Yerby thought to himself. No one, other than those who chose expediency over truth, could have doubted that Alaric, the son of the Gothic Lord of Tarrabella, Teudis, was Prince Kamil's father.

"Kamil," Lady Sumayla said to her son, "why have you ignored me for so long? You know I worry about you."

"You worry more about Nasr's plans for Cordova, I fear," the young punk said to himself.

Córdoba, the largest center of learning and culture outside of Istanbul in the mid-ninth century A.D. boasted over 200, 000 houses and 700 public baths serving over a million souls. The capital's workshops employed 13,000 weavers, armorers and leather workers who produced goods of renowned skill and craftsmanship. Thousands flocked to Córdoba daily to learn the trades valued throughout the civilized world. Merchants and farmers from all over Spain, from Galicia and Asturias to Andalusia and Estremadura, sell fruits and produce, livestock and goods to Córdoba's teeming masses. The capital stimulated prosperous trading activities between local merchants and others located all over the world. Goods flowed into Córdoba and thence down the Guadalquivir River to Seville and onto ships that crossed the Mediterranean, or caravans that crossed the North African desert. Western Europeans from France, England and the Gemanic territories, some of whose intentions were on peaceful commerce while others were bent on plunder and war, were drawn by tales of wealth and luxury to Córdoba.

It was against a group of war-bent European Christians, Viking Norsemen who attacked Córdoba from their fleet of armed ships, that Prince Kamil won great fame and glory in the eyes of al-Rahman II. In a great battle, Kamil defended the emirate with courage and valor. The Emir rewarded the young warrior by recognizing Kamil as his own cousin, a member of the royal family and a prince of the realm. Prior to this "official" recognition, Kamil meant even less to the Emir than the lowliest slave in the Alcazar. The so-called secret of Kamil's birth was the worse-kept secret in Córdoba. And certainly the idea that Kamil would have ever been invited into the presence of the Emir would have been as far fetched as the governor of Mississippi welcoming his uncle's "yard child" by one of the Negro sharecroppers into the family.

FRANK YERBY:

Kamil's bravery in the face of hordes of hairy beasts streaming out of their ships to destroy Ispahnia inspired many Moorish knights and fighters to repel the Christian invasion. The Vikings descended upon village and town, and massing together in a furious charge, struck down all in their path. They were so filled with savagery, war-like spirit and murderous intent that the only choice a Moor had when facing a Viking was *kill or be killed*. In *An Odor of Sanctity*, Frank described how Kamil's bravery and success against the Viking invaders earned him the Emir's friendship and gratitude. That the Emir was honor-bound to grant Kamil some recognition, some show of gratitude for his rescue of Alaric Teudisson during the struggle against the Vikings, was quite natural. Al-Rahman II and Alaric...who the Emir called Aizun al Qutiyya...were very close. The Emir's own son, al-Mundhir, married Alaric's daughter, Theodora.

But the Emir outdid himself in generosity and kindliness by not merely recognizing Kamil but bestowing upon him the position of secretary to the Emir's own vizier of correspondence in the Dimashiq, the palace of viziers. The Emir staged an elaborate court ceremony attended by members of the royal family including the Emir's uncle, Kamil's "father," Prince Abd al-Karim ibn al-Hixim, and dignitaries from all over the Emirate. At this ceremony, al-Rahman II bestowed upon Kamil a gorgeous robe embroidered with the golden symbols of his new office. The presentation of the *tiraz*, for so the garment was called, indicated that the Emir wished to honor Kamil in such a way that all would know that Lady Sumayla's son would soon occupy a high office such as vizier. The robe the Emir presented to Kamil was so wondrously extravagant that it left no doubt in anyone's mind the great love and esteem Emir al-Rahman II felt for his cousin, Prince al-Kamil ibn Abd al-Karim ibn al-Hixim. Futhermore the reason that Lady Sumayla saw so little of her son was that the office Prince Kamil held entitled him his own apartments in Dimashiq, the palace of viziers within the Alcazar, sitting close to the palace of the Emir himself.

"Yes, mother," the young prince replied, showing his exasperation. "I've been busy. There's a lot happening at the court. This religious disturbance of the Christians has kept me up reading and replying to correspondence almost every night."

"Yes," Sumayla carefully responded, "we have heard that you have been quite busy at night." His mother's attempted irony did not escape the young prince, but he decided to ignore her double meaning.

"You know that my duties at the palace take up all my time. The Emir did not appoint me to my post just so I can come and go as I please. Besides Nasr...."

"Oh, you don't have to tell me about Nasr," the princess sighed. "I know how he behaves sometimes. But you just have to tolerate him, poor thing. No man can be the same after suffering castration. And in him burns such hatred that even I who have known him most of my life still have not plumbed its depths. Yet, I owe him my life. But for him I would still be a slave and you, my son, would never have been born."

What a strange thing to say, Yerby thought to himself. *Of course he would have been born. Just not to you!*

"But look, Kamil, let me introduce Frank Yerby," Sumayla exclaimed. "He has come to unlock the future for us...and possibly your past as well."

Of all the young knights of Córdoba, Kamil far and away cut the most dashing figure. A superb horseman and skilled with both the scimitar and bow, the Emir's swarthy cousin whose green eyes and muscular body received stares from women, young and old, had displayed great courage and prowess on the battlefield. Moreover, Kamil was an accomplished linguist and interpreter. This skill came as a surprise to absolutely no one at the Emir's court, considering the great reputation and renown Sumayla enjoyed for her intellectual attainments.

The young prince turned to observe Frank Yerby more closely. "You really did it! You came to us!" he exclaimed. "I never believed it was possible, but you did it."

"Well, Frank, what do you think of my mother?" Prince Kamil asked.

"She is lovely, quite lovely…almost like some kind of a goddess," Yerby replied.

"Yes, she generally has that effect on people, all people…men and women," the young prince commented. "But all she dreams about is me becoming the next Emir, isn't that so, Mother?"

Lady Sumayla looked around nervously and then at her son. Kamil noticed her eyes narrowing, the way they did when his mother was cross with him…which always seemed to be the case.

"She fears it as well." The prince found a seat and called for some refreshments. "Mother really isn't equipped to handle all the complexities that the Christians are bringing to our civilization." Prince Kamil paused as if lost in thought. "But since my real father is a Christian, she believes that as Emir, I'll be able to handle them. But the day that I become Emir, I pray, will be a long way off."

Yerby noticed a quick tightening in Lady Sumayla's face. "There is still much that her son does not know," Yerby observed to himself.

"There are many types of Christians," Kamil continued. "Just recently we defeated Vikings from the far North. My mother's afraid that the Christians will not rest until they have conquered and en-slaved all our people here in Spain. And with that wonderful logic known only to women, she believes I am the savior. As Emir, I would unite these various Christian sects as well as the Jews and Muslims into one great religious faith which would practice toleration and brotherhood."

"He scoffs," Sumayla replied, "but the Arian Christians are bar-barians. They forbid intermarriage between themselves and anyone else, even other Christians. They even shun the Romans. They set themselves above every other people. They have sworn to dominate or exterminate. We cannot allow them to gain power. Someone good like you, my son, must be in charge."

Prince Kamil continued: "But the Christians have many forts and walled cities. Yes, I agree…if Christian fanatics continue their disturbances, the Emirate itself could face severe problems. But, I can't believe that the Christians would allow the Peace of the Prophet to be destroyed. Did not my own father suffer from grievous wounds received from Viking invaders seeking to overthrow the Peace of the Prophet? If I became the Emir, I would find a way for the Christians to have more say in the government and eliminate these religious troubles which serve neither Christian nor Moor."

"Yet, young Master," Yerby observed prophetically, "since the Christians do have many forts and walled cities, surely they intend to keep up this disturbance for some time."

Kamil considered Yerby's words without comment.

"Now," Lady Sumalya said, grabbing her son's arm and half dragging him over to her favorite reclining area set off from the reception hall proper, "come and tell me all you have seen and accomplished since last we talked. What have you learned of the people?"

But before the prince could say anything, the princess turned majestically to Yerby, clapped her hands, and said, "Please make yourself comfortable!" A servant immediately appeared as if from thin air. "Khalid will show you to your rooms and see to your needs." Then, gazing deeply into Yerby's eyes, the princess walked over and touched his forearm. Her fingers on his skin were warm and reassuring. "Don't worry, Frank…I will explain it all to you, but first I must talk with my son. It's very important."

CHAPTER TWO

Khalid was a bent and wizened little fellow with the round and protuberant potbelly characteristic of many eunuchs. But the rest of him was thin and wiry, his body hinting at a quiet strength which might not have been expected from someone of his apparent years. Actually, Yerby found it difficult to judge Khalid's age. The toothless grin Khalid flashed from time to time suggested that he might be in his mid-forties, ancient for a slave in ninth-century Spain. But the old servant's deeply sad and knowing eyes suggested to Yerby that Khalid had witnessed events and mysteries which occurred over several lifetimes.

"How long have you worked for the princess?" Yerby asked his escort as they left the reception area and begun to cross what seemed to be an endless number of corridors and doorways connecting the halls and apartments which comprised Princess Sumayla's palace. In truth, this palace was only somewhat less magnificent than the four palaces of the Emir and his court within the Alcazar. When Lady Sumayla first married Karim, the Emir's uncle, she had begged him to build their home here on the banks of the Guadalquiver River. She did so at the urging of Nasr, whose intrigues required that he have a meeting place hidden from the prying eyes of the Emir's network of personal agents and spies. Lady Sumayla's palace proved to be a convenient meeting place for the Emirate's arch-conspirator. Not hearing an answer to his question, Yerby repeated it, a little louder. "How long have you worked for the princess?"

But again, the shuffling figure ahead gave no response. In frustration, Yerby reached out, grabbed the little black eunuch and whirled him completely around. "How long have you worked for the princess?" he shouted.

The little man bowed humbly and moved his lips, but no sound came out; no sound at all. Khalid then made several simple gestures with his hand to his mouth that helped Yerby understand. Khalid had been a gift to Sumayla from Nasr, who made it a habit of having his household slaves' tongues removed in order to insure that they could never speak of their master's affairs. Once he was certain Yerby knew he could not speak, Khalid turned back around and continued leading the way down a corridor which ended in front of two massive doors. The little black man showed Yerby through the doors into a large circular vestibule around which were placed cushions and low furniture. Around the spacious room great columns supported an arched ceiling in whose center was an opaque dome through which the sun was filtered. Below this great skylight sat a fountain. Archways opened on opposite sides of the vestibule. To the left lay a bed chamber with bed and closets containing a wardrobe for a prince. To the right, a tiled bathing area held a great sunken bathing pool. Tables on the side held decanters of bath salts, oils and fragrances. Towels and robes lay neatly folded in closets on the opposite wall. The bathing room opened onto a patio with a private garden.

Yerby decided to take advantage of the bathing facilities. When he finished luxuriating, he found that Khalid had brought refreshments into the vestibule. Silently serving Yerby from silver plates, Khalid made certain that his guest wanted for nothing. Then, after indicating that a servant was stationed on duty outside his apartment, Khalid took his leave and Yerby was left to his own thoughts.

. . .

The Lady Sumayla turned her attention to the urgent matter she had to discuss with her son. In the court of Emir al-Rahman II, the most prized and sought-after females were the blond, blue-eyed northern Europeans. To many members of the dark-skinned races such as the Emir himself, only the milk-white skin, skinny hips and ponderous breasts of those barbarian wenches were really beautiful. *But who am I to cast stones,* she thought, *is not my own son's father, the fair Goth, Alaric Teudisson?*

With that she smiled to herself, remembering that only time of pure happiness, spent with her Goth lover when the two of them had produced her magnificent son, one who was now recognized as the Emir's own cousin and would soon contend for the throne. But now she must discuss this matter with her son, who like most black men would have little interest in her words because when he looked at her he saw nothing more than a face as black as night...not that Sumayla wasn't lovely. Her body was breathtaking. It was still quite slender and soft. Even with her forty-plus years, the Lady Sumayla still displayed the utterly harmonious lines of a classic feminine beauty. Her breasts were perfect, conical and firm with only the slightest tilt caused by their fullness. Her legs were long, ending in softly curving hips and a flat stomach. Her hair, however, was strange to the touch, rigid with no softness to it. Heated irons had pulled it into a hard, sculptured straightness. Her face was not uncomely. She had the high cheekbones and almond eyes distinctive of her Arabic forebears, for, in truth, she was a mixture of both African and Arabic races. But, since notions of beauty are formed by habit and custom, both learned and taught, few, including herself, could appreciate how truly beautiful Sumayla actually was. And today, she especially did not feel beautiful, she felt angry, really very angry, the kind of angry you feel when you feel betrayed, duped. The kind of angry only a parent who has lived a whole life through an only child can feel.

"What is this that I have been hearing about you and the Lady Tarub?" Sumayla fixed Kamil with a look that said she was serious and would not tolerate any lies. However, the young Prince decided that he would be as truthful about this situation as he must…but no more.

"Well, mother," her half-breed son began, "it's really all your fault, you know."

"My fault?" Lady Sumayla responded. *This is going to be worse than I had imagined,* she thought to herself, *and far worse than my-informant had reported.* But she decided not to let Kamil know how much she already knew. "How is it that I am responsible for you getting your head separated from your shoulders over Lady Tarub, the Emir's favorite wife?"

"If you had not trained me to be a linguist, like yourself," Kamil replied glibly and with a straight face, "I probably would not have been involved with the Lady Tarub."

"I think you had better tell me the whole story from the beginning," she said quietly. "And don't leave anything out."

Well, I certainly intend to leave as much out as I possibly can, Kamil thought to himself. *There is no reason to get mother any more involved in this thing than necessary. Where did it all begin?* And the answer came quickly, for it began as most of the intrigue in Córdoba did…with Lord L'Fath Nasr, the Emir's grand vizier.

Kamil's mind reached back. Some time ago he had begun to play a pretend game with himself. He pretended that he was unaware of the plots that Nasr and his mother were hatching on his behalf, so that he never really considered what he was doing. He just did as he was told…even though his only ambition was to perform his duties

FRANK YERBY:

for the Emir to the best of his abilities. He really liked what he was doing…and he really liked the Emir. But once he had begun this pretense, Kamil was not really smart enough to know when to stop playing…and get serious. Even when he knew he had gotten in way over his head with Umm Walad Tarub.

"Nasr told me that he wanted me to read to the Emir's harem. That he wanted me to try a new device invented by that scientist fellow the Emir brought from Alexandria."

"Read! To the Emir's wives? Impossible! How?" Sumayla asked, her curiosity piqued.

"With a device that would let me read aloud in one room and be heard in another," Kamil said. "Nasr had persuaded the Emir that his wives would profit by hearing the readings of the Koran and be entertained by other readings of poetry and of philosophy. 'It will be strictly for your ladies' entertainment and diversion', Nasr told him. 'Prince Kamil will read from one room and the sound of his voice, enhanced by the natural acoustics of wood paneling, will be heard in the adjoining chamber.' The idea appealed to the Emir, not so much because he wanted to cure the tedium of his wives, but because he was intrigued by any innovation developed by his man of science and Nasr knew that the Emir could not resist seeing a practical demonstration of a device which could reproduce sound."

"So how did the gossip begin about you and the Emir's wife?" Sumayla asked knowing that Kamil had not told the entire story.

· · ·

It had all begun so innocently, Kamil remembered. He would enter a room completely separated and hidden from the harem and read into a tube. The Emir's wives, completely hidden from him, could hear the reading in their quarters. No man who was not himself a eunuch could ever enter the harem and see the Emir's wives. However, from the very beginning, the deep sensual voice of the prince enchanted every one of the Emir's wives. Only those women whom the Emir had actually married lived in the Alcazar. The Emir's other women lived elsewhere and the Emir had scarcely any time for them. But his wives were a pampered spoiled lot. The Emir often found himself thinking of ways to keep his wives occupied. This was especially true for the Lady Umm Walad Tarub. The daughter of a wealthy Venetian merchant captured by corsairs raiding Christian merchants plying their way across the Mediterranean. She sold to the Emir for a king's ransom. And this slim, voluptuous Christian maiden was used to getting her way, especially when she was restless and bored. Although it was forbidden that the Emir's wives have access to the Emir's private meetings, Lady Tarub often would listen to the proceedings in the Emir's council chambers from a secret anti-chamber. "The one who reports on correspondence has a voice that stirs my soul," the Lady Tarub once remarked to Nasr.

Gradually, the Emir's harem cared less and less about the readings, and more and more about the reader. His voice, wondrous and sensual, enchanted them. The entire harem talked of nothing other than seeing the courtier with the wonderful voice. But Tarub, possibly because she was the youngest and the Emir's favorite, determined that she would find a way to meet the man in person. Nasr quickly realized that he had an opportunity to further his own plans and willingly encouraged the Lady Tarub to satisfy her own interests. And as things will happen where young passions are fired by a longing in their hearts, Tarub and Kamil found themselves meeting in secret for several weeks. Before long, after a succession of such meetings, the emir's handsome mulatto cousin and the emir's young blue-eyed, honey-blond wife fell helplessly in love.

Kamil remembered every meeting; it all happened so fast. For the past month, he had attended to his duties with scrupulous attention. He didn't want to arouse the suspicions of his master, Abu Kitab al-Mitar, the vizier of correspondence. But after dark, Kamil would sneak into the gardens of the royal palace through a secret connection from the palace of the viziers. During that magical time of the evening when hidden in the shadows of their secret garden, the two victims of Cupid's barbs made love...and plans.

"*Tarub,* " Kamil whispered, "for the sake of Allah, please..."

"Are you a coward?" Lady Tarub taunted. "I was told that in the battle against the infidel Vikings, you surpassed all others in bravery to save your father's life. Why does the sight of a woman weaken you?"

And what a sight was the Lady Umm Walad Tarub. Her flowing golden-reddish blond hair framed her fair sharply chiseled features with tiny freckles dancing on the tip of her nose. Deep blue eyes tantalized Kamil with their mocking gaze just above the filmy half veil that extended down a little below her chin. The veil, as transparent as spring water, made subtle mockery of the Prophet's command to maintain female modesty, for the ruby red lips glistening through the veil induced a delirium into Kamil's brain of dizzying proportions. Her body so close and perfectly shaped with legs that reached up to a tiny waist weakened Kamil's knees so that he had to reach out for support to keep from fainting. Tarub usually wore a short brocaded jacket opening to reveal a binding supporting her ample breasts. Kamil was certain that this binding was woven of a spider web, so fetching was the sight of the twin mounds of flesh pointing out their rouge-red tips dancing within easy reach just above her bare midriff. Tarub wore billowing silken harem trousers, revealing her long, shapely legs and bejeweled ankles. Kamil could scarcely control his own breathing so great was his desire to hold this all but naked Aphrodite.

"Coward!" Tarub taunted him. "Come here and kiss me. I haven't tasted those sweet lips for such a long time." Kamil drew her to him and slanted a little so that their mouths would fit. Slowly he moved his lips to hers, touching her ever so gently, but she swept his hands up behind his head and locked them and clung to him, grinding her mouth against his, her tongue darting serpent-like into his mouth and kindling a flame which soon turned into an inferno, burning his lips. She grounded the whole length of her scantily-clad body against his, scalding him with breast and thigh in a passionate embrace. And as she arched up to feel the entire length of his muscular manliness, he felt the terror of a man lost in passion, maddened by forbidden desire, and at the same time, utterly aware of the certain consequences of his terrible sin, his touching not just another man's wife…the Emir's favorite wife. *For this I will be killed*, he thought. But intoxicated by her scent and electrified by her touch, he determined that she was worth dying for. Boldly, he freed his hand, pushed aside the flimsy garment and caressed her bare flesh, roughly, almost brutally, as though she were his slave…which was what she wanted. But just as suddenly, he turned her loose. And as he turned away, her long reddish, blond hair trailed about his face like a veil.

"I'm sorry," he said.

"Don't be," she said almost calmly although the passion remained in her eyes as well as in her body. "You're the man I want, I must have! I would let you do what you like right now, if I thought we had time."

"By the Prophet's beard," he whispered, "there is no one lovelier than you!"

"Kamil, my love?" the Emir's wife purred.

"Yes, Tarub."

"You must come to my chambers."

"How can I do that?" the lovelorn prince answered, "even now we are in great danger and must soon part."

"Even so, " she replied. "I have a plan. If it works, we will be able to spend an entire night together. Don't you want to?"

"You know I do."

"Well, the day of the Breaking of the Fast will be in two weeks," she reminded him. "After the banquet, which you will attend, everyone will be dead tired."

"But what if the Emir wishes to visit you in your chambers?"

Kamil asked.

"I will arrange for a sleeping potion to be given to the Emir," Tarub responded calmly. "He will not want to visit me on the night after such a day's ceremonies and festivities. Besides I will be ill and not able to leave my chamber."

"One of the al-Khurs or a eunuch is certain to discover us," Kamil worried. "They would suffer the most terrible torture and death, if they were derelict and not to betray us immediately."

"We can do it," she responded. "Nasr will help us."

"Nasr!" he exclaimed.

Once again she held him in a passionate embrace, her breath rustled against his bare throat and breaking away, she whispered, "I must go…but remember, the night of the Breaking of the Fast, we will be together."

"But Tarub…," Kamil said weakly.

"Is it not worth the risk, my love?" she asked, fondling him.

"By Allah, yes…" Kamil answered, "but…"

"Then, until then, my sweet prince," she said gaily. And she slipped out of his grasp and wrapping a great grey veil about her, skipped out of their garden which had served as their secret meeting place for the past several months, into one of the many secret passageways which honeycombed the Emir's palace within the Alcazar. This last encounter with the Lady Tarub was all Kamil thought about, but, of course, he could tell his mother none of this.

· · ·

"I don't know," Kamil said to Lady Sumayla, innocently enough. "But you know how the servants talk. You can't believe half of what they say."

Yes, I know how the gossip flies within the confines of the Alcazar, Sumayla agreed to herself, *since most of those involved in gossip, rumor and the passing of secrets work for me.* One of the reasons that Nasr was so attracted to Sumayla from the very beginning was her highly organized and absolutely faithful network of spies and agents...a network that as a Christian Goth, Nasr could never have established. Her network started strictly by accident.

From her earliest days as a reader in Horeth's copy house, the copyists thought of Sumayla as a saint. Horeth demanded that the twenty or more slaves, most of whom were white, produce a minimum number of texts from her dictation each week. In addition, he demanded that the new texts be completely free of errors. Horeth would fly into a rage when he had to give a customer a refund or exchange a customer's text because of errors. He would beat a copyist whose work cost him money. After one of Horeth's beatings, a woman could remain maimed for life. Somewhat infrequently a copyist would die from such a beating. From the very beginning, Sumayla never failed to assist her copyists by proofreading their material and even dictating the text again, if necessary. In return, the copyists never failed to tell Sumayla what they heard was going on in Córdoba. Even after Horeth sold his copyists, which was not uncommon since Horeth always needed money, they would return to tell Sumayla what went on in their masters' and mistresses' beds and households. Sumayla always had the latest news for the markets and the juiciest gossip from the baths and the streets.

In the beginning, Nasr had been merely a low level administrator in the royal court. Always watching and listening, Sumayla would amaze him with all the intelligence she gained with her network of copyists. Not only did Nasr find the information Sumayla provided him useful, he organized her network. And in his climb to the pinnacle of power as the Emir's Grand Vizier the information provided by Sumayla's network proved essential. Nasr always seemed to know who was vulnerable to blackmail, how to eliminate his rivals without any suspicion being focused on him and when and where his own enemies intended to strike. Nasr actually brought Sumayla's network from the streets of Córdoba into the Alcazar itself. A full fifty percent of the female slaves and sevants within the Emir's own household belonged to Sumayla's network. So Sumayla knew almost as much about Kamil's affair as he did. However, when does a mother ever disbelieve anything her son tells her? Where her son is concerned, a mother listens with her heart rather than with her head.

You mean I can't believe half of what you say, Sumayla thought to herself. But she decided to keep her thoughts to herself. She knew that she had indulged her son far too much. It was not his fault that he behaved like the man she wanted him to be. Possibly her agent had embellished the story. So she said, "You know how dangerous it is to have anything to do with the Emir's harem, my son. You must be careful, especially now."

"Yes mother," Kamil said dutifully, "I will be very careful." And there Lady Sumayla let the matter rest…for the time being. But for Kamil the torment continued. It had only been two weeks since the young lovers had last sat together in one of the Alcazar's many secret gardens. By any account, Kamil's boldness was amazing, considering the fact that it was certain death for any man to even gaze upon any member of the Emir's harem, let alone to have touched and held her. Yet, anyone who remembers his own youth could understand how meaningless even the threat of death is to one in love. For as surely as the sun shone on the white and red tiles of Córdoba, Kamil loved the Lady Tarub.

Of course, Nasr did everything he could to encourage Kamil's affair with the Lady Tarub. He knew this path was very risky. Already the gossip was flying about the Alcazar. It was just a matter of time before all Córdoba knew. This was certain to reach the ears of the Emir himself. But I have no choice, he thought to himself; he was behind on his timetable.

Nasr's plot had probably been cleverly laid and well executed, with-

out any room for me to maneuver, Sumayla thought to herself. *He never makes any mistake when it comes to a power grab. And he has left me no room to maneuver to save my son.* Nasr would either replace the Emir with her son…or both she and Kamil would die.

CHAPTER THREE

U ncle, how will I rule over all of them?" a young al-Rahman II asked his favorite uncle. Abd al-Karim ibn al-Hixim stood by the new Emir's side as the long line of dignitaries, representatives and leaders streamed into the royal palace's great reception hall. From as far away as the great Egyptian city of Alexandria and even from Damascus and Constantinople, Arabs, Berbers, Moors, Africans, Egyptians, Christians, Jews, merchants, priests, generals, ambassadors, intellectuals, doctors, scientists all came to pay homage to al-Rahman II, the newly installed Emir of Córdoba.

"My son," the youngest brother of the late Emir replied, "Allah must show you the way. It is well known that you have not the disposition to oversee this multitude with the iron grip that your late father used. You will need intelligence and skill if you are to keep these vultures at bay."

"Just look at them, uncle," the young ruler said. "They eye me as if my head were already on a platter."

"It is your eye, my son," al-Karim observed. "They have all heard of the time when your father took you to your first public execution and how you were so frightened by the blood that you developed a nervous twitch in your eye. As they all come forward to prostrate themselves and present their gifts, they are curious to see if what they heard was true."

And indeed it was true, for al-Rahman II could never control the twitching in his left eye, especially when he was under the kind of stress he was this day of his ascension to the throne. He felt fortunate indeed that his uncle as well as his brothers were here to see him through this ordeal.

"They may take it as a sign of weakness," al-Rahman II's uncle confided to his nephew, "but you and I know they would be wrong. They will soon learn that you are far stronger...and wiser... than you appear. You will have no problem ruling."

al-Karim's assessment of his nephew was correct. Al-Rahman II was far smarter and more cunning than his subjects gave him credit for. And even though bloodshed was distasteful to him, the Emir never hesitated when matters of state required that someone's head be separated from their shoulders...whether it be male or female, Christian, Jew or Muslim. To be the Emir of Córdoba required constant vigilance and instant decisions. The collection of Berber and Moorish tribesmen, who had only recently converted to the Islamic faith, ceaselessly roamed about the Spanish hinterlands in search of plunder and booty. Their conversions to Islam and loyalty to their Arab ruler resulted less from religious belief than from promises of battle spoils. But their presence created a real danger to the stability of the Emirate in general and the Emir in particular. The Berbers and Moors were nomads. They were not interested in settling down or becoming domesticated. They warred for pleasure, respecting no man's wife, sister or mother, and made a virtue of treachery.

And these tribesmen who threatened the Emir's rule outside of the large cities were not al-Rahman II's only concern. The great amalgamation of conquered peoples, including Christians and Jews in addition to the Arabs, Egyptians, Africans, Persians, Tartars and other peoples seeking the Peace of the Prophet, made it impossible to guarantee the safety of outlying areas, roads or small villages against marauding nomads. No one blamed the Emir when a caravan or fortress was attacked. But, he was expected to maintain some security within the city walls. A relative peace was expected and necessary for the exchange of commercial goods and services. Traders, merchants and businesses of all descriptions took the Peace of the Prophet within the walls of the great cities of Spain for granted; and so did the Caliph of Damascus, the Emir's lord and master. So all threats against property or person and any criminal breaches would be swiftly punished. The Emir ruled less by the agreement between similar peoples who shared similar beliefs and values and more by the manipulation and subjugation of dangerous peoples always looking to take advantage. Thus al-Rahman II had to be continually watchful and vigilant.

"Are you really prepared to appoint Nasr to the post of Grand Vizier, Rahman?" Karim asked his nephew. "This will not be popular in Damascus." Several viziers served Abd al-Rahman II, each responsible for some aspect of the Emirate's administration. They collected taxes, operated courts, transcribed and received official correspondence, administered justice and supervised all the Emir's building projects. Headquartered in their own palace within the Alcazar, these men, whose decisions affected millions, sat upon their own carpets and administered the Emirate's affairs. But one vizier outstripped all the others in power and influence. He sat on a higher throne and he gazed down on all the others. His word was absolute law to everyone save the Emir's family and the Emir himself. This vizier was allowed direct contact with the Emir without awaiting a summons. In addition to his title of Grand Vizier, he held the additional title: Hajib, "doorkeeper."

"The Caliph is concerned only with the Peace of the Prophet," Rahman replied to his uncle. "Has not Nasr proved his loyalty and usefulness many times over?"

"Yes, but he is a Goth," al-Karim replied slowly. "They can never be fully trusted."

"He volunteered for castration just to serve my father." It was true. Nasr himself chose to be castrated. He sacrificed his manhood just to obtain a position in the Royal Court. It was necessary; none but the royal family were permitted access to the Emir without having his maleness cut away. And this was not the only sacrifice the ambitious Goth was forced to make. After entering the Emir's service, Nasr was occasionally forced to perform humiliating sexual acts for members of the ruling circle, the lords of the land. He especially caught the eye of Prince al-Mugira, the Emir's brother. Al-Mugira was well known for his homosexual preferences. "He has renounced the Christian religion," Rahman continued, "and adopted the true faith. Certainly, this proves his loyalty. Besides, look at the intelligence network he has built up over the past three years. There's been no plot or conspiracy that the Christians have dreamed up that he has not revealed to us. There is no business venture that the Jews can put together in which we do not participate. What greater proof of his value do we need?"

"That intelligence network is not his. It belongs to that enchanting woman whom he freed from Horeth, the copyist," al-Karim replied. "Sumayla is her name."

"You mean that black one?" al-Rahman II asked. "She looks like midnight on legs. I don't see why he spends so much time with her. If I didn't know that he has no genitals, I'd think they were lovers…and he a Goth. Don't they believe blacks to be related to monkeys?"

"My son, you have much to learn," al-Karim said sharply. "That woman is a prize beyond measure. All the praise you heap upon Nasr properly belongs to her. Did you know that she can recite the Koran by heart? This woman speaks many languages, has mastered advanced mathematics and writes poetry."

"My uncle, you seem to have been enslaved by a slave," al-Rahman II smiled. "Since you have complained so often about your own wives, why don't you marry her? Possibly she can do for you what all your other women have failed to do."

"What is that, nephew?" the elder man asked softly.

"Give you a son," the Emir laughed out loud. Al-Karim took no offence for well he knew of his nephew's passion for white women.

That his uncle could consider marrying a woman as black as Sumayla caused al-Rahman II to indulge in a laughing fit he could barely control. The Emir was as susceptible as any in the Islamic empire to craving for white women. Arabs, Moors, Egyptians and Berbers alike all treasured the fair-skinned slave women. They paid huge sums for the thin-lipped, narrow-hipped maidens. White owmen were being kidnapped and stolen out of northern Europe and sold into harems across the Islamic empire by the thousands. The idea of siring fair-skinned, blue-eyed children tantalized Islam's Negro rulers. And this desire for white women spilled over into an interest and desire for anything white. This was the actual reason al-Rahman II wanted Abu L'Fath Nasr, a white Goth and former Christian, as his Grand Vizier. In his mind, appointing Nasr as his Grand Vizier made al-Rahman II a most powerful ruler indeed.

Al-Karim, a philospher and a lover of the arts, had been searching all of his life for a woman like Sumayla. He wanted to discuss things that really mattered to him with a woman who loved him and shared his life. None of his other wives had any knowledge of these matters. As none of them had been able to give him a son, his life had become a continual struggle between desperate wives trying to get as much as they could in preparation for his advancing age as well as their own. And so it came to pass that both men got their wish. Al-Rahman II, Emir of Córdoba and ruler of Spain appointed Nasr his Grand Vizier and Abd al-Karim ibn al-Hixim, his uncle, married the black former slave, Sumayla, whom Nasr had sometime earlier freed. Both were quite pleased.

Never had al-Karim met anyone, man or woman, Arab or infidel, as wise and knowledgeable as Sumayla. He could listen for hours to her discourses on al-Farabi's translations of Aristotle and Plato or find endless pleasure in her original poetry or even listen to her own interpretations of the sacred Koran. Al-Karim could take his wife's interpretations to the court and amaze even the Emir's venerable imam, reputedly the holiest and wisest man in the Spanish Emirate. Happily had Abd al-Karim ibn al-Hixim elevated Sumayla to the status of a princess of the realm.

And yet, Sumayla never felt secure. She shared the same fears that haunted al-Karim's other wives...that when her aged husband died, which could be at any moment, her status as princess would be immediately terminated and she would find herself back on the slave market. Her marriage was temporary, but her black skin was permanent.

"He loves my mind, not my body," Lady Sumayla had complained to Nasr. "He wants me to recite verses and weave intricate arguments of philosophy! But sooner or later the novelty of a woman who can think will wear off. Then I won't have anything to keep him from truly looking at me! Before he tires of me, I need to give him a son. If I could but give him an heir, I could avoid being cast out by one of those other she-cats he married. After all, old men can father children. I would be secure, for my son would be his only heir."

But her wish had seemed impossible since, at the time of their marriage, Abd al-Karim ibn al-Hixim was already an old man.. No matter—in order to secure her position against her husband's inevitable death, Sumayla was determined to give her husband a son and an heir. And as usual, when she needed assistance Nasr was available to help.

"My Lord Abd al-Karim ibn al-Hixim," Nasr addressed the Emir's uncle one day after Sumayla had petitioned for his help, "I have noticed how sad the Princess Sumayla has been over these many months, is there some service which I can offer which may be of some assistance to you?"

"I am afraid that not even you with all of your marvelous powers can help in this matter," al-Karim replied distractedly. "The Lady Sumayla wants to have a son, as do I…and for many years now, Allah has not seen fit to grant this wish to any of my wives."

"Well sir," the crafty vizier replied, "I have most wondrous news. I have been aware of your troubles for some time now. I have sent messengers far and wide to seek anyone who can assist you."

"And?" the old man asked, already eager to become a willing accomplice in Nasr's scheme.

"I found someone who is willing to assist Your Royal Highness with what he said was a trifling problem." With that, Nasr convinced al-Karim to make a trip to the mountains. There in an isolated health camp established by one of Nasr's own men, the Emir's uncle underwent a regimen of exercise and diet to build up his sexual potency…or so he was told. In the meantime, back in Córdoba, for an entire month, Nasr arranged that Sumayla enjoy passionate bliss with the fair-haired, blue-eyed Goth Alaric Teudisson as Yerby tells the story. When Sumayla was certain that she was pregnant, Nasr brought the elderly but invigorated al-Karim back to his wife and several months later the old man announced that he had sired a son and heir, al-Kamil ibn Abd al-Karim ibn al-Hixim. And the kindly old man and fervent philospher remained grateful to his black wife until the day he departed this life to rest in the bosom of Allah…which was not long after Kamil had been honored by the Emir for his defense of the Emirate. In this way did Sumayla insure her position as being the mother of al-Kamil ibn al-Karim, first cousin to al-Rahman II, Emir of the Emirate of Ispahnia. And Nasr had Sumayla securely in his debt.

• • •

"If he is here, I want to see him, immediately! Wake him!" A high-pitched, almost hysterical screech burst into Yerby's dreamless sleep, shocking him into consciousness. It was as if a sudden blast of Gabriel's trumpet had sent a call throughout Yerby's nervous system. "Prepare to meet your maker!" it shouted out. L'Fath Nasr, Grand Vizier of al-Rahman II, Emir of Cordova, was personally calling on him.

"Ah, Frank Yerby." The high-pitched voice screeched his name like the noise a crow makes calling to its mate. "Please join Lady Sumayla and myself…we have urgent matters to discuss with you." Quickly, Khalid dressed Yerby in a silk robe and a pair of embroidered slippers. With that there was a whirl of silken robes and a line of torches streamed out into the hall with Yerby ushered between them as he was escorted to Lady Sumayla's audience chamber.

"You told me that he could give us all the information we needed to ensure our success." Nasr was screeching at Sumayla, stomping his feet like the pompous little ass that he was.

"My Lord Nasr," Lady Sumayla replied, "you must be patient. He has only just arrived. I wanted to make him comfortable and give him time to adjust."

"Time to adjust!!" Nasr shouted, "we have no time to adjust! The priest's execution is tomorrow. Everything is in place. We have to know now."

Yerby listened to the conversation with an odd sense of disinterest, as if their problems really didn't matter to him. And as his mind wandered, he idly speculated why Prince Kamil was not present. And then he heard Lady Sumayla say: "You see, he's drifting away. We are losing him, he's not interested."

"Frank…" Lady Sumayla was speaking to him. "Can you hear me, Frank?"

"Milord," the Lady Sumayla said sternly to Nasr. "You're going to have to leave and let me handle him. Don't you realize that I am just as interested in a successful outcome to our adventure as you are?"

"But you don't have the Asturians and the Emir breathing down your neck," Nasr replied.

"No…but I have my life and the life of my only son depending upon a successful outcome. You must trust me. I haven't let you down yet…have I?" She smiled at her patron and went over and rubbed his bald head, a trick she used whenever she wanted her way with him. Like many eunuchs, Nasr was given to fits of emotional outbursts. Only calming and soothing words ever worked when he was in this agitated state. Motioning to his bodyguard, he prepared to return to his palace in the Alcazar. Then, pausing at the door, he turned and glared at Sumayla and whispered, "If Yerby cannot predict our safe future then we must kill him and take fate into our own hands!"

CHAPTER FOUR

It was a beautiful sunny day and Córdoba teemed with sights and sounds. Its streets were lined with tents of shopkeepers selling everything imaginable. Córdoba attracted merchants from all over Spain, and from Alexandria to Istanbul, Baghdad to Damascus, Rome to Athens…in fact from all over the known world. But today even more people crowded into Córdoba's streets and headed for the Great Square just outside the walls of the Alcazar. Today the great event, the execution of the Christian priest, Prefectus, would take place. His head was to be hacked from his body for the high crime of blasphemy against Islam and its holy prophet, Muhammad. The Lady Sumayla had ordered her carriage bearers and escort to take her to the execution. So now, Lady Sumayla not thinking about the prosperity and wealth all about her, with Frank Yerby walking by the side of the carriage, was headed towards the Great Square to witness the execution.

Sumayla thought only of the task Nasr demanded of her that Yerby be forced to tell all he knew about future events though Sumayla knew that it was too soon. Yerby had to be brought along gradually. He had to be willing. *What did Abulafia say?* she asked herself, recalling her sessions with the Jewish doctor turned mystic. *Contact requires faith and a desire to believe.* Sumayla especially recalled the old Jew's warning: "Your contact with Yerby will only be maintained if he desires the contact. You must keep him interested."

In the past, Moses Abulafia's confidences had been very helpful, she thought to herself. His instructions in Jewish mysticism were simply amazing. Sumayla had been the recipient of this knowledge simply because the Jews themselves had barred all women from religious and magical studies. Moses Abulafia believed that this prohibition was not only wrong, it worked a great harm on the Jewish people themselves. "They have even denied the truth of the *Shekhinah*," the heretical Jewish physician decried. "They want to deny the goddess, the purely feminine embodiment of Life, itself."

"She is the intellectual fire, the animating principle of the world. How can these men hope to control the Goddess of Life? The Jewish race will pay for this blasphemy with everlasting damnation unless they recant."

Whatever his reasons, Abulafia had given her information regarding the Hekhaloth guide to the Merkaba, which she combined with her own intuition and knowledge. As a result Sumayla acquired incredible powers. Abulafia told Sumayla that one of the reasons that men feared to give women instruction was because women needed no seals or passports. "Women have direct access to magical powers," the Jewish mystic told her. "All women need do is to make the journey." And Sumayla had...on several occasions. But letting her enthusiasm get the best of her, Sumayla shared her knowledge with Nasr, and the grand vizier suggested that she use her power to summon Yerby and see whether or not the author could predict their future. *That was a mistake* she thought to herself. *That little eunuch is going to ruin everything.* So now she was bringing Yerby to the priest's execution to see whether or not it would stimulate him. Would Prince Kamil succeed to the Emir's throne as they planned...or were they all to lose their heads?

"So, Frank," she asked as he walked alongside her carriage, "is this your first visit to Córdoba?"

"No," Yerby responded, "I have been here many times."

"Yes, but not during the time of the Peace of the Prophet, I would guess," Sumayla observed trying to interest him in the surroundings.

"What?" he asked.

"This will not do," she said to herself.

"Halt," Sumayla cried out to her bearers. Smoothly all four of the massive Negro carriage bearers came to a stop. Sumalya alighted gracefully from the carriage. Instructing the bearers to return to her palace, Sumayla continued on foot taking her place next to Yerby. "This is much better, don't you think?" she asked demurely.

Yerby nodded noncommittally. With the princess' guards forming a protective circle, the two resumed their journey towards the Alcazar and the Great Square.

"See over there," Sumayla pointed out, "I used to work at master Horeth's copy house." Yerby was noncommittal. "But you already know that, don't you? Scholarship is valued, here in Córdoba," she continued. "The Emir's own library boasts of over four hundred thousand volumes of learned works from all over the world. Some are as old as antiquity itself. Córdoba is emerging as the greatest intellectual center in the world. Here we find learned professors, students from every country. And many booksellers are flocking here."

In the distance, Yerby could hear voices from the many different readers dictating to the copyists enslaved in there. Yerby nodded. But he was rather uncomfortable dressed in Arabic robes. He wore light pantaloons with a wide sash and a tightly wrapped turban. Most uncomfortable were the cloth sandals that were not made for walking. But Sumayla knew that walking forced Yerby to concentrate on his surroundings and prevented him from drifting back.

Though Yerby was only half listening, Sumayla's plan was working and Yerby began to attend to the wealth of exotic sights and sounds of this city formed of Arabian culture. He began to focus on the shops and stalls from which industry flourished. Gold and silversmith workers everywhere were seen creating wondrous pieces of jewelry and works of art; weavers producing woolen and silken goods; glass, paper, and leather goods were everywhere in abundance. Through the maze of jewelers, exotic fragrances of perfumes and incense stirred Yerby's olafactory senses with thoughts of romance and languid pleasures. Everywhere the sights of industry, learning and culture amazed the visitor. Finally, in some of the stalls they passed, he found sweetmeats and delicacies that delighted both the nose as well as the palate. Yerby was hooked.

"I had no idea Córdoba was such an advanced society," Yerby said, his mouth now filled with candied figs and crunchy walnuts. And as he spoke, they turned onto a street above which rose the towers of the dazzling palaces just beyond the walls of the Alcazar.

The Alcazar, a city within a city, actually contained four palaces: al-Imara, al-Rassafa, Dimashiq and al-Rawa. Each of the palaces and the Alcazar's commons opened onto lovely gardens, lush green lawns and miniature groves. The perimeter of all four palaces was lined with stables, armories and quarters for the thousands of slaves, soldiers and officials who owed their personal allegiance to the person of the Emir Abd al-Rahman II, himself. The great walls surrounding the Alcazar were dotted with guardhouses located at regular intervals. Adjoining the Alcazar stood Córdoba's great Mosque with the mighty Guadalquivir River flowing majestically behind both the Mosque and the Alcazar, re-enforcing the protection afforded by the walls. In front of the huge double gates marking the entrance into the Alcazar lay the Great Square, a wide, flat area now filled with thousands of onlookers who along with the Lady Sumayla and Frank Yerby had come to witness the execution of the priest. Prefectus.

Even before approaching the Great Square, Yerby became aware of the insistent cries of the mob. But now as they entered the square,

Lady Sumayla's retainers, forcing the crowd to give way, the roar became deafening. In the seating area reserved for dignitaries, they spied Prince Kamil, who broke away from the group of young noblemen he was with to come over to greet them.

"Some show, eh?" the young prince observed excitedly. "Most of Córdoba must be here."

"Good morning, Kamil. I trust that you have been minding the Emir's affairs and honoring the trust he has placed in you." Sumayla greeted her son calmly, betraying none of the anxiety and fear she had on his behalf.

"You need have no concern on that matter, mother," the young prince replied. "I am the Emir's most faithful servant." Kamil lied. Only recently had he come from a secret tryst with Tarub. Neither correspondence nor statecraft occupied Kamil's mind now. His only thoughts were of the Lady Tarub. His feelings ran so deep that nothing and no one other than she mattered. He had fallen ill to a sickness that could be cured only by the complete release of that gigantic tide of sexual energy lying deep within him. But for the time being Kamil knew he had to act normal and attend to his mother and his duties as a member of the Emir's personal staff. As Kamil escorted Lady Sumayla and Yerby to seats on velvet cushioned chairs under the shelter of a billowing umbrella, attendants bowed as they as members of the royal family took their seats. The crowd continued to roar, excited by their anticipation of seeing Prefectus' bloody head lopped from its body. And in an instant of reflection rare in a young man whose hormones are popping, the incautious young Kamil thought to himself, *This could well soon be happening to me.*

"From the looks of the crowd, people have come from as far away as Seville and Toledo," Sumayla observed.

"Yes, and many of them are Christians," Kamil observed, "who would use force to stop the execution if given the opportunity. The al-Khurs will certainly have their hands full today."

"Do you think we are safe here?" Lady Sumayla asked in calm, even terms though inwardly she was apprehensive at the thought of a pitched battle here in the Square between Christians and Moors.

"Don't worry, mother," Prince Kamil confided. "In addition to the al-Khurs, Nasr has a regiment of soldiers clothed in civilian garb mingling in the crowd with their clubs, daggers and swords beneath their robes. If anything happens that the al-Khurs cannot handle, the soldiers have orders to use as much force as is necessary to put down any disturbance by these Christians. If the Christians attempted any disturbance here in the Square none would survive."

"But my son," Sumayla said showing some anxiety, "I do not care to be on a battlefield." Sumayla was well aware that Kamil, like most men of power, could not feel pain and death. Their feeling of invincibility, of distance, insulated them from what many assumed to be natural feelings of sympathy and mercy. Few understood as well as Sumayla that men of power think no more of human life than swatting a fly, smashing an ant or killing an animal...they wrap themselves in the invincibility of power. To the nobility, a battlefield is a neccessity...one that most women fear. Lady Sumayla was far too intelligent not to see the telltale signs of the coming end of the peace of the prophet. *The beheading of this frail, foolish white priest,* she said to herself, *certainly gives the signal to anyone who can see. The end is inevitable but do I have to be on the battlefield?* But she knew the answer she had to prepare Yerby for Nasr.

"These screaming, yelling Christians will be no match for the Emir's crack troops," Kamil declared. "But as you can see, the al-Khurs seem to have everything under control. Don't worry. Enjoy the spectacle."

It was true. Black-robed al-Khurs in squads of six or more milled about everywhere. Parting the crowds, they beat and arrested anyone foolish enough to display the least inclination to do anything other than bow and get out of their way. Everyone knew that if the al-

Khurs arrested you, whether you be man, woman, boy or child, you would end up as a galley slave and the remainder of your short miserable life would be spent on a rolling green ocean, your salt-scraped chafing body beat down upon by a hot Mediterranean sun, chained to a heavy oar with your back being lashed to ribbons by a gigantic Negro. The prayer of one arrested by the al-Khurs was for a quick death…and most got their wish, for few lived scarcely more than two months as a galley slave.

Many al-Khurs were Negroes; the rest were Bulgars, Tartars, Slavs. But no al-Khur, whatsoever, was ever an Arab, a Berber, a Muladi or a Mozarab. Their officers were Franks, because the Frankish variety of the Romance dialect was, with difficulty, still comprehensible to the populace. Over time, the emirs did all in their power to prevent the al-Khurs from learning either Arabic or Romance. The emirs decreed that no al-Khur should speak or understand Arabic or Romance. They did not want the al-Khurs accessible to the public. No plea or bribe could divert the Emir's police from executing their orders. The al-Khurs depended upon the Emir for everything, including their lives. It was a lifetime job without any pension. The Emir paid them well, considering that they wanted nothing. Everything was already given to them. However, their pay allowed each al-Khur to gamble and gambling possessed the soul of every al-Khur. The less lucky an al-Khur was, the more certain that his pay was insufficient and that he would be very active in providing Christians to the galleys. The Emir supplied their beds with fine willing slave girls, tied, just as the al-Khurs themselves, to their profession for life. Many learned that once their looks faded and younger women became available, they would be thrown out and have to make it as best they could. A few used their looks to acquire a hoard of gold, silver and precious stones from the al-Khurs who had plenty of everything. The al-Khurs ate well but were allowed no alcohol. They could be absolutely depended upon to put down a Christian riot with a precise thoroughness that even the Goths would admire.

After awhile, the roar of the mob began to swell as the gates of the Alcazar opened and the procession of Córdoba's officialdom poured out. First to appear was the head executioner dressed in a hooded black robe. Next came a gigantic Negro wearing nothing on his huge bare chest other than a golden medallion attached to a gold chain. His mighty arms rippled with muscles. Cradled in the black man's hands was a gigantic scimitar. Next in the procession came the *cadi* who had presided over the trial. Behind trailed all of the Emir's official witnesses; they included the royal court, viziers, secretaries and clerks. Nasr, as usual, was undistinguished, a roly poly little man with an evil face. But, of course, Nasr sat on a dais set above everyone else who stood on the platform. Taking his place on the execution platform, Nasr made only a half-hearted attempt to remove the look of satisfaction from his face. It was not that this execution helped in his bid for power. Rather Nasr, like everyone else, just wanted to see a man beheaded.

Once Nasr had been seated, in came a frail-looking priest dressed in a brown coarse knit cassock cinched around the middle by a single white knitted cord. He was surrounded by the Emir's own personal guard. The priest's arms were heavily manacled behind him and he wore shackles on his feet. Stringy white hair flew about a face lined with wrinkles and covered with gray stubble. On the priest's chin a mass of whiskers lay in a matted mess. The priest's pale blue eyes, which had often danced with gaiety, now wore the dull and lackluster look of certain death. However, there was no indication that the prisoner had been subjected to any torture or humiliation, unlike those Jews who would fall into the clutches of the Christian Inquisition some centuries later. These Christians would subject their prisoners to beating, gouging, tearing and burning. Afterwards the victims were paraded through the streets riding backwards on a jackass. Barely conscious, bleeding and dazed, the condemned wore fool's caps and humiliating signs. The crowds were invited to pelt these victims with rocks, garbage and even excrement. But now, in ninth-century Córdoba, the Emir tolerated no such treatment of the condemned.

The *cadi* raised his arms. The roar of the crowd diminished abruptly and then finally hushed. Then he intoned: "Inasmuch as the Christian priest, Prefectus, publicly mocked Islam, our great and true belief, and has steadfastly refused to recant his blasphemy against Allah and His Prophet, Muhammad, let him now be put to death."

With that proclamation, the crowd roared out with one voice until its howling shook the very walls of the Alcazar. But, it quickly died away as Prefectus cried out in a reedy voice the terrible words of a Christian martyr:

"I declare an anathema upon your Prophet and all his works! My God will punish him for the many souls he has seduced into hell! Upon you, Nasr, apostate of the True Faith, castrate of the spirit as well as of the body, I reserve my dying curse! You will not live until today's anniversary. You will join Satan, thy true Lord, in his sojourn of eternal pain. My blessings for all those who believe in the Lord Jesus! And upon all those who follow that black devil, Muhammad, my curse! And now executioner, strike well!"

Once again, the crowd burst into a deafening roar as the Negro raised his mighty arms. Holding the great steel blade, gleaming into the sun for a fleeting instant, the black agent of death sent it whirling in a great arc. Knifing it down with ferocious power, the axeman aimed his blade at the old priest. A clear swishing and cracking sound issued forth as the axe sliced its way down through the thin, wrinkled neck. The black-robed official executioner reached down and grabbed Prefectus' gory head. The eyes and mouth were still wide open, still screaming now silent curses. The executioner held the head up to the crowd. The mob exploded into a bestial cry that reached the heavens and glazed over the noonday sun.

"Let's get out of here!" the Princess Sumayla said, her face pale with horror. She quickly signaled her retainers. They formed a wedge and Lady Sumayla, Prince Kamil and Frank Yerby moved back through a path parted by several squads of al-Khurs who, in their turn, bowed to the royal party. They retreated back towards her palace. Once Sumayla had gotten over the savagery of the execution and fear of the consequences, she focused on whether it had the desired effect on Frank Yerby. "Did any of that seem familiar, Frank?" Sumayla asked.

Shaking his head, Yerby replied, "No, I don't believe I have ever witnessed anything like that before. What did that old priest do?"

"Daily, the Peace of the Prophet rains down blessings upon all the inhabitants of the Emirate of Spain," she explained, "but Arian Christians like Prefectus blaspheme Islam, curse our Prophet and even ridicule the Emir himself."

"Our imams and other religious fanatics have not been altogether innocent," Kamil commented. "They have done their share to goad these Christians and provoke the situation."

"Yet Arian Christians urged on by their priests as well as their own hatred of anything which does not model Teutonic supremacy continue to assault the Peace of the Prophet," Lady Sumayla responded. "So the Emir has been forced to retaliate and execute some of these fanatics." She watched Yerby for any sign of recognition. So far she couldn't tell. There seemed to be none.

"Surely you recall this controversy, Frank," she declared matter-of-factly. "You are aware that these Christians are proclaiming those that have been executed to be martyrs of the Christian faith."

"They are martyrs," Kamil said. "And now the Emir has given the Christians their first martyred priest. Did you hear the curse Prefectus put on Nasr? I'll bet that fat little castrate is trembling in his slippers."

"Somehow, I don't think so," the black princess said. "Besides which, Nasr could not allow any blatant challenge to Islam pass. Otherwise it would have been his head on the executioner's block."

"That still makes them martyrs," Kamil persisted. "They have a list of grievances and they want them heard."

Sumayla looked over at her son. *Why are you persisting in this stupid line of reasoning?* Then she remembered. One thing lay between mother and son that prevented perfect understanding between them. The one impassable gulf was that her son was a Christian in belief and outlook. "Oh yes, I forgot, Kamil, your father is a Christian."

"Yes, my father is a Christian," Kamil replied proudly, "as well as an honored confidant of the Emir who calls him Aizun ibn al-Qutiyya, his friend."

"Friend or no friend, the Emir will not allow these fanatical Arian clergy to complain with impunity. They are not going to recite their list of real or imagined wrongs from their pulpits, or in meetings with their followers or in their Christian councils, with impunity. The consequences would be disastrous for his regime. Isn't that right, Frank?"

"I really do not know," Yerby replied. "This situation doesn't have anything to do with me. I'm still trying to figure out how I got here...and why. I'm not religious and all this is just a bunch of nonsense to me."

Sumayla concentrated her powers; she had to make Frank Yerby focus. "Frank, listen to me. What do you think is going to happen here? Do you believe these Christians will overthrow the Emir?" Sumayla was trying to probe Yerby's memory and force him to remember. After all, much of what Yerby wrote in *An Odor of Sanctity* concerned this very issue. Then and only then could they pry it out of him.

But just then a party of three distinguished gentlemen, one wearing a priest's cassock and the other two the rich garb of gentlemen of commerce, the sort normally worn by important Christians and Jews, drew near, Kamil recognized Garcia, his own brother-in-law. Garcia was married to Munia, daughter of Alaric Teudisson and Kamil's own half sister, providing another link between Kamil and the Emir. Al-Rahman II had enthusiastically approved the marriage between his son, al-Munhir, to Alaric's daughter Theodora. Kamil and Garcia hastened to one another. Hailing, they clapped each other on the back and embraced each other vigorously. "My brother Garcia," Kamil exclaimed eagerly. "How are you?"

"Kamil," Garcia cried out with just the barest hesitation as if somewhat embarrassed by the chance meeting. Though Garcia exercised his most courtly manners, inwardly he raged at having to associate publicly with this ape who happened to be his father-in-law's son. This fool does not even have the decency to be discreet when we meet in public, Garcia thought...and they said that Kamil was educated! Garcia planned to take great personal satisfaction in watching this half-breed blackamoor, standing in front of him, writhe in agony when they burned him at the stake. And Garcia intended to make certain Kamil got the death sentence whether or not Nasr succeeded in overthrowing the Emir. But for now, Garcia needed to be patient and endure this African lavishing affection on him. Accompanying Garcia was Alvaro, the ex-Jew and recent Christian convert, and the fiery Father Eulogius.

Observing the formalities, Kamil introduced each in his turn to his mother and Frank Yerby.

"Were you present at the execution?" Eulogius addressed Yerby. "This is a great day...the beginning of the end."

"How is that?" Yerby asked.

"Long have I prayed for this vindication of the One True Faith! Outnumbered, surrounded, corrupted, seduced by Muhammad's subtle wiles, we children of God have long needed proofs of our rightness as was seen in the Square today! If I could raise such a crop of martyrs as the good Father Prefectus, I could drown all these Moorish dogs in blood. In neverending files, we'll bow our necks to the axe, accept tortures and the cross itself, until the truth of the One True Church of Our Lord Jesus Christ would be revealed to all."

"How can you take pleasure in such a sad event?" Lady Sumayla asked. "Can the sacrifices you contemplate really be worth the paltry gains that you would win? Certainly you are completely free now to practice your religion without interference."

"I would think that you would rejoice with us," Eulogius retorted, "considering all you have at stake!"

The Lady Sumayla ignored his obviously snide remark concerning secret efforts on her son's behalf. *Are there any truly well-kept secrets in Córdoba?* she asked herself. "Even so," she continued, "how can you work for such evil ends when you have complete freedom of worship? Christians are not victims."

"Our young Christian scholars delight in the poems and romances of the Arabs. They study the works of Islamic theologians and philosophers, not to refute them but to acquire an elegant Arabic style. Our most talented young Christian minds are being captured and held hostage because they know no other literature or language save Arabic." Eulogius began reciting the litany of well-known grievances. But in reality, the concerns were always the same. The priests would not tolerate losing control over Christians, especially the young men.

"Not to mention," Alvaro broke in, "that we good Christians are forbidden to parade our sacred images in holy procession through the streets of Córdoba. We may not sound the bell to call worshippers to prayer. Muslim *cadis* offer insulting interpretations of our Christian faith, but when we attempt to defend our faith we are threatened with death."

"How often have we been stoned by children," Eulogius broke in again, "and spit upon by the mob because of our clerical garb?"

"The mobs that you are complaining about," Sumayla spoke up, "are made up of your own children and grandchildren. You Christians lose converts to Islam, daily, not only from the lowly who wish to improve their material lot but you are losing those young Christian men you have enrolled in the ranks of your brightest and best Christian minds." But Sumayla smiled to herself since the answer was far simpler.

If you were a pretty smart young man and you had a choice between two religions, which one would you choose? One choice would have you living in a cold single cell and sleeping on a few pieces of straw strewn on a stone floor. Your life would be one of continual drudgery. Every day you would be obliged to do exactly as you were told under threat of physical punishment or even death…and loss of your immortal soul. To live this life one would stay a Christian. On the other hand, another choice gave the young man access to the economic activity of the empire and in addition access to as many women, slave and free, as he could desire. Every day the challenge would be to be as successful as your skill and intelligence would let you. This choice meant embracing Islam. Sumayla knew what choice the majority of the Christian boys made. The outcome could be easily predicted by how greatly the royal court treasured and valued white skin. As the young, formerly Christian, Goths converted to Islam there developed a privileged class distinct from the court that could assume the mantle of legitimacy over the masses without the royal court or the Emir himself, being aware of it. Sumayla said nothing of that. Rather, she raised the issue of choice and competition.

"You Christians complain that your children are seduced by Islam's luxury," Sumayla said. "That is why you want to overthrow, not Islam, but the happiness it gives to the people of Islam. Christians suffer and are guilty of wanting to suffer. Christian priests want their people to suffer, otherwise there would be no need for Christian priests. Your ignorance and backwardness cannot compete with our culture and learning. You burn and hide books rather than read and understand them. That is why you need martyrs…you are planning to kill your own people."

"Don't you know," Kamil said in the attempt to play mediator, "that this religious struggle is harming Christians as well as Muslims. Is that what you want?" His position as a member of the Emir's inner circle gave Kamil insight into the impact the ongoing religious struggle was having on the Emirate. Dogmatic intolerance inflamed angry mobs on either side with a savage ferocity and self-righteous anger that was horrible to witness. Christians unfortunate enough to fall into the clutches of an Islamic mob might end up being beaten or torn apart or even crucified. On the other hand, Christians prowled the streets, evading the roving squads of al-Khurs in search of an unsuspecting and defenseless Moor they might kill.

Listening to the discussion, Frank Yerby permitted himself a comment, to both the astonishment and delight of Lady Sumayla. "Your tactics do seem a bit extreme, given the mild conditions under which you live," Yerby observed.

"Extreme!" Alvaro shouted at Yerby. "You dare say extreme!" The raised voices attracted several onlookers from the waves of people now filtering back from the Square.

"Look," one man cried, "it's the blessed Father Eulogius. He's challenging those black Moors."

"We can't let them get away with killing another of our holy men," cried another. The Christians prepared to charge. But a crowd of Moors also attracted by the voices streamed over. "There's another of those Christian infidels," the cry went up.

Kamil looked at his mother and said, "I believe this little party should be adjourned…and quickly." Grabbing her by the arm and signaling his mother's retainers, he steered her away just as the Christians and the Moors turned to face each other. Hurrying away, Sumayla, Kamil and Yerby heard the angry words "infidel," "heretic" shouted back and forth.

"In my day, the words will be 'nigger' and 'whitey'," Yerby thought sadly.

Zig-zagging through Córdoba's narrow streets with Garcia, Alvaro and the rabble rousing Eulogius close behind, Kamil and his mother hurried out of danger into Cordova's Jewish Quarter where her friend, the physician, Moses Abulafia, lived.

"We will avail ourselves of Moses' hospitality," she decided.

"I must return to the Alcazar." Kamil announced. "I've been gone far too long. We who work for the viziers are as much prisoners of the Emir as all his other slaves and servants." And embracing his mother and Garcia, who required all of his courtly charm to hide his disgust as well as nodding to Yerby, the prince took off.

"We, too, must take our leave," Garcia said, and bowing to Lady Sumayla, he, with Alvaro and Eulogius headed back to the Christian Quarter.

Sumayla then led Yerby to the modest home of Moses Abulafia where Judith, his portly and friendly wife, opened the door and gave them admittance. Judith served Moses as nurse and pharmacist. When Sumayla first began visiting, Judith told Sumayla that Eve planted the tree of Good and Evil. Adam plucked the forbidden fruit and Eve cast Adam out of the garden. Judith descended from the Jebusites, the original Canaanites who secretly worshipped the Goddess Anatha after whom the village of Bethany is named and whose sacred lioness had mothered the tribe of Judah. Every Passover, the Jebusites still mourned Anatha's murdered son Tammuz, the God of the Barley Sheaf.

"My darling, daughter," the old man exclaimed as they entered. "Come in, come in." Abulafia's welcome was warm and genuine. Sumayla was one of his children. Then looking directly at Sumayla's companion, he asked, "And who is this fine looking gentleman? You couldn't be Frank Yerby, could you?"

"Yes sir, I am," Yerby responded.

"Oh my, oh my," the old Jew cried. "This is unbelievable… unbelievable!" Turning to Sumayla, the mystic asked "He answered your summons according to the laws?"

"Yes," Sumayla replied. "He came of his own accord."

"Amazing," the physician replied. Abulafia was old and careless about his appearance. His stained and spotted robes had been washed, but not in recent memory. The sparseness of the gray hairs on his head contrasted with the fullness of his great beard. But his eyes twinkled with merriment and he hopped about with the energy of a child.

"Have you questioned him yet?"

"Some…"

"Well, Frank, how do you feel about being here?" the old Jewish physician asked. "You do realize you are not in your own reality, don't you?"

"Of, course," Yerby replied huffily. "I'm just waiting…"

"Waiting for what?" Moses Abulafia replied.

"Waiting to wake up," Yerby replied. "This is a dream, isn't it?"

"Yes," Abulafia answered, "you could call it a dream…but this is a special type of dream."

"How so?" Yerby asked.

"Sumayla summoned you…."

"Sumayla summoned me?"

"Yes…and you came," Abulafia replied, gleefully. "You came of your own free will."

"I did?" Yerby asked. Yerby was beginning to become a bit uncomfortable. He could not understand how a character, his character, his creation, could summon him into a dream. And yet this dream was real. These were real people and he was experiencing real events.

"But how can this be?" Yerby exclaimed.

"You did it, yourself," Abulafia explained. "Through the discipline of your own mind, you have created bridges in time. And because they are your creations, you have the ability to cross over these bridges any time you wish. All you needed was the desire and intent."

Intent… Yerby remembered the practices of ancient Mexican shamans. They intentionally empowered all their behaviors with remarkable concentration by withdrawing into an inner world or a separate reality. By using their intent, these shamans developed an awareness linked to a universal force existing outside the realm of time and space. This power link was the warrior's connection to the binding force of the universe.

"I do not believe that this is possible," Yerby replied. "People that accomplish these things require discipline and years of practice…and I have neither."

"Oh, but you have, my friend," Abulafia said. "You have enormous discipline. That's how Sumayla was able to call to you. You imparted that discipline to her. And since you were within hours of your death, you had no choice but to answer her."

Yerby remembered a passage from Carlos Casteneda: "Death is the eternal guide always to our left and an arm's length behind us. Death advises only the warrior. Whenever the warrior feels that he is about to be annihilated, the warrior turns to his death and asks, 'Is now the time?' Death always tells him: 'Nothing other than my touch matters…and I haven't touched you yet.'" And Yerby realized that death had not touched him yet.

"Why did you summon me?" Yerby asked Sumayla.

We need you to tell us about the future, she began to say, but the Jewish physician turned mystic silenced her. Abulafia knew that now was not the time for Yerby to reveal the future. So much of what she wanted to know was conditional. Man's fate was never immutable. To ask Yerby about the future as he knew it, could change what he knew. This was not the time to ask for any pronouncement from on high. The world still did not know that the creator was not almighty. The creator needed the creation as much as his creation needed him.

"Tell me, Frank," Abulafia smiled, "now that you are facing death, do you still believe there is no God?"

Yerby had to consider that question. How many times had he said that the only reason that man invented the gods was because of his fear of death? Now, he realized it was true. Yerby didn't fear death itself; but he did not want to face the thought of his own annihilation, or extinction. That his body should become food for worms was of no concern, but that his creative mind would be reduced to nothingness, and the greatness of his dreams would cease their wonderful creations, was unacceptable. Yerby had often said that man bore the heaviest burden of all creation: the knowledge of his own approaching death. That was why Yerby believed that man had been forced to invent gods.

"It's just that I believe that life is meaningless as it is," Yerby replied, defending himself. "It's up to us to give it significance. Only we can make our lives meaningful to others and ourselves. We do this to be as happy as possible. By creating rites and ceremonies, inventing glorious myths, dignifying the struggles of our brothers in sorrow, we mitigate our condition of insignificance. But by filling our minds with lies, merciful though they be, including the one about a god who cares about us but does not need us—the first and greatest of all myths—trivializes the efforts each of us makes on our own behalf, which is our only gauge of happiness."

"So how do you feel now?" Abulafia asked. "Do you still deny the existence of God? Or do you believe that your death is the end of your own existence?"

"I don't really know," Yerby said with a degree of honesty and humility he had not felt for many years.

"Frank," Sumayla said hesitantly, "there was another reason for your summons."

"My summons?" Yerby replied in an annoyed tone. Yerby found it strange that any of his characters could control him.

"Yes, Frank," Abulafia cut in. "The Lady Sumayla summoned you at the request of Nasr."

"It was not a request," Sumayla broke in, "it was a command. Nasr wants you to tell us what you know about the outcome of our plans for my son, Kamil."

"What is it you want to know," Yerby responded.

"Do you know why Nasr plots against the Emir?"

"Of course," Yerby responded. "Nasr is one of those twisted

people, the kind that so often turns against his master."

"But why?" Lady Sumayla persisted in her questioning. "Abd al-Rahman II is a kind and generous ruler. Nasr enjoys the Emir's confidence and trust. Nasr is the most powerful man in the Emirate with the exception of the Emir himself. Why would Nasr jeopardize his position, not to mention his life, in this mad scheme to destroy the Emirate?"

Yerby thought awhile. The truth was that he didn't know any more about what was about to happen than Sumayla, Nasr or any-one else.

"You want to know why Nasr is risking everything including his life, to assassinate the Emir?" Yerby asked Sumayla, trying to sort out his thoughts.

"Yes," Sumayla answered.

"Because Nasr is a Goth," Yerby explained, the words easing from his mouth carefully and slowly. "And not only is he a Goth, he is an agent for the kingdom of Asturias and in direct contact with King Alfonso II. Alfonso is an Arian Christian and he is building up an army of Christian knights and soldiers. They flock to his banner from Northern Europe for a military campaign against the Spanish Emirate." *Now how did I know all of that?* Yerby asked himself.

But this brief moment of reflection ended with a banging on Moses Abulafia's door. Shouts and threats were exchanged with Lady Sumayla's armed retainers stationed in front of Abulafiah's residence, and the black-robed al-Khurs who came bursting through it. The al-Khurs' captain gave a stiff bow and said, "Forgive the intrusion, milady, but the Lord Nasr has ordered us to escort you and your guest…" indicating Frank Yerby, "…safely back to your palace. He wants to make certain no harm comes to either of you."

CHAPTER FIVE

In the Christian quarter, the Archbishop of Córdoba summoned the newly appointed pastor of San Acisclo's parish, the elderly, yet mentally alert Father Juan. The Vatican had sent a papal legate to investigate the religious disturbances in Spain. The Holy Father was very concerned about the outbreak of so-called martyrdoms, of which the death of Father Prefectus was just the latest. The papal legate directed the Archbishop to convene a synod. "We must investigate these matters in order for me to report back to the Holy Father," the papal legate directed the archbishop. It did not take the synod long to discover that Father Eulogius and his "Exalted Ones" were stirring up their parishioners to publicly insult the Islamic religion, and the *cadis* willingly put the offenders to death. The Vatican wanted these martyrdoms stopped, immediately. The Christian church existed at the pleasure of the Emir of Spain and Eulogius' rabble rousing would not only set off a round of reprisals that not only could destroy Christianity in territories controlled by the Moors but also disrupt all the Vatican's carefully laid plans to recapture Spain, as well.

"Father," the Archbishop addressed his newly appointed pastor, "what is your opinion of Father Eulogius?"

"Father Eulogius means well, Your Eminence," Father Juan respectfully replied to the Archbishop.

"The road to perdition is paved by 'good intentions', my son," the Archbishop remarked. He wondered whether he had made the right choice in replacing Prefectus with this doddering old man. *I might have just replaced one fool with another,* the archbishop thought to himself. *Father Juan might not be the right person for an assignment as delicate as this one.* But the Archbishop knew he had no choice. The Vatican wanted immediate results and the papal legate was there to get them. So the Archbishop addressed the elderly cleric standing in front of him once again. "Good intentions are not what I want to discuss with you here today," the Archbishop boomed out harshly. "Nowhere do Christians gather together where the Emir's informants are not present, as well. The Emir even is informed of discussions between priests and leaders of the Church." The old priest's blank look did nothing to convince the Archbishop that Father Juan had the vaguest understanding of what the Archbishop was talking about.

"Father Eulogius is on a mission," Father Juan replied. "I don't believe he thinks about who is watching him."

"Father Eulogius is on a mission, all right," the Archbishop responded. "But he seems to have fallen into grievous error and sin. Father Eulogius is unable to control his passions. He seems very angry and behaves out of hate rather than love."

"Your Eminence," Father Juan responded, "Father Eulogius has a powerful faith. He believes that he is doing God's will. Certainly we can't condemn him for that."

"He has taken the vow of obedience," the Archbishop remarked, "as have you." Though the Christian church of the ninth century knew none of the asceticism of later years with its emphasis on poverty, silence, celibacy and mortification, the early church did have a primary rule of obedience. Not only was disobedience frowned upon, it was grounds for the severest punishment the Church could inflict: excommunication.

"Forgive me, Your Eminence," the old priest replied. "I had no intention to challenge your authority."

"Yes, Father Juan," the Archbishop chided him, "sometimes a sudden elevation makes a person forget their vows and their duties. I would warn you against trying to be too fond of your own ideas and pray for humility."

"Yes, Your Eminence, please forgive me."

"That is better, my son." The Archbishop felt a little better about Father Juan's loyalty, but was resolved to continue to watch the old priest. "Now tell me, how did Eulogius get Father Prefectus caught up into this trouble?"

"Actually, Father Prefectus was not a member of Eulogius' Exalted Ones, as they call themselves," Father Juan began. "He was tricked into becoming a martyr." One would have thought that the archbishop would have known as much or more than a simple parish priest. One might have even asked: Where are the archbishop's spies? The simple matter was that the parish priests and the pastors were the source of the archbishop's information, just as the Pope got all of his information from his archbishops and papal legates. In general, archbishops and papal legates tried to work together so that whatever was reported to the Pope would be reviewed by both prior to submission to the Pope. The archbishop and papal legate called the synod so as not to be accused of collusion. And the findings of the synod agreed to by both the archbishop and the papal legate were delivered by the Pope. The Roman Empire had been "holy" since the conversion of the Emperor Constantine. Having been given the prediction *in hoc signo vinces,* Constantine won many battles when his soldiers and knights wore the cross on their armor and weapons. Now the empire was in the hands of the pope and he intended to resptore it to its former greatness.

To manage this great restoration of the Roman Empire, the Pope required information from all over the world. And once one unified Holy Roman Church dominated the entire world, all information reaching the Pope would be accurate. However, in ninth-century Spain, the Christians were not in control. The archbishop knew little or nothing of what transpired in the Islamic community. He had to probe his pastors for information. Just as the archbishop and the papal legate would agree upon what to tell the Pope, *the pastors and priests agreed upon what to tell the archbishop.* There was a very good reason for this: Arianism had infected a large segment of the priesthood. And the Arian priests were sadistic, homicidal, psychotic killers whose victims were innocent members of the Christian communities. At first it was easy to identify the Arian priests—they were the ones obsessed with obedience and blood, and they stood out from the many gentle and spiritual priests.

They stood out, but they were not eliminated. Soon bishops who wanted absolute control over their Christian communities found the Arian priests useful. The Pope himself found priests dedicated to violence and war useful. Thus the Holy Father assembled legions of such priests under the rule of the Knights Templar (though they recognized each other as Teutonic Knights of Arthurian legend). Early bishops found the ability of the Arian priests to keep their congregations in line very useful.

"Tricked!" thundered the Archbishop. "My God, the situation is worse than I imagined. A priest of the One True Faith is tricked by a group of ignorant savages. Tell me, Father Juan, just how was Father Prefectus tricked into publicly blaspheming Islam and its Prophet and getting his stupid head cut off?"

Father Juan began his tale very carefully. "A group of Muslims engaged Father Prefectus in a debate upon the relative merits of their Prophet and Our Lord. The Muslims promised Father Prefectus that the discussion would be a private affair between scholars. But soon they were shouting at each other. After the Muslim clerics denied Christ was

God, the good father lost his temper and quite attacked the Prophet as a blackguard and an adulterer. How the al-Khurs were summoned I do not know, but as loud as the good father was bellowing his insults, any passerby could have heard him and reported him to the *cadi*."

Father Juan decided to end the story there. He did not tell the Archbishop the complete story. He did not tell the Archbishop about Father Prefectus' good friend the Abbot Spera, pastor of San Zoil's parish. Abbot Spera claimed that he had found a way to demonstrate the falsity of Islamic teachings to anyone with an open mind. One day the abbot even made the idle boast to his good friend, Father Prefectus, that he, Spera, could even convince the heretics of the truth of Christian beliefs.

. . .

As one of the Abbot's closest friends. Prefectus spent many hours with Sperta developing what they considered to be an irrefutable argument. They convinced each other that they were in possession of facts that, in their minds, no reasonable person could deny. Daily, Spera and Prefectus discussed their points of view, admitting no demonstrable proof that might counter their arguments that Christianity was the only true religion and was destined to rule the world. They argued down anyone who offered the least challenge to their "irrefutable logic." The two old men fully supported each other in their belief that no conceivable counterargument against Christianity even existed. Certainly no Muslim cleric could withstand their carefully assembled "logical proofs."

Eulogius and Alvaro studied under Spera. Eulogius and his Exalted Ones praised Spera and Prefectus throughout the Christian quarter, declaring them to be prophets of God who had discovered the "Truth." But this was not all. Spera and Prefectus confounded their arrogance by assembling their logical absurdities into a collection of writings. These written "proofs of the false teachings of the Prophet Muhammad" made very tempting targets for any Muslim thinker wanting to have a good laugh at the two fanatical Nazarenes. Thus, when Father Prefectus, who had never intended to be either reasonable or rational, was challenged and his truths all but destroyed, he adopted the dogmatic, anti-intellectual stance that had motivated him from the very beginning; the very arrogance that had now caused him to become an "accidental" martyr. None of this did Father Juan tell the archbishop.

. . .

But the archbishop had heard enough. "Do you know what the Emir's informants tell him, Father Juan?"

"No, Your Excellency."

"They tell him that a conspiracy exists among Christians to overthrow his rule. They name Garcia, Alvaro, a renegade Jew turned Christian, and, above all, Father Eulogius as the leaders of this group of insurrectionists called the The Exalted Ones. That's what the Emir is being told, Father Juan." *I hope this feeble old fool can grasp the seriousness of this situation*, the archbishop thought. Father Juan hoped that the archbishop would get no closer to the truth than he was now. The archbishop continued. "Soon these mad fools will exhaust the Emir's patience, and his al-Khurs will bend their stiff necks beneath his executioner's scimitar. They and their group of Exalted Ones, of which every third man is one of the Emir's spies, will cease to exist. But do you want to know what my concern is, Father Juan?"

Father Juan said nothing. The archbishop assumed he was too overwhelmed to respond.

"I fear for the rest of our Christian community, Father Juan," the archbishop said with the proper amount of emotion, the older priest observed.

"What would you have me do, Your Grace?" Father Juan asked the Archbishop, adopting a pose of complete deference and obedience.

"We must convince the Emir that the Christian Church is not behind this disturbance," the archbishop replied. "He must learn that we are doing everything within our power to stop it." The Archbishop stared at the old priest. These rabble rousers were able to manipulate many of the old priests as easily as the people of their congregations. It was hard for the archbishop to know whom to trust. He did not have the power to compel absolute obedience that the Church so eagerly coveted. But what could he do living under the rule of these heathen blacks? For now, the archbishop had to bargain and cajole Christians to do as they were told. One day, the archbishop prayed, all that would change. "The Emir must not see Christians of Spain as a group of ignorant and dangerous troublemakers. Do you understand me, Father?"

"Yes, Eminence."

"You must immediately communicate this message to Father Eulogius," the Archbishop commanded. "Do you understand?"

"Yes, Your Eminence," Father Juan replied bowing low. And offering his ring to the lips of the old priest, the archbishop dismissed him...but not without some trepidation.

Back at his parish, Father Juan lost no time in summoning the rabble-rousing priest.

"The first duty of the Church is to survive, my son," Father Juan told the younger cleric. Eulogius had agreed to meet with the older priest as much to convince the synod of the rightness of his position as to demonstrate his obedience to the higher authority. "You and your followers, those madmen you call the Exalted Ones, could provoke the Emir into destroying us altogether. You recognize that he has the power to do it, don't you?"

"Still, Father," Eulogius replied slowly, "might does not make right. If we do not resist these blackamoors, they will destroy us—not all at once, but by wearing down our faith, by stripping our churches of penitents and by showing our young men an Islamic heaven where each has six concubines." The younger cleric had to try hard to restrain his natural arrogance and respond respectfully. Father Juan represented the power of the synod. This is my opportunity to win them over, Eulogius thought to himself. Soon they'll be offering me everything I want. So Eulogius presented a very humble image to his superior.

Father Juan continued. "You, Eulogius, Alvaro and your entire band of exalted followers are going to bring down the Emir's wrath upon the whole Mozarab population…and when you do, you will be guilty of murder."

"And if we, ourselves, are martyred?" Eulogius asked.

"When a man embarks upon a course of action that deliberately causes his own death, he is committing suicide. Suicide is a grave sin," Father Juan chastised the young man.

"I find this line of reasoning strange," said Eulogius, allowing some of his smugness to show. "You could have made the same accusation against the saintly martyrs of the early Church."

"No, Father Eulogius," Father Juan remonstrated. "These early martyrs were true victims. They suffered for being Christians; they resisted to the death the blasphemy of worshipping the Emperor as a god. Here nothing of the sort takes place. Here, you and your fanatics are bent upon provoking a slaughter of Christians in the land where we dwell in perfect peace and in the full exercise of our faith. We are not forced to worship Allah; we do not have to hail the Emir as a god. We've been, for the most part, able to keep our churches open, say Mass, hear confessions and bring our children up in the Christian faith, without hindrance. Why must we provoke martyrdoms here? Here you can only produce martyrs by insulting an Islamic faith that hath treated Christians most kindly."

Father Eulogius rolled his eyes to the sky as if to pray for guidance and then responded, "We are the guardians of our flock. Daily our flock chafes under the heel of this dusky tribe of Africans who extort life's toil from our men and cheat their children of their patrimony."

"Your meaning is unclear, my son," Father Juan said.

"We have met with many of the Christian nobility. One of their chief concerns is the taxes they must pay to the Emir."

To this, Father Juan answered, "We all must suffer from the burdens imposed on us by the taxes. But taxes do not threaten the existence of the church! Taxes would be imposed even by Christian rulers."

"The Emir has enacted a prohibition against the sweet sound of church bells; he has forbidden the passing of holy images in solemn procession through the streets," Eulogius continued.

"Martyrdom is justified when the faith's in danger, my son," Father Juan replied. "Here in Córdoba, our faith is protected by the highest power of the state—and endangered by mad fools like you."

"I may be mad," said the fanatical priest, "but I am far more interested in saving our faith here in Spain than you realize. You think the battle here is between the Christians and Muslims! But everywhere heretics, schismatics and apostates assault the One, True Catholic Faith. We must deal with Gnostics, Manicheans, Dolomites and, worst of all Arians. Yes…the True Church is being threatened by extinction, but not by these sons of Ham who will soon be back where they belong. It is a battle between the heretics and the true Christians. And in this battle, no quarter can be asked or given."

The elderly priest took pause and reflected. Of course, he had heard of these heresies. The archbishop and the papal legate were certainly concerned with these great heretical attacks against Christ's true Church. *Was this fanatical priest*—soon to be bishop of the diocese of Toledo and afterwards a martyr—*trying to link these matters?* Father Juan asked himself. But withholding comment, he said quietly, "Go on my son."

Eulogius knew he had him. *This pious, obedient but hopelessly backward priest knows nothing*, the young man thought. Eulogius knew that many of the older clerics had fallen into the mistake of believing in their own superior knowledge. That clever device the Christian church used so effectively, known as the sacrament of penance, made the priests complacent. Every week the clergy listened to the faithful confess their sins and in the process provide the pastor an incredible amount of intelligence about the lives, families and doings of their parishioners. He knew so much about the intimate details of so many people's lives; information that could be used to make a person do just about anything...even become a martyr. Control over so much information about what went on in his parish gave the pastor a certain feeling of omnipotence. However, that was as far as it went. The pastor knew very little about what was going on *outside* his parish. Only those who were permitted to sit on the synod had even an inkling of the weighty matters the Christian church considered in its deliberations. Father Juan wanted to know more of Eulogius' thinking.

"You see, Father Juan," Eulogius continued, imitating the legendary patience that the Abbot Spera used to capture the imagination of his young students, "we have a choice whether or not to be victims."

"How is that, my son?" Juan responded, now really intrigued.

"Victims have one thing in common: they believe in the finality and permanence of the world. They have no intellectual ability to look into the future and 'see' what can happen, what will happen, what must happen. It is the victims' own intellectual shortcomings which force them into a soulless existence where there is an insufficiency of dreams, imaginings, ambition to carry out the destiny that God has ordained for them."

Father Juan eyed the young priest with a dawning appreciation for his intelligence. "We of the True Catholic Faith," the older cleric said, "must, as you say, contend with dangers which threaten our very existence, heresies, schisms as well as the plots that secular powers hatch to further their own ends. But we cannot lose priests and dedicated Catholics at a time when our numbers are yet small and growing smaller."

Eulogius replied with a craftiness that Father Juan had failed to appreciate in the brief time he had known the younger man. Later others would realize they, too, to their disadvantage had underestimated Eulogius' intelligence. "Father, let me explain the Abbott Spera's teachings."

With that Eulogius launched into a discussion that he believed deeply impacted Father Juan's thinking, making the older priest a convert to the cause. Eulogius explained that man lives always on the verge, always on the borderland of something more. "Man is the only animal who has built restlessness into a religious principle," Eulogius said. "Even in the practical sphere, he is restless in ways that mark him off as distinct and unique in all of God's creation. Human desires, winged by imagination, fly beyond the scope of natural instinct and mock our efforts to satisfy them. But even when—perhaps especially when—we succeed in satisfying our basic needs, our feelings of a beyond and the urge to wonder about it remain. Indeed, the idea that there is something more, something beyond the horizon, beyond our grasp, is lodged in the very root of our awareness. But this awareness is not just a state of being, a state of existence like the existence of a rock or a tree. This awareness requires intent, the act of being intelligent. This awareness requires that the individual focus beyond and testify that some kind of beyond actually exists. Awareness means always to be on the verge of entering into this beyond but never getting there because, of course, only the soul can enter heaven."

Eulogius felt that he had captured the parish priest's imagination. "Father," Eulogius concluded, "you must tell the synod that I, too, fear for the existence of the True Faith. But I know that the threat comes not from the Emir and his dusky African brethren. They have not the intelligence to build a lasting civilization. They are not smart enough to defeat us. Their only purpose is to give us the resources and the time necessary to defeat our real enemies. Our real enemies, if given the opportunity, can and will destroy us! Even as we speak, agents from the kingdom of Asturias are gathering the intelligence necessary for the conquest of Spain by Arian Christians. This conquest will eliminate the Moors and establish the rule of the Goths under Arian Christianity. And the One, True Catholic Faith has no worse enemy than this Arian heresy. I believe that even the archbishop and the papal legate agree that it would be far better to sacrifice the blood of martyrs in order to prevent the re-emergence of that heresy that once before almost succeeded in supplanting the Catholic Church itself."

. . .

And in this Eulogius was quite correct. The Arian heresy all but destroyed the Catholic Church in the fourth century. The Catholic Church was saved by the accident of Julian becoming ruler of the Roman Empire in 361 A.D. Julian's disdain for all forms of Christianity caused him to reject it as the state religion and withdraw Roman support. The new emperor's indifference enabled the Catholic pope to direct an attack against pockets of Arian Christians throughout the empire. Yet even under the persecution of the Vatican, Arianism survived. It survived as the faith and belief adopted by the Teutonic inhabitants of northern Europe. Ulfilas, a disciple of Arius, himself, spent forty years preaching Arian Christianity to the Goths. From the Goths, Arianism spread to other German tribes including the Vandals, Burgundians and Lombards. As the Roman Empire crumbled under successive waves of German invasions, Arian beliefs and values dominated Christian faith and practices. Arianism spread within the Christian community like a virus. The Vatican made stamping out the heresy the Church's number one priority. Roman Christians purged anyone, cleric or lay member, from their community found to favor Arianism. Once the Roman Empire had been destroyed in the west and Germanic barbarians established their rule in Italy, Africa and

Spain, the Germanic ruling classes practiced Arian Christianity while their subjects remained Roman Catholics. The Arian nobility forbade intermarriage between themselves and any other people, especially the Roman Catholics. Taxes for Roman Catholics were higher than for Germanic Arians. Roman Catholics paid higher fines and even suffered capital punishment for crimes which Germanic Arians received lesser punishments. Arianism became the uniquely Teutonic form of Christianity that sanctioned all social and political differences on the basis of their racial superiority. Gradually the believers in Arianism held that Christianity was the distinct and unique religion of pure Arian peoples. Arianism taught that Christ himself intended that all peoples of the world be subject to the will of their Arian masters.

In the sixth century, the Holy Roman Emperor, Justinian, hurled his armies against the Germanics, and stamped out Arianism in Italy and Africa by the sword. However, in Spain, the invasion of the Muslims during the eighth century kept Arian Christianity alive on the Iberian Peninsula. Islam tolerated all forms of Christianity. Islam's religious tolerance and regard for anything white left it without any ability to appreciate the real distinctions between the two Christian beliefs. And so it was in Spain that Arianism remained dormant in the breasts of the teutonic knights, awaiting the opportunity when it could emerge once again and suppress and destroy the hated Roman Catholics.

But in the ninth century, Rome still remained Arianism's most aggressive foe. Arianism obstructed the Popes' ability to rule over a universal "catholic" church. Arians would not recognize Rome's authority. Eulogius counted on this fact. His movement helped Nasr. And that meant Eulogius was helping himself, because Eulogius was very ambitious…the mark of a true Arian. Arians believed neither in heaven nor in hell. They especially did not believe in retribution, divine or otherwise. This was why the Arian takeover of Christianity had been such a calamity. They seemed to have counteracted Christian values to the point that heaven and hell had become subjective realities in the present life. Christians soon accepted that those who fell into the clutches of the Arian priests and were forced to suffer cruel tortures and painful deaths were examples of Christians who suffered from the pains of their sins. Those who lived in grand mansions, wore the finest of clothes and dined at sumptuous banquets, were without guilt and entitled to heaven's blessings. For Eulogius this struggle, the martyrdoms, opened a path for him to a bishopric and, perhaps, an even higher position. And here in front of him, Father Juan was offering the opportunity.

"You must convince the synod that there is much to do and we have not much time," Eulogius said to Father Juan. And with that Eulogius departed.

• • •

And as Eulogius knew he would, Father Juan lost no time preparing his report…a report that neither the archbishop nor the papal legate expected to hear. And as might have been expected, later in the week, the archbishop summoned Eulogious to a hastily called meeting of the synod. The archbishop had no idea Arian Christians could sweep down from the kingdom of Asturias and wipe out not only the Muslims but the Catholics as well. And as Eulogius expected, the papal legate was extremely concerned. The Holy Father would discover that he could not rely upon the Christian church of Spain to be completely loyal to the One Holy Catholic Apostolic Church. The Vatican would question the loyalty of all Spain's Christians. The clergy, themselves, must be suspected. Had not Eulogius intimated that Arian informants and collaborators could be found throughout the Spanish Emirate? The archbishop and papal legate were forced to rout out the Arian heresy from Spain's Christian community before the Holy Father took action to remove them.

Awaiting the pleasure of the synod, on the day set for his meeting, Eulogius felt more powerful than ever before. He was well prepared. If matters went according to plan Eulogius could emerge as the most powerful cleric in Spain. Therefore, going into the meeting of the synod, Eulogius was filled with enthusiasm and high hopes. Standing before his superiors, Eulogius addressed them in slow steady tones. "My lord archbishop and distinguished members of this Holy Synod, agents of the Arian heretic Alfonso have issued a prediction that Islam will be defeated by Alfonso. Even the black Moors themselves have heard the prediction. Listen to the words of their prophet:

'...We have an Amir who desires Bougie for a Zanata Dynasty
which has appealed and which has manifestly seized power,
And [from] a region of Spain, then...
The Banu Nasr came, and victory followed
Rulers, Knights, and people of wisdom,
If you wish, write them down. Their region is empty...
If you wish, represent it in Latin without linguistic error,
And Alfonso and Barcelona...
And the Arabs, our people, have been weakened'."

"Who would utter such blasphemy?" asked the papal legate.

"Abu L'Fath Nasr, the Emir's own Vizier," replied Eulogius. "And, if this defeat comes at the hands of the Arian, Alfonso, what hope will there be for the One True Catholic Church in Spain?" Eulogius looked around and knew he had the attention of the synod

"My lords," Eulogius continued severely, "that castrate, Abu L'Fath Nasr, spreads this vicious plot among the Christian heretics serving Alfonso. The plot he hatches against the black Moors will keep him in power under the rule of Alfonso. If we of the True Catholic Faith do not act, those Asturian barbarians will spread Arianism throughout Spain at the point of a sword."

"What do you recommend?" the archbishop asked Eulogius.

"We must look to the learned Abbot Spera for guidance," the

ambitious young priest replied, looking over to his mentor and giving a slight bow. The abbot returned his protégé's nod.

"My Lord Abbot?" the archbishop addressing his fellow synod colleague.

"Your Excellency," the elder cleric replied, "Father Eulogius has shown us the way. Those heretics that Alfonso has placed among us must be compelled to give a testament to the True Faith, by their own martyrdom, if necessary. And the plot against this Emir must be foiled."

"What is the nature of the plot, may I ask?" The papal legate asked.

"Nasr plans to overthrow the Emir and put his cousin, al-Kamil ibn Abd al-Karim on the throne. This person is the illegitimate son of the Goth, Alaric Teudisson. His seizure of the throne will pave the way for King Alfonso's invasion," Eulogius spoke out to a hushed synod.

"My Lord," the archbishop exclaimed, "do you think they will succeed?"

"With God's help," Eulogius exclaimed, "we will defeat them."

"May I address the synod?" It was Father Juan who spoke up.

"Speak, my son, " the archbishop said,

"Your Eminence, I believe that Father Eulogius has brought to us one of the greatest challenges facing the Church since the time of the great persecutions and the catacombs. Since then, our struggles have been minor, struggles involving the choice between good and good where both sides are somewhat wrong and only God, Himself, can decide which side is actually in the right. But this coming struggle is between rightness on one side and wrongness on the other. The differences between the two sides are immense. This struggle will be in defense of civilization, of a Christian world order, the rule of our Lord and his faithful and the One True Religion. If we lose this war, a night of barbarism will settle not only over Spain, but the entire European continent, over the whole world. And it will last a thousand years."

"What is your recommendation, Brother?" the archbishop asked.

"I recommend that we appoint Father Eulogius to lead us in this struggle," Father Juan responded, "and that he be appointed to fill the vacant post left by the late bishop of Toledo."

The synod approved Father Juan's recommendation immediately although none of the members were quite sure how sending Eulogius several hundred miles away would help in this struggle.

CHAPTER SIX

The al-Khur sentries should have been watching more closely. Then they might have noticed a solitary figure lurking about the wall, tall, bearded, arrogant like the monkish priest, he was, for all of his age. The priest cautiously groped his way toward a secret entrance, wrapped in a magical black robe. The robe was not the brilliant, shining black kind worn by the great and wealthy, nor the stern overpowering black worn by the al-Khurs. The robe was a dull, lightless black: a sorcerer's cloak of invisibility. A cloak that absorbed light so that invisibility was all that remained; this was the purpose for which it had been designed. The priest's presence did not go completely unobserved because he was expected. Silently, an entrance slid open and in an instant the priest was through the wall. Within a matter of minutes, the priest was shown into the private apartment of the Grand Vizier, Abu L'Fath Nasr himself.

"Welcome, Father Juan," the head eunuch said expansively. "Please make yourself comfortable. What news have you?"

Nasr's apartment occupied an entire wing of the vizier's palace. The high domed reception area, covered with the intricate designs and beautiful architecture, held a battalion of slaves standing attentive to their master's every desire. Mountains of fruit, meats and pastries served in plates of gold lay on the sideboards; wine, white, red, was available in golden goblets. Musicians, dancers and other varieties of entertainment were available in this place of luxury and ease.

"My Lord Lengvold…"—as that was Nasr's Gothic name, "I bring news. At Eulogius' insistence, the synod's decided to institute an inquisition against us."

"Were you not successful in getting him out of our hair and appointed as the bishop in Toledo?" Nasr asked mildly. "I was led to believe that all Eulogius wanted was to be a bishop."

"Yes, milord," Father Juan replied, "but even so, he declared that we who serve good King Alfonso are heretics and the synod authorized him to take measures to root us out."

"I feared as much," Nasr replied thoughtfully. "Eulogius was never a man of his word. Ambition dominates men and makes them untrustworthy. They take success as a kind of omen that allows them to dare anything. Eulogius is as much of a castrate as I. He is blinded by his own ambition and power. So now he thinks that he can outwit me."

"Eulogius means to capture our informants," Father Juan replied, "he means to blind us." Nasr held his hand up to his visitor indicating that he should be silent. Nasr pondered Eulogius' daring. After several minutes he nodded to Father Juan to continue. "Eulogius has put himself in a very strong position, mi'lord. He knows we can't touch him or else he'll make our plans known to the Emir. And…"

"And both of us will loose our heads," Nasr completed the Arian priest's thought. "But intelligent men will leave nothing to chance. There is only one kind of luck: bad. That one must be eliminated… or soon he will be our undoing."

"As you know," Father Juan stated, "I am a true servant of my God and a loyal subject to our liege lord, King Alfonso, but as I stand here, I believe we can make much use of Father Eulogius. I believe him, in his heart, to be a true Arian. Once we begin our march, he will serve us well."

"How so, Father?" Nasr asked dryly.

"Eulogius wants to destroy Arab rule over Christianity," the priest observed. "And in this endeavor, I believe him to be right. It is not God's will that Moors rule over white men. We will not be their victims. Arabs are not concerned with the rule of law. They are not concerned with deterring people from misdeeds. They care only for property that they take by looting and by taxes. Under the rule of Arabs, we Christians live in a state of anarchy, without law, as victims."

"And your point is?" Nasr sneered.

"We must not make war on Catholics," Father Juan said, "we must win them over to our cause."

Priests, Nasr thought to himself. *They need to moralize everything.* As a Teutonic Knight, Nasr had been taught to mistrust priests…all priests. Priests envied the warrior class for their love of war, adventure and hunting. They envied the warrior's vigorous and free spirit, unfettered by any sense of morality. The priest hated the warrior because of his own impotence. *To priests, good is not what is noble and powerful; only the wretched are 'good'; the poor, the impotent, the lowly alone are 'good'. The priests believe that the suffering, the deprived, the sick, the ugly alone are good and they, alone, are blessed by God. How wrong these priests are! The powerful and the noble, on the contrary, are blessed of God. The cruel, the lustful, the insatiable rule through all eternity by the will of God; and through all eternity, God has placed the unblessed, the accursed, and the damned under the control of priests.*

Nasr needed to remind the priest of the major tenet of Arianism. "We of the noble races must take back the innocent conscience of the beast of prey. We rule triumphant. We emerge from murder, arson, rape and torture with an exhilarated undisturbed soul that our God Jesus Christ provides us. For in the sign of the cross, the sign of power and the sign of death, we will conquer. *In hoc signo, vinces.* Our deeds provide poets and historians with material for song and praise. The noble race, the beast of prey, the splendid blond beast prowling about avidly in search of spoils and victory, must erupt as the beast he is so that our civilization continues to grow and expand. You, of all people, must remain true to our faith."

"Of course, you are right, milord," Juan replied with a sigh. "How quickly we forget the old ways and the old beliefs living under the decadent rule of these black devils, I think."

Nasr interrupted. "Until we have taken control, Eulogius is to be considered an enemy. After all, Eulogius could disrupt King Alfonso's plans."

"So what is it that you propose, milord?" asked the Arian priest. "What should I report back to our liege lord, King Alfonso?"

"Tell him that we are proceeding with all due haste. Tomorrow, I will inform Lady Tarub that she is to begin her preparations." With that Nasr dismissed the Arian priest. *Now to return to that unfinished business with Mr. Yerby,* Nasr thought to himself. *He will either tell me what I want to know willingly, or be persuaded by my expert torturers.*

. . .

The next day Prince Kamil sat at his assigned place in the vizier's palace idly completing his assignments. Rather preoccupied, rather distant, mooning like the lovesick calf that he was, completely un-aware that everyone around him also knew that Kamil was in love. But Kamil, the son of a former black slave and a white Goth whose illegitimacy was overlooked only to please the kindly uncle of the Emir, was not just in love with *anyone*. Kamil was in love with the favorite wife of the Emir himself, the Lady Tarub. Their love could disrupt Nasr's carefully laid plans and deliver them all to the royal executioner. Prefectus would have the final say. But even if Nasr's plans were successful, how long would Kamil remain on the throne before he and his mother, too, suffered the fate of having their heads separated from their bodies?

Ironically, Kamil's position in the Emir's court gave him a great amount of insight into the problems facing the Emirate in its quest to bring the Peace of the Prophet to all its subjects. Having access to the Emir's personal letters and official correspondence, he was familiar with the various state secrets. He knew how Damascus drained the treasury continually. Attacks by the nomadic Berbers against Goth forts were increasing and the Goths were threatening retaliation. And religious disputes between Christians and Muslims were increasing. Kamil also knew the Emir's mind on most issues. He knew which issues the Emir considered important. Kamil liked the Emir and respected his decisions. But that wasn't strange, because Kamil liked everybody and everybody liked Kamil...even the Emir. The other members of the royal family were languid, distant, bored. But Kamil was always alive, intent and intelligent. Al-Rahman II liked that in Kamil. But tonight was the night when all things would change forever.

Kamil turned the whole thing over in his mind. Even being caught...even the torture. It was folly and worse, and Kamil knew it. But his whole body could still feel her body; the fragrance of her perfume enveloped him. His oversensitive nerves remembered the feel of her moving against him, he tingled... and the ache in his loins was as real as death. More real since he knew that he *would* die. His chances of escaping were one in a thousand, he knew. But first, he would spend a night of ecstasy with his Umm, the Lady Tarub.

Nasr and Tarub had set their plans in motion. As Yerby describes it in *An Odor of Sanctity*, Nasr himself had directed al-Harrani, the royal court physician, to prepare a poison that Tarub would put into the Emir's drink on his next visit to her chambers. The poison had been delivered. However, the royal physician's lifelong dedication to healing made it difficult for him to kill the Emir. Al-Harrani loved and respected the lofty figure of al-Rahman II. In truth, the royal physician believed that His Royal Highness, Abd al-Rahman II, was the noblest figure that his race and times had yet produced. At the risk of his own life, the physician attempted to send a warning to the Emir through his lovely concubine, the Lady Fakhr. This enchanting princess of the Kingdom of Egypt had been the Emir's favorite wife until the fair-skinned Tarub displaced her. Now the Emir did not trust her. He was well aware of Fakhr's hate for Tarub, and Fakhr could not warn her lord. The Emir knew how all of his wives hatched their petty intrigues, which he delighted in exposing. But the Emir had refused Fakhr access, so the court physician's warning went unheeded. However, the danger for Lady Sumayla and her foolish son continued to increase.

· · ·

"Thank you for attending me, milady," Nasr said. He was sitting on Lady Sumayla's own dais in her palace's great reception hall. Nasr was a man of medium height, but he appeared smaller because of the girth of his middle. Nasr dressed in the resplendent robes of a Moorish nobleman. From the round paunch that marked his waist hung a bejeweled dagger with which his fingers continually played. Beneath his close fitting white turban, Nasr's cold, piercing steel blue eyes gazed out into a reception hall empty of everyone other than household servants and the household guard. Then he hurled a penetrating look at the person he meant to crush into submission: Frank Yerby.

"Lord Nasr," Lady Sumayla advanced towards the grand vizier. "This is an unexpected surprise. To what do I owe the honor of this visit?"

"I think, Lady Sumayla," he said in the high whining voice characteristic of castrates, "we must move quickly with our plans."

"Why the suddenness?" the Princess asked. "It seems that the recent execution of Father Prefectus would make the Emir very cautious. He'll take extra measures."

"I shouldn't have to remind you that I am responsible for security," Nasr said, darkly. "I have complete control over the al-Khurs. And now that we have given Eulogius his martyr, we must begin the next phase of our plan, immediately." Nasr's blue eyes literally danced with excitement. The revenge he had planned for so many years was nearly here. "You do want your son on the throne, don't you?" he said with oily glibness knowing for certain what her answer would be. "Everything is in place," Nasr said. "Before we are finished, Eulogius and his Exalteds will have created so much confusion and instability that, after the Emir's death, Kamil will be welcomed on the throne."

Then Nasr smiled and glanced over at Frank Yerby. "And with him, we have the final piece to assure our success. What information have you gotten from your guest?"

"I've been hesitant to approach him with any specifics," Lady Sumayla confessed. "I have not your complete confidence…as you well know."

Nasr eyed his long-time protégé with an amused concern that only his emotionless soul could understand. How often he wanted to rid himself of the only person who knew him inside and out… knew his sinister nature. How often he wanted to destroy this woman who knew more then he. Each time Nasr was certain she had outlived her usefulness Sumayla came up with something new. If he could control this Frank Yerby person, Nasr would have his own crystal ball to the future. Sumayla continued to keep Nasr interested. He chuckled to himself, but sooner or later this black woman will outlive her usefulness and I will enjoy seeing her die…slowly, while she is thinking about it. But he said out loud. "As the Lady Sumayla knows, we have labored long over our mutual goal of putting her son, Prince al-Kamil, on the Emir's throne. Has this not been uppermost in your mind since his birth?"

"Yes," Lady Sumayla responded truthfully, "it has been my earnest desire to see Kamil on the throne. But how can he become Emir if he is dead?"

So Kamil has told you about his affair with Tarub, Nasr thought to himself. *That's been the most dangerous part of this entire affair. All these women talk. The Emir will hear about Kamil and Tarub soon. And then we'll all be undone. I must move quickly.* Nasr stared at the princess coldly. "Yes," Nasr replied, "your son had an indiscreet relationship with the Lady Tarub. I have been wondering how the two of us might save him. I am afraid that once the Emir hears about his indiscretions Kamil's head will belong to the executioner." Sumayla gave a start and Nasr knew she was caught.

Nasr glowed with satisfaction. He loved having Sumayla completely in his power. "What I propose is that we eliminate the Emir before he learns of Kamil's indiscretions. What do you think?"

Sumayla looked about helplessly. "What is it that your lordship would have me do?" she asked in resignation.

"I want you to learn from your friend, here, whether or not we are gong to be successful."

Turning to Yerby, Sumayla asked, "Frank, do you have any information which will help Lord Nasr save my son?"

Yerby knew exactly what Nasr wanted to know. But in reality, he didn't know any more than anyone else. Sure he could look at this situation and tell how it was going to turn out, not because he could see the future but because he could see the present. And he could see that these flimsy, poorly planned conspiracies and palace revolutions were doomed to failure. But Yerby decided to be discreet. Nasr still had power over him.

"How is it that you are aware of my existence?" Yerby asked the vizier.

"You are the creator of this world and all who dwell in it," Nasr replied.

"I did not create your world," Yerby replied, "it existed long before me."

"Whether it existed before you or not," the vizier snorted, "you know things that I would know...that I *must* know."

"All that I know," Yerby replied matter-of-factly, "is that I was lying in a hospital in Madrid and then I began to have these experiences, which I neither understand nor control."

Nasr stared at Yerby for some time. This was not what he wanted or expected. Nasr always expected prompt obedience and quick replies. It angered him when he did not get what he expected. Yerby read Nasr's anger as hesitation and doubt. So seizing the initiative, Yerby continued, "As my Lady Sumayla summoned me; perhaps it is in *her* power to answer your questions."

"Why do you say that?" Nasr asked.

"Because we are bound together," Yerby replied. "She is fearful for her son and I am fearful for...."

"Yes, what do you fear?"

"I fear that everything I have created will disappear. That no one will remember me or you, you are but a being conjured up in my mind and you live only within my novel."

"So you need Sumayla to rescue you from oblivion, is that it?" Nasr asked.

"Yes," Yerby admitted. "But, in reality, I believe I am here to learn something about how true intelligence can rescue my soul."

Facing Nasr squarely, Yerby finished. "So if there is something you need to know about your own fate or your own future, my response is that you must find it within the plan itself. For no man who tempts fate can know the outcome until it happens."

"Mr. Yerby," Nasr said, "I need to know how successful my plans will be to assist my lord Alfonso, furthering his ambitions for reconquering Spain. This is the information I want from you, now."

"OK, I get your drift," Yerby responded somewhat disinterestedly. "But this is the type of intelligence that folks like you always seek in their pursuit of power."

"Don't you mean as societies become more immoral, more savage?" Sumayla asked. She had been listening and observing the interchange between Nasr and Yerby with much interest.

"Well, yes" Yerby responded, "that, too. But, getting information has always been savage. You torture and kill for it. You spy; you steal information; you plant dis-information. You blackmail. You pimp pretty women... or pretty boys. You force people into chemical dependency."

"Well," replied Nasr, "I have enjoyed our little discussion, but since I have not gotten the information that I need I must go to work on Mr. Yerby, here and now."

Clapping his hands, two burly Negroes, whose muscular arms and broad chests bespoke great physical strength, clasped Yerby squarely by his loose-fitting robes and dragged him down into the dank lower region of Lady Sumayls's palace. There they locked Frank Yerby into a small cell. And the danger that he had feared suddenly became very real. Nasr decided to give Yerby a few minutes to think as his inquisitors prepared their implements and started up the fire. Nasr sat there, anticipating the pleasure he would get from seeing the wounded flesh, and hearing the screams of torment. But before the torture could begin, a messenger darted inside and prostrated himself before the vizier and proffered a message. Nasr barked orders to his retainers and guards and disappeared from the dungeon and out of the palace.

Later another servant hurried into Lady Sumayla's private chambers and whispered to her. Sumayla nodded. The servant disappeared only to quickly re-emerge in the company of a eunuch. Like Sumayla, the eunuch was black. His hawk eyes glanced quickly about before he knelt down and kissed the hem of Sumayla's robe. It was Quissan, who had known Sumayla for most of his life and who would give his life in her service. In the beginning Quissan worked with Sumayla in the copy house of Horeth. After her marriage into the royal family, Quissan begged Sumayla to get him a position in the Alcazar. He voluntarily became a eunuch. But since the castration was done voluntarily, only his instrument was removed and not his sacs. Quissan had much less of the flabbiness characteristic of those who had been subjected to the knife that separated them from their manhood. His livery indicated that he was one of the Emir's own personal servants.

"My lady," the handsome eunuch bowed low to his protectress, "you asked me to watch and listen for word of any plot against my master, the Emir."

"Yes, Quissan," the Princess replied, "what news have you?"

"My master, the Emir, sent the al-Khurs to fetch the fair-skinned Goth, known as Aizun ibn al-Quitiyya, before him," Quissan reported.

"Why would your master send for Aizun?" Lady Sumayla asked.

"My master desired," Quissan continued, "that Aizun explain his marriage to Natalia, the daughter of my master's youngest brother, al-Wallid. For, as you know, a Christian man cannot marry a Muslim woman without the woman renouncing her faith, in which case in the eyes of Allah she has committed heresy. For this crime, the punishment is death."

Sumayla gasped! Sumayla knew how rigid the rules of religion were, especially when the punishment was death. Even the Emir would not shrink from executing his own niece where the religious forms had not been observed.

"Do not fret, milady," the eunuch quickly continued. "The Lady Natalia's mother, Umm Walad Goissuintha, also a Goth and a Christian raised Natalia as a Christian and so no heresy occurred."

"That's a relief," breathed Lady Sumayla. This time Natalia's life was spared. The next time under Eulogius' influence that she violates a religious code, her head will tumble from her body, as Yerby tells us in *An Odor of Sanctity*.

"Yes, especially for my master, for he dearly loves his young niece," Quissan said.

"So what have you come to report, Quissan?"

"The Emir held a private audience with Aizun," Quissan continued. "Before Aizun left, my master thanked him for the warning. Though Tarub had become much bolder than any of the others, she was not so evil at heart as she seemed," the Emir said. "However I will appoint a royal taster. I'd even have her taste a few herself, if I didn't know that it would kill the silly trull!"

"So, the Emir knows of the plot," Sumayla summarized.

"Yes, milady," the eunuch replied. "The Emir knows."

Sumalya sent her guards down to the dungeon to free Frank Yerby, and retired to her own chambers. "Frank," she said more calmly then she actually was, "now the purpose I called you for is clear. You must accompany Quissan, here, and help rescue Kamil. My son's life is in your hands."

CHAPTER SEVEN

Abd al-Rahman II, Commander of the Faithful and Emir of Córdoba, was careful to cultivate the image of what he believed a Moorish prince should look like and he believed that a Moorish prince should look like him. Al-Rahman II was very dark; his skin had the hue of burnt copper; he was tall with a nose as thin and beaked as some bird of prey. The Emir had red hair, dyed each day by his personal barber. His long beard, on the other hand, was as black as the night. And so were his eyes. One of al-Rahman II's eyes winked ceaselessly. In his youth, al-Rahman II had been forced to witness the execution of several prisoners by his father, the former Emir, Abu'l Asi al-Hakam. The sight of so many heads falling to the headman's axe caused one of the eyes of the future Emir to suddenly begin twitching. From that time onwards his eye never stopped its nervous twitch. Some believed that this permanent affliction was why the Emir permitted as few executions as possible.

Yet, in defense of his throne and to maintain his rule, al-Rahman II learned to appreciate the value of public and private executions. After awhile, though his eye continued to twitch, it merely camouflaged the Emir's complete detachment and utter indifference to the spilling of blood and taking of life.

"Bring in those dogs!" the Emir cried out ceremoniously.

Immediately, the gigantic doors leading into the throne room in which the Emir and his court sat, opened. Two files of al-Khurs marched in, escorting between them ten heavily manacled Negro slaves. All were naked except for cloths covering the areas where their genitals should have been. However, since they had all been castrated, their loincloths covered only scars and memories. Two of the eunuchs marched in, tall, proud, looking neither to one side or the other. But the others came in gazing about wildly. Some sought to forestall their fate by half walking, half stumbling and finally dropping to the ground, forcing their captors to drag them the final distance. These were the eunuchs charged with guarding the Emir's harem. They had allowed Prince Kamil access to Lady Tarub and now they would lose their heads. One by one, at the foot of the Emir's throne, each had his head placed upon the block and the headman's axe flashed, and the severed head rolled from its trunk.

Al-Rahman II's two brothers, al-Mugira and al-Wallid, sat on cushions and enjoyed the show. Each cast sly glances at the official just in front of them whose quaking knees and wide eyes betrayed his absolute state of terror. Only that morning had abu Kitab al-Mitar, the Emir's personal secretary, the Vizier of Correspondence, heard rumors that his assistant, Prince al-Kamil, was engaged in profane behavior towards the Emir's wife, the Lady Tarub.

"Take those heads back to the eunuchs' sleeping quarters," al-Rahman II ordered. "I want all to know the fate of any who fail in their duty to me." An army of servants bore off the severed heads and trunks of the unfortunate harem guards. The slaves soaked up the blood flowing over the exquisitely ornamented tiled floor using mountains of cloth. So quickly did the slaves scour the floor that within a brief space of time, no trace remained to bear witness to the horrible slaughter that had occurred only minutes earlier.

Now the Emir turned his terrible gaze outwards on to his court. He allowed it to wander over the assembled nobles and dignitaries before allowing it to rest upon the unfortunate Vizier of Correspondence, abu Kitab al-Mitar. Then the Emir thundered, "Seize him!"

"My Lord," screamed the Emir's private secretary, "please—have mercy. I am innocent. I have served you faithfully. What wrong have I done?"

But the Emir's pitiless, black eyes glared at the hapless secretary. "You have cost me a most talented and gifted secretary," the Emir said to al-Mitar, "I doubt that I will find your like again." Al-Rahman II then nodded to the headman. And, al-Mitar's head was forced down onto the block, as quickly as before the axe flashed, and the head rolled away from the body.

"Put it in the viziers' palace," the Emir ordered, his left eye blinking wildly, "as a reminder to those who would forget that they have taken the oath of allegiance." With that he dismissed the court, leaving only his brothers in attendance.

"I rather enjoyed that," al-Rahman II said as he and his brothers adjourned to a comfortable salon immediately behind the throne room. "That should put some fear into those slackers over in the Dimashiq," referring to the viziers' palace. "Did you see their faces?"

"Yes," al-Mugira concurred, "it did go rather well. But why you indulge that woman, Tarub, I don't know. You are too kind and indulge your women far too much."

"I agree," al-Wallid chimed in, "we have real problems to deal with without having to deal with that white witch. She gives the Christian community a bad name."

"Not to mention that uncle warned you about Nasr," al-Mugira continued.

"Yes, yes, I know!" al-Rahman II moaned in mock gravity. "Neither of you two want me to have any fun. I like playing with my wives. What's wrong with that?" Neither al-Mugira who was blatantly homosexual nor al-Wallid, himself married to Aizun's own daughter, commented. They knew that despite the grisly executions, al-Rahman II was really quite gentle. He wished nothing more than to provide the Peace of the Prophet for his subjects and to play with his wives. Unfortunately, his wives always played rough which was the way he liked it. "It makes the lovemaking afterwards so much more interesting," al-Rahman II explained to his brothers.

Al-Rahman the kind, the Emir thought, *Yes, I am very kind but how else should an enlightened ruler behave.* Certainly al-Rahman II was kind—but he was not a victim of his kindness.

Normally, visits to his harem were the highlight of his day...and today was no exception. The Emir luxuriated in his bath and took time to say his prayers, thinking of the delight he was to enjoy in the company and charms of his wives. He would take a great amount of pleasure in reading the looks on their faces and hearing them murmering among themselves, especially today. Finally the moment came when he could delay visiting his harem, and especially his lovely Tarub, no longer.

When al-Rahman II entered the outer chambers of the harem he noticed how quiet it was. Normally when he walked in, his wives were all chattering at him like delightful little children, all with their petty problems real or imagined with little to distinguish between them. But now it was quiet, serene. *I like that*, the Emir smiled to himself. *Having quiet respectful wives is a blessing*, he sighed. This was the only place where he had no servants and no guards...only wives. Today al-Rahman II's many wives maintained a discreet distance from their lord and master. Some preoccupied themselves with simple tasks, sewing or weaving, tasks for which they had no skills. Others merely lounged about quietly talking between themselves. All the time, they cast sidelong looks at their lord and master, weighing his mood and wondering whether his wrath would cost them their own heads. Fakhr, the Emir's alluring Egyptian, whose charms never ceased to hold the Emir's attention, even dared to absent herself altogether. She remained in her own apartment. She knew that there was scant chance in risking the Emir's displeasure. The old goat was having too much fun, she thought. Where else could a man play bogeyman as well as champion to the world's most beautiful women?

al-Rahman II made himself comfortable in the common area, a great circular space filled with lush cushions, reclining and straight-backed chairs and tables where he received his wives. Only the delightful Tarub seemed completely unaware that anything was amiss. She raced into the room and fell upon the Emir with her usual exuberance.

Tarub was a true daughter of Aphrodite, one hundred and twenty pounds of wickedness and sin. She had been a gift of the Sultan himself. When Tarub was in the room, al-Rahman II just could not see any other woman. Tarub completely captivated and enchanted the Emir. She was beautiful, her white skin delicate as alabaster, golden hair tumbling down her tapering shoulders and sensuous lips. She was all his and that was all that mattered. But even for all of Tarub's charms and ability to entice and distract him, al-Rahman II sensed a certain strangeness in her. *Is it some unknown, intangible, indefinable feeling of fear that she has come to know for the first time?* al-Rahman II asked himself. *How wonderful that this woman who I certainly love will begin to fear and respect me*, he smiled to himself. But to her, the Emir was silent.

Tarub was unaccustomed to not having her way with the Emir anytime she wanted. But today his behavior bothered her. *I'll be glad to get rid of this old man*, Tarub thought. *Then Kamil and I can be together whenever we please.* So in her most enticing and seductive voice, she purred, "Please, milord! How have I displeased you? Come, let me serve you." As she spoke, Tarub used her full arsenal of feminine powers. She exhaled her full seductive breath into his face filling his lungs with her presence. Her scantily clad body seduced his mind with promises of ecstasy and exquisite sexual fulfillment in her arms, as did the touch that she placed lightly on his hands and arms as well on his neck and face. But the Emir remained impassive.

Clapping her hands, Tarub directed her slaves to bring a golden goblet filled with the dark red wine forbidden to the faithful but which the Commander of the Faithful thoroughly enjoyed. "Drink, milord," Tarub said, attempting to enchant her master with her beautiful eyes, the color of a cloudless blue sky. With but the briefest hesitation, al-Rahman II motioned to his personal body servant who took the goblet from the Lady Tarub's hands. Striding out of the harem, the Emir's body servant gave the golden goblet to Adin, the newly acquired royal taster, who stood outside in the hall awaiting his master's pleasure.

Until just recently, Adin had been a homeless street urchin, spending much of his miserable sixteen years of life begging for the meager fare upon which he lived. Now he declared that his only desire was to serve the Emir. "I will undergo whatever trial he asks of me." So it was to Adin, the ill-fated royal taster, that the wine from the golden goblet was passed. The drink brought a warm glow to Adin's still emaciated body, infusing him with a sense of satisfaction. But then slowly his vision blurred and his legs and arms went rubbery and he began to lose his balance. And as the young victim, never to see his seventeenth year, fell to the floor, oblivion closing upon his eyes forever, his last act was to praise the name of al-Rahman II, his lord and master.

When Hasan returned to al-Rahman II with the news of the taster's death, in words as calm as the whispering wind the Emir said to Tarub, "Your betrayal has been discovered." Then he called to his guards who were posted just outside the main entrance of the harem. "Escort the Lady Tarub to her quarters where you will attend her while awaiting my pleasure." Knowing that the plot had been discovered but betraying not the slightest trace of fear, Tarub marched away to her multi-room apartment where she remained undisturbed by what the Emir might think or do. And as his guards escorted Tarub off, all the Emir could think was, what a perfect woman she was and how much he enjoyed her.

Pausing only to throw the briefest glance at the Lady Fakhr who made her regal appearance in the common area where the Emir could scarcely ignore her, al-Rahman II abruptly stormed out of the harem. He and his guard returned to the public chambers. *What a wonderful woman also is Fakhr*, al-Rahman II said to himself. *Very soon, one of these days, I'm going to have to tell her so.*

In the reception hall where his brothers had assembled the court including his viziers and advisors, al-Rahman II thundered, "Bring me Abu L'Fath Nasr!" Then looking over at al-Mugira, he said, "Now you see why I love her so much? I haven't had this much fun in months."

"Brother," al-Wallid spoke out, "the only thing I see is that we're finally getting rid of Nasr, for which Allah be praised!" Al-Wallid had agreed with his uncle's opinion of Nasr all along. The Goth was too dangerous for al-Rahman II to play games. But al-Wallid knew that his brother, ever the experimenter and tinkerer, kept this traitor around just for his amusement. *One day, Rahman will go too far*, al-Wallid thought to himself. And now al-Wallid as well as al-Mugira were satisfied seeing Nasr being marched into the hall between two rows of al-Khurs. "Put him down," al-Mugira shouted, "the Emir does not wish to see his face." Now the man who had been the second most powerful prince in the Emirate was freed to grovel before his master.

"Milord vizier," the Emir said quietly, only his constantly blinking eye masking his smiling face, "please rise and drink from this golden goblet that is forbidden to the faithful but which brings such enjoyment to your people."

"But, milord," Nasr protested, "thou knowest that I converted to the true faith and wine is forbidden."

"Yet," the Commander of the Faithful replied, "well do I know that in your own apartments, much wine do you keep which on special occasions you share with your visitors, especially those who come from the kingdom of Asturias."

Nasr's face paled and his body gave an involuntary shudder. Yet, for all his scheming and plots, the soon to be ex-vizier was no coward. Stiffening his shoulders, Nasr accepted the cup. Turning about, Lengvold took one final look at the royal reception hall that as an Arian Goth he believed was his by right that he had tried to claim by force. Then turning once again to face his master, Abu L'Fath Nasr, known as Lengvold to his true master, the Arian King Alfonso of Asturias, bowed deeply and drained the poisoned cup of wine completely.

· · ·

Of course with news of the executions, al-Khurs, guards and retainers hurried back to their organization to brace themselves for the maelstrom of violence and mayhem that was certain to follow Nasr's fall. The entire security force was uncertain of what to expect and who to trust. Some of Nasr's people had been rounded up, with more to follow. Some would be executed, others would be sold as galley slaves. Nasr's organization extended into every aspect of Córdoba's religious, economic and intelligence community of spies, police and interrogators. The Emir appointed his brother al-Mugira Grand Vizier in place of Nasr. The number one task the Emir gave his brother was the total elimination of Nasr's entire organization. But the Emir displayed considerable restraint by not permitting the situation to degenerate into an internecine war involving al-Khurs, guards and retainers, all warring against each other. He put a minimum number of victims on the list of those to be executed and these only because of family disputes, past gambling debts or personal jealousies. Of course, this number did not include the many names that al-Mugira himself put on the list either because of personal reasons or as a request from other family members. So even though the Emir tried to keep the number of victims as few as possible, several thousand names were on the list of those to be executed. Everyone involved in the security organization was affected. Many chose to keep a low profile and wait until the turmoil ended. Others, on the other hand, chose to leave Córdoba. The roads were choked with al-Khurs, guards, retainers and their families. Many of these would form little farming communities and withdraw from the Grand Vizier's recall.

One name which topped the list was Sumayla's son al-Kamil who at this moment was standing knee-deep in one of the Alcazar's many cesspools. Kamil trembled in the damp, dank cold and nearly fainted from the stench. Kamil was waiting for Frank Yerby to come back. Yerby and Quissan had found Kamil sneaking through a secret passageway trying to get back to Tarub.

"You must return to your mother's palace with us," Yerby told the young Negro.

"I must get to Tarub. The Emir will have her executed. I cannot let that happen."

"I don't see how you can prevent it," Yerby said matter-of-factly, "you can't even get yourself out, not to mention the Lady Tarub." Kamil considered the matter and finally was forced to agree. He didn't know how to escape. So now he found himself in this rank, foul-smelling pit. "I will return soon," Yerby had said. "We need to get you some less distinguished garb without the Emir's mark on it. Quissan will go ahead and mark the best and safest route out of the Alcazar."

Kamil had been waiting several hours now. He was nauseous and faint…and the sewer rats continued to worry his feet so that he had to continually ward them off with kicks and jabs.

"Kamil! Come quickly…" Yerby hissed at him. Kamil must have dozed off because he had been unaware that Yerby had removed the cesspool's cover and had been trying to get his attention for some time. Lowering a rope that Kamil tied around his waist, Yerby dragged the exhausted fugitive up through the opening. Keeping a considerable distance away and averting his face, Yerby held out several towels.

"Take off your clothes, and put these on…quickly." Yerby handed the fugitive a ragged pair of pants, a rough-spun hairshirt and a black cloak of invisibility with hood. "As soon as you've dressed follow me."

"How is it that you know how to get out of here?" Kamil asked Yerby.

"Quissan is marking our escape route," Yerby replied. "The al-Khurs are everywhere…they know you haven't left the Alcazar. And Quissan said that the Emir has ordered every floor of every apartment and every room of every palace searched. The Emir intends to find and behead you. Quissan believes the best escape route is taking one of the channels flowing under the Alcazar wall into the Guadalquivir River."

The Guadalquivir River flows through Córdoba to Seville and into the Atlantic. The Emir's engineers built canals from the river under the Alcazar's walls to take advantage of the river's many drinking, sanitary and irrigational uses. A mill pumped clean water from the Guadalquivir River into the Alcazar and pumped wastewater out. But Kamil feared the water and never went near it. "The river?" he shuddered. "I'm not going to get in the river…I don't know how to swim."

"Don't worry. All we need to do is get to the canal without being spotted, take the canal under the bridge and we'll be safe," Yerby said.

Many years later, Emir al-Rahman III divided Córdoba into four self-contained quarters with separate walls around each quarter. Al-Rahman III declared himself independent of Damascus and established the Caliphate of Spain. Preoccupied with security, al-Rahman III built walls around the entire city. However, at present, only the palaces of the Alcazar were walled. Channels within the Alcazar met and formed the canals to the river under the Alcazar's walls, upon which sentries paced between towers. Once he had passed the walls, Kamil could escape Córdoba with the thousands of other former members of Nasr's security organization who fled the Emir's wrath.

They crept down the dark passageway marked by Quissan until it dead-ended into a small alcove partially hidden by tapestries. Kamil knew that behind the tapestries a secret door led into the private gardens; he and Tarub had met out there on several occasions. He could still smell her scent. The entrance was locked, but Kamil found the key in a recess in the wall where it usually was. Once in the garden, Yerby looked about. "What are you looking for?" Kamil asked,

"Quissan's marker," Yerby replied. After groping around awhile, he called out, "Found it! I think we go this way." Kamil came over to Yerby. "We can make our way that way"—pointing toward the wall—"through the gardens down to the canal," he said. They crept along the labyrinth of private gardens separated by high hedges, trees and flowerbeds. At critical points, Quissan would leave his telltale marker. Over a somewhat roundabout route, the fugitives were able to work themselves toward the canals flowing under the Alcazar's wall into the Guadalquivir.

As they passed out of the gardens, the danger increased. Now between them and the outer walls lay the stables and armories and kitchens and sleeping quarters of the thousands of slaves and servants working in the Alcazar's palaces. Kamil and Yerby had to pass through this maze of buildings and there was a great possibility that at any moment they would be detected. However, people were scurrying back and forth all over the area and everyone seemed to be looking over their shoulders. The al-Khurs who were checking were so busy that Kamil and Frank easily avoided them by keeping to the shadows, they slipped through this area completely unnoticed. Then they approached the outer wall itself and heard the heavy tramp of patrolling sentries who challenged everyone they saw, and observed everything that moved. Seeking the darkest spots, the fugitives soon reached one of the irrigation channels that disappeared under the outer wall joining the canal to the Guadalquivir on the other side. The channel openings under the wall were broad enough, but they were very low with hardly enough space for a man to squeeze under without completely submerging himself.

"Now young master," said Yerby, "you must do as I tell you. Remove your shirt and slippers and wrap them in your cloak, just as I am doing." Quickly Yerby removed his own clothes.

"Breathe deeply and then hold your breath and get into the water." The channel was shallow. Kamil found that the water barely reached his waist. Taking the long corded rope he carried beneath his cloak, Yerby tied one end around Kamil's chest and under his armpits and the other end around his own waist.

"Now we will go under the wall. Hold your breath and hold on tightly to this rope and we will make it through," Yerby said to Kamil. And then to his own surprise Yerby prayed silently, *Please don't let this young fool drown me!*

Kamil did as he was instructed. Manfully overcoming his fear of the water, he carefully slid into the channel with just the faintest gurgle. Once in the water, Kamil followed Yerby under the wall. Actually the water did not completely cover Kamil's head. Midway through, Kamil found that there was room between the water and the bottom of the wall for him to take several additional breaths with relative ease. And in merely a matter of minutes Kamil and Yerby emerged on the other side.

However, on the other side of the wall where the channels joined together in the canal, the water was considerably deeper. Kamil lost his balance and sunk completely beneath the surface. Frank Yerby had to rescue him by pulling the half drowned prince to the side and up onto the bank, all the while trying to keep Kamil's kicking and splashing from being heard by the al-Khur sentries on the wall. Fortunately they got safely ashore without being spotted. After taking a short rest to catch his breath, Yerby got up, wrapped himself in his wet cloak and said, "We must be going. It will be light soon."

But Kamil just looked at his rescuer and said. "Frank, I must go back."

"What?" replied Yerby. "Are you mad?"

"I must go back. Tarub is in danger. With Quissan's markings and you showing me the way under the wall, I can now save her."

"Kamil, you can't save her! You are going to be caught and they will cut off your head. You must get out of Córdoba."

"Please tell my mother…" Kamil seemed to choke up. "Tell her I will catch up with her in Seville."

"But, Kamil…," Yerby protested.

"Go!" hissed the determined would-be Emir. Taking up his sodden bundle with cloak, shirt and sandals and hiding them in the underbrush, and tying the knotted rope around his waist, he plunged back into the canal and disappeared below the waters under the walls back into the Alcazar.

CHAPTER EIGHT

Yerby had failed. Now he had to tell Lady Sumayla of his failure. "Kamil was determined to go back for Tarub," Frank told her. "He said that he would meet you in Seville."

They're going to kill him," Sumayla said sounding a note of finality. "They're going to kill my son! Never again will these eyes rest on his face…the face of my son." But with dignity and fortitude Lady Sumayla directed her slaves to prepare for her escape. What else remained to her? Only that she behave as she knew she must…she must behave as a princess and protect the lives of her household as well as those who served her all over Córdoba as well as other parts of the Emirate. Sumayla was responsible for all of their lives. So now what remained to her was her intelligence and her responsibilities. She would have to look to her grief later. And while she and her household hurriedly made their preparations to flee, a company of al-Khurs came directly up to her palace and pounded on the doors.

"Open for the Emir's emissary," the al-Khur captain shouted out. Quickly Sumayla directed one of her servants to open the doors for resistance would be pointless. The Emir's emissary was sent directly by al-Mugira.

"The Emir has no fondness for nor interest in executing women," the Emir's emissary said to Lady Sumayla after the formal greetings were given. "Nor does he want the incident between the Emir's cousin and his wife discussed."

"What does the Emir command of his humble slave?" the Lady Sumayla asked, prostrating herself before the royal emissary. She knew that the Emir could not have the story of his being cuckolded by his own cousin spread further than absolutely necessary. The Emir meant to have anyone rash enough to repeat the story to be within the headman's grasp. He was not a vain man, but he could allow no man…or woman…daring enough to repeat such an insult to keep his head. If the story circulated, the jackals would make bold with challenges of their own. But the Emir also feared that the quickest way to spread the story was to begin wholesale executions. How many heads would have to fall before every tongue in Córdoba would wag and every household would be seeking vengeance for a lost father, son or brother? That was the way of madness, the Emir believed. It was far better for all concerned that Lady Sumayla be allowed to escape, creating as little attention as possible.

"The Emir would be grateful if the Lady Sumayla acknowledged the generosity of the Emir in saving her life to all her friends, family, servants and slaves," the emissary announced. "His Majesty would be grateful for any dispatches that the Lady Sumayla might send out regarding the Emir's generosity as well."

"You may tell your Master that word has been sent." With that Lady Sumayla summoned one of her servants. After whispering briefly in his ear and providing him with a signet ring and a pouch filled with gold coins, the servant backed away with a bow. With that, Sumayla transferred the loyalty of her not insignificant network of copyists, readers, household servants, water carriers, eunuchs and even al-Khurs from the late Abu L'Fath Nasr to the new Grand Vizier and brother to the Emir, Abd al-Mugira. "The Emir has always admired the Lady

Sumayla," the emissary said. "He is especially grateful to her for bringing so much happiness to his uncle in his declining years."

"I only tried to return a small part of the happiness and joy my husband gave me," Lady Sumayla replied simply.

"Al-Mugira still holds you in great esteem. He desires that the details of your departure be handled without any concern on your part. Furthermore, al-Mugira proposes that your servants remain on his staff as permanent liaison between yourself and his royal highness."

Al-Khurs assisted Lady Sumayla's servants and slaves in packing a caravan of many carriages, wagons, mules and horses. Furniture, carpets, pots and pans, clothing and jewels, and hundreds of other personal and household items to be transported to her palace in Seville. Quissan and the al-Khur captain planned her journey. The final plans for Sumayla's voluntary relocation were approved by al-Mugira and his staff. Safe conduct was arranged for the party; a company of the Emir's own guard provided escort. All over Córdoba, the name of al-Rahman II was praised, as the Lady Sumayla was seen leaving the capitol under the Emir's protection.

Two days into their journey a royal guardsman caught up with the caravan. "My cousin who guards the Emir's prisoners has informed me that your son, Prince al-Kamil ibn Abd al-Karim, was captured and thrown into a dungeon just after sunrise yesterday," he announced to Lady Sumayla.

Kamil's mother gasped involuntarily. "Is he all right?" she managed to ask.

"When the Emir was informed of your son's capture," the guardsman continued, "he ordered your son executed, immediately and in secret. Your son's body lies buried in an umarked grave. Those who buried him have gone to their graves as well."

Upon hearing this news, Sumayla's charateristic stoicism left her, and she fainted. And after Sumayla's servants returned her to consciousness, her cries and moans were most piteous. "Everything…everything gone," she cried. "My son, my life." But deep in her soul, she heard her own voice saying, *But are you not the guilty one?*

. . .

"So, Frank, did you learn anything from your little journey?" Pride Dawson's voice preceeded a vague awareness and then the absolute certainty that he was once again in Pride's Castle. Pride Dawson sat a chair-length away, glaring at him.

"No, I didn't," Yerby replied. He looked about the castle's gloomy interior and tried to get his bearings. *Pride has lost none of his arrogance*, Yerby grimaced to himself.

"What do you mean by that?" Pride asked. "You mean you met no victims? Or none of the victims you met was guilty? Speak up, man!"

Yerby smiled. He refused the favor of reacting to Dawson's insulting language though he felt that he had just been splashed with a bucket of ice water. "You, Pride Dawson," Yerby said, "are a victim if I've ever seen one. Not just because your family were some clay-eatin' dirt farmers from the backwoods and not because you were poor once. You are a victim because no matter how much money you make, you still are the backwoods hick you've always been." Yerby stared directly at Pride and let his comment soak in. Then Yerby continued, "Don't pretend with me. You've lost everything. Even this house doesn't belong to you. You live here on charity of your wife, don't you?"

Pride Dawson crushed men for less than what Yerby had said, but, understanding the game Yerby was playing, Dawson merely shrugged and said "I have had a run of bad luck, you might say." With that he pulled at a golden rope with a beaded tassel. Almost instantly, the Negro butler shuffled in. "Chester, bring me a port that is above mediocrity. Would you care to join me, Frank?"

Yerby nodded.

"And bring Fran...I mean *Mr. Yerby* a glass, as well. And you hurry it up. I don't want any of your nigger dawdling. Mr. Yerby is on a mission and he hasn't much time." The butler left and returned with a decanter of port wine. Pouring out two glasses, he served Pride and Frank. "That will be all, Chester. Leave the bottle and get out of here," Dawson harshly dismissed the old black retainer. The servant retreated out of the room, quietly closing the door behind him. "Got to keep them darkies in their place, don't you agree, Frank?" Pride Dawson sneered. Thus the robber baron assured himself that the Arian ideas of the natural order of things still prevailed. Sipping his port in silence, Pride Dawson continued to watch his reluctant visitor. Finally Dawson said, "I apologize for being such a bore, but, of course, that is how you *created* me. But I think now the two of us should try and get along as best as possible so that you can complete your mission."

"My mission?" Yerby asked. "What mission? Who has given me a mission?"

"Don't you get it yet?" Pride once again said just the right thing to set Yerby off.. "We called you! We called you! *You are working for us...doing what you are told?* Do you understand that?"

"So you did," Yerby affirmed Dawson's statement. "So you did. Well, since we are working together, old chum, what do you expect me to do? How do you expect me to help you gain immortality? I haven't the power to change anything."

"We are not asking to change anything." Dawson twisted his face into a look of skepticism mingled with a gleam of hope. "We only want you to participate in this work. Face the *demons* we face. Give us some insight into that brilliant mind of yours. "

"You want me to participate in this piece of very bad writing!" Yerby replied hotly. "As you said, I am not here because I want to be here. I was forced into this by what power I do not know. Besides, the plot of this book is too convoluted for my tastes. My novels always have happy endings and I can see no good resolution to this tale."

"That's because you always wrote like a white man," Pride purred. "This one here writes like a *nigger*."

PART TWO

*Akhenaten loved debauchery and sexual perversion.
He remains a god to this day, but prefers to be known as
Papa Legba. He roams the world with a swollen penis
that can never be satisfied. Papa Legba's only pleasure
is tricking humans into behaving like animals
while he eats their brains.*

CHAPTER NINE

The first thing Yerby noticed was that Pedro's home was anything but pleasant; it was a typical *bohio*, the kind of hut lived in by all Cuba's blacks, even those who were free. This hut had a dirt floor with the fronds of palm trees for a roof, and clapboard and mud for walls. Yerby had a feeling that he was no longer in Córdoba.

Pulling himself off of the floor and brushing himself off, Yerby went out the hut's single entrance into a bright Caribbean sun. In front of the hut, Yerby found a muscular young black man reclining in a hammock tied between branches of a *ceiba* tree. The massive *ceiba* dwarfed both the black man in the hammock as well as the man's nearby hut. The *ceiba* tree's undulating truck reminded Yerby of the coils of Damballah. Near the hammock reclined a beautiful woman within the folds of one of the *ceiba's* coils. The woman's mixed ancestry produced such a sultry, natural beauty that it would have been appealing to either the white or black races. Carlota simply took a man's breath away. She was very tall, but thin with full hips that swayed as she walked, as if she were in complete harmony with the rolling Caribbean itself. Her honey creamed skin glowed; a great mass of reddish brown hair flowed about her in continual ringlets and curls like the cascading of petals in glorious sunflower. Carlota's eyes were mysterious and shy, reflecting the innocence of her soul. Her eyes, her heart and her soul belonged to Pedro. Ever since he had deposited the glow of life between Carlota's legs, her face glowed each time she touched the slight protrusion in her stomach. Carlota prayed that Pedro's child would be a boy child, a perfect gift of love.

"What place is this?" Yerby asked the reclining figure in the hammock.

"This is Guanabacoa, Señor Yerby," the young man said. "And I am Pedro."

"How is it that you know me?" Yerby asked, looking around, somewhat disoriented. He did not know quite where he was, but he didn't think that he was any longer in ninth-century Spain.

"My uncle Tolomeo, Babaluaye, of this village called for you," Pedro answered. "You are here to assist us in our revolt against Spain. No?"

"I am here to assist you in your revolt against Spain, *no!*" Yerby replied. *From a revolt in Spain to a revolt against Spain*, he murmured to himself. Then once more to the black man in the hammock Yerby said, "Guanabacoa. Is that Guanabacoa, Cuba?"

"Si, señor," Pedro replied.

I was afraid of that, Yerby thought. *There is going to be a dandy little rebellion here, soon. Just what I wanted! To die proving that blacks were guilty of being victims.*

Close to ninety percent of Cuba's population was black and of that number, eighty percent were slaves. Mainly, the blacks labored for the *hacendados*, the Cuban plantation owners. All but a few of the *hacendados* plantation owners were *criollos*, native-born Cubans of Spanish descent. But the true masters of Cuba were the *peninsulares*, the Spanish aristocrats whose appointments to the various posts from captain-general to governor and ambassador were made by and on behalf of the Spanish Crown. These aristocratic *peninsulares* insured that the wealth of Cuba flowed into the coffers of the Spanish Crown, while at the same time generously helping themselves to the generous bounty the Crown allowed in payment for faithful service. Profits from Cuban tobacco, molasses and cane sugar were exorbitant. The amount of gold bullion passing through the port of Havana on its way to Spain was unimaginable. There was no wonder that Spanish galleons laden with the treasures of the new world were continually stalked by raiders from England and Scandinavia as well as pirates from all over the Asian and African continents. The *criollos* did not enjoy any of the benefits from their plantations. They were not slaves but they might well have been, so well heeled were they to the *peninsulares'* boots. The *criollo hacendados* were forced by law to sell their products to the *Factoria*. The *Factoria* was the government monopoly owned by the Spanish Crown. The *Factoria* purchased all of Cuba's produce at far less than fair market price, yet any *hacendado* attempting to sell sugar cane or tobacco or any other produce to anyone other than agents of the *Factoria* was guilty of smuggling, punishable by fines and imprisonment. A black man caught smuggling tobacco out of Cuba would be summarily executed. Despite the penalties, smuggling was the primary occupation of free blacks such as Pedro and their *criollo hacendado* suppliers. Thus to any disinterested observer, it seemed to be a reasonable statement that if *criollos* and blacks joined together, there should be a great possibility that they could overthrow the rule of the *peninsulares,* even considering the latter's absolute control over the Spanish military and naval presence in Cuba. So if there was any time or place to test Yerby's oft-quoted statement, especially in *Griffin's Way,* that blacks who did not want to be slaves didn't have to be slaves, this was it.

"Who is he and why does he stay in your *bohio?*" Carlota asked Pedro, referring to Yerby.

"I was feeding Chango at his Royal Palm," Pedro explained to

Carlota. "All at once Chango called for the drums. I answered and answered. I stayed there all night answering Chango's call, beating the drums until exhausted, I collapsed. The next morning, there he was, laying there in front of me."

"Who is he?" Carlota insisted.

"Señor Frank Yerby." Pedro replied making the introductions.

Carlota did not believe Pedro, but she stopped questioning him. Pedro seemed more irritable with her than usual. Sometimes she wondered if he wanted their baby. *I will keep my eyes on you, señor Yerby,* Carlota vowed to herself. And so, Carlota who had been so much a part of Pedro's life for such a long time, formally to be married in a *Lukumi* Voodoo ceremony, was forced to keep her distance. Now instead of nestling together with Pedro in his *bohio,* Carlota was forced to stay in her own and only allowed to visit with Pedro when the stranger was not around. For that reason, Carlota hated señor Frank Yerby. And it did not matter. Yerby might help Pedro lead the entire secret *Lukumi cabildo* sect in a victorious rebellion over Spanish slavery. Slavery did not matter to Carlota; the only thing Carlota wanted was Pedro.

From before she could remember, Carlota had loved him…loved him completely. They were soul mates. Like Pedro, Carlota was an orphan. But unlike Pedro, Carlota didn't have an Uncle Tolomeo, Babaluaye of the *Lukumi* sect of the dread Voodoo cult. She had no family whatsoever. Carlota's mother, a *mulatta,* died giving birth to the child whose father was a passing Spanish soldier. The child, Carlota, whose remarkable beauty was a curse, lived in the village with her elderly *abuela,* her grandmother, so-called by all the orphans she had taken under her care. "You see my woman is very suspicious, señior Yerby." Pedro said.

"Everyone seems to be waiting for something," Yerby commented.

"Yes," Pedro responded. "They are waiting for my uncle. He is the village fisherman. The entire village depends upon my uncle to return with a boatload of mackerel."

"He must be a very good fisherman," Yerby observed.

"Yes," Pedro observed, "my Uncle Tolomeo is an excellent fisherman. But he left early this morning not only to catch fish for the village of Guanabacoa, but also to catch sight of the promised *americano* ships...the ships that will bring American fighting men, guns and supplies to support the Cuban insurrection."

"You are expecting Americans to come here to Cuba to fight for blacks to be freed from slavery?" Yerby asked.

"Si, *señor*," Pedro replied. "We just do not know when the *americanos* are coming."

"When will the *americanos* come?" Tolomeo had been asked this question hundreds...no, thousands of times by his people. They asked Tolomeo because he was the one who had promised them that the *americanos* were coming in the first place. As Babaluaye of the *Lukumi*, Tolomeo was important and respected. He was thought to possess unique powers and control the spirits. But even his staunchest supporters, villagers in Guanabacoa as well as elsewhere, were becoming impatient. Some even whispered that the Babaluaye was responsible for Aguero's earlier failed attempt at overthrowing the Spanish. "They would not have revolted if they didn't believe that the *americanos* were coming to help them," some villagers said.

"So your uncle is beginning to lose support because he promised *americano* support for the insurrection?" Yerby asked.

"Si, *señ*...I mean Frank," Pedro replied. "A month ago, on July 4th, Joaquin de Aguero, a *criollo*, issued a proclamation declaring Cuba free of Spain's control and free of slavery and took to the hills. Aguero and forty-four *criollos* were accompanied by several hundred blacks both free and slave, most of who were *Lukumi* warriors. They did it because my uncle, the Babaluaye of the *Lukumi* had promised the *americanos* would come as soon as they heard about the Cuban insurrection."

Many of the *criollo hacendados* were committed to overthrowing

Spanish rule. Their group met surreptitiously at a saloon known as the Havana Club. The club raised a million dollars for the sole purpose of bringing 5,000 American mercenaries to fight for Cuban independence, that is the independence of *criollo hacendados*, creole planters, from the Spanish Crown. The Havana Club sent Ambrosio Gonzales to the United States to recruit *americano* mercenaries. The Havana Club was not the only group desiring the overthrow of Spanish rule in Cuba. In the time when the Spanish monarchy was overthrown by Baldomero Espartero who proclaimed himself Caudillo of Spain, Narciso Lopez was one of the Caudillo's generals. His reward was a governorship of one of Cuba's rich provinces. Narciso Lopez became extremely wealthy. He was forced out of office when the monarchy was restored in Spain. Lopez took his wealth to the United States and raised a force of American mercenaries in 1850. Lopez landed his army at Cardenas where he was beaten by superior Spanish troops. Now a year later, Lopez was trying to raise another force of American mercenaries to overthrow Spanish rule in Cuba. But little of this, if any, did the Babaluaye Tolomeo or his *Lukumi* followers know. All the *Lukumi* knew was that Americans were coming to overthrow slavery. That was what the Babaluaye Tolomeo and his Pedro, a favorite of the Orishas, had told them. So each day for the past month, *Lukumi* asked the Babaluaye "Have the *americanos* arrived yet?"

"My Uncle Tolomeo likes to spend his time on the water," Pedro explained to Yerby, who now was stretched out in one of the folds of the ceiba tree. "He likes fishing best."

"What else does he do?" Yerby asked.

"He is a smuggler," Carlota laughed. "Pedro's uncle takes cigars and tobacco from the plantation owners to tobacco dealers in Florida." Pedro gave Carlota a twisted look. "Well, you said he is here to help. He needs to know everything, doesn't he?" Carlota has a way of making Pedro sorry he had shared so much of his activities with her. At times she was not very discreet, like now.

"Sometimes my uncle serves one of the *hacendados* by selling his tobacco to *americanos* in Florida," Pedro said. "But the Spanish have so many ships, smuggling is too dangerous right now.

"Your uncle trusts the *hacendado*," Yerby asked.

"Oh, yes, he is a very good man. He is working with the other plantation owners to get *americanos* to come and fight to end slavery here in Cuba. He guaranteed that *americanos* would arrive right after Aguero's uprising."

. . .

It certainly was possible that the 'good' *hacendado* from whom Tolomeo and Pedro got their information was not in possession of all the facts. Tolomeo's 'good' planter was not privy to official dispatches and correspondences from the Spanish consulate in New Orleans warning Jose Guiterrez de la Concha, the Captain-General of Cuba and the Spanish Crown's personal representative, about a plot to instigate a slave insurrection which would be supported by an armed force of American mercenaries. So when Aguero and the *Lukumi* declared an end to Spanish rule, de la Concha had already deployed his troops to control the insurrection. Armed with advance intelligence, the Captain-General of Cuba turned the first stage of the insurrection into a massacre. The Spaniards were armed with the most modern weapons: muskets, revolvers and artillery…while the insurgents were armed with machetes, clubs and a few flintlock muskets and pistols. The outcome was never in doubt. By July 22nd, Aguero and his followers had all been killed or arrested. Some of the slaves considered valuable were returned to their masters, the others were executed. All the while, the Havana Club's representative, Ambrosio Gonzales, continued recruiting American mercenaries. On August 19th, a 435-man American mercenary force under the leadership of General Narciso Lopez sailed out of New Orleans in the leaky steamer, *Pampero*. This pitifully small force was about to meet 8,000 of the best trained, best equipped and best controlled fighting force in the Americas. As the *Pampero* sailed towards Cuba bound for Morrillo, General Lopez and his officers believed that the insurrection of black slaves and *criollo* planters against the Spanish aristocrats was going strong. None of any of this was known by Tolomeo, or Pedro, or Carlota, or any of the black *Lukumi* waiting for the drums that would signal the long awaited insurrection. All they could do was wait. And each day, Tolomeo went out in hopes of catching sight of the long awaited *americanos*.

• • •

"Frank, did you know that Pedro is going to lead the *americano* attack against the Spanish?" Carlota said in a laughing voice whose manner indicated a certain amount of seriousness. "His uncle predicted a great future for Pedro. So Pedro thinks that the *americanos* are going to let him lead the insurrection. What do you think, Frank?"

"I think it is unlikely that when the *americanos* come they will follow you, Pedro." Yerby observed.

"Pedro's a dreamer and he truly loves me," Carlota said, "and like most dreamers and lovers, my Pedro loves his people and wants his people to love him. So he dreams of ending all this." She waved at the poverty, illness and ignorance all around.

Yerby saw what she saw; a people brutalized beyond imagination, living a marginal existence, needing the basic necessities of food, clothing and shelter. Only the smouldering anger visible in their eyes gave a hint of their total obsession with and commitment to some great insurrection. "I think Pedro does not understand that it will take more than driving the Spaniards out of Cuba to change all of this."

All the while, Pedro lay in the hammock, listening. "What's wrong with wanting to help your people?" Pedro said loudly. "Somebody needs to help them."

"I think what Carlota is saying," Yerby observed, "is that she is concerned that you will be harmed before you are able to do good for your people."

Yerby's attempt to smooth over what was obviously a sore subject between the two lovers failed. Pedro believed that crushing Spanish domination would solve all the problems facing his people. He was the Cuban revolutionary ready to lead his people to freedom and prosperity. Pedro took Yerby's presence as an omen of success. Pedro intended to lead black Cubans to freedom when the *americanos* arrived with the guns, supplies and men. *Now that the Babaluaye Tolomeo has provided me with the services of Frank Yerby,* Pedro thought, *the insurrection cannot fail.* And once Cuba was free, Pedro smiled to himself, as if he were party to some great secret soon to be revealed. The natural bounty of the island will insure that everyone will enjoy a life without want or fear, Pedro vowed to himself. And deep in his soul Pedro believed that he would be successful.

· · ·

In many ways, the idea that he was destined to be a military leader may have arisen from some deep recess in Pedro's long suppressed memories, for rebellion ran in Pedro's blood. As an infant, Pedro was one of the few survivors of the massacre at Fort Negro in the First Seminole War. His parents, both runaway slaves, were members of the Seminole Nation that took refuge in the dense Florida Everglades. In 1816, communities of runaway slaves calling themselves Seminoles took over an abandoned British fortress on the Apalachicola River. The three-walled fortress manned by black men was able to protect the black families who cleared land, raised crops and tended cattle. The fort attracted Native Americans as well. These were survivors of the systematic elimination of Indians throughout the Carolinas, Georgia and Alabama who sought to escape the white settlers who were killing them and stealing their land. On infrequent occasions, the blacks and Indians would launch a raid on white plantations. The raiders would take supplies and free as many slaves as were willing to join the "Seminole" community.

General Andrew Jackson was given the responsibility for suppressing the Seminoles occupying Fort Negro. Jackson ordered five hundred Creek Indians, assisted by regular army and marine troops, to attack the fort. Gunboats in the river supported the attack with a massive naval bombardment. Suddenly a roar of flames mushroomed into the air over the fort. Red hot shot landed inside the fort's ammunition dump. Instantaneously hundreds of barrels of gunpowder ignited. The resulting explosion killed, mortally wounded or maimed over three hundred people...including Pedro's father. Tolomeo had been able to evacuate Pedro and his mother from their cabin before Jackson's attack. But Pedro's father decided to stay and defend the fort. Tolomeo brought Pedro and his mother here to Guanabacoa. Six years later, Pedro's mother died. Now almost thirty-five years later, Pedro was a tried and true black rebel. He had lived by his wits as a free black, evaded arrest and earned the respect of *Lukumi* all over Cuba. No amount of ridicule from Carlota would divert his attention away from his destiny to be leader of the insurrection.

· · ·

But now Carlota, shielding her eyes against the sun reflecting off of the waters, stared out toward the Caribbean and asked, "Is that not your uncle coming in now?" Even as she spoke, the thing that had been a blotch only moments ago began to resolve itself into the shape of a small fishing boat. The solitary figure maneuvered the boat into the small inlet that served as shelter. By the way the gulls circled and squealed out, the hold of Tolomeo's boat was filled with mackerel.

As soon as they spotted him, many of the villagers raced down to the beach, laughing and waving at Tolomeo. Pedro walked down to the sandy beach followed by Carlota as well as Frank. Uncle and nephew hailed each other good-naturedly. Then each fell to the task of securing the good-sized fishing boat onto the wooden docking structure midway up the beach. Tolomeo's boat had a cleverly contrived keel that could be raised. Without this keel, called a centerboard, sailing upon the Caribbean would have been impossible. However, withdrawing the keel allowed Tolomeo to beach his fishing boat safely, fitting it snugly on a wedged sled. Then with the aid of a wooden winch and block and tackle, Tolomeo and Pedro pulled the boat onto the secure docking structure.

"Any sight of the *americanos?*" Pedro asked, giving his uncle a warm hug.

"No, not yet," Tolomeo replied "but they will be here soon." Tolomeo was confident. The *americanos* would arrive. "But, for now, let us get these mackerel out of the boat and ready to distribute," he said to his nephew. They leapt over the side of the boat and lowered nets into the great barrel built into the bottom. Then they began scooping out the mackerel from the barrels in the hold and lowering the fish to the beach. Carlota and several other women transferred the fish into the community pool where anyone wishing a fish could take one. Others joined in and soon the beach was alive with laughing men and women, singing and playing while preparing and distributing Tolomeo's hardy catch.

"Your people are happy with you today, Babaluaye," Pedro said.

"Today, yes, they love me today. They have fish today. But tomorrow, who knows about tomorrow," Tolomeo replied, looking at his nephew, of whom he was very proud. *What a strong black man he is, How proud his parents must be.*

"Tomorrow!" Pedro answered. "Most certainly they will love you tomorrow as well. Tomorrow you will lead us in victorious battle against the Spanish. Yes, most certainly, we will all love you then. They will love you for giving them revenge for the floggings they have received, the sons and daughters they have lost, for the labor forced upon their bodies and the shame they have harbored in their souls. Oh, yes, Babaluaye, they will love you tomorrow."

CHAPTER TEN

*T*he slave who is brought to this new world no longer is a human being. Rather the slave becomes a beast to be sold and traded as the master sees fit. If the master is kind, the slave will eat and live to work. If the master is cruel, the slave will work until the slave dies.

Night sings a Yoruba song and a handmade drum replies. Voices join more drums. The dancing starts and old movements are recalled. Chants and dances settle quarrels. Rhythms unite, tribes join, all transform and give birth to something new, and make love to each other.

The root man looks after the sick and he can see the future. He chooses prayers, offerings, sacrifices. He knows what foods the gods like and which women attract them. He kills enemies with a handful of powder.

The white man wearing a black cassock comes.... His white god doesn't talk. His white god doesn't visit. His white god hates singing, dancing, food and drink. He hates the feel of the soft velvety flesh and the laughter in the night. The white god makes no miracles; he only takes life. His is the sign of the cross; the sign of death.

Secretly, the old priest teaches the young initiate the ancient rites. They are treasures. Nannies croon African prayers. White babies fall *asleep to stories of black gods. The babies grow up with the dance and the belief.*

The Spanish Inquisition comes to burn and kill. They say there is only one god. His priests are monsters; they love to torture and debase and kill.

The slaves smile. They worship Chango, Obatala or Oshun as they kneel in church. They also believe in the white god and his saints as well. The more love and respect they give to all the gods, the greater protection do all the gods provide. Chango, the invincible warrior chief, the whoring god of storm and lightning, shows his sense of humor. He becomes St. Barbara. Everyone feels much more protected now that Chango is a warrior as well as a female saint inside the church. The slave owners see that after a religious festival there is peace and harmony on the sugar plantations. White mothers have their children brought back to health by black root doctors. Young women swear by love potions. They show off husbands as proof. White priests thinking about the slave uprisings in Haiti and the massacre of white priests assure the Catholic laity that a little drumming in the night is absolutely harmless.

· · ·

Still Yerby had little respect for religion whether Christianity or Voodoo.

"The *Lukumi* believe that just because they listen to the drums," Yerby told Pedro one day, "they know what the drums say." This was a serious challenge to Tolomeo's authority, but it couldn't be helped. The coming insurrection was a serious matter. It was so serious that if possible Yerby would rather avoid it altogether. But if there was going to be an insurrection, Yerby felt very strongly that the most important thing the *Lukumi* could do to increase their chance of success was to find a more accurate way of communicating than by beating on the drums.

It was not that Yerby disliked the drums. He found Pedro's drumming imaginative and rhythmic. But with all of the drum beating reverberating over hundreds of miles all over the island, Yerby was convinced that no two villagers could interpret the message the same way. It was as if Yerby was dealing with children and the recess bell at a school. When the bell rang most of the children knew that they were supposed to do something, but the children did not quite know what. As a means of communication, the drums left much to be desired. Yerby continued. "I've asked around the village," he said. "I ask them what the drums say. One says that the drums say hide...another that the drums say come to the meeting place. I am certain the drums told one of the villagers that the *americanos* were going to drop from the sky." Saying this Yerby stared deep into Pedro's eyes. Yerby had been visiting with the villagers. They were simple, trusting folk, most preoccupied with those tasks necessary for survival: Foraging for food and clothing; trying to make repairs to their huts; trying to keep as much dirt off themselves and their children as possible. But the villagers also listened to the drums and what they said. The subject fascinated and mystified Yerby. He learned that the ill-fated Aguero insurrection was signaled by drums.

Pedro smiled. He liked this Frank Yerby. Yerby spoke directly and gave you the facts. Pedro had never had anyone explain anything to him. He was always trying to figure it out, until after awhile it was so much easier to give into the gods, the Orishas, and let them ride us as they may, Pedro thought. *Now that the Babaluaye has brought this powerful Orisha to live with us we must follow his instructions. This thing with the drums, yes, it has always been that way. I should know, since I am the drummer,* Pedro chuckled to himself. *I should know what the drums say. But I just let in the Orisha who wants his message out. Whether it be for war or love, I just play. I don't know what rhythms and beats will come out of the drums until I hear them myself. But I didn't really know this until Frank explained it to me.* And Pedro looked over at the author who had created him. Between them there passed an understanding. *Yerby would always be there to tell the truth.* Nobody knows what the drums say, not even the drummer.

"Did you signal Aguero and the *Lukumi* to take to the hills with your drums?" Yerby asked Pedro.

"No, *señor*, Frank," Pedro stated emphatically, "I did not signal the insurrection."

"Well, who did?" Yerby asked.

"I do not know," Pedro said with a shrug.

"Did you, yourself, hear the drums calling the *Lukumi* to join Aguero?"

"No, *señor*. I did not hear the drums calling the *Lukumi* to join Aguero," Pedro said emphatically.

Which was why this insurrection will leave blacks in no better situation then Aguero's did, Yerby observed to himself. When, or rather if, the *americanos* come, they will expect communications far more effective than drums. Yerby had long concluded that the villagers beat the drums because illiteracy prevented them from using more effective communications. Frank stared at this ragged black idealist dreaming of leading his bedraggled followers of marginalized slaves and former slaves against one of the best-equipped and successful armies anywhere in the Americas. With the directness and seriousness this statement deserved, he told Pedro, "This means that your people, the *Lukumi,* will fail in any attempt to overthrow the Spanish."

Pedro eyes widened in a look of disbelief. "But surely we can learn what we need to know from the *criollos.*" Pedro turned up his hands in a gesture of resignation, as if to say, "what else can we do?"

"Neither the *hacendados* nor the *americanos* want to free the slaves," Yerby explained.

"But then how do you explain *Señor* Aguero and those white *cubanos* who gave their lives for a free Cuba?" Pedro asked.

Here was the dilemma for most black people. Any white person who lost his life in the insurrection was proof that he was genuinely concerned with freeing the slaves. There could be several alternative explanations. Aguero certainly overestimated the ability of the black insurgents to defeat the Spanish army. So one of the explanations was that Aguero was just stupid. Yerby answered Pedro as best he could. "Aguero did not give his life. He risked his life believing that 5,000 *americanos* were coming. Aguero made an incorrect assessment of his chances of success and it cost him his life."

Pedro sort of understood what Yerby was saying, but, in reality, all Pedro understood was that when the *americanos* arrived, he would lead the insurrection that would drive the Spanish out and liberate his people. Pedro could not concentrate on anything else right now. Like the other *Lukumi* all over Cuba, Pedro believed the hour of their liberation from the Spanish had come, which was why he and Carlota had not gotten married yet. Pedro had a one-track mind. His dream gave hope to all of the hopeless villagers as well as the hopeful *Lukumi*…and to him most of all. But Yerby was right. Liberation was not at hand; the Spanish were merely preparing another trap. This time the trap was for the *americanos* and their *Lukumi* allies, alike. And in this situation Frank could find himself losing not only the insurrection but his life as well.

"The Babaluaye Tolomeo told us that the only way for Cuba to be truly liberated," Pedro explained to Yerby, "is for us to forget color differences between whites and blacks. We are to remember that we are all *cubanos*; white *criollos* suffer from the Spanish just as much as blacks."

"The Spanish enslave the *criollos*—*sí?*" Yerby asked mildly. It really was not much of a question since there was no time in the memory of any Cuban black when a *criollo* was forced into slavery.

"Yes…in a way," Pedro responded. "But that is not the issue."

"What is the issue?" Yerby asked.

"The issue is that once Cuba is free, there will be no more slaves…black or white," Pedro smiled.

"No more slaves?" Carlota asked

"No more slaves," Pedro repeated. He turned his back on Frank and went into his *bohio*, putting an end to that particular conversation. So here was Yerby in Cuba, awaiting a force of indeterminate size from the United States with an island full of *Lukumi* Voodoo practitioners, poised for an insurrection against the military and naval might of the Spanish Crown which was armed with the latest military weapons available and informed by the most up to date intelligence reports from Cuban and American sources. So as he sat on the beach outside the hut, gazing up into a starry night and listening to the softly rolling Caribbean, Yerby wondered, *just why am I here on this mysterious island, looking into a gathering storm?*

· · ·

Yerby reflected that Pedro was in many ways not unlike Kamil. Both were cast in the role of leader of revolt against the established order without the remotest possibility of success. Had Kamil really believed he would become the next Emir? Why not? *Pedro believes that American mercenaries are coming for him to lead against the Spanish. What drives men like Pedro and Kamil to take the road of rebellion and insurrection rather than the way of intelligence and planning?* Yerby wondered. *What would drive these miserable wretches here to contemplate insurrection and rebellion before they have the means to communicate in the most rudimentary manner? More victims,* Yerby sighed. He felt some of the pain his creations suffered. And then from deep within himself, he heard the voice shout, "Monster!"

"That is what you called God…isn't it?" the voice said, "when you wrote in *An Odor of Sanctity* that God is all powerful and God is all knowing. He knows the future and he knows the past, you said. God gives freedom of will so that His creations may choose between the good and the evil inside themselves. If His creation chooses goodness,

God reserves a place in heaven forever. If His creation chooses evil, He pitches the offender into Hell where sins are punished by endless torments." With his condemnation of God, Yerby had grown angry and insolent. "God, you knew eons of years prior to men being born that certain men would fornicate with other men's wives even as Kamil had done," Yerby had said. You have always known that some would murder, rape and rob. Others would lie, cheat and conspire to break their own word. Some others would abandon their children and brutalize their wives. Still others were so weak willed as to commit suicide."

"You broke your contract with Your creation!" Yerby had raged. "Mankind has no choice! God, You have always known what choices each man will make...these choices mankind could not help since choice is a matter of the nature which You gave them rather than the intelligence which they acquired through their own efforts."

And not satisfied Yerby had continued. Art thou First Cause or no? If Thou art, does not all choice ultimately reside in Thee? If Thou knew that there are those who would choose evil, You allowed them to be born. Neither did you stretch out Your merciful hand to stay them from doing evil. Now by what right do You create the foul pit of hell for punishment? Is hell Your attempt to absolve yourself of Your own guilt? Or must the innocent suffer because they are guilty of being victims? Or have You created hell because You delight in cruelty, in pain and in the piteous screams echoing down through time. Is it not that the cries of victims are music to Your ears...Monster?"

So now in the silence of his own soul, Yerby heard the brokenhearted, grief-stricken voice of Lady Sumayla shout out: "Monster!" And when he looked into Carlota's innocent and trusting eyes, he heard the inner shout, "Monster!"

And in the darkness of his own soul, Yerby responded, *I gave them intelligence; they must use it or suffer the consequences.*

CHAPTER ELEVEN

Ross Pary stood with the other officers on the foredeck of the decrepit steamer, *Pampero*. The ship was barely seaworthy. It leaked. A collapsed exhaust pipe had burned out one of the boilers. So now the *Pampero* lumbered across a moonlit Caribbean towards the Cuban coast at a painfully slow eight knots. U.S. warships sailed under presidential orders to stop the *Pampero*, by force if necessary, as soon as she could be located. A flotilla of Spanish warships were scouring Cuba's coast for any sign of the *Pampero*. Each Spanish captain prayed for the opportunity to send the *Pampero* to the bottom of the Caribbean. From his vantage point, Pary could see what a clear horizon the moon made on the sea. A heightened anxiety over this dangerous situation began to replace his annoyance at the steamer's slow pace. Ships of either the American or Spanish navy could see her and overtake her. But Ross Pary was less concerned for his own safety than for the safety of Conchita Izquierdo, the daughter of a Cuban *criollo hacendado*. Ross loved Conchita more than life. When Conchita's father, Eduardo Izquierdo, learned of Aguero's insurrection, he left New Orleans as soon as he could to support his friend and the cause. As soon as Conchita learned that her father had joined Aguero, she booked passage on the next ship out of New Orleans bound for Cuba. *And now I'm here chasing across the Caribbean with a boatload of adventurers recruited on a killing matter so that I can rescue the both of them*, thought the young Mississippi planter. For well he knew that the daughter would never leave without the father. Ross was unaware that Eduardo had already been killed in Aguero's premature uprising. *My love, why didn't you wait for me?* Pary shouted silently to his fiancée wishing with all his heart she could hear him. Then his thoughts turned morbid. She wasn't thinking of me at all, he said to himself. She was only thinking of her father and this idiotic idea of a free Cuba...a free Cuba, indeed. He looked about the deck at the rough group of officers, grizzled veterans of the many conflicts with Mexicans and Indians. These boys intend to turn their free Cuba into a slaveholding state.

· · ·

Conchita Izquierdo actually was thinking of Ross Pary when she left New Orleans for Cuba. She was thinking of how she was lying in the arms of her *americano* lover, while her father was being slaughtered by the Spanish. She was thinking of how she made love to a white planter who believed in the superiority of the white man while her father, cripple that he was, was defending the idea of the equality with his blood. Conchita Izquierdo's father was committed to ending the institution of slavery. He paid dearly for his commitment.

For each slave Eduardo freed, the Spanish levied a heavy tax on him. Eduardo was forced to sell his plantation to satisfy his tax debt. Almost penniless, he immigrated to the United States where he was introduced to General Narciso Lopez. Lopez found that Eduardo's reputation and support for a free Cuba gave the former Spanish general legitimacy in the eyes of the black *Lukumi* insurrectionists. Since Narciso Lopez spoke no English, he offered Eduardo Izquierdo a position on his staff. But while the general valued the father, he earned the goodwill of every Southern cavalier he met, who made it his duty to try and seduce Eduardo Izquierdo's very beautiful daughter. Not only was she beautiful and gay, Conchita was also a bit of a flirt. She could not help herself. Conchita was a Cuban *criolla*. She had been raised on Catholicism and Voodoo, she loved the drums and the dance. She also loved New Orleans. It was an exciting town. She loved the social life with its continual round of parties. Narciso Lopez' personal wealth and his promise to pay a million dollars for the recruitment of American mercenaries for his Cuban campaign gave Lopez access to the cream of Southern society, beginning with the Governor of Mississippi, John Quitman. During the 1850s, nothing was dearer to a Southerner's heart than gambling, women and politics. So wherever General Narciso Lopez and his staff were invited, the vivacious Conchita Izquierdo found herself the center of attention from the most eligible and not-so eligible of Southern society.

But while Conchita was a gay favorite during the social season, she was equally disinterested in her suitors. After all, these men had only one interest: the expansion of slavery. None of them interested her in the least...until she met Ross Pary. As Yerby describes it, the politics of an up and coming white Southern planter and the daughter of a *criollo* revolutionary in no way prevented their love. Ross Pary, who spoke to her in his wonderful blend of Castilian Spanish and Southern English, captivated Conchita from the very beginning. Afterwards where her love for Ross Pary was concerned, Conchita was shameless. She lied to her father and she made love to this dashing white man who owned slaves and fully supported the institution of slavery. Thus Eduardo had been unable to contact his daughter to tell her that he was returning to Cuba to join Aguero because Conchita was making love to Ross Pary.

So it was not honor or duty or even adventure that drove the young architect to leave his Mississippi plantation to join with General Narciso Lopez's American mercenaries in an invasion of Cuba.

Not for the great cause which has inspired so many of these others, Pary thought to himself, but to save the one person who is more dear to me than life.

Staring out towards Cuba's yet invisible shoreline, Pary became aware that a young officer seemed to approach him directly. "Excuse me, sir," the gentleman said, his voice boyish, his face exuberant, "but aren't you, Ross Pary of Natchez?"

Ross studied the young man with reserve. He expected to know few people on this trip. As a matter of fact, the only men Pary knew on the *Pampero*, other than General Lopez himself, were the brothers George and Henry Metcalf, who also came from Natchez, Mississippi. They were quartered below decks with the other men. But, Ross realized that where he was going, he would need as many friends as possible. "Why yes…yes, I am," Ross answered.

"Well, sir, I am William Crittenden of Kentucky," the young man introduced himself. "I had the pleasure of meeting you at the Brittany's dinner. I especially remember your remarks to Governor Quitman, about the European reaction to nullification in the South."

"Of course," Ross Pary said, beginning the chivalric affectations that Southerners, especially social climbers like Ross Pary whose antecedents were definitely below Mississippi's planter class, so love to display. "As I remember, you were a member of General Narciso's party that evening," Pary said, giving a slight bow.

"Yes, sir," the youth replied, "I've been with the General since last year. I met him in Nashville at Governor Quitman's secession convention. My uncle…."

Ross Pary, ever ready to pounce on a chance for advancing himself blurted out, "Yes, Crittenden…are you related to John J. Crittenden, President Fillmore's Attorney General?"

"Why yes, I am," young Crittenden responded, apparently feeling no irritation at being interrupted. "John Crittenden is my uncle, but some of my family, including me, do not agree with his views on holding the Union together."

"Please forgive my interruption," Pary said, realizing that the young man seemed to need to talk to take his mind off of this slowly chugging steamer and the bright Caribbean moon. "You were saying your uncle…."

"Yes, my Uncle Ted…Theodore O'Hara, has been serving General Lopez since 1849," the young Crittenden said proudly. "My uncle led a company of Kentuckians for General Lopez in the attack at Cardenas last May and was wounded in action."

"In the attack on Cuba?" Pary said, beginning to get a deeper appreciation for the real dangers he was to face.

"Yes…he was shot in the leg and his men had to carry him back to their ship. They just barely escaped a Spanish man-of-war," Crittenden said proudly. "In Kentucky, my uncle is very famous. Did you know he wrote the poem *Bivouac of the Dead*?"

Pary had not even heard of *Bivouac of the Dead*. However, out of respect to Crittenden's uncle, Ross exclaimed, "So you have famous men on both sides of your family." Yep. Uncle Ted is quite an outstanding person," Crittenden said, "and I wanted to follow in his footsteps so I got him to introduce me to General Lopez and I've been with the general ever since."

"Well, try not to be too much like him," Ross Pary said with mock concern, "don't want you getting all shot up, now, do we?"

"No, sir," the young adventurer agreed. Ross Pary liked Bill Crittenden. It was just like having another brother. For his part, the young Crittenden was happy to have a friend…someone who wouldn't mind if you told him how scared you were. Most of the other officers were veterans of the Mexican War who had become maladjusted to civilian life. Killing was what they did best. They were happy to sign on for the thousand dollars Narciso Lopez promised. These old campaigners intended to "liberate" more than just the land during the Cuban campaign. In the Mexican War, many of their friends had gotten very rich. These officers did not intend to let another opportunity slip by. They were far less idealistic about Narciso Lopez's upcoming campaign to free Cuba and far more mercenary in their intentions to gather up the spoils of war. Young Crittenden was chilled by what he learned about their plans for the upcoming campaign.

"You know," Crittenden said to Pary in a confidential manner, "when I met you at that banquet, I do not recall that you had any particular interest in politics."

"I didn't then and I don't now," Pary replied.

"As I recall you even tried Governor Quitman's patience on certain points touching on whether the South should nullify its relationship with the North," the young officer smiled.

Bill Crittenden's remembrance of Ross Pary's remarks was as delicately put as they were kindly meant. Ross Pary's political opinions had won him few admirers among Natchez's planter class. Pary's origins as a mill worker's son were humble, but his parents' ambitions for their younger son made it possible for Ross to study at Oxford and travel throughout Europe. Ross especially loved Spain where his ability to learn and speak fluent Spanish won him many admirers. Wealthy Mississippians tolerated Ross Pary because of his talent as an architect. They willingly overlooked his humble background as long as he could design and build houses with the old world grace and charm of a Finiterre, the plantation home which he had completed for his friend Lance Brittany and Lance's wife, Morgan.

"If you are not here for politics," the young Bill Crittenden observed, "you must be here for love. Am I not right, honorable sir?"

"You are right, my young friend." Ross Pary replied, gaining a better appreciation for the young Kentuckian's intelligence. "Do you remember Eduardo Izquierdo, the Cuban patriot whose entire life was dedicated to Cuban independence?"

"Yes…"

"Then you must remember his exquisitely beautiful daughter, Conchita?"

"I certainly do remember her. She had lovely sea-green eyes and a sultry walk. Every man at that banquet, young and old, fell madly in love with her," Crittenden said.

"Even you," Pary asked with a laugh.

"No, not I," Crittenden replied, defensively. "You probably do not remember, since you only had eyes for the lovely Ms. Izquierdo, but I was accompanying Miss Lucy Holcombe of Texas. Miss Holcombe, who happened to be a visitor of Governor Quitman's family, and I became engaged that evening."

"Congratulations, sir," said Pary, giving a salute.

"And are you engaged to the beautiful Ms. Izquierdo, as well?" Crittenden asked.

"I have asked for her hand and now this terrible business in Cuba threatens my happiness," Pary said somberly. "That is why I'm going on this mission…to save her and her father if I can."

"To save them?"

"Yes," said Pary, "it's complicated."

"How so?" Crittenden asked.

"When Eduardo Izquierdo, freed his slaves, the other *hacendados* threatened to kill him. The *hacendados* want to get rid of the Spanish; they don't want to get rid of their slaves. Eduardo was a man of honor. When he promised his slaves freedom, he actually meant it."

"So the slaves on the other plantations expected the other *hacendados* to free them as well?" Crittenden asked

"Right," Pary replied. "But instead, the *hacendados* ran the Izquierdos off."

"So what happened?" Crittenden asked.

"Conchita and her father came to the United States, but many of his former slaves became tobacco smugglers and kept in contact with the Izquierdos. That is how Eduardo knew of Joaguin de Aguero's uprising. Eduardo returned to Cuba to join Aguero. When Conchita learned that he had returned to Cuba, she left as well."

"So now you are going to save her?" Crittenden asked.

"Yes," Pary replied, "that's about it."

"Your mission is even more noble than mine...I go to Cuba for glory, you go for love." And Bill Crittenden gave Ross Pary, his comrade in arms, a salute. And as Pary was about to respond, the dignified General Narciso Lopez himself came onto the deck. The imposing figure and military bearing of the handsome white-haired Venezuelan general inspired confidence in officers assembled on deck. Lopez had led military campaigns on three continents, but Pary still had mixed thoughts about this Cuban revolutionary.

"How much do you know about the General?" Pary asked his young companion.

"Not a lot," Crittenden admitted. "He speaks no English and I speak no Spanish, which limits our conversation."

"So you know nothing about him?" Pary stated, more as a question than as a fact.

"I know he is originally from Venezuela, where he was a general in the Spanish army," Crittenden said. "When Venezuelan revolutionaries kicked the Spanish out and won Venezuela's independence, Lopez escaped to Spain."

"So why is he leading a revolt against the Spanish now?" Pary asked.

"In Spain," Crittenden said, "Lopez allied himself with General Baldomero Espartero who led Spanish troops, and fought insurrections in the Americas. Espartero was not very successful."

"Why do you say that?" Pary asked.

"Because he returned to Spain and led a *coup* against the monarchy. After the civil war, Espartero becomes the *caudillo*, dictator of Spain."

"I guess Espartero had enough money to buy the army," Pary

observed.

"And you would be right," Bill Crittenden laughed. "Espartero appointed all *ayacuchos*, former military commanders who served with him in America, to important government posts. He appointed Narciso Lopez governor of Valencia. Then in 1841, Espartero appointed Lopez governor of the Cuban province of Las Villas. His villa occupied most of the town of Trinidad."

"I still don't see why Lopez is leading an insurrection against Cuba," Pary stated.

"You will, if you let me finish," Crittenden said good-naturedly. "When Espartero was overthrown by military officers loyal to the Spanish Crown, Lopez not only lost his governorship but, threatened with arrest, he was forced to flee to America for safety."

"So he's as much of an adventurer as anyone on this seagoing wreck," Pary observed.

General Lopez, looking around the deck and spotting Crittenden and Pary, strode over to the two officers. Crittenden noticed that the general's usual interpreter, Cirilo Villaverde, was absent.

"Good evening, Gentlemen," General Lopez's liutenant haltingly said. "The general wishes the best to you for yourselves and the task ahead."

"Thank you, General," Ross Pary replied in Spanish, "it is good to get off on the right foot, *empezar con buen pie*, no?"

"Si, *Señor* Pary," the general beamed, "I am happy you have joined us. That you speak Spanish will be useful for us. I have risked everything, me *juge el todo por el todo*. Now I will speak to the men. Will you translate for me?"

"I would be honored," Ross Pary bowed low.

The officers gathered around the general. Ross Pary translated the general's remarks. "We are embarked upon a great enterprise to free Cuba. As you know we could not wait any longer. Many are impatient for action. You are impatient for action."

A great cheer went up from the men.

"This is no scheme of conquest. We do not go to rouse the natives to rebellion, but to aid them in driving from their land the oppressors who control Cuban soil. The people are weary of their bondage, their chains cause festering wounds. They will welcome us for their liberation."

Once again the men cheered.

"Fear no consequences. The Cuban people have given their promise that their actions will match yours. Their revolt has already given you their commitment that we will depose Spanish tyranny and raise the Cuban flag over a free Cuba!" It was just what the men needed to rally their spirits. They clapped and cheered the general. In his turn, the general beamed at his men and then, waving, abruptly returned to his cabin.

After the general left the deck, Ross Pary turned to Bill Crittenden and asked, "How confident are you about this mission?"

"Why do you ask, Ross?"

"I don't know, maybe I'm just jittery…but something doesn't seem quite right," Ross observed.

"Well, I sure did expect to see a lot more men," Bill said thoughtfully.

"What do you mean?"

"There's only four hundred and fifty men on board."

"And so what does that mean?" Pary asked expectantly.

"We have been recruiting people all over the South. I personally signed up more than six hundred volunteers from Kentucky alone. Yesterday, I signed up over a hundred men on this ship from New Orleans. They were just hanging around the docks with nothing to do. I asked them if they wanted to go to Cuba and they volunteered."

"So where are all the other men you recruited?" Ross Pary asked.

"That's a good question," Bill Crittenden replied thoughtfully. "I don't know."

Pary began thinking about their situation. "What you are saying, Bill," Pary summarized, "is that after having recruited hundreds if not thousands of men who have left their homes and signed induction papers to join this expedition, only three hundred are actually on this boat...plus the hundred or so from the docks of New Orleans who have no military experience whatsoever?"

"Yes," Crittenden replied, "I think that is what I am saying... And another thing, Ambrosio Gonzales is not on this boat."

"Who is Ambrosio Gonzales?" Ross asked.

"You met him at the banquet. He is the general's aide and second in command. But he is not here with us." Crittenden seemed to go into a trance and then blurted out, "The cannon..."

"What do you mean, the cannon?" Pary asked.

"There should be cannon on board," Crittenden said. "When I was recruiting, some of the men wanted to volunteer for artillery duty."

"So?" Pary asked.

"Cirilio Villaverde, the general's aide and translator...who, by the way, also is not on this boat," Crittenden said, "told me to tell anyone wanting to volunteer for artillery that we would have cannon right out of the Mississippi and Georgia arsenals. But I didn't see any cannon put on this ship."

The two men again lapsed into silence. The thump, thump, thumping of the *Pampero's* engines barely disrupted their thoughts. Now, at eight knots, the Pampero seemed to be losing the race with the morning's light to the Cuban shore.

CHAPTER TWELVE

The manor house of Monmouth Plantation flaunted the Grecian architectural style that excited the imagination of many of Mississippi's wealthier planters. Tall and gracefully white columned, Monmouth manor reflected the aspirations of a culture dedicated to gentility through a strict adherence to what the Southern gentry called the *natural order*. It represented everything that was pure, chivalric and beautiful. Monmouth was the 'Southern way of life' to the world. The plantation reflected its owner, John A. Quitman, a general in the Mexican-American War and the former governor of Mississippi.

At Monmouth, one found rare and exquisitely handcrafted furnishings; the best Europe could produce. There were marble mantelpieces adorning every room; delicate glass for the sides and fanlights of the doors; crystal chandeliers and bronze lamps with hand-etched glass-blown globes; gay Brussels carpets; hand-blocked wallpaper; gleaming tall tiered mirrors with gold-leaf frames; silver knobs and gold fittings for the doors; gold window cornices; elaborately carved and richly upholstered mahogany furniture; rosewood chests; heavily brocaded draperies; exquisitely hand-knitted lace curtains; bronzes;

marble sculptures; silver plate that gleamed from the sideboards; delicate china and crystal gracing banquet tables. Monmouth Plantation served as a showcase of Arian pride.

Outside on its thousands of acres of land, Monmouth Plantation boasted of even more wealth and affluence. Fields of cotten, corn, oats and barley lay in neatly lined rows; a hardy rice crop overgrew its wetlands; pastures fed herds of sheep, goats and cattle; pens burst with pigs and chickens, and stables boasted the pride of all Southern plantations: horses, magnificent thoroughbreds, horses for coaches and wagons, plow and field horses and ordinary saddle horses. And supporting all this wealth and culture were thousands of plantation slaves who made the 'Southern way of life' possible.

Indeed, John Quitman determined that Monmouth Plantation would be the legacy to his almost fanatical commitment and active involvement in slavery's expansion throughout the Americas. As a matter of fact, slavery was his family's business. His grandfather, the Governor of Curacoa, ran the island's slave concentration camp for the Dutch West India Company. Shortly before his birth, Quitman's parents moved from Curacoa to New York, bringing their slaves with them. Though he spent most of his childhood in New York, it was in Mississippi that Quitman found the political climate and social atmosphere conducive to his rise as the chief architect of the social organization establishing white supremacy. This was his principal and dominant worldview for blacks as well as whites. Quitman maintained an unwavering commitment to the ordering of all social and political relations throughout the Americas, so no person of color whether African, Indian or Hispanic could rise above the status of a slave. Quitman dreamed of consolidating the Americas into one great slaveholding empire. All his activities were directed to the fulfillment of this dream. He was the driving force behind the Mexican War that he had hoped would bring far more slave states into the Union than it actually did. And even though he was no longer a general in the army and had been forced to resign as Mississippi's governor because of a federal indictment, John A. Quitman, by all accounts, remained one of the most powerful men in the United States.

Today Quitman sat in his study, busily dictating a mountain of correspondence to his personal secretary. The Governor paused to look out the window. The view was quite lovely. He wished he could spend more time enjoying his land. But, although the federal indictment forced him to resign as Mississippi's governor, Quitman still remained quite busy. Quitman's correspondence still affect many and decided much.

President Zachary Taylor had personally directed that Quitman be indicted for violating the United States' neutrality laws. When President Taylor had denounced Quitman for supporting Narciso Lopez's invasion of Cuba in 1850, Quitman hurled the gauntlet at the President of the United States by calling the Nashville Convention to discuss secession from the union. "I'll hang every secessionist I find starting with Quitman," the President declared. Taylor then demanded Quitman's indictment for violations of the United States Neutrality Act. But the indictment was quickly dismissed after President Taylor's bizarre death, and Quitman's secession conference was an overwhelming success. All the Southern and border states sent official representatives. Many states, including South Carolina, passed resolutions endorsing secession. So now correspondence poured in from all over the South. All the leading pro-slavery politicians in the country, it seemed, looked to John Quitman for leadership.

Politics was not the only reason Quitman had so little time for his plantation. His fraternal commitments were equally demanding. Quitman was the Grand Master of all Masons in Mississippi. In addition, he was the Grand Sovereign over all the Southwest Masonic Lodges. Quitman was also the Grand Inspector General of the 33rd Degree Ritual for the Masons' Southern Division. Finally, John Quitman sat as the founder and charter member of the Supreme

Masonic Council for the United States. Correspondence from all of these fraternal responsibilities was massive. Each day Quitman found himself facing a mound of correspondence that daily grew bigger and bigger. But doggedly each day, Quitman spent hours reading and dictating responses to this correspondence pouring in from all over the country. And so on this August day in 1851, the knock on John Quitman's study door was a welcome interruption.

"Yes!" Quitman boomed imperiously.

In shuffled an old black slave dressed in the finest livery of a century earlier including white silk stockings, brocaded sky blue frock coat and powdered wig. The old servant, whose body after so many years of service was bent into a permanent stoop of humility, announced in a voice eerily similar to that of his master: "The Honorable Caleb Cushing."

And immediately, a distinguished looking gentleman pushed past the servant into Quitman's study. The former governor rose up from his desk and greeted his guest warmly. "Caleb, my dear sir," Quitman said expansively and seized his visitor's proffered hand, giving it a vigorous shake in a manner known only to his society's most elite inner circle. Like Quitman, Caleb Cushing was also a Northerner, born in Massachusetts and a graduate of Harvard. Cushing was a member of Boston's elite social class known as the Brahmins. But unlike Quitman, Cushing was not a soldier. He was not one to march off with men under his command who were willing to kill and be killed to seize land and power. Cushing was a behind the scenes manipulator and a government diplomat who amassed his wealth as did many of his fellow Brahmins through slave trading and opium dealing. Cushing's familiarity with the opium trade caused President John Tyler to appoint Cushing the United States representative at a peace conference in China. The British had won the First Opium War and U.S. opium distributors needed Cushing to negotiate the land and labor concessions from the defeated Chinese for them.

Cushing was successful and the American drug dealers who had not even participated in the First Opium War received the same concessions the British had forced upon the Chinese.

"Governor, I heard the great news. The Lopez expedition left for Cuba several days ago." Cushing spoke with the distinctive Boston twang that sounded like a cross between an Irish brogue and an English whine. "I came down here to salute you in person, sir, and offer you my heartiest congratulations."

"That is mighty white of you, coming all the way down here and leaving your duties as a representative of the Massachusetts legislature," Quitman replied cordially.

"Nonsense! Few men in the country or even the entire world could have pulled off the Lopez expedition as deftly and as satisfactorily as you," the portly little Bostonian said.

Quitman was appreciative of the man's obvious admiration, but what he liked most was Cushing's absolute loyalty. Few slave traders and drug traffickers were trustworthy, even among their own fraternity. Treachery, lies and ruthlessness were the keys to success for those dealers in human misery. In the business of human bondage, seldom could confederates be trusted. But, Caleb Cushing's loyalty had been proven many times. He had taken the most solemn oaths and agreed to the most terrible penalties, for Cushing, too, was a member of that most ancient of fraternal societies whose roots can be traced back to the Temple of Solomon and the Priory of Sion. Later on in the evening, after each of them had had more alcohol than they should, Quitman and Cushing would preside over a ceremony with the formal rituals associated with their fraternal order. But now all too briefly, the two fraternal confidants would enjoy each other's company in a leisurely Southern way.

"You are most kind, sir, most kind, indeed," Caleb Cushing said to his host. "For that reason, sir, I am proud to call you my most worshipful grand master." They exchanged the secret signs and traditional greeting with good feelings and jovial cordiality.

"Thank you for your kind words and faithful support, Caleb," John Quitman said. "It is often very lonely for those of us who must carry out our mission and our goals. The very need for secrecy, even from our own, makes it hard for those of us who are charged with the duty of bringing order out of chaos."

"That will be all for today, Adams," Quitman said dismissing his secretary. Then tugging at an inconspicuous cord, he summoned the butler. "Bring me my usual, Scipio," Quitman said when the black slave shuffled in, "and, I believe, a whiskey for Mister Cushing. That is correct, isn't it, Caleb?"

"Whiskey would be fine," Cushing responded heartily. "A man needs whiskey to clear the dust from his travels out of his throat!" And the two men chuckled.

Having received their drinks, the two men once more observed the ritual toasts and awesome pledges of their order. Finally, each settled back into a great overstuffed chair and sipped his drink in an atmosphere of contented comradeship. Each could feel his increasing power. Because of their fraternal ties they could go on accumulating power and creating even greater successes through the mystical relationships promised as a dawning 'new world order'.

"It was simply amazing," Cushing said, "how you used that pompous Spanish peacock to accomplished so much for our cause."

"We, my good friend," Quitman reminded Cushing, "...we. If you had not brought General Narciso Lopez to me in the first place, none of it would have happened."

"You're right, most worshipful master," Caleb said with a little giggle, "but I almost slipped up on that one. At first I couldn't understand what he was talking about. You know that Narciso doesn't speak any English."

"You knew enough Spanish to understand *one million dollars*," quipped Quitman.

"I believe if it looks like a turkey and says 'gobble, gobble,' it must be asking to become Thanksgiving dinner," Cushing shot back gleefully.

"But even so," Quitman said, "you are to be congratulated."

"It was only after our Cuban brothers got Lopez's friend, Cirilo Villaverde, out of prison and up here to the United States that I began to appreciate the opportunity that had fallen into our laps." Cushing smiled and took a sip of his whiskey. It's good to have the respect of the Supreme Grand Master, he thought to himself. Lopez had heard what the *americanos* did in Mexico during the Mexican War. He was convinced that the *americanos* would have no trouble in Cuba; it was not even a quarter of Mexico's size. Five thousand *americanos* would have no problem ousting the Spanish from Cuba. So Lopez promised Cushing one million dollars to help him raise an *americano* army—as he called it. And Cushing realized that he had been given a once in a lifetime opportunity. And he took full advantage of it.

As he sat there, knowing that few could boast of enjoying an afternoon visit with the Supreme Grand Master, suddenly the idea of a free Cuba seemed funny. Maybe it was the whiskey or the long drive or the hot weather, but all of a sudden, Caleb just couldn't stop laughing. "A free Cuba, ha, ha," Cushing cried with mirth, "Lopez is as interested in a free Cuba as I'm interested in free darkies."

With that Quitman joined in the laughter. "Actually the darkies are free," chuckled Quitman, "it just costs so much to get them to do anything." With that the two men exploded in laughter. They grabbed their sides and tears rolled down their cheeks.

Sometime later, when they had gained some composure and had their glasses refilled, Quitman asked, "Those Cubans who are paying us, what did you call them?"

"*Hacendados?*"

"Right, *hacendados*," Quitman said barely able to control himself. "Those Cuban *hacendados* sent us Ambrosio."

"Ambrosio Jose Gonzales…" Cushing pronounced the name with mock dignity.

"Ambrosio Jose Gonzales offered us three million dollars not to have Americans come down and invade their island," Quitman recalled, still amazed at the offer. Then once again, the fact that General Lopez offered them a million dollars for 5,000 mercenaries and Gonzales offered them three million dollars not to send them, struck the two men as funny. With that these two powerful captains of war, holders of high public office and grand masters of the most ancient and secret fraternal society, once again begin laughing so hard that it was as if the great god of mirth, himself, held them in his clutches. Again tears streamed down their cheeks. Nor could they look at each other, for when they did, the laughing fits continued.

Finally Cushing said, "The *hacendados* gave us three million dollars to do nothing."

This seemed to settle Quitman down, because his reply was bitter, "Yes, but that Lopez only gave us a little more than three hundred and fifty thousand dollars. The little bastard cheated us." This sobered up Cushing as well. He didn't care so much about the money, but he knew that Quitman hated to lose at anything. Cushing always worried about the issues that concerned the Supreme Grand Master. "It's not as if we didn't have expenses," Quitman observed. "We had to put on a good show and that wasn't free. We had to do a lot of recruiting and then there was the matter of securing weapons and ammunition. And then there were the newspaper articles that needed to be run, especially in those northern papers. "

"Well, sir," Cushing replied, his eyes twinkling in merriment, "I don't think you will be able to get any more money from our friend, General Narciso Lopez. He's going to be busy for quite a while. And I still say it was the finest piece of bamboozling this old boy ever did see." And the laughing began once again.

Quitman and Cushing had planned the campaign well. Contacts in the national and international press did their work. The fraternity organized a few demonstrations in major cities both North and South. 'Good old boys' from Kentucky went across the county creating the illusion that recruits from across America were marshalling for a Cuban invasion. Soon the upcoming 'filibuster' invasion against Cuba was front-page news on every major newspaper in America. On April 25, 1851, the *Newark Advertiser* published an article about an expeditionary force of 600 men in Jacksonville, Florida, set to sail for Cuba within thirty-six hours. "Cannon, gun carriages, rifles, muskets, ammunition and the furniture of an army," the article reported, "were being loaded from local warehouses. Along with stores of provisions and large quantities of resin and firewood to fuel the steamer, *Pampero*, men and horses are being prepared for embarkation. The officers are brave men and the volunteers are veterans of the Mexican War. Some of these troops are the same Cubans involved in last year's 'Cardenas' affair." Many Northern papers reproduced this article, including the *Philadelphia North American* and the *Louisville Democrat*.

The United States government lost no time warning the Spanish government of the impending "invasion." The U.S. Secretary of State sent a wire to the Spanish Minister to the United States reassuring him that America "…wholly condemned any planned invasions and would earnestly do everything possible to defeat these plans." The next day the Spanish Minister chartered a schooner and personally delivered intelligence on General Narciso Lopez's invasion to Cuba's Captain-General, Jose Guiterrez de la Concha. That message sealed the fate of all those moving towards Cuba on the decrepit steamer, *Pampero*.

"Still, it's a shame that we have to lose so many fine boys," Cushing reflected.

"Yes, but they are casualties of war," Quitman observed. "We needed some of them to go over to Cuba with Lopez. We had to make it look good. Beside we didn't send many…just enough, it seems to me. Most of those boys were recruited from the docks in New Orleans. None of those boys has any real fighting experience, so we didn't really lose many fighting people."

"I understand John Crittenden's nephew, William, went," Cushing reflected matter-of-factly.

"Yes, he did…yes, he did." Quitman repeated himself absent-mindedly. "He will be sorely missed." The governor thought about Lucy Holcomb. The young beauty had been his guest here at Monmouth Plantation. How happy she had been when her engagement to the young Crittenden had been announced, Quitman remembered. *I'm gonna make sure that that young man will never be forgotten*, he decided. *People need to know the sacrifice that fine boy made for our cause.*

"Well, at least we saved Teddy O'Hara," Cushing observed. "Now that was a fighting man…and we're gonna need all the fighting men we can get before long."

"I'll drink to that," Quitman said. After a silent spell, Quitman said, "We also got that young upstart, Ross Pary, on the boat."

"Pary?" Cushing asked as much to himself as to Quitman. "I don't believe I recall a Ross Pary."

"No matter," Quitman drawled, "he wasn't much of a fighting man."

　　　　　　　　　　　　　　　　　　　　　　　　FRANK YERBY:

CHAPTER THIRTEEN

P edro! Wake up! Wake up!" Tolomeo burst into the *bohio* where Pedro and Carlota slept. "The *americanos* have landed!" Clearing the sleep from his eyes, Pedro rolled out of his hammock and focused on what his uncle was telling him. "Yes, the *americanos* are here!" Tolomeo shouted.

"Where are they, Uncle Tolomeo?" Pedro asked. "Who told you?"

"The *hacendados* sent a messenger. The *americanos* landed in Bahia Honda two days ago," the Babaluaye Tolomeo said.

"But uncle," Pedro asked, "how can that be? Bahia Honda is the home of the Spanish fleet."

"I know, I know," Tolomeo said shaking his head.

"Did you question the messenger?" Carlota asked with a yawn.

"Yes," Tolomeo responded. "I asked him several times. He only repeated what he was told. 'The *americanos* have landed at Bahia Honda.'"

"It's just not possible," Pedro exclaimed. "They were to meet us in Mantanzas. I don't believe the *americanos* would attack the whole Spanish fleet.

"Nor do I, " Tolomeo said. "They might have landed at Morrillo;

it's close by."

"It's close by," Pedro agreed, "but isn't it further west? Nobody can help them out there. That's on the far western end of the island. There's nobody there."

Yerby was awakened and joined the others. "Maybe these Americans have enough men and ships to attack Cuba and don't need the *Lukumi*," he reasoned. "They must have one huge force since they have chosen to attack Havana and the might of all Spanish military forces in Cuba."

"Not need the *Lukumi*," Pedro shouted. "The *Lukumi* will lead the rebellion. I will lead the *Lukumi* and we will free all the slaves. Let us sound the drums, now!"

"Bahia Honda! We expected them in Puerto Principe. Aguero's uprising was over three hundred miles away in Puerto Principe. Why would these crazy *americanos* land in Bahia Honda?" The more Pedro thought about it, the angrier he became.

"No matter where they are," Tolomeo said, "we've got to find them."

"What about the drums?" Pedro asked. "Shall I sound them?" Yerby's comments notwithstanding, Pedro loved the drums. It was through the drums that he talked to his people. *No one… not even the Babaluaye Tolomeo, himself,* Pedro believed, *has as much power over his* Lukumi *as I and my drums.* There were hundreds, maybe thousands of drummers in Cuba, but only Pedro was known far and wide. To the *Lukumi* and other Cuban blacks, when the gods wished to talk to their people it was Pedro who beat their drums. The Orishas, the Voodoo gods of the *Lukumi*, loved Pedro. He was handsome, courageous and the gods blessed him and his drums. But one of the Orishas, Papa Legba, was always very difficult even for someone like Pedro. Papa Legba was a Trickster and had to be respected, fed but, most importantly, watched very carefully. Papa Legba hated complacency even in those he loved. If Papa Legba caught someone like Pedro not paying attention, the god would play a dirty trick on him. But, for some reason, when he heard that the *americanos* were coming Pedro forgot all about Papa Legba. *What about the drums?* Pedro repeated.

"I don't think the drums should sound until we know where the *americanos* are," the Babaluaye Tolomeo decided, much to Yerby's relief. *The last thing we need is a general insurrection and a massacre of these brave yet ill-equipped, poorly led and wholly ignorant Lukumi,* Yerby thought to himself. *If I have anything to say about it maybe they will not become the victims of a senseless slaughter on this day.*

Pedro's face frowned in disappointment, but he made no comment. "We can sail around to Bahia Honda," Tolomeo said. "Once we contact them, we can offer our assistance."

"I will lead them to victory over the Spanish," Pedro replied eagerly. "But, come on, let's hurry, we must be off. Joining us, *Señor* Yerby?"

"Of course," Yerby replied. "I wouldn't miss this for the world."

Carlota had been listening. Fear rose into her throat. She could not breathe. Fear clutched at her very soul. Even under normal circumstances, Carlota never wanted to leave Pedro's side. With the rebellion and the *americanos* losing their way and landing in the middle of Havana's entire garrison, Carlota feared that if Pedro left her now, she would never see him again. The thought of losing him was unbearable. She loved Pedro. And now that she was expecting a little *niño*, Carlota wanted nothing to separate them.

Carlota's love for Pedro was a desperate kind of love…the kind of love that masks deeply held terrors and fears. She had the kind of love that reaches out and holds on for dear life; the kind of love that smothers the loved one. That was how Carlota loved Pedro.

The other women called her "crazy Carlota." "No one should be that crazy over a man…not even over Pedro who was the god's own messenger," one of the village women said. But nothing they said mattered. Carlota only wanted to remain by Pedro's side…and be his lover and have his children. So as Tolomeo, Pedro and Frank prepared to meet the *americanos*, Carlota planned to go with them and meet the *americanos* at Bahia Honda or at Morrillo or wherever they were.

But Pedro had other ideas. "No, no, no! Dear one!" Pedro smiled." This is not the trip for you, or for my son. You should know better. Now be off before I ask Tolomeo to cast a spell and lock you in a *ceiba* tree until we return."

"You would not lock me in a *ceiba* tree," she said, defiantly. But Carlota was not brave enough to test a curse by the Babaluaye. So reluctantly, she decided to do as she was told. She picked up her things and made a great pretense at withdrawing to her *bohio*. Tolomeo, Pedro and Yerby had to pull the fishing boat out of its dock and slide it down a barely visible channel and into the Caribbean. Once they were out to sea, Carlota was all but forgotten.

They sailed due west towards Bahia Hondo where they hoped to rendezvous with the *americanos*. It wasn't far from Guanabacoa to Bahia Honda, barely 60 miles. On the other hand, there was the entire Spanish fleet. Several Spanish warships trained their cannon on Tolomeo's fishing boat. Even the fortress, Castillo del Morro, guarding the entrance to the Havana harbor, opened its gun ports and rolled out long-range cannon when the fishing boat came within range. The fortress could sink Tolomeo's fishing boat with a single salvo. But neither the fortress nor any other Spanish ship fired upon Tolomeo's fishing boat. The Spaniards had bigger quarry in mind. No captain wanted to be laughed at for sinking a pitiful little fishing boat owned by three ragged blacks. The Spanish warships wanted to catch a steamship coming from America in support of those Americans already caught in de la Concha's trap. The little fishing boat continued sailing westward. And the further west they sailed, the more Spanish warships they saw with gun crews prepared to fire at a moment's notice. "They must have sent a mighty army," Pedro said, awestruck by the sight of the mighty Spanish fleet..

"It could not be too large," Tolomeo said, "otherwise the Spanish wouldn't have so many warships guarding the port."

. . .

Indeed, the *Pampero* landed the pitifully small American invasion force at Morrillo ten miles west of Bahia Honda. Narciso Lopez left 125 men with Lieutenant Crittenden to guard their supplies of food, weapons and ammunition that had been unloaded from the *Pampero* and were now still sitting on the beach. They were the 125 wharf rats that Crittenden had recruited from the docks of New Orleans. Lopez took the remaining three hundred men into the Cuban interior to find the welcoming party and transportation. Against these three hundred American invaders, de la Concha dispatched his entire army of 8,000 regular soldiers, dragoons and cavalry. These units were supported by artillery and an armada of ships with a full complement of sailors.

De la Concha quickly choked the Americans from their supplies by landing seven hundred and fifty Spanish marines under General Manual Enna at Bahia Honda from the warship *Pizarro*. This force blanketed the entire five-mile coastline between Bahia Honda and Morrillo. De la Concha then sent Colonel Joaquin de Rada Morales by railway with four hundred troops and one hundred and twenty dragoons to intercept the Americans from the east. Finally, the captain-general directed another division under Colonel Angel Elizalde to march directly on Narciso Lopez from the town of Pinar del Rio in the southwest. So as Elizalde attacked from the south, Morales blocked the Americans from moving east towards Havana and Enna blocked their retreat to the sea. An army of fifteen hundred well-armed Spanish regulars had completely surrounded Lopez's three hundred-man invasion force. Within a matter of hours, Enna's marines exploded upon the Americans guarding the supplies on the beach. Lt. Crittenden's New Orleans wharf rats were completely overwhelmed. Over half were killed in the initial attack; the remainder, including William Crittenden, were captured and marched the fifty miles to Havana to be imprisoned at Castillo del Morro. How did someone with the status and family background as William Crittenden come to such a sad end, an innocent victim?

William Crittenden had everything to live for. He came from one of Kentucky's first families; he was young and bright. His fiancée, Lucy Holcombe of Texas, was one of the most beautiful and intelligent women in the South, and she adored him. But the young Bill Crittenden had a rival. Eugenia Holcombe had taken her daughter on a visit to Mississippi as the guest of Governor John Quitman. Lucy Holcombe, the Rose of Texas, captivated many hearts on that trip. One of those politicians smitten by Lucy Holcomb was the fifty-year-old Francis W. Pickens, an arch-secessionist and political ally of John Quitman. Pickens accompanied the lovely Miss Holcombe all the way back home. Pickens was the governor who led South Carolina out of the Union and inaugurated America's Civil War by firing on Fort Sumter. But as powerful as he was within the slaveholding faction of the Democratic Party and important as he was to the new world order built upon slavery, Francis W. Pickens had absolutely no chance, whatsoever, to win the affections of Lucy Holcombe. Lucy Holcombe loved the young, dashing William Crittenden. John Quitman promised to help his South Carolina ally and send Bill Crittenden on a mission to Cuba from which it was guaranteed he would not return. And soon afterwards, Lucy Holcombe of Texas became Mrs. Lucy Pickens, wife of the governor of South Carolina. And William Crittenden became the innocent victim of treachery!

Long after the slaughter of Lt. Crittenden's men, Tolomeo navigated his little fishing boat past the warships crowding the Spanish harbor of Bahia Honda and less than an hour later, he landed at Morrillo. On the beach, they saw destruction and death everywhere. Corpses sprawled about in a grotesque tableau of men frozen in death.

Sightless eyes staring in terror at the burned out craters and charred rubble that were all that remained of the invaders' supplies. The corpses with hands and arms distended trying to ward off the final bayonet thrust or the final musket shot. The pungent smell of gunpowder mingled with the odor of charred human flesh nauseated Tolomeo, Pedro and Yerby as they gaped at the battlefield. The three Negroes climbed over the sides of the fishing boat, each wondering whether the entire American force had been destroyed…had there been survivors. But before they were able to speak, Spanish marines from the *Pizarro* with muskets at the ready and bayonets fixed surrounded them.

"What is your business here?" An officious looking sergeant directed the question at them.

"We are but poor fishermen, *señor*," Tolomeo replied to the sergeant in a pleading tone. "We just pulled into this place for the evening. Tomorrow we go out to catch the mackerel."

"You don't look like fishermen to me," the Spanish sergeant said suspiciously. "Where are you from?"

"Guanabacoa, *señor*," Tolomeo replied. "We come here to fish because, as the captain surely knows, the mackerel do not swim on the other side of Havana." Tolomeo had taken off his tattered straw hat and, with downcast eyes, looked very much like the itinerant fisherman he pretended to be… and sometimes was.

"You look like rebels," the sergeant said, "I'd better take you to my captain, he'll know what to do with you."

Suddenly there was a stirring from the boat. Another figure jumped over the side and raced over to where the soldiers detained Pedro, Tolomeo and Yerby. "No, no, *señor*," Carlota said. "Do not take them. They only came here to Morrillo for me. I needed a rest from the sea." Carlota looked up at Pedro with a mischievous smile, "You see, I am with child."

Pedro had all he could do to control his anger. *Will this woman ever do as she is told?* he asked himself, but he already knew the answer.

The Spanish officer stared first at Carlota and then at Pedro suspiciously. Pedro had no choice; he had to follow Carlota's lead. "Yes," Pedro spoke up, "my woman gets sick when she is at sea too long." Glaring at her, he continued, "And she is too stubborn to remain home as she has been told." Pedro gave Carlota a look that was meant to wilt her; she returned his angry look with a smile.

The Spanish officer stared at Carlota a long while. He was not above relieving his sexual desires on whichever mulatto and black wenches happened to catch his eye. Small enough compensation for the pitifully small wages he received. But recently, he began to draw the line at pregnant women. He told his men that his newfound moral scruples stemmed from feelings for his wife and daughter whom he hoped to see again one day. In reality, the marine sergeant had become squeamish after his last rape of a pregnant woman, who suffered a miscarriage while he was still in her.

The sergeant ordered his men to inspect the boat. Three marines disappeared over the side of the fishing boat but shortly reappeared reporting that they found nothing other than fishing nets, bait and tackle. The officer paused to think about what he should do. But in the end, he knew how little his captain wanted to be bothered with trivial matters.

"Okay," the sergeant said, "I will let you go, but get out of here before I change my mind."

Tolomeo made a deep bow and with profuse thanks, turned and climbed back into the boat. Yerby not far behind him, Pedro turned to grab Carlota. He wanted to drag her back into the boat by her hair. But as the Spanish officer continued to eye him, Pedro, in a quick motion, picked up Carlota and, lifting her over his back as if she were a sack of potatoes, climbed back into the boat. Hoisting the sails, shoving the boat off the beach and lowering the keel, Tolomeo had his boat sailing out of the inlet and back onto the Caribbean Sea before the Spaniard was able to consider whether he had made the proper decision.

"Carlota," Pedro groaned once they were out of earshot, "whatever are you doing here?"

"Does it matter?" Yerby asked. "Had she not been on board, we could well be on our way to a Spanish prison."

"Do you believe that any of the Americans survived?" Pedro asked his uncle anxiously.

"There were signs," Tolomeo replied, "but the signs were not good."

"Yes," Pedro said. "With all those Spanish troops, it looks as if all the *americanos* are either in prison or dead."

"No," Yerby replied, "some of the Americans have survived."

"If so, we need to find them," Pedro stated emotionally. "And the *Lukumi* and the Creoles must be warned about this disaster." Pedro didn't know who offended him more, the stupid Americans who landed three hundred miles from where his *Lukumi* stood ready to help them or Carlota who continued to disobey him. *How can I love such a woman?* Pedro asked himself, but he knew the answer was simple. He just did...or so he thought because he really didn't know. He really didn't know what love was. But right now Pedro had no time to deal with Carlota.

"You're right," Tolomeo replied. "Someone needs to find out what has happened."

"I'll go back," Pedro said. "Just get me close to shore and I'll swim the rest of the way."

"No, no," Carlota wailed. "Do not go, do not leave me...and your child. I know I will never see you again."

"Don't say that," Pedro replied. "I will return to you."

"No you won't," Carlota cried. "I had a dream...you and I will never see each other again." She was frantic. And fell to sobbing. Tolomeo loved Carlota like she was his own daughter, but there was nothing Tolomeo could say to console her that night...or in the nights to come. There was no choice, Pedro had to search for the surviving Americans before the drums sounded or else much *Lukumi* blood would be shed in vain. Somehow Pedro believed it was his destiny to lead the *americanos* out of de la Concha's trap. Tolomeo guided the fishing craft to a secluded spot of shoreline a couple of miles west of Morrillo. From there Pedro could swim to shore.

"I'm coming with you," Yerby said as Pedro prepared to slide into the water.

"*Si, Señor* Yerby," Pedro replied, "I am happy for the companionship." Pedro made no attempt to console the grieving Carlota. Her slender body, swollen with child, continued to heave with her sobs. As he and Yerby swam towards shore, Pedro took a last look at the woman who had been so much a part of his life for as long as he could remember. The only woman he had ever had or had ever wanted. "She is such a pain," Pedro thought to himself, "I will make it up to her when I return." But Pedro would never keep his promise; for he would never see Carlota again… nor would he ever forget her last cries of anguish.

CHAPTER FOURTEEN

It was mid-afternoon. Lopez and his men had marched a good distance inland and had arrived at the sleepy little village of Las Pozas. The village was empty; all the inhabitants had fled when they got word that the *americanos* were coming. This was not the reception Narciso Lopez expected. *Where is everyone?* he wondered.

"General!" Lopez's orderly and interpreter hurried over to where Lopez directed his headquarters to be located. Lopez noted the worried look on the officer's face. "General, the scout you sent to check on the supplies and Lt. Crittenden has just reported back."

"Tell him to go back and instruct Lieutenant Crittenden to move the supplies up; we'll camp here until we can meet up with the leaders of the insurrection. They should send someone out to meet us very soon, now."

"General, the scout has bad news," Lopez's orderly reported. "The Spanish attacked Crittenden on the beach. He and his entire command have been annihilated. Furthermore, the scout reports that you have landed on the western side of Habana. From the looks of all the Spanish ships sailing about, I'd say our army is right in the middle of the Spanish army.

Narciso Lopez had little time to think about his situation as his officers began shouting orders and the men began to form a line of battle. "General, a detachment of Spanish dragoons are heading this way." The dragoons were an advanced force attached to Colonel Elizalde's division that was striking out at the American invaders directly from Pinar del Rio. The officer in charge of the lightly armed dragoons wanted the glory of inflicting the first wounds. But at first the Americans' greater numbers and superior firepower easily beat off the attack of the charging Spaniards. The victory was short-lived. More Spanish troops are coming, Lopez was told and Las Pozas sat in the middle of a flat area that was completely indefensible. The Americans could not defend themselves against a larger Spanish force. Lopez called his officers together. "We must get away from here before we are surrounded," he told them through his interpreter. "Get your men up the hill as quickly as you can." There was a lot of grumbling from the ranks, but the officers got them moving before any more Spanish soldiers arrived. The Americans retreated up through the Cuban foothills and into the Cuban jungle. Fifteen dead remained behind including the scout who had originally reported on Lieutenant Crittenden. De la Concha had the Americans in a noose.

Spaniards love no sport more dearly than bullfighting. True Spaniards love to see the bull tormented and wounded and drained of blood until at last the poor animal is mercifully killed. And this was exactly what de la Concha intended for the Americans. Now he could engage in the delightful game of slowly tightening the noose around the invaders, killing them slowly until they no longer existed.

After several days of constant retreating, Lopez began talking to himself. *What happened to my support?* The former general of the Spanish army murmured to himself over and over. *Where are Cirilo and Ambrosio? Where is my transportation? Where is everybody?* Only now did he begin to realize why his good friend and translator Cirilo Villaverde failed to meet him on the *Pampero*. The plan was that

Ambrosio Gonzales would have the other American mercenaries recruited for Cuba ready to board the *Pampero* when it returned to Florida. Only now did he realize that Ambrosio would not be arriving with reinforcements. Only now when it was too late did he realize that he had been betrayed.

In only two days the American force, disciplined veterans intent in slaughter, had been turned into a cowardly unruly band desperate to escape. Their few supplies of food or water dwindled and with them order and discipline. Where once they fought in ranks, now at the first sign of attack the Americans ran for their lives. And so the retreat became a rout. Enjoying their sport, the Spaniards pressured the Americans deeper and deeper into the Cuban jungle...killing slowly, methodically, as in the bull ring, when those too exhausted or too severely wounded prayed for death. The Americans could not forage for food or even find suitable drinking water and every time they thought it was safe to stop and rest, Spanish troops would appear from nowhere and attack. De la Concha and his general staff took endless pleasure in tormenting these invaders. Like torturing the bull, de la Concha attacked Lopez with *torero, banderillero* and *picador*. He ambushed them; he charged his cavalry at them; he shelled them with field artillery.

Lopez directed his men to hack through the *manigua*, spiny thorns of the subtropical Cuban cactus that tore through clothes and ripped great wounds in the flesh. It took no time for these wounds to begin to fester and ooze in the Cuban sweltering heat. And the oozing discharge attracted all manners of bugs and insects. These once proud veterans of the Mexican War and the war for Texas independence who came to Cuba expecting an easy victory and lots of plunder were reduced to a band of starving, thirsty fugitives running for their lives and facing their inevitable deaths...like escaped slaves being chased through the swamp. They had but one chance. If they could get through the jungle and up the foothills skirting Havana, they might find support. But Lopez himself was lost. His former position of provincial governor had not given Lopez any familiarity with the Cuban jungle nor the rocky hills leading away from Havana down to the plains of San Cristobal. Narciso Lopez's familiarity with Cuba was limited to Havana and his own palatial residence in Trinidad. So he continued stumbling about with the group of Americans mercenaries in their hopeless retreat.

. . .

"They've got to be around here somewhere," Pedro said to Frank.

"Whatever the Spanish leave won't be much to find," Yerby replied. They had continued their search for the American mercenaries by following the carnage and death of battle. At first, they would come up on the American dead as they lay fallen in battle. Now they followed a trail of dead American bodies, some hacked to pieces, other trampled under horses, and still others impaled on stakes.

But Pedro was persistent and after almost a week of searching, he found the sorry band of ragged Americans, all that remained of Narciso Lopez's invasion force, hiding in one of the caves up in the Cuban highlands.

Ross Pary watched the two blacks as they made their way into Narciso Lopez's camp. The Americans were sprawled about. This was not the army that Pedro hoped to find. Not even a single sentry had been posted. The Negroes entered the camp unchallenged. "Where do you come from?" Pary croaked, his throat parched from the lack of water.

"We come from Guanabacoa, a small village on the other side of Habana," Pedro replied. "We were told you would be landing in the vicinity of Puerto Principe; many of us were prepared to assist you."

"Where are they? Did you bring food?" Pary asked, somehow relieved that the natural order of things had begun to reestablish themselves once more. "Who sent you here to save us?" Pary asked. The irony of this situation escaped Pedro but not Yerby. Of course, the idea that these blacks were here to save the men that the pro-slavery faction of the American South had sent to re-enslave them was quite natural for Ross Pary. After all, of what importance was a black's life other than to serve whites and further their interests? *Where would we be without our niggers to get us out of trouble?* Pary laughed to himself, relieved that the prospect of his death was not so imminent as before. "You boys, come with me and I'll take you to the General." Pary now served as Narciso Lopez's interpreter. The general's original interpreter was killed in the battle at Las Frices. Spanish troops with bayonets fixed had charged the Americans from the rear. Inside the lines, Lopez stood with what remained of his staff. The line broke and several Spaniards bore down on the General, their bayonet prepared to taste his blood. The general's interpreter died protecting him, receiving several bayonet wounds to the body while Lopez emptied his revolver into the charging soldiers.

"General," Pary said, "these, Negroes, say that they have come to help us."

Pary addressed a little man sitting on a rock at the edge of the cave. The man's eyes were lackluster, looking off in the distance. His face was haggard and covered with gray stubble. His uniform, once so fine and perfectly fitted, was shredded and tattered covered with stains, mud and blood. But with all that said, General Narciso Lopez still stumbled to his feet and offered his hand to these two emissaries of the insurrectionists. "Welcome, my friends."

Pedro gazed about at the ragged men sprawled about. He could not lead these men to free Cuba. Pedro's disappointment was profound, *I will not be the saviour of my people*, he thought bitterly. Then out loud he shouted at Narciso Lopez, "How did you come to this place? Don't you know that you are surrounded by the entire Spanish army?" Narciso Lopez looked at Pedro helplessly.

"Did you intend to land west of Havana?" Yerby asked. "Couldn't you see that this was a trap, that you had been betrayed?"

But the general shrugged. "Who sent you, my friends?" he asked. "Can you help us escape?"

"We were sent by the Babaluaye Tolomeo," Pedro replied. "He sent us to lead you to the *Lukumi*. They want to participate in your war against the Spanish."

Lopez looked about at what was left of his mercenary force. Of the three hundred men he led off of the beach at Morrillo, less than fifty remained. "These men, *muchachos*," Lopez said, "cannot attack the Spanish."

"Then, general," Pedro said, "you must act quickly and leave here. We must get into Matanzas if you are to have any chance of surviving. We can show you a way through the jungle and down onto the plain of San Cristobal and away from the Spanish."

"I will tell the men," Pary volunteered and turning he called the men to assembly. But when Pary explained their good fortune, the men began muttering, "No! No goddamned more marching. We've had a bellyful. We'll stay right here—it's safer. We can hide in this cave." It was two of the remaining officers who spoke out. They had agreed to relieve Lopez of command. They were hoping that Lopez would leave with Pedro and Frank. Then they would assume command of what was left and try to fight their way out of this trap. No matter that Ross explained that Pedro could lead them to safety, the officers were adamant and determined to stay.

"General," Pedro said, "we must go now!"

"Then you must go," Lopez said, "and leave us to our destiny, for I will not abandon my men." With that the would-be liberator of Cuba bowed his head and returned to the rock that served as his temporary headquarters.

Ross Pary convinced George and Henry Metcalf, his friends from Natchez, Mississippi, to join the escape with Pedro and Yerby. "These niggers are going get us out of here," Pary told them and the two joined up. The Metcalf brothers were practical; they wanted to save their hides. So, even though they were just as hungry, just as thirsty, just as exhausted as all the other surviving American mercenaries, Ross Pary and the Metcalf brothers found the will and the strength to followed Pedro and Frank up the rugged hills, through the Cuban jungle. They walked until all they could do was stumble. They stumbled until all they could do was crawl. The *ceiba* trees, bougainvillea, thick vines, bamboo groves and *manigua* presented a barrier that only a person who willed it could penetrate. And by willing a passage through this age-old Cuban jungle, they would endure the pain from innumerable scrapes, cuts and gouges from the jagged rocks and prickly bushes, sharp cactus and tough bamboo. They fought the jungle, pushing through where they could, hacking through where they couldn't. The next day in the distance, echoes of guns firing, men screaming and bugles blaring sounded up from where they had left their companions. "Well," Pary said looking at the two brothers, "I guess that's the end of that." And they were correct. Narciso Lopez's expedition had come to its inevitable end...the end planned by de la Concha. Like the bull in the ring, the Americans sat in their cave just waiting for death. But when the Spanish made their final assault, after a brief fight the Americans surrendered Narciso Lopez and themselves. The Spanish draped their American prisoners in chains and drove, dragged and beat them all the way down to Havana where Cuba's Captain-General had planned a fit reception for his prisoners. Many Americans did not survive the trek...some of those who did, later wished that they hadn't.

But through sheer will and determination Pedro was able to lead the three white Americans up to the top of the foothills and down onto the plain of San Cristobal. Once they got down onto the coast, *Lukumi* transported them across the Gulf of Batabano on a fishing boat to Matanzas.

News of Narciso Lopez's invasion swept over the Cuba like wildfire. Yerby hoped news of the Americans defeat got to the *Lukumi* before the drums sounded. The fate of many *Lukumi* warriors was held by a thread. If the drums sounded signaling the arrival of the *americanos, Lukumi* from all over the island would revolt. And the Spanish soldiers would be waiting. They would cut the *Lukumi* down like stalks of sugar cane. Pedro prayed that the Babaluaye Tolomeo would wait before sounding the drums. He had sent *Lukumi* to warn his uncle as soon as he arrived in San Cristobal. "Do not sound the drums!" was his message. And the *Lukumi* were fortunate because Papa Legba remained content with his people and the drums did not sound. From plantation to plantation news of the Americans' defeat spread. And the *Lukumi* put away their knives, machetes…and dreams of freedom.

. . .

Conchita knew that her Ross had been rescued. She was determined to go to him, but where to go? *The captured* americanos *are still being marched to Havana,* she thought, *maybe I can learn something there.* She darkened her skin and wearing the tattered rags of a free *mulatta* slipped into Havana. And as it happened, she recognized Bill Crittenden as he was being paraded through the angry mob lining the streets of Habana. Going up to him in mock anger, wielding a machete, she whispered, "Is there someone I can contact for you?"

"Who are you?" the young Kentuckian asked back.

"I am Conchita Izquierdo; I met you at the dinner in Mississippi for Governor Quitman, do you not remember?"

"He came for you, Conchita…." Crittenden whispered as a soldier came up.

"No my little one, you may not harm this *gringo* now. The Captain-General has other plans for him and his friends—si? Maybe after awhile." With that he pulled Conchita away from Bill Crittenden. "Now off with you," the soldier said.

Ross, where are you? Conchita shouted silently to herself. *I must find you!*

Havana bustled with excitement. The streets were filled with onlookers, whites and blacks, *hacendados* and slaves, *criollos* and *mulattoes*, all anticipating the executions, all eager for any news about the capture of the other *americano* invaders they had been told about. Mingling in the crowd were de la Concha's soldiers, spies and agents. Conchita Izquierdo was well known to *criollos* and *peninsulares* alike. The longer she remained in Havana, the greater the danger that she would be recognized and arrested. If she were arrested, Conchita Izquierdo would certainly be executed. "Señorita Izquierdo!" From within a narrow alley, Conchita heard a woman's voice beginning in a shriek, but ending in a whisper. A pair of black hands reached out and grabbed Conchita's skirt, pulling her into a narrow alley. These black hands belonged to one of her father's former slaves. This woman had been very dear to Conchita. The two of them had been playmates growing up on her father's plantation.

"Oma!" Conchita cried, tears streaming from her eyes as she hugged her friend.

"Oh, *señorita*, you must leave Havana, and quickly," Conchita's former playmate pleaded. "Everyone speaks of nothing but the rebellion. Your poor father, who was such a saint, was killed with Joaquin Aguero. And now you are in great danger, *señorita*."

"Yes, my father died bravely," Conchita sighed. "And I know danger lives here. But I search for a tall, blond *americano*; he was not captured with the others. His name is Ross...Ross Pary. Have you seen such a one?"

"No, *señorita*," the black woman replied. "All the *americanos* are dead or will soon be. They lie in Moro Castle and will be executed within the week."

"Is there no one to whom I could turn who would know where they have taken the *americanos* who have survived?"

The black woman thought for a moment. "Si, *señorita!* Go see the Babaluaye Tolomeo. He could tell you what you want to know. But now you must hurry and leave here before someone else recognizes you. Please, leave now. *Adios, por favor, señorita!*" And so saying, she gave Conchita a shove back towards the road out of Havana. Guanabocoa was not very far away. *He is not dead*, Conchita convinced herself, *he is not dead and I will find him, my Ross...the Babaluaye Tolomeo will help me find you. Stay safe, my love; please stay safe until I find you, my love.*

· · ·

Ross Pary and the Metcalf brothers had reached relative safety in the province of Matanzas. They were forced to darken their skins with burnt cork and remain hidden during most of the daylight hours. But black Cubans, the *Lukumi*, vowed to give their own lives to protect these white men from Natchez, Mississippi. This is what the Babaluaye Tolomeo wanted and this is what they would do. It was as if these white Mississippians were under the protection of the Voodoo gods. But in reality it was only Papa Legba playing another one of his tricks!

"Ross, my love!" Conchita Izquierdo screamed as she raced across the patio of the big, old fashioned house of her father's friend here in Matanzas. When Tolomeo told Conchita that her *americano* was in Matanzas, she asked the Babaluaye to direct a *Lukumi* messenger to bring the *americanos* to her friend's home. Conchita herself had only just arrived. Flying into her lover's arms, Conchita held on and wept with happiness. "My love! My love!" she cried, "I thought I would never find you."

"I knew I would find you, *mi amor*," Pary responded, kissing her passionately. "I am here. I came here to find you. And here I am."

"But why did you come here?" Conchita looked deep into his eyes.

"Because I love you," Ross replied, "and I could not bear the thought of being without you."

Ross Pary looked pitiful. He was bedraggled and cut up. His fair skin was now completely covered with burnt cork. The *Lukumi* were assisting them all. Henry and George Metcalf collapsed to the ground. They had to be helped into the house. *Lukumi* women gave them food and drink and helped them to hammocks. Pedro held back. Watching the reunion between Ross and Conchita, Pedro began to feel something rise up from the pit of his stomach, something like fear…actually something more like terror. And then one word that came rushing to his mind and on his lips, "Carlota!"

Pausing only to fill a gourd with water and to accept some dried fruit and flour *tortillas*, Pedro plunged back down the hilly path, back through the *manigua* towards Guanabacoa, his woman and their unborn child. Pedro had helped this *americano*, this Ross Pary find his woman, but what about his own woman and their unborn child. *No!* he said calming the desperation inside. *I am not afraid. She is safe at home where she belongs. And everything will be fine between us again.* But for some reason, just as Yerby remained at his side, so too did the mindless terror that refused to leave him.

. . .

On de la Concha orders, fifty of the captured Americans, including Bill Crittenden, were shot outside Havana's Castillo Atres. Witnesses claim that the firing squad did not shoot to kill the americano mercenaries, but only to wound them. Then the Cuban mob, enraged by the invasion of their homeland, was allowed to finish the execution with knives and machetes by hacking the invaders to death.

The following day, de la Concha ordered a black slave to strangle Narciso Lopez by garrote. A wooden scaffold was built high above Habana's main public square. The crowds pushed and jostled each other *to get a view of Narciso Lopez's execution. The self-proclaimed Cuban liberator was pinioned on the scaffold and a thin steel band attached to hemp bindings encircled his neck. A huge Negro slowly twisted the lever, causing the binding hemp to crush the steel band against Lopez's windpipe, ending in death by slow, painful strangulation. So courageously did Narciso Lopez endure his execution that de la Concha decided not to turn Lopez over to the mob but allowed the garrote to settle the manner. Afterwards he gave his defeated enemy a dignified, if simple burial. After all, the Cuban Captain-General thought, we don't want the Americans to think we are uncivilized.*

CHAPTER FIFTEEN

As soon as Pedro arrived back in Guanabacoa, he ran about the village going from *bohio* to *bohio* shouting, "Carlota! Carlota! I have returned!" But his cries went unanswered. No beautiful woman, bursting with life from their unborn child, came rushing into his arms. After he had made several passes around the village, Pedro finally stopped and sank to his knees in the white, sun-bleached sand, great tears rolling down his cheeks.

"She is not here, my son!" Tolomeo tried to calm Pedro down. And Pedro looked up to his uncle and asked, "Where is she? Where is she?" Pedro held his sides and rolled about, with the most piteous moans and whimpers pouring from his mouth.

Tolomeo looked down at Pedro and explained what had happened. "After leaving you, Carlota and I returned here to the village. Carlota did not stay here one night, before she decided to sneak back out after you. When I found her gone, I sent *Lukumi* after her. They found her body by the side of a road on the other side of Havana. She lay as she had been left, her partially nude body ravished and mutilated. The *Lukumi* buried her there where they found her."

Frank and Pedro had been in Guanabacoa for more than a week.

The great sadness Yerby felt over Carlota's death overwhelmed him still. Such a lonely death for such an innocent black woman was almost more than he could bear. Until now, Yerby believed himself immune to the tragedies suffered by other black people. But now he felt Carlota's death as if it were a great personal tragedy. Possibly he was distraught because Carlota had been pregnant...but Yerby didn't think so. It might have had to do with the fact that Carlota was not one of his characters...one whose fate no matter how horrible, Yerby already had considered and permitted to take place. Yerby had not pre-ordained Carlota's fate. He had not condemned her...and yet she suffered rape and murder. Had Carlota's fate been written in the script of a more powerful author...one who held the same inexorable control over humanity that Yerby held over the lives of his characters? Some powerful being whose existence Yerby, himself, doubted? Whatever the reason, for the first time in many years, Yerby could feel wet, salty tears running down his cheeks and emotional tremors shaking his body whenever he thought of Carlota.

Even in his sorrow, Yerby's characteristic arrogance directed the bitterness and anger he felt towards Pedro. Yerby believed that Pedro was much less affected by Carlota's death than he, himself. As a matter of fact, Yerby believed that after the initial shock of finding Carlota gone had passed, Pedro was little more affected by Carlota's death than by the deaths of all the other blacks who died at the hands of their Spanish masters. In the evenings, whenever Frank heard Pedro playing melancholy chords on his three-stringed guitar, an anger directed against Pedro boiled up inside of him. The three-stringed guitar had been a gift to Pedro from Carlota. When Carlota's grandmother died just after Carlota's eighth birthday, the eight-year orphan stood alone at the burial site. Touched by a great outpouring of sympathy, the twelve-year old Pedro went over to Carlota's side and took her hand. Pedro remained by Carlota's side until her grandmother's funeral ended.

Afterwards Carlota gave Pedro the only possession of value to her, a three-string guitar that had belonged to her grandmother. Just to please Carlota, Pedro taught himself to play the guitar. But his music seemed to come not from the guitar but from the wind, from the water, from the trees and from the sky…as if those sounds had found refuge in his instrument and Pedro merely took the time to collect these notes inside his three-stringed instrument and then magically set them free. Flowing from the minds of the gods through his own soul and down into the souls of the people, Pedro's music lifted up their spirits and dared them to dream of the day when they would be their own masters. Pedro used his three-string guitar to fix the *Lukumi's* attention on the mysterious powers of the Orishas, their Voodoo gods. His music inspired and empowered them. Even Yerby was overcome. This may have been the source of Yerby's hostility towards Pedro…that Pedro could play the guitar like that. It almost put Pedro, artistically, at the same level of Yerby. Soon, Yerby found himself drowning in a sea of self-pity and doubt. At that point, Yerby decided to stop playing "god." He released all of the control he believed he had. And then, slowly, without him being aware of it, the healing began. After awhile, Yerby reconciled himself to Carlota's death and found the ability to forgive Pedro. Since Pedro saw Yerby as an Orisha, he did not have any need to challenge Yerby's authority. He accepted his role in Carlota's death, but also accepted her death as the will of the gods.

"Do you still believe that blacks are guilty of letting themselves become victims?" the Babaluaye Tolomeo asked Yerby. It was a question that Frank did not want to answer. It challenged Yerby's own deeply held belief that blacks actually submitted to whites because of their deeply ingrained racial inferiority…an inferiority to which blacks like Frank Yerby were not susceptible. The question suggested that his own success resulted not from some ability he had to overcome the inferiority of his black genes, making Yerby superior to all the other blacks…at least in his own mind. Was it possible that Yerby's flight from the United States did not demonstrate successful resistance on his part but rather something closer to the opposite was more the truth? This was an unsettling thought.

Without waiting for Yerby's reply, Tolomeo continued, "It is quite easy to make judgments about what someone else should or should not do, isn't it, *Señor* Yerby? As long as you don't have to live with the consequences."

I could have saved them, Yerby rebuked himself. The death of Carlota and her unborn child still affected Yerby, profoundly. He was surprised how much so. *I could have saved them, their fates had not been written.*

"Guilt?" Yerby replied to the subtle probing from the Babaluaye Tolomeo. "I do not recall charging Pedro with anything." And he thought to himself, *How quaint! This old man is trying to enroll me in his Voodoo superstitions as if I were one of these backward black slaves.*

Tolomeo looked at Yerby with a sadness of eye and compassion of soul. "You," he said, "have been so filled with your own pride that you have squandered the great gifts the gods have given you. What you feel is not sadness but remorse."

"Remorse," Yerby replied. "Possibly you're referring to the 're-morse' that you and Pedro feel over the death of poor Carlota."

Yerby looked directly at Pedro as he spoke. Pedro gave no indication that he had heard Yerby's accusation. He merely continued to strum Carlota's three-stringed guitar and stare out at the gently rolling Caribbean. Yerby continued, "If I don't accept the beliefs of Christians whose beliefs give white Europeans the right to become masters of the universe, how can you, expect me to succumb to your Voodoo beliefs?

"You've already *succumbed*," Tolomeo replied with a smile.

"What do you mean?" Yerby asked sharply.

"How do you think you got here, if not for our beliefs in the Orishas, our Voodoo as you call it," the Babaluaye asked. The Babaluaye looked at Yerby with the deep penetrating gaze of knowledge and insight. "How did you put it," Tolomeo continued, "let me remember. Ah, yes, you said that the only race that you believed in was the human race. Not only do you have no pride in your own black race, you do not believe the black race exists. You said that you would have preferred being born a Commanche, an Iroquois, or a Sioux, because 'they preferred to die before accepting slavery.' Isn't that what you said?" Yerby nodded his head in agreement; those were the words he had written in *Speak Now*, but how did this Voodoo priest know that, Yerby wondered? "So what *have* you learned from your stay with us?" Tolomeo asked.

What have I learned? Yerby asked himself. One thing I haven't learned is how to break these creatures' hold over me, he thought. But on the other hand, I'm still here *stretching time*, holding onto the only life I know. And, Yerby had to admit, he was enjoying himself. There was something about actually seeing how white people's ironies, plots and conspiracies gave black people everywhere opportunities for advancement. If only they could see and understand, Yerby thought to himself. He wanted to tell the Voodoo priest that the only thing the slaves and former slaves here in Cuba had done was support those whose only interest was to continue slavery in Cuba. But he told Tolomeo that the white *americanos* came to Cuba to maintain slavery, not end it: "The *criollo hacendados* of the Havana Club paid the *americanos* not to harm the existing Spanish rule in Cuba. So they sent a small detachment of men, not enough to do any harm, just enough to get you and your *Lukumi* exposed and killed. Your insurrection was one of Papa Legba's jokes."

If Yerby had intended that his remark have some impact on the Voodoo witch doctor, one look at Tolomeo's careworn face told him that he had missed the mark. The Babaluaye Tolomeo seemed unimpressed by Yerby's supposed revelation. Yerby continued, "If the drums had sounded, the Spanish would have slaughtered *Lukumi* all over the island. So I have a question for you. Now that you have this information, how can you trust these *hacendados?*" Yerby knew he had him. If Pedro and Tolomeo had not been involved in this silly insurrection and Pedro had remained with Carlota…she would not have died. Here was Frank Yerby's victim's guilt.

"I must tell you, my lord," the Babaluaye replied. "We knew the plan was a charade. Our people who visited Florida told us they heard many different stories at the tobacco auctions and at the trading houses about what the *americanos* were going to do in Cuba."

"You *knew!*" Yerby replied trying to keep the surprise from his voice.

"Yes, Narciso Lopez promised to pay a million dollars for *americano* mercenaries and supplies. And the Cuban *hacendados* who greatly feared Lopez's plot promised Quitman and his people three million dollars to betray Lopez." Tolomeo detailed the outlines of the plot.

"If you knew, why did you go along?" Yerby asked. "It was like suicide."

"We knew some of the plans of the *hacendados* and the *americanos* as well as the Spanish. But it made no matter to us. Our people are enslaved on this island. Those of us who are not slaves go hungry. We cannot hold land. We cannot grow food. Trading for food or tobacco is a crime; if we are caught the punishment is death. We are tormented constantly. *What difference did it make?*"

"It makes a great difference," Yerby exclaimed. "If you knew of their plans, why did you allow your *Lukumi* to follow Aguero? You knew they would be killed!"

"There are some things more important than death!" Tolomeo smiled as if he were privy to a well-kept secret. "Possibly you will learn this lesson before too long. Besides, aren't you the one that praised the Indians who fought senseless and useless battles only to be destroyed in the end?" Tolomeo asked. "Why would you object to the death of a few of the *Lukumi* whose fate it was to fight for a free

Cuba? Is it your belief that a 'victim' must senselessly throw his life away…without purpose, without plan? Is your notion of the *victim's guilt* the same thing as the whites saying that *'the only good Indian is a dead Indian'*?"

Yerby fixed the Babaluaye with a look that bordered on fear and shame. Something like self-doubt entered his mind. Tolomeo continued, "Those fighters who followed Aguero did the most significant thing that they will ever do in their lives. They stood up and behaved like men…not like slaves. Why should I or anyone else deprive them of the opportunity to throw off their shackles and act like men?" The Babaluaye paused and gave Yerby an opportunity to weigh his words. "Those men who fought and died with Aguero were freer than you ever were, playing golf with your fascist friends in Spain." How often had Yerby boasted that he was freer in Franco's Spain, where he was welcomed on the golf course, than he was in America where he was denied access even to public accommodations. What Tolomeo told Yerby was that everything he believed about his having overcome was an illusion. Whether in America or Spain, *Frank Yerby was still a nigger* whether he knew it or not! And white folks did not hand out awards to niggers unless it was in their interest to do so. Yerby had a difficult time with that.

"Besides," the Babaluaye continued with a smile, "we did not sound the drums. We did everything we could to bring the *Lukumi* back. Many returned, but some did not." It was then that Yerby began to realize he was out of his depth. The Voodoo priest was toying with him. Possibly trying to lead me somewhere, Yerby thought. In any case, Yerby decided to do the only intelligent thing he could possibly do under the circumstances…he remained silent and decided to listen.

"What should be of interest here," Tolomeo continued, "is that love drove Ross Pary to give up his comfort, his safety and possibly even his life to save the *criollo* maiden, Conchita Izquierdo. Is this not so, *Señor* Yerby?" Of course, Yerby had to agree. That was why he put this "damsel in distress" story in *Floodtide*. "Yet my poor nephew over there was so unthinking, unfeeling, unloving, that he sacrificed Carlota. In this, I think, lies the meaning of 'a victim's guilt'…no?"

Yerby could only nod, fearing to give words to his own feelings.

"They are very much in love, no?" stated Tolomeo.

"Yes, they are," Yerby agreed.

"Just as you intended…"

Yerby gave an involuntary shudder.

"But…" Yerby attempted to say.

"No buts, you intended it to be that way," Babaluaye Tolomeo said, "I know who you are. What I don't know is what you intend to happen?"

"So you believe I am here because of some type of guilt?" Yerby said.

"I don't know," Tolomeo replied. "You Orishas live in your own world. But what I do know is that you are not being honest with yourself or me. Do you really believe Pedro's indifference to Carlota's death is a sign of guilt?"

Yerby lowered his head as he tried to think about his own motivations, but now his mind was confused and he could not think as clearly as before.

"What concerns you is that neither I nor Pedro is acting in a way that you planned for us. What really disturbs you is that you don't understand us at all!"

Now Yerby really felt anxious. This thing had gone on long enough…suddenly he was very tired and wanted to divorce himself from all this drama and intrigue. He wanted to WAKE UP! His characters had become monsters in a nightmare that had become far too real. Now Yerby really felt intimidated.

"But *Señor* Yerby," Tolomeo said softly in a voice that seemed to come from within Yerby's mind, "you *are* awake." Then the black man gave him a jab in the side that made him jump. Yerby winced from the pain in his side. "You are a very strange person, *señor*," Tolomeo shook his head. "You have created all this and yet you behave as if it does not exist. Very strange, indeed." And with that the Babaluaye abruptly got up and walked away, leaving Yerby alone, trying everything he could to wake himself up…unwilling to believe that he was trapped in this world…in this creation of his own making.

. . .

In the meantime, the brothers Metcalf, Ross Pary and Conchita Izquierdo had left their Matanzas location and now were hiding with Tolomeo, Pedro and Yerby in Guanabacoa. It was late afternoon and Yerby lay in his hammock tied to a *ceiba* tree considering the situation. Suddenly the screams of village women pierced the stillness of the afternoon and the sounds of gunfire echoed about. In a nearby hut, he could hear Pedro's voice urging Ross to flee.

"Quick, *Señor* Ross," Pedro implored, "you and your friends must be quick."

"But Conchita!" Ross Pary replied.

"Don't worry, she will be safe," Pedro said, "but now you must hurry…run."

"You must leave, my love!" Conchita shouted at her lover as she skipped off in the opposite direction. "Stay safe and I will find you!"

All of a sudden, Spanish soldiers seemed to appear from everywhere with rifles pointed and bayonets. This Spanish patrol under the direction of a mounted Spanish officer was searching for the remaining *americano* invaders one village at a time. The officer had no particular reason to suspect the *americanos* were actually hiding in this particular village. So once the white *americanos* were whisked away to another village where they would be safe without being spotted, the inhabitants of Guanabacoa were relatively safe. The soldiers probed, searched and intruded into every *bohio* in the village.

They herded the black men, women and children into the clearing between the *ceiba* trees and the huts that served as Guanabacoa's meeting place. During the search, the Spanish soldiers did what they usually did. Shouting out orders, the soldiers fired their guns into the air or into *bohios* or into the villagers themselves as they went about their business. It was a matter of little importance to the officer whether any or all of the villagers were harmed or killed. His mind was on completing his assignment and getting back to Havana as soon as possible.

But nowhere in Cuba were the *americanos* safe. De la Concha vowed to kill or capture them. Spies were everywhere, patrols of soldiers scoured the width and breadth of Cuba; anyone suspected of giving them support was summarily executed. As soon as she could, Conchita followed Ross and the Metcalf brothers. They joined a little band of *Lukumi, mulattoes* and *criollos* living in the mountains that had prepared to fight for a free Cuba regardless of support from Americans. The *Lukumi* had wanted to fight this war for a long time. Now was the time. They sent word to Pedro to join them. "Beat the drums," he was told. And though the *Lukumi* knew that the *americanos* had failed, many of them answered the drums, as Tolomeo knew they would.

Pedro led the insurrection. They began by ambushing Spanish patrols and "liberating" needed supplies and weapons from the soldiers…and then disappearing into the hills. As news of Pedro's success spread, new fighters flocked to join the band. After a time, their band grew so large, they had to move into the high mountains, the only place capable of providing them protection. From Villa Clara, Pedro directed the struggle. At long last, he was leading his people in a struggle for freedom. And not just black people, whites and brown Cubans also fought side by side to destroy Spanish tyranny. But as might be expected, more blacks joined than any of the others. They wanted to avenge deaths of family, friends and loved ones. Pedro understood this need. He needed to avenge the death of Carlota and his unborn child. On the battlefield, Pedro was merciless: *kill or be killed*. Pedro planned and led all of the *Lukumi* band's attacks. Hundreds of Spanish soldiers were taken completely unawares in Pedro's lightning raids. Many soldiers were wounded, some mortally...many more were killed. The Spanish soldiers were unprepared to deal with armed blacks charging out from an ambuscade, screaming and howling, hacking with heavily weighted razor sharp machetes that could decapitate a man in a single stroke and firing captured Spanish muskets. The *Lukumi* were intent on slaughter. The Spaniards could not match the furious hatred and emotional outrage bursting forth from the blacks. So after many encounters, Pedro's band made certain that Cuban soil drank deep of Spanish blood. But for Pedro not even an ocean of blood could make up for his loss of Carlota and their child. Nor would a river of blood wash away the guilt Pedro carried deep in his soul.

The rebellion was very successful... at first. Pedro's "hit and run" guerrilla tactics kept the Spanish soldiers off balance. The *hacendados* were furious. They had worked with the Captain-General and paid a lot of gold just to avoid this kind of uprising. De la Concha had promised an end to the disturbances. Now the *hacendados* demanded the Captain-General squash this uprising immediately. Every day more of their slaves ran away from the plantations and joined the rebels. De la Concha was furious for having lost control. He quickly realized that he must resort to the one ploy that always worked against these uprisings. He directed that his network of informants send spies into the mountains to join Pedro's band of insurrectionists.

Quickly de la Concha's spies reported when and where Pedro planned his next attacks. From then on, the insurrection was doomed. When Pedro and his rebels attacked a small Spanish patrol in the southern part of Matanzas province near the Bay of Pigs, de la Concha launched a counterattack with his far superior Spanish forces. In the counterattack, a combined force of a thousand light cavalry and dragoons accompanied by a regiment of regular soldiers completely routed the *Lukumi* fighters and their *criollo* and *hacendado* allies… killing or mortally wounding three-quarters of the guerrillas. Once the issue had been decided, the whites, including Ross, Henry and George Metcalf, and Conchita surrendered. Only the promise of a substantial reward for any captured *americanos* saved them from immediate execution. Conchita's beauty captivated the Spanish officer in charge. This colonel was being transferred back to Spain and he wanted to take Conchita back with him. The Spanish officer promised Conchita that if she agreed to accompany him back to Spain, the colonel would spare Ross' life. Though Conchita agreed, the Spanish officer had no intention of keeping his word. He ordered Ross to accompany the Metcalf brothers back to Havana where a public execution not unlike the one suffered by William Crittenden and his men awaited them.

"We must save them," Pedro entreated the Babaluaye *Lukumi* Tolomeo.

"Why must we save them, Pedro?" Tolomeo asked, fixing Frank Yerby with a questioning stare. "Are they our responsibility?"

"Yes," Pedro responded, emphatically. "Yes, they are our responsibility."

"And so, *Señor* Yerby," Tolomeo said, "we come to the moment of truth. Answer if you dare. Does my nephew, Pedro, who is dearer to me than life itself, have any choice not to save these white men?"

You lie in Your holy teeth, Almighty, when You say that you, or Satan Your brother, gave me choice! Yerby's own words from *An Odor of Sanctity* came ringing back to him. *Would You say that You didn't know, up there in Thy Cloud, an eon ago—which choice I'd make, which choice I could not help but make, having the nature which You in Your total wisdom gave me? Are You trying to absolve Yourself of Your own guilt, which consists of playing ducks and drakes with human be-*

　　　　　　　　　　　　　　　　　FRANK YERBY:

ings created in Thy image? Or You in theirs—for who knows which came first, chicken or egg, egg or chicken? … Are You First Cause or no? If You are, does not all choice ultimately reside in You? You knew that I would choose evil of my own volition and You let me be born to choose evil. Neither did You stretch forth Your merciful hand to stop me from doing evil. Why then do You hurl me into Your pit? By what right? Answer me, why? Answer me not. Allow me to tell the answer! Because You delight in cruelty, in pain. Those piteous screams echoing unending throughout all time have been music to Your ears!

"So, *Señor* Yerby," the Babaluaye said accusingly, "you have guilt, no?"

To which Yerby could only bow his head in recognition. He wrote those words as he knew he must, for Frank Yerby now recognized that he, too, was a victim.

"Come, Pedro," Tolomeo said. "Let us prepare the boat. We will rescue these *americanos* and deposit them safely back in the United States. This has all been pre-ordained."

Pedro, Tolomeo and their *Lukumi* rescued the *americanos*. The Spanish soldiers had not expected the attack. Ross and George and Henry were brought back to Guanabacoa. All three had endured torture, and Ross was barely conscious when Tolomeo set sail for Florida. They landed on Key West and found refuge on the plantation of Harry Linton, an associate of Ross. Pedro decided to remain in Florida with *Señor* Pary. And in this as well, Tolomeo knew that Pedro had no choice; Yerby had written his fate. But in Pedro's mind, he thought: "It was for this *americano* that I sacrificed my Carlota… and I intend to find out the reason why."

CHAPTER SIXTEEN

Papa Legba owns the roads all over the world. Those serving Papa Legba live on street corners, in the woods, on the banks of the river, on the shores of oceans, at garbage dumps, at the gates of cemeteries. Papa Legba uses these, his followers, to watch passersby and listen to their hearts. Papa Legba is most cunning and the father of guile. Everyone, even the other Orishas, try to stay on Papa Legba's good side. The Lukumi *hope that Papa Legba will not put obstacles on the path of any* Lukumi *traveler, so the* Lukumi *always feed Papa Legba first. Papa Legba loves the* Lukumi; *they are his own. As with any father, Papa Legba wants his children to be successful and make him proud. And those who are successful, Papa Legba helps; the others, he teaches.*

In less than a month, Henry and George Metcalf had recuperated well enough to catch a steamer heading for New Orleans and from there, a riverboat up the Mississippi to Natchez. Ross Pary lingered on Henry Linton's plantation in Key West. According to Yerby, afterwards Pary steamed up to Isle of Hope Plantation in South Carolina where he continued his convalescence under the loving care of Cathy Linton, Harry Linton's niece. Harry did everything possible to assist Cathy's plans to marry Ross Pary. But after six months with Cathy,

Ross Pary fully recovered from his Cuban ordeal and also returned to Natchez…back to his own plantation, Moonrise, and his architecture firm. His adventure was concluded.

Pedro remained in Key West with Harry Linton. Harry was quite unique for a Southern white man. That is to say, Harry Linton did not believe in the inherent superiority of the white man. Harry believed in the business opportunity every man presented. Harry Linton was a thoroughgoing capitalist and never allowed anything as mundane as racism to get in the way of his making money. Harry's own personal heaven was his plantation where he indulged in the great capitalistic activity of buying, selling…and making money.

Harry loved to smoke a good cigar. And nowhere in the world could one find any better smoke than one provided by a good hand-rolled Cuban cigar. Harry loved being around men who enjoyed a good Cuban cigar. And he was happiest when he could make a profit bringing fine Cuban cigars and tobacco to the American smoking man. Harry cared not for the social taboos, legal impediments or international laws that prevented him from accomplishing his life's work…that of making money. Early in his life, Harry determined that he would use whatever means available to achieve wealth and earn recognition from his family and friends. Furthermore, Harry genuinely liked most Negroes. And because he liked them, his relationships with them usually benefited him financially. When Harry Linton met Pedro, he knew that he had hit the jackpot.

The only legal source of Cuban tobacco was from the *Factoria* owned by the Spanish Crown. The *Factoria's* prices were exorbitant. And even though Harry could always sell his Cuban tobacco products, both his profits and inventory were always low. Harry spoke excellent Spanish. In less than five minutes Harry realized that Pedro had access to all the Cuban tobacco he needed. Furthermore, Pedro could have the tobacco delivered to Harry's Key West warehouses. Harry's costs would be a quarter of what he paid the *Factoria,* with no transportation costs. Through Pedro, Harry Linton stood to make a fortune. Within months, Pedro's *Lukumi* built a profitable enterprise smuggling Cuban tobacco and cigars to Harry's Key West plantation. Tolomeo himself, became a major supplier. With this new source of product, Linton could offer a variety and grade of tobacco products which few other tobacco importers or growers could match. Once the *Lukumi* found they could trust Harry, tobacco products from every *hacendado* on the island found their way to Harry's warehouses on Key West. Within six months Linton tobacco became the most eagerly sought after and traded product at Key West's monthly to-bacco auctions. Tobacco buyers and dealers from as far away as New England flocked to the Key West tobacco auction houses for the opportunity to buy some of Harry Linton's product. Harry Linton began to make a lot of money.

"I can handle everything you can bring across," Harry Linton told Tolomeo. Harry had his slaves assist in the unloading of a very nice shipment of Cuban panatellas, hand-wrapped with distinctive indi-vidual bands. "I'll pay you fifty cents for each box of cigars," Harry Linton offered Tolomeo. "If you bring more cigars over on each trip you will get paid more." Harry was getting greedy. He was selling out at every tobacco auction; he needed more tobacco products. Harry was wheedling Tolomeo in the same way he tried to get every *Lukumi* tobacco smuggler to bring in more on each trip. "*Señior* Linton, there are many reasons for us not to bring too much tobacco over at one time," Tolomeo replied. "A sudden storm could rise up and the excess weight could capsize the boat before we could toss it overboard, or we could be pursued by a Spanish warship. If they found the tobacco, they would execute us as smugglers…which is what we are." Harry's concerns did not include the dangers the *Lukumi* smugglers faced; he was concerned about increasing the amount of Cuban tobacco and cigars he could sell. Tobacco smuggling endangered everyone involved… the *hacendado* who sold the tobacco to the *Lukumi*, the tobacco workers who transported the contraband tobacco, and the smugglers who brought the tobacco to Linton's Florida plantation. "This is risky business, *señor*," Tolomeo said. What he didn't say was: *And what will we do with all this American money we earn? Give it to the Spanish?*

The Cuban *hacendados* were also pressing Tolomeo and the *Lukumi*. They also wanted the *Lukumi* to increase their tobacco purchases. The *hacendados* could grow a lot more tobacco, but for what? The *Factoria* would just take it. Now if the *Lukumi* would buy more, they would grow more. "You barely take half a load over," one of the *hacendados* complained, "You should double your cargo and double the amount of money you make."

"And how do we get the gold that you demand up front for your tobacco?" Tolomeo asked. "We hardly make any money now, we are not bankers, *señor*."

Tolomeo warned his children about becoming slaves to the white man's gold. This was just a way of re-enslaving themselves to the white man. The Babaluaye offered sacrifices, incantations and *gbo* to warn the *Lukumi* about the danger of having too much wealth. However, some *Lukumi* smugglers ignored the Babaluaye's warnings and increased their shipments…causing Harry and the *hacendados* to increase their pressure on the others. Tolomeo decided he needed a plan to keep his *Lukumi* from suffering from their own success.

"It's just as much in your interest to try to bring more tobacco over, as it is in mine." This time it was Pedro's turn for Harry to "jawbone" about getting the *Lukumi* to bring in more tobacco. "Just think, we could fill these barns with tobacco and become richer than anyone around these parts. You really ought to get your uncle to think in bigger terms, my dear boy. There must be some way to increase the supply." Gradually Harry had shifted the responsibility for the entire operation to Pedro. He unloaded the boats as they arrived and stored all the tobacco in Harry's warehouse. Once stored, the products had to be counted, itemized and valued. After a while, Pedro accepted the responsibility for delivering the tobacco products to the winning bidder after each of the monthly tobacco auctions.

When he was buying from the *Factoria*, Harry always auctioned off each shipment as a single lot, which simplified his storage and delivery problems. However, the *Lukumi* products mixed in a higher grade of tobacco with the regular grades. Shipments of *el supremo* cigars, never before available in the United States, began to appear in Linton lots. So merely by taking the time to sort his tobacco into separate grades, Harry found another profit increase. He increased Pedro's responsibilities once again to include separating and grading each tobacco shipment.

"How does *Señor* Linton expect me to do as he has asked?" Pedro complained to Frank. But even so, Pedro found the work challenging and fun. He enjoyed the tobacco business because it helped his people in Cuba. More importantly, Pedro enjoyed the close contact with the black slave community on Linton's Key West plantation. Harry's slaves were treated as well as any slave anywhere in the South. They were not beaten. They lived in a private segregated area on the Linton plantation where the only white man permitted access was Harry himself. Harry's slaves had their own vegetable plots and gardens. They had barnyards where chickens and pigs were raised and other farm animals kept. Harry's slaves raised and grew their own food. Harry's slaves did not work from before sun-up until after sundown; they worked a regular twelve-hour six-day a week work schedule. On Sundays, Harry's slaves were allowed to do whatever they chose. Harry kept his slaves contented and his plantation prosperous. He even opened a little dry goods store near the slave quarters where they could purchase against what they earned. The smugglers were given the same credit as Harry's own slaves, solving the problem of what the *Lukumi* did with their extra money. The paid it to Harry in the form of interest on their purchases which were made against their earnings. But since Harry Linton's brand of capitalism was practiced with the religious zeal of a true believer, everything worked out well for the slaves as well as for Harry Linton.

Pedro took full advantage of the situation. He taught those who wanted to know about the Orishas. Some of them became initiates and made the preparations necessary to join the *Lukumi* cult. On this particular day, Pedro and Frank Yerby were inspecting the latest shipment of tobacco and Pedro seemed not very interested in his responsibilities. "Look at this, there's tobacco everywhere," Pedro complained.

"Pedro, why don't you make some of Harry's people responsible for sorting and storing?" Yerby suggested.

"Certainly, *Señor* Yerby," Pedro agreed, "but how does one accomplish this?"

"You have already prepared some to join the *Lukumi*," Yerby replied. "Put your *Lukumi* initiates in charge."

Pedro thought about it and said, "That's a good idea, *Señor* Yerby."

When Pedro approached Harry with the idea of appointing foremen who would share the responsibility for sorting and storing the tobacco, Harry quickly agreed. He kept accurate account of the proceeds from his auctions and he paid the *Lukumi* fairly.

After a bumpy start where one foreman had to be replaced because he would not do the work and another because a delivery was lost in transit to the purchaser, the system began to work reasonably well. Pedro spent more time in the slave quarters than at his own residence. He had to get Harry to accept the idea that a certain amount of tobacco would be "lost" from the warehouses and "distributed" among the workers. After all, white Americans were not the only people who could enjoy a fine Cuban cigar. Yerby suggested that some of the "loss" be given to the slave's community's church to support the sick and those unable to work. He also suggested that they set up a school for their children and make improvements to the community's sanitary and drinking facilities.

Rumors of Harry Linton's niggers belonging to a Voodoo cult began to make the rounds of some of the Key West tobacco dealers. But since Harry's tobacco had increased the prosperity of the entire island and the whites didn't really believe in nigger mumbo jumbo, they left Harry Linton to arrange his own activities. What the niggers did on Linton's plantation was no concern of theirs. As long as the good Cuban tobacco continued coming in, there was no need for the white men to go onto Harry Linton's plantation and disturb things…even if it was being run by a bunch of "voodoo niggers." And for a while Harry Linton's plantation in the deepest South came close to achieving a state of harmony and prosperity envied by even the most idealistic of the New England utopian communities. But after more than a year, Pedro became restless.

"Frank, I have begun to think about Carlota and our unborn son more and more recently," Pedro told Yerby one day. "I know that Carlota's death was my fault and a heaviness weighs on my soul and nothing seems to ease it."

"Carlota took her chances trying to find you," Yerby replied.

"I want to go to Natchez and see *Señor* Pary," Pedro announced.

"Why do you want to go there?" Yerby asked.

"I sacrificed Carlota to save him," Pedro said. "I want to know whether or not the sacrifice was worth it. Besides, someone or something is calling me to Mississippi."

Yerby could see torment on Pedro's face, hear the pain in his voice. "I should not have left her," Pedro said with a heavy sigh. "You see, *Señor*, I am not as wise as my uncle nor as brave as my mother and father, but Carlota made me strong. I never knew that all the time I felt that I was destined to lead the rebellion, it was her all the time. She made me want to be a man, want to be a free. And I deserted her. The longer I stay here, in this new-found life of ease and comfort, the more I feel ashamed of myself for Carlota's sacrifice."

Yerby made every attempt to dissuade Pedro from his decision. "If Carlota had obeyed you," Yerby rationalized, "she would be alive today."

"If I had stayed with her or allowed her to stay with me," Pedro replied, "she would be alive today." And both knew that each was partly right, and absolutely wrong.

Harry Linton was not at all happy about Pedro leaving. "Who will run the business while you are away?" the plantation owner complained.

"Don't worry," Pedro replied. "Each of the foremen will attend the auctions. They can deliver whatever you sell."

"How long will you be?" Harry asked.

"As long as it takes," Pedro answered.

"You will need a letter…possibly several letters," Harry concluded. "Letters to a steamer captain, sheriffs and police and to the Mississippi paddyrollers. "I would wear shabby clothes, if I were you," Harry warned Pedro. "It will be best if you act real humble-like; the white folks hereabouts are real touchy when it comes to uppity niggers. As long as you act quiet and humble-like, you shouldn't have any problems."

"I'll go with him," said Yerby.

They decided that Pedro and Frank needed three letters, each saying the exact same thing; that they were free Negroes from Cuba taking a message on behalf of Harry Linton, upon whose plantation Pedro resided, to Ross Pary, at Moonrise Plantation outside Natchez, Mississippi, signed, Harry Linton, Key West, Florida. In addition, they needed an itinerary that any white man who wanted could trace. When the day of departure came, Pedro waved goodbye to his friends, shook hands with Harry Linton and boarded a steamer for New Orleans.

The trip from Key West to New Orleans was uneventful. By the time Pedro disembarked in New Orleans his heart was lighter and he could hardly control his anticipation. Pedro could feel Carlota with him. In New Orleans, Pedro located a paddlewheeler leaving New Orleans in two days and making a scheduled stop at Natchez. When he reached Mississippi, Pedro was thankful for Harry Linton's preparations. Blacks in Mississippi were the most downtrodden, oppressed and dehumanized people Pedro had ever seen. No black whatsoever was ever allowed to behave with any dignity around white people. Such behavior was branded as "uppity" and at a minimum required a sharp reprimand, if not some physical punishment. All blacks were expected to walk with a shuffle, to smile and grin continuously, to say sir at the beginning and end of each sentence and to display only the humblest of attitudes. To a white Mississippian, a nigger could never be too humble. Each white person had a civic duty to degrade niggers as often as possible. Blacks' purpose on earth was to serve white people...this held for free blacks as well as the slaves. In Mississippi, there was but one social status for all blacks, the status of a sambo. The only protection a black enjoyed resulted from giving good and faithful service to some white person. As long as Pedro was on a mission for a white man, he could gain entry into Mississippi. But not even his worst experiences in Cuba prepared him for dealing with the Mississippi white man.

"Sheriff, my friend Pedro and I thank you for your accommodations," Frank Yerby said as the sheriff opened the door to their cell.

"Well, nigger, if you keep talkin' like that, I might just keep you here another night and mind you some manners!" Sheriff Wilson did not like the looks of these two foreign niggers coming into his town without him knowing anything about them. The papers the niggers carried looked real. *But them niggers sure act funny*, Sheriff Wilson thought to himself. *One couldn't even speak English...the other spoke English too damn good for my likin'.* Sheriff Wilson sent out telegraphs to Natchez and to the other towns Pedro and Frank had to pass on their way to Moonrise. "Two foreign niggers are on the way with a message for Ross Pary at Moonrise," the message said. Some of the sheriffs detained them; others after questioning let them pass. The riverboat captain put them ashore some distance from their destination. And a journey that should have taken a couple of days on foot took the two Negroes over a week while having to endure the frequent questionings and incarcerations as their stories were "checked."

In addition to their continual encounters with the law, their journey was punctuated with stares, abusive language and threats of physical violence from the white people themselves. It was commonplace to be called a nigger by every white person they met. Pedro feigned an inability to speak English and ignored them. If he were pressed, Pedro would show them the letter from Harry Linton and mumble "Moonrise...Pary" and then lapse into a *Lukumi* dialect that Pedro knew not even Ross Pary who was fluent in Spanish would understand. Actually Pedro spoke English quite well. Pedro began to learn English as soon as he landed at Key West. He understood that the secret to learning a second language was just about learning *new words*. Since a person always learns to speak a language before he can read or write it, learning another language for Pedro was like calling his *bohio* a hut and the *Orishas* gods. Pedro quickly learned that Obatala was Our Lady of Mercy or *La Virgen de las Mercedes*; Chango was St. Barbara, and Oshun was Our Lady of Charity or *La Caridad del Cobre,* Cuba's patron saint. Pedro did not know Papa Legba's *white* name. Papa Legba did not want anyone to have a hold over him. Nor would a wise person want to have a hold over Papa Legba. That was how Pedro learned English and how the black slaves on Harry Linton's plantation learned about the *Lukumi*. But none of this did Pedro allow the whites to know.

Yerby was not as fortunate. The whites learned that Yerby spoke English a bit too well, and this had been the initial cause of their problems. Yerby's manner was inappropriate for a black man in the

State of Mississippi, the home of America's "peculiar institution." Yerby attracted the wrong kind of attention. And it took several sessions with local sheriffs for Yerby to learn to practice far more humility. White Mississippians loved to play their white supremacist games. Each white person competed with each other in demanding more and more infantile and sambo-like behavior from their black slaves. It was simply a status symbol for white Mississippians who never got too attached to their slaves. Yerby received most of the abuse. He learned not to look white people directly in the eye, and deflect most of their hostility. Yerby was continually engaged in a battle of wits with the white people of Mississippi. He had to forget his heroic notions of a "victim's guilt" in favor of a more accommodating, self-effacing attitude of a "victim's survival." Imperceptibly, Yerby began to mimic the typical behavior of an Uncle Tom or more appropriately an Uncle Frank…and deemed it a personal victory at the end of each day that he was able to have evaded anything worse than verbal insults. It was not long before Yerby slipped easily into his role as a victim, worrying less about any "theoretical" idea of manhood and more about the practical need to keep the white folks off of his butt. Yerby began to learn how to "shuffle along" with the best of them. And it was with this attitude and in this posture that Frank and Pedro arrived at Ross Pary's Moonrise Plantation in Natchez, Mississippi. And as luck would have it, Pedro spied Ross Pary and immediately started running towards him.

"*Señor* Ross!" Pedro laughed; "I found you! It was a journey of formidable distances and of an immensity of trouble; but I have found you."

"Yes, yes, Pedro," Ross Pary replied with a carefully controlled friendliness. "I heard that you were on the way."

"You heard that I was coming?" Pedro replied. "But how?"

"In Mississippi, we have our ways. But welcome to my home where you will, of course be my, my guest."

"I knew you would not forget me," Pedro began…

"Yes, yes Pedro," Pary cut him off. "I am afraid you mustn't babble on. My Spanish is not as good as it once was. Tell me, why did you come here?"

"I want to stay here with you, *señor*," Pedro replied. "I saved your life, I feel responsible for you. Possibly, you could make me your body servant and pay me whatever you believe is fair. I trust you." Just seeing Ross Pary, Pedro felt better than he had in months. "I trust you, *señor*."

"I thank you for your trust," Pary said, sincerely… at least as sincerely as any social climber from Natchez-under-the-hill who wanted to break into Mississippi's planter class could be. Pary had no intention of defying local customs in any way, just because this nigger had saved his life. After all, what else were niggers good for!

CHAPTER SEVENTEEN

rank," Pedro announced decisively, "I'm going to initiate a band of *Lukumi* right here in Mississippi." A worried look flashed across Yerby's face. He had been thinking that this might happen. Once again, Pedro was restless. Pedro never seemed to be able to relax or take a break. He was restless from the time Yerby first met him. And he was restless now. Being restless in Natchez, Mississippi, Yerby believed, was not such a good idea even for Pedro, who came and went as he pleased to the chagrin and downright displeasure of the local whites. Pedro interacted with all the slaves on Moonrise Plantation. He visited plantations nearby and in adjoining counties. Pedro told the slaves on plantations all around about the gods. The response was much greater than he had hoped, black people still remembered their gods. And if they remembered their gods, Pedro reasoned, they could learn the *Lukumi* way. "I'm going to have a *Kari Ocha*," Pedro declared.

Kari Ocha is the ceremony that the *Lukumi* call "making the Saint." This is the grand ceremony when an initiate's guardian angel is "crowned" on the initiate's head. The guardian angel always helps and protects the initiate, bringing blessings from the Orishas to the initiate and prayers from the initiate to the Orishas. Sometimes the guardian angel takes away some terrible disease. The Orishas use the guardian angel to choose an initiate for the priesthood. The priest or priestess has *Ocha* crowned on their head; they receive the *Ache* of the Orishas, and they become a medium for them. Often the initiate carries messages both in the trance and in the normal state. The Orishas are always there and often wish to speak to their initiate. Priests and priestesses are the only ones the gods trust to intercede for others. Everyone else, the gods believe, prays only for himself or herself. While it is a great honor to be chosen to be a priest or priestess in this fashion, Papa Legba is fully prepared to punish even his priest for the least inattention.

Pedro had been so honored and was one of Papa Legba's priests. And the mighty lord of the roadways loved Pedro. Papa Legba helped guide Pedro's dealings with Obatala. And since Obatala controls reason and justice, he has the most authority over human beings, Pedro would need all the assistance Papa Legba could give. Obatala was not just the creator of humankind, but the creator of the earth. As the oldest Orisha, Obatala is due respect from all the other Orishas. In their turn, the Orishas freely give their respect to Obatala. After all, Obatala is their father too. *Much respect for the King of the White Cloth.*

"So, Pedro, you believe that Papa Legba has chosen you to be his priest?" Yerby asked. "You deserted your first congregation in Key West? They needed you then…they need you now!" Yerby wanted Pedro to return to Florida.

. . .

Tom Pary, Ross' brother, Tom's wife, Jennie, and Ross and Tom's sister, Annis, all lived at Moonrise plantation. None of them liked Pedro. He always avoided them and pretended not to understand English. No matter how loud Tom, Jennie or Annis screamed at Pedro, when they did corner him, trying to get him to do something, he would always reply back, "*No entiendo*—I don't understand." Tom thought of Pedro as a menace. A free negro, a hoo-doo man giving the slave niggers ideas isn't good, Tom reasoned. "He's a nuisance, " Tom complained to his brother.

"Oh, Pedro's all right," Ross replied. "Have I told you how he saved my life in Cuba?"

"Yes, several times," Tom said. "You need to lay down the rules. He can't just go wandering about anywhere he wants with not so much as a by your leave. It looks bad…like we owe him something."

"I do owe him something," Ross explained to his brother patiently. "I owe him my life."

"Some folks might not think that's important enough to let some uppity Cuban nigger walk all over us, threatening our women and acting like he's the master." Tom could see what a struggle this was for his brother. "I know you are a decent person. You have a good heart," Tom said. "Let me do what's necessary. You won't have to be involved. You better let me take him down a peg now or else these other darkies might get ideas."

"Just give him a little time," Ross said. "He'll adjust. He hasn't been in any trouble, has he?"

"No, not yet," Tom answered, "but it's just a matter of time."

Pedro had enjoyed a special status at Moonrise, but the time limit on that special status was rapidly approaching. So Yerby knew this was not the time…nor the place, to seek initiates for a Voodoo cult. Pedro needed to think about returning to Florida; his days were surely numbered in Mississippi. Yerby used every argument and tactic he could think of to convince Pedro to return to Florida immediately.

"*Señor* Yerby, why do you want me to leave when so much more must be done?" Pedro asked.

"What do you think you can do here?" Yerby asked. "Isn't your neck hurting just a little bit with all this bowing and scraping?" Every time he had to lower his eyes, buck his teeth, bow his head and answer "yessir" and "nosir" to every white person in sight, including three year old children, village idiots and town drunks, he lost a little more of his own self respect and suffered additional twinges of guilt.

"You have been doing most of the shuffling, grinning and "yessir"-ing and "no sir"-ing. It is of little importance," Pedro replied. "What does it matter whether I must accept this treatment as long as I know who I am on the inside and I serve my Orishas?"

"And do you know who you really are on the inside?" Yerby asked.

Pedro paused to think about the question. But being an honest person he quickly reached his conclusion. "Not really...but I believe that I'm here for a purpose, Carlota's purpose. Carlota gave her life for some reason...and I came to Mississippi to find out why." Pedro was in earnest. "Besides," he continued with a sly smile, "I have met someone and I think I am in love."

"What," Yerby exclaimed. He didn't know whether or not Pedro was just the village idiot or an absolute fool. Pedro had fallen in love with Bessie, Morgan Britanny's personal maid. Morgan's husband, Lance Brittany, owned the plantation known as Finiterre that Ross had built. From the moment he first saw her, Pedro knew that Bessie was the reason he had come all the way to Natchez, Mississippi. Mulatto-born, Bessie was blessed with a unique beauty. From her African roots came her magnificent body, thin yet sensuous, with legs which gave her a graceful walk of tall grass blowing in the savannah. From her white roots came pale green eyes, fine features, and a shock of thick reddish-brown hair, which tumbled mischievously about her face, twisted into a unique style that few ever saw since Bessie usually kept her hair tied up in a yellow bandana. Bessie's beauty was tinged with a wildness that bordered on the feeling of abandonment at the moment of achieving sexual orgasm and at the moment in prayer when the utter feeling of helplessness and aloneness suddenly disperse in great waves of understanding and enlightenment. Pedro thought of it in simpler terms. "Bessie has the soul and mind to become a *Lukumi* priestess. She had been chosen." Morgan Brittany must have been able to see this power; it was one of the reasons why she hated Bessie so much. Bessie had the fire. Pedro invited her to meet his *Lukumi*. When she arrived, three others accompanied her.

"How many initiated *Lukumi* do you have now?" Yerby asked. He was surprised how quickly slaves from Mississippi plantations in the area responded to Pedro's call.

"There are thirteen of us," Pedro replied. Though he was no Babaluaye, Pedro had recruited slaves from several plantations in the area into his *Lukumi* band. The slaves worshipped the Orishas and honored their own ancestors. Pedro taught them how to listen to the drums…how to hear what they were saying. Every so often, the call of Pedro's homemade drum would echo out in the dead of some Mississippi night. It called initiates to serve and feed the Orishas. The sound of the drum unnerved the white folks. Paddyrollers made many unsuccessful attempts at finding the nocturnal drummer… without success. Pedro conducted his *Lukumi* rituals each Saturday night after the full moon and the Orishas seemed to favor his efforts. "Why don't you come to our next meeting?" Pedro asked Yerby.

Thus far Frank had declined Pedro's invitations to join any of Pedro's *Lukumi* bands, whether in Cuba, Florida or here in Mississippi. *There are some mysteries*, Yerby counseled himself, *which are best left to the initiated*. "I'll think about it," Yerby told Pedro slowly, "but what with the blood and that nasty tasting other stuff, I need a very powerful incentive to want to join your group. I prefer bread and wine; did you know I'm a Catholic?"

"You can always come as an onlooker," Pedro said. "The Orishas will be happy for your presence, as long as you are respectful and offer gifts."

"Certainly, if I come," Yerby said solemnly, "I will bring gifts for the Orishas." Yerby had not fully comprehended the *Lukumi* voodoo practices, but there was no doubt in Yerby's mind that the Orishas had a powerful impact on all people, believers and non-believers as well. He intended never to offend the gods whether he believed in them or not.

One day while Morgan was out riding, Pedro went over to Finiterre to visit Bessie. "See what she did to me," Bessie said to Pedro, holding out her left hand. Through the top of her hand, just below the knuckles, there was a hole. Around the hole, the skin was scarred and discolored. Tendons of the ring finger had been completely severed and her finger hung downward at an awkward angle. "She stuck a scissors through my hand 'cause I done her hair wrong. She kicked me down the stairs because I was a little slow," Bessie told Pedro. "And that's not all that woman's done. I'll take you up to the attic. She has a special place made where she can chain a slave to the floor and give herself sexual pleasure by beating him."

Up in the attic, Bessie showed Pedro the globs of dried blood still visible on the floor. On the wall hung several whips. Some were long with leaded tips; others were short and thin. Morgan had a custom-made riding crop, a thin flexible piece of metal encased in a leather that cut through skin with the slightest stroke. And there were other implements of torture, knives and picks and saws. "Just last month old Lucas was whipped to death up here," Bessie said. "Come with me and I'll show you where she buried him." Bessie took Pedro back downstairs and out behind the barn. Pointing to a rounded mound of freshly dug dirt, Bessie said, "There's where she had Lucas buried." Her emotion enhanced Bessie's beauty in Pedro's eyes. He locked this image of her away in his heart where once only Carlota had lived. Pedro vowed that from this time onwards, his fate and Bessie's were linked together.

· · ·

A full moon bathed the remote hill in an eerie white. The Orishas loved to appear on nights of a full moon. The initiates could feel the magic of both good and evil. They wore white, which especially pleased Obatala. An area marked by a circle was set off for the gods. Inside the circle of the gods various symbols and signs marked the way up to a wooden altar. Upon the altar were gifts for Papa Legba as well as for Obatala, the Father of all gods. The altar also held gifts for Chango and Oshun, his wife. The air was heavy with the scents of Spanish moss that curtained groves of cypress and magnolia, competing with the sickly-sweet smell of wild orchids. Surely this spot was sacred to the gods. It was an accidental knoll that poked up from the murky Mississippi swamp on a very gentle slope. The knoll was completely surrounded by a murky swamp that in places was over six feet deep. It could hold twenty or thirty people comfortably. Finding this spot was hard if you did not know exactly where Pedro had positioned his two flat bridges. These flat bridges, barely visible during the day and absolutely invisible at night, crossed from dry land over the swamp to the knoll from two opposite points.

Pedro had found this spot by navigating his canoe up the waterway of one of the many dismal swamps spawned by the mighty Mississippi River. Pedro had penetrated to the deepest, most inaccessible part of the swamp. So overgrown was the waterway, with gray cypress and other watery trees, that even at high noon the sunlight never directly shown on the water. The water was infested with several varieties of venomous snakes, including cottonmouths and water moccasins. The swamp also happened to be the favorite breeding ground of alligators. It was one of Damballah's gardens, a perfect meeting ground for Pedro's little band of *Lukumi*.

Calling to the *Lukumi*, Pedro alternated between a Latin beat strummed on his three-string guitar and a conga beat on his handmade drum, each calling the Orishas to a feast prepared according to Pedro's instructions. *The Orishas will soon make their presence felt*, Pedro thought to himself, *the Orishas are pleased. I can feel it*. The altar held the candles, the dishes of herbs, the incense, the whiskey and wine. Pedro prepared the *Omiero*, the exotic drink of the gods, himself. Cooked foods brought in pails, and fruits and vegetables in straw sacks, all had been laid out on the altar as well. Pedro continued to play; his *Lukumi* passed the time in quiet conversation, jokes and plantation gossip. After awhile the Orishas began to make themselves felt. Pedro drew symbols on the ground and invited the gods to eat and drink. He took the whiskey and offered it up; he did the same with the wine. Then he lit two cigars and put them each in a separate ceramic plate on the altar. Next he sacrificed a chicken, a lamb, and a goat. The animal's carcasses were discarded after their blood was sprinkled.

Several women quickly brought up dishes of prepared meats from animals sacrificed at an earlier ceremony. Finally, after the gods had eaten and drunk their full, the initiates were invited to share the *Omiero*, the wine, the whiskey…and the blood.

The gods accepted two more initiates into the *Lukumi* cult. Then other mysterious ceremonies were performed where Pedro revealed to the *Lukumi* the secrets of voodoo, the tapping into the source of power, the casting of spells and the controlling of an unbeliever's mind. Far into the late night, the ceremonies to the gods were performed. Only after all the initiates were almost exhausted did Pedro end the *Kari Ocha*. And when all the voodoo worshipers had slipped back to their own plantations, some having come from several miles away, many whites pretended not to have heard the beat of the voodoo drum and the chants of the Voodoo priest.

Pedro looked around the abandoned *Lukumi* meeting ground. Bessie remained. She and Pedro together engaged in those rites which have initiated men and women into the mysteries of life since time immemorial.

Over a period of months, Bessie and Pedro had explored the mysteries of each other's mind, soul and bodies far more often than

FRANK YERBY:

once a month. They were superbly matched to each other physically. Without the hunger of youth, each was capable of exploring, enjoying and nurturing human feelings long after their bodies had convulsed in passionate fulfillment. Pedro made love to Bessie as if she were his three-string guitar from which he could so expertly and lovingly coax out the sweetest sounds. Their union, culminating so often in moments of pleasure beyond endurance, made the lovers lose all sense of reality, believing they were the only two humans in the world—only to learn too late that they were quite mistaken. It was afterwards while each gazed at their reflections in their lover's eyes that Papa Legba was always the Trickster.

Sometimes the person you love can quickly turn it into hate… which was exactly what Bessie was doing to Pedro. But actually it was Pedro's fault…he had made the mistake of telling Bessie about his Orisha, Ayagunda, and gunpowder. "Ayagunda demanded gunpowder at last month's meeting," Pedro told her, "and what do you think happened?"

"What?" Bessie replied disinterestedly.

"Two men came to tonight's meeting with a rifle and a pistol," Pedro replied. "They were very fine guns, good quality, almost new."

"Black men have guns!" Bessie almost shouted, "God almighty, God almighty!" As Pedro had noted earlier, Bessie had the fire, which was something that Yerby was certain they didn't need right now. "God is preparing to wreak vengeance on the white man for all the wrong he has done. And it's going to begin right here in Mississippi!!" she exclaimed. "There can't be no better sign than black men getting guns." The over-powering image of black men getting guns, getting power, becoming men capable of fighting the white man, simply overwhelmed Bessie's imagination. She did not know what to make of it. And in the end, Bessie made much more of it than she should have.

This poor abused plantation-bred, mulatto daughter of some white vagrant could not know, nor could she be expected to know, that there was more to fighting whites than having guns. How could she understand that the last act of a war is to seize weapons and prior to this act, the outcome of the war has already been decided? In Bessie's overtaxed imagination, she believed that black men with guns meant black liberation from bondage. And nothing could have been further from the truth.

"We could get enough guns to arm every slave in the county," Bessie told every black slave who would listen to her prattling. "Nuthin' these white folks gonna do when we black folks have the guns. All the whites gonna run away when all the black men have the guns." Pedro could do nothing to make Bessie more discreet. There was nothing he could do to make her keep her mouth shut. Papa Legba filled Bessie with hate for her white mistress and she wanted her revenge. Bessie did not understand that the great problem with her plan was that the white folks would not "all go away." Of course Bessie did not know that. How could she know? She lacked any practical experience. She had limited knowledge. She didn't know that the white folks had no fear of black men with guns; they'd welcome it. White folks were born to kill. They kill for the pure pleasure of killing. They kill for conquest. They kill in order to steal. Killing is a way of life for them. Their ability to kill gives white folks a belief in their own invincibility. Black men with guns would be a welcome diversion for the white men of Natchez. *A nigger hunt sounds good to me*, they would say. The white men would have more guns, better guns and lots of bullets as well as the skill and practice you needed when shooting niggers.

The problem with Bessie's plan, was the plan itself. The last thing Bessie should have wanted was for black men to have guns. Bessie confused freedom with revenge. The one had absolutely nothing to do with the other. To achieve one's freedom is extremely difficult; to get revenge is absolutely impossible. Hate blinded Bessie when love should have opened her eyes. Bessie saw Pedro as a giant, a mighty warrior, Chango himself. The whites saw Pedro as just another nigger who needed bringing down to his "proper" place. Bessie didn't understand what she was unleashing; yet Pedro should have understood.

But Papa Legba had caught Pedro not paying attention.

At the next midnight meeting of the *Lukumi*, more black men brought guns, rifles and even a few cutlasses, machetes and clubs. Of course, the guns were stolen from their masters. That meant that on plantations in two counties white men were discovering guns missing. And a sudden rash of missing guns around Natchez was a sure sign that the niggers were up to something.

"Pedro, your power is great," Bessie insisted. "You are strong enough to lead an uprising."

"Lead an uprising!" Pedro replied skeptically. "I've got a better plan. Why don't you come back to Key West with me?" Yerby's pleas to return to Florida had begun to have an impact on Pedro.

"Don't tip them off that we know something is going on," one of the senior members of Natchez's civic club said. "Let's let them make the first move, but we'll be ready." Anything and everything happening in Natchez was usually discussed at the Natchez Civic Club. And when the old boys got together in their elite club, they clucked like a chicken coop filled with hens. "Well, I know one thing, any blubber-lipped burr-headed coon who looks at me sideways, I'm gonna blow his bubble-eyes out the back of his head." The speaker showed off a pair of Colt revolvers. "Just see what happens if they try to put their hands on these." The planter looked about the room until he spied a black waiter. "Hey you, boy…" the planter called.

"Me, sir?" the black waiter quailed fearfully.

"You, nigger!" the planter shouted, having drunk enough to make him even more belligerent then he normally was. "Come over here!"

The black servant shuffled over to the planter's table, but just before he got there, the planter's friend put out his leg, and not seeing it soon enough, the old waiter went tumbling down to the floor. His eyes were frozen in fear; his gray hair stood straight out on the back of his neck. "See," the planter said menacingly as he pulled out one of his revolvers. "If that nigger's eyes even twitch the wrong way, I'm gonna spill his brains all over this floor."

"Oh, just calm down, Charlie." The voice came from another table, "Let's not make a mess. I would prefer not to have to leave the club while they take God knows how long to clean up after some dead darkie. We get your point."

• • •

Without even knowing about the missing guns, Morgan Brittany began to suspect there was problem. Her slaves weren't talking back or refusing to work or acting defiant, but there was something in their attitude that seemed different. "Every time your Pedro nigger visits my gal Bessie," Morgan complained to Ross, "she becomes absolutely impossible. She's always talking in riddles about freedom and white people running away."

"Sounds like she's just afraid of you, Morgan," Ross Pary said. "I thought you said you would free the slaves if you could."

Morgan eyes confirmed her bloody secret. "That was before I realized that the "Southern way of life" gave one so many interesting ways for diverting oneself. And you know how I love my little diversions," Morgan's eyes smouldered with the evil oozing from her soul and her breath quickened. "Anyhow, Ross," she said emphatically, "I want you to keep your nigger, Pedro, away from my Bessie."

"Okay, I'll tell Pedro that he is no longer welcome on your property," Ross agreed. He immediately sent his personal servant, Wallace, out to Moonrise to fetch Pedro and bring him back to Pary's bachelor flat in town. Ross wanted to tell Pedro, himself, that he was no longer to visit Bessie; he wanted there be no misinterpretation. Ross had to agree that Pedro was taking far more liberties than he should. *It is time I had a talk with him. The darkie should know better.*

After all this is Mississippi. I should turn the whole thing over to Tom and let him handle it. Sooner or later, Pedro would have to learn. But this matter had to be handled soon, Ross concluded, *or else the consequences for Pedro might be more than the simple lashing that Tom wants to give him.* Pary told Wallace to make haste and find Pedro. And in all of Natchez, Mississippi, there could have been no worse Negro for Bessie to rave about black men with guns than Pary's man Wallace. Papa Legba could not stop giggling.

It so happened that the very day that Ross sent Wallace for Pedro, Bessie had that entire afternoon free. This was not strange, for as Yerby wrote in *Floodtide*, Ross Pary was screwing his best friend's wife, Morgan Britanny. So anytime her mistress went into town, Bessie knew she would have the afternoon to spend with Pedro. When Wallace arrived at Pedro's cabin to deliver Ross Pary's message, it was Bessie, not Pedro, who met Wallace at the door. The stodgy and quite condescending black body servant was scandalized to find the tall, youthful beauty lounging about Pedro's cabin.

"Gal, where's Pedro?" Wallace spat out at Bessie, his eyes rebuking her for being where she shouldn't be. His eyes also told her that he had every intention of letting Morgan Brittany know where Bessie had been spending her time.

"He's here 'round abouts," Bessie replied. "What you want him for?"

"Ain't no business of yours," Wallace said, "but if you must know, Marse Pary wants to see him right quick. So if you know where he's at, you'd better tell me before you get in more trouble than you already in."

"Trouble? What you mean trouble?" Bessie asked. "I does what I pleases when Miss Brittany's ain't around. And pretty soon she ain't never going to be around, no more."

"What you talking about, girl?" Wallace exclaimed. "You'd better get them foolish notions out your head before your Mizzus lays a whip to your sassy black hide."

"I ain't scared of her no more," Bessie said with a toss of her head and a quiet laugh. "Pretty soon she ain't gonna be able to whip me and nobody else, either. Soon black men gonna have guns and they ain't gonna stand for white folks beating up on their women."

"I done asked you, what are you talking about girl?" Wallace repeated himself contemptuously. "You talking crazy and crazy talk like that could get you and that nigger Pedro strung up real quick."

"Well, you heard what I said, you old shuffling nigger," Bessie said. "You just wait and see. One day we is going to be free!"

To say that Bessie frightened Wallace with her talk of freedom would not only be an understatement, it would miss the essential fact that nothing frightened Wallace more than the idea of not being able to serve white people. Being considered a faithful slave was Wallace's purpose for living. All he wanted in life was the chance to earn the respect and…possibly, even the love of his master. There was nothing Wallace would not do to serve not only Ross Pary but any white man. Wallace had no mind, no soul, no will, other than that he needed to do as he was told and to serve all of his master's needs and desires. Life held no greater pleasure for Wallace than being able to anticipate his master's wish and satisfy it before his master could make the request himself. The idea of being free to Wallace was like looking into the face of death. And the idea of black men with guns and white people running away could mean that he, Wallace, would be a homeless outcast without anyone to care for him.

So the more Wallace listened to Bessie, the less fearful and more angry he became. Wallace had never heard such dumb talk. He had been privy to many of the planters' discussions. Wallace knew which of Mississippi's first families were doing well and which ones were tenants on their own property. Wallace overheard conversations involving the price of cotton on the European market and the cost of furnishings being imported from Europe. Wallace had access to information that

Bessie could not have ever imagined existed. Though Bessie had the heart and the courage, she was as dumb as a door knob when it came to knowing what it would take to make white men run away.

These dumb cotton pickers think that they've got the brains to beat these white folks, Wallace thought to himself. *Only thing these niggers are gonna do is get a bunch of people killed. And I will see this Cuban nigger swinging from a tree before I let him ruin my life.* Wallace knew exactly what he had to do. "You tell Pedro that Marse Ross wants to see him, right now," he told Bessie. "And then, if I was you, I'd take my black behind back to where it belongs as soon as I could." Wallace left immediately. *I could be hung just knowing these crazy niggers,* he thought, watching Betsy retreat back into Pedro's cabin.

At first, Wallace decided to tell Ross Pary about the whole plot. *But then, somebody might think it was me, Wallace, Marse Pary's man, who was behind this trouble,* Wallace thought to himself. So rather than telling Pary about the plot, Wallace decided to distance himself from the whole affair. Then he thought about Cobb. He and Cobb shared the same way of thinking. They boasted to the other about how important their masters were. Cobb was the butler for one of the circuit judge. He was always looking for news to tell his master.

I'll tell Cobb. Wallace chuckled over how clever he would be. Cobb never wanted his master to know the name of any other "good nigger." *Cobb will want to take all the credit and he'll leave me out of the whole mess,* Wallace thought, *and no one will know it was Wallace that told.*

But once again, Papa Legba intervened and Wallace's scheme went awry. Cobb did reveal the source of his information to the circuit judge. Wallace was summoned in front of the judge to tell all he knew. "Now, boy," Judge Smith said, towering over Ross Pary's quavering manservant from behind his great courthouse desk, "what did this gal tell you about this nigger uprising?"

With trembling knees and beating heart, Wallace told Judge

Smith everything Bessie had told him. "Your Honor, sir, the niggers been talking to this hoo-doo man from Cuba who done told them to go steal guns from their masters. The hoo-doo man told them once the blacks have guns, the whites will run away."

"Whites will run away!!!" Judge Smith exploded. "This Voodoo man gonna put a hex on us White men so that we just run away from a bunch of liver-lipped, burr-headed jungle bunnies?"

"Yessir," Wallace mumbled. "I come and told as soon as I heard, sir."

"That's a good start, boy," the Judge said sternly, "but you'd better come clean and tell me all you know, or I'll have you beaten bloody."

"No sir," Wallace wailed. "You don't have to beat me. One thing I always know is that Master Pary will take care of old Wallace. Master Pary loves Wallace as much as Wallace loves Master Pary. I could never betray Master Pary and Master Pary would never betray me. So Judge, you can trust Wallace."

"I hope so," Judge Smith said sternly, "...for your sake!"

Judge Smith kept Wallace in the courthouse jail for a week while he and the leading planters discussed how they would handle this situation. They decided that within two weeks all the slaves involved in the plot needed to be identified and killed. The Natchez Civic Club would raise an indemnification fund for any planters who lost slaves.

"Ross Pary ought to pay," one of the planters said. "He's the one who brought that Cuban hoo-doo man here."

"Pary didn't bring that Cuban nigger to Natchez," Lance Brittany said, "he came of his own accord. Besides, how would it look after all Ross went through in Cuba for him to be ruined by those of us who stayed home?" Although some of the planters grumbled, it was finally decided that Ross Pary would be treated the same as any of the other planters. If he lost any slaves in the uprising, he would be compensated. "But not for Pedro," Judge Smith decided. "That nigger is gonna swing and that's that."

"Let's invite the blacks with guns to a shoot out," another planter hooted. "Every sporting white man within three counties will participate. We could raise money for the fund by charging a fee for every dead nigger. The boys won't mind." They finalized their plans. Judge Smith had Wallace brought before him. "Nigger, we want to know the next time those niggers with guns meet."

"Well, sir," Wallace cried piteously, "I don't rightly know when they meet. I don't know nothing more than what I already done told your Honor."

"Wallace," Judge Smith shouted at the cringing slave, "if you don't get me the information about these niggers with guns, I'm going to have every inch of flesh beaten off your black hide. Do you hear me, boy?"

"Yessir," Wallace wailed, "I'll certainly find out when they's gonna meet next."

"And Wallace," Judge Smith said," make sure it's within the next two weeks."

"Yessir, Your Honor," Wallace replied dutifully.

"We can't be waiting on you niggers, do you hear me boy?" Judge Smith thundered.

"Yessir," Wallace quailed. "Wallace is your nigger awright. Wallace won't let you down."

• • •

"Right now, "Yerby told Pedro, "is the time to bid Mississippi adios."

"But, señor," Pedro asked, "what do I do about Bessie?"

Yerby agreed that the problem with Bessie was serious. "Pedro, my brother, the time has come for us to leave Mississippi," Yerby said. "You must understand, the situation is very dangerous now."

"Yes," Pedro said, "I am aware that Wallace spent many days as the guest of Judge Smith. The judge wants Wallace to get *Lukumi* to reveal themselves within two weeks."

"Now understand, my friend, "Yerby exclaimed. "We need to get out of here quickly,"

"That's not the problem, *señor,*" Pedro said. "It's Bessie! Something needs to be done about everything she is saying. She won't listen to any plans to escape. She only wants to talk about the number of guns black men have. I am afraid it is only a matter of time before the whites will be on us, Papa Legba protect us."

"You need to give her a choice to run away with you now, or you will leave her," Yerby said. "In any case, it's her choice." Her choice? Yerby knew that neither Bessie nor Pedro had a choice; they were doomed.

"But I cannot leave her," Pedro replied, "I would not leave any woman again, no matter what. But I simply can't leave Bessie. Don't you understand that I love her?" Maybe it was Carlota that Pedro saw in Bessie, it made no difference now. The living guilt about Carlota still ate at Pedro's insides.

"I don't know how you're going to do it," Yerby said, "but there will be a boat going down to New Orleans in five days. *We need to be on that boat.* "Yerby took a gamble and said, "I'm going to let Wallace know that Saturday next, blacks with guns will gather at the meeting ground. By then everyone should have been warned to run away. And we should be safely downriver on our way back to Key West, Florida."

"What do I tell Bessie?" Pedro asked.

"That, my friend is up to you," Yerby replied.

Surprisingly, Pedro nearly met Yerby on the New Orleans riverboat heading back to Florida on the scheduled day. Pedro had convinced Bessie to run away with him on that very night. "But," she said, "we need to warn all the black men with guns to try to escape as soon as they can." Pedro agreed and signaled all the *Lukumi* to come to the sacred meeting ground. However, when they were all together, instead of telling them to run for their lives, Bessie suggested that they attack Finiterre and kill her mistress, Morgan Brittany. "After I have burned that bitch's house down, then I will leave," Bessie vowed. "After that, Pedro, I'll go wherever you want me to."

Judge Smith sent out runners to the plantations in Adams County, Jefferson County and Franklin County. The call went out to the Knights of the Golden Circle. These 19th-century cavaliers possessed an array of firearms and weaponry that would have been envied anywhere in the world. And the men possessing these weapons were veterans of wars, raids and duels, cold-blooded killers, men who lived for an opportunity to kill niggers. Bessie could not have been more wrong about what the whites would do when faced with blacks with guns. Over a hundred men showed up to indulge their passion for mankilling.

Bessie and Pedro led the *Lukumi* attack on Finiterre. And as Frank Yerby described it, their attack failed. The blacks with guns who were not shot outright were hanged. Ross Pary and George and Henry Metcalf without remorse, and with a certain amount of relief, all aided in the hanging of Pedro and Bessie. But the instant the whites jerked him into the air, Papa Legba appeared to Pedro and whispered in his ear. Pedro only smiled.

CHAPTER EIGHTEEN

*Z*eus fell in love with Nemesis, but fearing his lusty, perverted nature the goddess fled. Zeus pursued Nemesis over the oceans and through the forests. Finally, when Nemesis took to the air as a wild goose, Zeus changed into a swan and triumphed over her. Afterwards Nemesis delivered to Leda, the wife of the king of Sparta, a hyacinth-colored egg that Leda hid in a chest. When the time arrived, Helen of Troy was hatched. When Helen became known as the most beautiful woman in the world and married the Spartan king, Menelaus, Nemesis returned and took vengeance for having been ravished by Zeus by urging Paris to seduce Helen. From then onwards, the world has continued to suffer through continuous wars from which it has yet to emerge. The Druids took upon themselves the task of preventing the world from ever forgetting the rape of Nemesis. They desired to overthrow that Olympian plunderer and return the world to the bosom of its Mother. Every spring the Druids search the seashore for a blood red egg, called the glain.

. . .

Once again Yerby found himself facing Pride Dawson in his

great stone manor house.

My nemesis, Yerby thought to himself, *the one who had vowed to seek his vengeance on me.*

"I see you have returned," Dawson said, "find any guilty victims, yet?"

"No," Yerby answered. He thought about Pedro and Bessie. Their fate was their fate…nothing could change that. But Carlota and the child? What about them? "None of the victims of a terrible fate could in reality be judged guilty. As a matter of fact, some acted quite courageously."

"And what about you, Frank?" Dawson exclaimed.

"What?" Yerby asked defensively. He knew what Dawson was driving at. Yerby remembered his writings about how Negroes should have stood up and confronted the white man. He certainly did not want to be questioned about his behavior…or about how quickly he became as much a sambo as any other black, slave or free.

"Did you believe that you had any choice? Did your believe that somehow you could resist becoming a 'victim'?" Dawson asked, a faint smile playing around the corners of his mouth, enjoying fully the discomfiture of his creator.

Yerby thought about how he fled the Spanish in Cuba and adopted the attitude expected of a black in Mississippi as a matter of survival. "No," he replied hesitantly, "there was no way that I could have behaved in any other way than as I did."

"Right you are," Pride Dawson announced exhuberantly. "You were as likely to resist being victimized in Natchez, Mississippi, as I was able to resist victimizing myself in my own *castle*." And the smile disappeared from the New York robber baron's face as quickly as it appeared. "But you knew that, didn't you?"

Yerby honestly never considered Pride Dawson a victim. Dawson was a multi-millionaire whose holdings included silver and copper mines, railroads and steel mills. His wife, the former Esther

Stillworth, daughter of his mentor Black Tom Stillworth, had inherited a fortune many times greater than Dawson's own. Yet Dawson considered himself a victim nevertheless. But in this case, Yerby argued to himself, Dawson was certainly guilty.

"We were beginning to think that you would never get the point," Dawson said.

"Get the point?" Yerby asked stiffly. "You mean to tell me that there was a point to all this?"

"Well, of course there was a point," Dawson said with a touch of well-justified sarcasm.

"Then why didn't you just come out with it?" Yerby asked in an exasperated tone. "Why did I have to go through all of this rigmarole?"

"Would you have accepted it?" Dawson asked.

Yerby's face was as blank as his mind. He had no honest response other than he really didn't know.

"And frankly," Dawson continued, "I'm still uncertain whether or not you've really learned anything."

The fact that he had to listen to this arrogant white boy lecture him about anything was almost more than Yerby could bear. But Yerby realized that it was a test. No one was almighty, not even the author of the book or the teller of a tale. "What point did I miss?" Yerby asked.

"Actually there are a couple of points that we have been trying to make, Frank." Dawson said. "The first is that before anyone can recognize the genius of Frank Yerby, Frank Yerby must recognize that he is no better than anyone else. It has been a long time since you really thought or cared about anybody or anything other than yourself. Once you cared, but now you have no sympathy for anyone or anything. Perhaps you have seen too many bull fights."

But Yerby knew that was in the long past. *I cared!* Yerby said defiantly to himself, *I cared! I cared too much.*

It was as if Dawson could read his mind. "Well, the simple fact is," Dawson said, after taking a deep draw from his cigar, "if you had cared about anybody other than yourself, then that somebody would have cared about you, don't you think, Frank?"

Yerby sat back in the overstuffed armchair; Dawson's words hit him like a cold shower.

"Since nobody seems to have gone out of their way to memorialize you, in any way, it seems to me that you didn't do very much for anyone else. It's as if you thought you were better. And that's the point, Frank. You are a brilliant writer, but you're no better than anybody else. That is point number one."

"What's point number two?" Yerby asked quietly. This wounding of his pride depressed Yerby.

"Can't you guess what point number two is?" Dawson asked.

"I'm not very good at guessing games," Yerby said with a touch of exasperation.

"That is not the point," Pride Dawson said with an air of indifference. "Try again. This time put your ego away and use that mind you seem to be so proud of."

It was not hard for Yerby to guess. Actually, he knew it all the time. He just did not want to say it; it was too difficult. Frank Yerby found it very difficult to admit to having made a mistake. "If I were to guess," Yerby conceded, "it would be that I was wrong about the *victim's guilt.*"

"Bingo," Pride Dawson said. "Absolutely correct. Frank, there is no such thing as a victim's guilt...if a person is guilty, that is not a victim. Innocence is the essence of being a victim. A criminal is guilty and, therefore, cannot be a victim. However, a person punished for a crime that person did not commit is a victim because that person is innocent."

Yerby thought about arguing the point but thought better of it. Instead he asked, "But how does that fact help either me or you?"

"It helps restore your faith." It was not Pride Dawson speaking.

Rather the voice came from a black man.

"You remember Bruce Randolph, don't you, Frank?" Pride Dawson asked.

"Of, course, I remember Dr. Randolph," Yerby responded.

Dr. Bruce Randolph was very dark and very intelligent; he had a bachelor's degree from Oberlin College and a doctorate in education from Harvard, "You've no faith in your people, Frank." Randolph continued, "...nor in yourself."

"I've complete confidence in myself," Yerby replied.

"You have confidence that you can survive in a white society, but that's not the kind of faith that I'm talking about," Randolph smiled. "Do you remember these words from *Griffin's Way?*"

"*The horsemen filed by Indian style making no sound. Their horses' hooves were padded with rolls of cloth, so that the animals seemed to be wearing turbans on their feet. The riders hadn't covered their heads with the tall conical hoods yet, so the fifty faces, one by one, showed up clearly in the moonlight as they rode. Each rider bore a terrible look matching the rider's intent to commit terrible deeds. These men really weren't any different from any other fifty men picked at random from any section of the land. They varied in age from forty downward to less than twenty. Some were thin, some fat, some rather handsome. They did not seem to be fiends incarnate out of hell just a group of average, rather ordinary men, riding quietly through the night.*

What made them look so terrible was not their robes, ridiculous coverings of sewn-up bedsheets, nor the hoods they carried, nor the whips coiled around the saddle horns nor the guns in their holsters nor the knives and swords. Their faces were terrifying because their faith was unquestioning. Faith sustained these Klansmen's belief that the pigmentation of their skins, or rather the lack of it, was a God-given badge of superiority. This superiority allowed them to commit acts of obscene barbarity without the faintest tinge of remorse. Their cause was holy. The Christian God was on their side. The Christian God and all His angels stood smiling their approval while masked fanatics whipped Negro women to death, burned schoolhouses, and made war even upon children. And throughout history it has been this way: Arian Christianity has left rivers of blood and mountains of skulls and bones as their legacy of racial superiority. The legacy of a civilization whose reality is evil and whose victims are innocent."

"Do you remember those sentiments?" Bruce Randolph asked Frank Yerby.

"Vaguely," Yerby replied.

"You have never had that faith," Randolph asserted, "and so you could not instill it in any of your readers."

"I haven't the faintest idea what you are talking about," Yerby said rather disinterestedly.

"But soon, I hope you will learn soon, Frank," Bruce Randolph replied, "both for your sake as well as ours."

PART THREE

CHAPTER NINETEEN

Two dark figures blended into the shadows of Squire and Dame Matthews' two-story brick house. They crept around carefully to avoid exposing themselves in the moonlit Massachusetts night. Each, wearing the shabbiest of clothes, was ill prepared for the biting New England cold. Pants cinched in the middle with a piece of rope, shirts ragged and torn, jackets that flapped about their emaciated bodies like the wings of some great black birds scavenging for food. The younger man was shoeless, while the older had shoes that had outlived their usefulness years ago. Now they were little more than worn out leather leggings with paper soles. Their scarred faces and frizzy hair, matted and sprinkled with bits of grass and leaves testified that their only abode was the damp earth, itself. The elder of the two had a hideous scar in the place where his right ear should have been. Under his tattered shirt, huge whelts and jagged pieces of lacerated skin crisscrossed his back, covering most of his body. Slowly the two fugitives inched their way around towards the rear of the house where the barn and chicken coop were situated. All day they had watched this house from a vacant field across the road; they had seen no dog guarding the chicken coop. The two fugitives had escaped from a Virginia plantation and made their way to Baltimore, where they had stowed away on a ship bound for Boston harbor. Now after having been in Boston for three days, they were starving. Now, the fugitives were about to add chicken theft to their list of crimes. No matter, they had to relieve their persistent hunger pangs somehow. But just as the former slaves were about to reach their goal, a large dog roared and suddenly the night was filled with the sounds of the dog's barking and growling as it rushed the two would-be chicken thieves. The noise alerted other dogs and the Boston neighborhood was filled with a chorus of howling, yapping and barking. The fugitives raced out of the yard, chased by the dog, and back across the field just as the Matthews' Negro servant came out the side door. "Here Pete! Come here, boy!" Pete's basic nature was friendly and he needed no additional encouragement. He stopped chasing the men, but continued to bark several more times until satisfied that the intruders were gone for good. Pete then turned and came back, wagging his tail proudly behind him. "Good doggie," the servant said, patting Pete on the head, "just let those two fellows be, they've got a lot of troubles without our adding to them."

. . .

At the same time, in that same moon-drenched Massachusetts night, Wesley Parks sat outside the Dexoxo cult house he had built for his Tau Vudun, his great ancestor gods. A fire burned in a pit in front of the structure, and a sacred circle joined the cult house, the fire and Wes into a mysterious union. Sitting inside the circle and stripped to the waist, Wes pulled a clucking chicken out of a cage. Chopping off its head, Wes sprinkled the blood around the fire and intoned the mysterious chants of his people. Then he threw the chicken's carcass into the fire. Wesley Parks, also known as Hwesu, former governor of one of Dahomey's richest provinces, completed his preparations for his three souls to call upon his ancestors who had become gods. Twice more he sacrificed a chicken while continuing to intone sacred chants. But when he pulled out the fourth chicken, instead of sprinkling its blood about, he put a huge finger into the spurting blood and drew a number of mysterious symbols on his forehead, chest and stomach. Then, draining the remainder into a earthen cup and tossing the carcass onto the fire, he drank the chicken's blood.

Reaching into a small pouch, Wes drew out a dirty gray powder that he scattered in a broad arc into the fire. Immediately, a great cloud of inky smoke arose from the flames and formed great figures, that remained transparent rather than becoming solid. Wes could see the Dexoxo cult house through them. But even though they remained shadows, the specters gained in weight and mass. Wesley Parks immediately flattened himself on the ground before these great ancestral apparitions. The shadowy spirits flowed down toward the prostrated Dahomean and enveloped him in a fond embrace. Then they directed him to sit on a fallen log while they billowed and flowed around him. While the fire glowed, Wes Parks' father, grandfather and great-grandfather talked with their son, Nyasanu Hwesu Kesu, son of Gbenu, as Wes had been known in Dahomey. And gravely, though often flashing ghostly smiles, Wes' Tau Vudun ancestor gods counseled him. Once his Tau Vudun had concluded their talk and had withdrawn, Wes looked up to see a handsome colored man with a well-trimmed mustache and beard. His close-cropped hair, slightly graying at the temples, was wavy, what many black people called "good hair." Never before during the rites when Wes conversed with his Tau Vudun had any stranger intruded. But Wes' ancestor gods had prepared Wes for this visitation.

"Good evening, sir," Wes said to the stranger. "You must be Frank Yerby. I was told to expect you."

...

Wes Parks enjoyed reading the *Boston Globe* newspaper when taking his breakfast. He had just introduced Yerby to his wife, Ruby, when Ben ran into the dining room and shouted, "Dad, they're taking the fugitive slaves down to the waterfront now. I'm going down to see. Are you coming? Mom, are you coming?"

From somewhere in another room, Ruby replied, "No, dear, I'll just stay here and pray for them." Ruby was a runaway slave…like so many of Boston's free black community. And like many of them, with the passage of the Fugitive Slave Law Ruby was afraid to go anywhere outside. Wes had read that Boston was one of the cities the slave catchers were targeting. Ruby was very afraid that the slave catchers might seize her. It was October, 1850, and the Fugitive Slave Bill that had been law for less than a month had sent shock waves through Boston's free black community. Already many black families had packed their belongings and fled to Canada. The newspapers detailed the responsibilities that whites had to inform authorities of any escaped slave known to them. While the newspapers' sentiment favored the fugitive slave, newspaper articles were quick to point out that "for some time now the problem had steadily worsened. Only a short time ago, fugitive slaves passing through Boston fleeing the south numbered two and three a week. But the number of fugitives continued to increase until now it was not unusual for as many as fifty slaves to pass through Boston in one week…and that figure was rising."

Wes looked over at his sixteen-year-old son, Gbenu, named for Wes' father. After his first session in the AME church school, when neither Gbenu's classmates nor teacher was able to pronounce his name, Wes' son became known as Ben.

Gbenu the elder had been mayor of Alladah, a provincial capital in the kingdom of Dahomey. Wes had taken many heads in the king's war, and he even saved the king's life. The king rewarded Wes with an appointment as *gbonuga*, governor, of the entire province of Alladah. But out of jealousy, Wes' brother, Gbouchi, murdered Wes' mother, his four infant children and his wife, Dangbevi. Then Gbouchi sold Wesley Parks into slavery. All of which seemed eons ago. Now Wes, living in Boston, was a rather successful author and a respected landowner and businessman. Wes rarely thought about the past. However, this new Fugitive Slave Law shook many like him in Boston's free black community out of their complacency.

Wes' daughter, Phoebe, considered herself *colored*. She had golden brown skin, lighter even than her mother who had a white granddaddy. But Phoebe was too dark to pass for white. In Boston, if you had to be born as a Negro, the ultimate blessing was to be able to pass...like her cousins Louise and Elaine. Phoebe hated the fact that her father was an African who spoke with a Southern drawl interlaced with unintelligible africanisms. She considered her father the ultimate embarrassment. He was black, ebony black, black like the panther who stalks at night, black as velvet. Phoebe could barely tolerate her mother's color. Although Ruby was hardly darker than a white person with a deep sun tan, she was still too dark for Phoebe's liking. But her father was just *too* black. Phoebe's cousins had told her what the proper skin color was for colored people in Boston.

"Dad! Can I go with Ben?" Phoebe asked her father, already knowing the answer. Her father never denied her anything. *He's so predictable*, Phoebe thought to herself, *no challenge at all.*

"Ben, look after your sister," Wes told his son.

Then Ruby walked into the room. She was grace herself, for all of her thirty-seven years. "Do you think they should go out there by themselves?" Ruby asked Wes, hesitantly. Once more the whole family was crowded into his small study. Wesley had been struggling to keep them out. He had barely enough room for his growing library. Every time they came in there, something got broken or torn or one of his books would be missing. This was where Wes retreated to read his newspapers. He not only read the Boston daily newspapers such as the *Boston Globe*, but also Garrison's *Liberator*, as well as James Russell Lowell's *Atlantic Monthly*, a leading abolitionist magazine. Ruby was not nearly as literate as her husband. Although she could read some of the headlines in William Lloyd Garrison's *Liberator* newspaper, she did not have to read the newspapers to know about the Fugitive Slave law. Slave catchers arrived from the South daily. They prowled about, ready to seize any poor unfortunate black without subsistence or support.

"We're just going up to Spyglass Hill," Ben said. "No one is going to be around us. But do I have to take her, Dad? I'm meeting Tommie and Carlos, and..."

"If you want to go," Wes said sternly, "look after your sister!"

Ruby still looked worried but she decided to hold her tongue.

"Thanks, Dad," Phoebe said, giving her father a big kiss on the cheek and smiling inside when she saw how misty her father got over the sudden show of affection. She quickly caught up with her brother who raced out the door and down towards Boston Harbor. The special federal commissioner was sending his first group of fugitive slaves back to Charleston, where they would be returned to masters eager to inflict severe punishment for having escaped.

"They come for you at your house, or at your job..." Ben was saying.

"They even kidnap you off the street," Tommie blurted out. Tommie and Carlos met Ben and Phoebe at their special meeting place. The four of them raced up to Spyglass hill that overlooked Boston Harbor. They were just in time to see the pitiful group of blacks, wearing manacles on their wrists and dragging leg irons, limp down to the wharf. A squad of blue uniformed federal soldiers, carrying muskets with fixed bayonets gleaming in the sun, escorted the five unfortunate captives. The mass of Boston citizens gathering for the send-off gave mixed reactions. In general, the whites approved of extraditing the fugitives. It was not as if they supported slavery, which of course was wrong. But they couldn't have groups of unruly niggers wandering about the Boston Common, stealing what they could and doing heaven knows what. But there were a number of whites who protested the extradition with little effect. The fugitive slaves were rushed across the gangplank onto the federal cutter that had been commissioned as a slave ship to deliver fugitives to slave pens and auction houses in Charleston.

"Does this mean that they can come into our house and take us away if they want to?" Phoebe asked.

"I guess it does," Tommie responded. Tommie was a year older than Carlos and Ben, but Tommie and Ben had been friends since before they knew who was older. And besides, Ben and Tommie had become blood brothers, following an Indian custom where they cut their fingers and mingled their blood.

"They beat slaves horribly," Phoebe said. "Have you seen Dad's back?"

"Yes," Ben replied. "They'd have to kill me before I'd let them beat me like that."

The black teenagers watched the whites putting the slaves into the hold of the ship. Each of the teenagers was lost in his own troubled thoughts about the world they were facing in 1850. The law gave any white the right to put any black person in restraints and sell them into slavery. "They'll never put me into slavery," Ben vowed, "not if I must escape to Canada, not if it costs me my life; not if I have to *kill*." And at the same time, Phoebe thought, "As long as I am as much like the white folks as possible, they will never make me a slave. Slavery is for those *black* niggers." But about that Phoebe Parks was wrong. And like Phoebe, most blacks have never understood that to whites it is not about skin color; it is about social class.

• • •

Daily, men, women and children were caught up in the cavalcade of government-sponsored misery. People of color were extradited back to the South by ship, by rail, by cart and by foot. Not all of these unfortunates had black faces and kinky hair. The heart-rending wails and cries of women, mothers losing their children, wives losing their husbands, resounded around Boston Harbor on a daily basis. Without a white person to stand up for them in court, these colored fugitives received no due process. Coloreds could not testify on their own behalf, nor could a colored person testify on behalf of an accused Negro. Only a white person's testimony had any standing in court. The parade of fugitive slaves, manacled and shackled, continued unabated from the city jail into the federal courts and into the custody of the slave catchers. Having been recaptured, the only hope for these unfortunates was to be sold to someone entirely new. If they were returned to their original masters, the captured runaways could expect at a minimum a vicious beating. But after the beatings, many suffered brandings, cuttings and dismemberment as well. Over time, the return of a runaway slave became great sport for the slave masters. They called on each other from neighboring plantations to see who could outdo the others in inflicting pain and suffering. And as the daily drama played itself out, the white citizens of Boston found themselves sharing the interests of the slave master.

· · ·

And yet for all of that, most if not all of Boston's free blacks worked for these whites as personal servants, maids, cooks, or porters and coachmen. They labored on the docks loading and unloading the white folks' goods, making Boston one of America's economic dynamos. Blacks sawed wood, shoveled coal, dug cellars, moved rubbish from back yards, and scoured cabins and served as barbers and waiters. These free blacks needn't fear the slave catchers...they were already indentured, working twelve to eighteen hours a day for wages to pay exorbitant rents and purchase food at inflated prices.

Wes Parks' family was far better off than most of Boston's free black community... as well as many whites. Wes was independently wealthy. Dwight Ingraham arranged to have Wes' African folktales published for a remarkable sum, and Wes supplemented his literary income with a metalworking shop that he owned and operated. In his native Dahomey, Wes had belonged to the metal-working clan and had learned the skill of turning gold and silver into artistic and intricately crafted jewelry. He also could forge the heavier metals, iron and brass, into wheels, gears and machinery parts.

Wes' family lived in a two-story brick house on the north slope of Boston Common behind Beacon Hill. Their home sat on several acres of land that contained both orchards and gardens. Among the hard-headed businessmen of the Beacon Hill crowd, the Boston Brahmins as they were known, Wes Parks was known as a solid businessman with quality products. The white folks became very proud of Wes Parks; they took credit for his success as they took advantage of the consistently high quality of his work at a third of the cost others charged. The Brahmins who formed the Saturday Club found many occasions to invite Wes to participate in their literary discussions; this former African slave who was so adept at Yankee capitalism fascinated them.

Over the years, thousands of blacks had fled the South. Many of them were honest, hardworking people looking for a place to live, work and raise their families. But others, brutalized and debased, sought not only freedom but also vengeance. They posed a threat that Northern whites could hardly ignore. These fugitives caused Northerners who did not necessarily agree with slavery to find the Fugitive Slave Law the lesser of two evils. As blacks flooded into the North, without money, clothes or food, without any means of support, whites quickly realized that something needed to be done. Either there needed to be an effort to return all fugitive slaves back to their former slave masters or there needed to be a way of moving the fugitives somewhere else… anywhere else just as long as it wasn't Boston. And the white citizens of Boston were not alone. Every city north of the Mason-Dixon line experienced this same problem. Every major city in the North was experiencing the same growth. Blacks were streaming into New York, Philadelphia, Pittsburgh and Albany as well. And at the same time, thousands of immigrants were arriving from Europe… especially Italians and Jews, and Irish.

. . .

Later in the afternoon, Ruby brought a young black man, with hat in hand, into Wes' study.

"Mr. Parks," the visitor said respectfully, "the Vigilance Society will be meeting tonight and beg to know if you will join them?"

Wes Parks had known for days that Boston's Interracial Vigilance Society would be meeting tonight. Wes knew that the matter must be of some importance for a special meeting to be called and his attendance to be requested. He replied, "Please inform the committee that I will be present at the meeting tonight."

CHAPTER TWENTY

In 1850, Boston had the largest population of free blacks in America. This group did not include the significant number of Bostonians "passing" for white…including Joe Collins and his sister Ellen. Joe and Ellen were the "yard" children of Barton Collins, owner of the Mississippi plantation known as Collinswood. As told by Frank Yerby in *A Darkness at Ingraham's Crest*, Wes had arranged for both Ellen and Joe to escape Collinswood. Wes prepared a hoodoo drug which made Ellen appear to be dead. Dwight Ingraham, who was madly in love with Ellen, then whisked her off to Boston. They were married and together settled into a comfortable, if not completely secure, existence.

Next Joe Collins, Wes Parks and Ruby escaped. Abigail Collins, the white daughter of another Mississippi planter, Wilks Thomas, and Barton Collins' first wife, Susanna, joined the trio on their flight north to Boston.

Abigail loved Joe Collins from the beginning. A young, foolish woman, Abby abandoned her family and her "Southern" way of life to live with her fancy colored man. But even after marrying Joe Collins and living in Boston these many years, Abby couldn't shed her

Southern values and beliefs. Nor could she continue to put up with Joe's habit of chasing every woman that caught his fancy. Abigail Collins still thought of herself as a white woman married to a "nigger." And after so many years had passed, Abby couldn't even remember why she had fallen so desperately in love with him.

"I thought the slave catchers had got you for sure, honey lamb," Abby said to Joe, sitting across from her at the breakfast table. She couldn't help needling her husband about his one great sensitivity.

"Oh, you mean last night," Joe replied without looking at her. "I stayed at the shop. We had a couple of orders that had to get out first thing this morning and you know how darkies are. If you don't stay on them every minute, nothing gets done." Wes Parks had taught Joe how to tailor men's clothes. Wes also lent Joe the money to open up a tailor shop. But Joe's Southern upbringing did little to instill in him either the desire or the perseverance to become a successful Yankee tradesman. His tailor shop was marginally successful. It would have done better had Joe Collins not been forced to hire a journeyman tailor as well as an apprentice.

"Oh," Abby exclaimed, "I thought my little Joey's disappearance was due to the attention paid to the clothes of some of his female callers. Possibly you are considering going into the dressmaking business, my love."

Joe Collins' Southern manners, handsome good looks and nonchalant, devil-may-care attitude were in striking contrast to the stiff, strait-laced disposition of most Bostonian males. Abigail Collin's octoroon husband was irresistible to much of Boston's female population.

"Well, my dear," Joe replied, "you know that most of my clients are women ordering clothes for their husbands. You would not have me turn away my customers, would you?"

"What shall I bring you for breakfast, ma'am?" Lucinda, the Collins' black serving maid, entered the room. Abby knew that Joe would have nothing to do with black women and so she had insisted on hiring Lucinda, instead of the Irish colleen Joe had selected.

"Just coffee, thank you, Lucinda," Abby replied. Turning to her husband, she continued, "Well, honey pie, you'd better be careful…you know now that they've passed that Fugitive Slave Law, they could come and pick you up and take you back to Mississippi any ole time."

"No one's taking me anywhere," Joe replied testily. He didn't like the way Abby taunted him. *What did she want from me anyway?* he had asked himself more than once. *What does she expect from me?* Hadn't he given her a good home and a degree of comfort far above what she could have expected? When they had arrived in Boston, he'd been penniless. Now he was prosperous and in some quarters, even respected. Joe Collins expected his wife to behave like a good Southern woman and overlook his wandering eye. What Joe Collins failed to realize was that Abby was not a "good southern woman"—if such a person ever even existed. Neither was Abby a rich white planter's wife and neither did she live in Mississippi with a regiment of slaves. She gave it all up for him. But Joe Collins neither understood nor cared for his wife. Joe Collins used Abby like he used all women…to get what he wanted…which was usually to get other women.

As much as Joe Collins, the ex-slave who looked like a white man, loved Boston, Abigail Collins hated it. Boston was cold and damp even in the summer. And when the Boston weather warmed up, it was still different from the Mississippi heat Abby loved. The streets in Boston were narrow, winding and dark even during the day. The atmosphere was reminiscent of the days when Massachusetts' women were terrorized by the threat of the Salem witch trials. *No wonder, Edgar Allen Poe signed his first book, "A. Bostonian,"* Abigail Collins thought to herself. Boston's melancholy environment was the perfect setting for one of Poe's frightening tales of revenge and retribution.

Abby hated their house; it was small and cramped, unlike the manor she'd grown up in. It creaked and groaned at night and

Joe was never there to comfort her. When they had first moved to Boston, Abby's love for Joe had helped her to ignore the cramped housing. Then came her daughter, Louise, who Abby just loved to death. Louise was a beautiful child and had grown into an even more beautiful young teenager with flowing hair and mysterious eyes that enchanted everyone who knew her. But now, even Louise could not distract Abby from her miserable life. Slowly her love for Joe turned into hate and malice.

Out in the hallway, the big brass knocker attached to the front door sounded its dull, ominous thud. Within seconds, Ellen Collins Ingraham swept into the dining room. Ellen greeted Abby with the sincere affection she retained for the "sister," now sister-in-law, she had known since birth. Turning to Joe, Ellen demanded to know, "Have you heard yet?"

"Heard what?" Joe asked, disinterestedly.

"They have passed the Fugitive Slave Law," Ellen almost shrieked. "No one is safe. "

"Yes, I've heard," Joe said looking over to his wife, who sat there staring back with a gloating look spreading across her face. "But I don't see what it has to do with me." Joe maintained his supercilious air of white arrogance. "I am sure that our father, the honorable Barton Collins, has no interest in sending a slave catcher after his own bastard children. Remember, Ellen, he believes you're dead. I don't think there's anything to worry about."

"But what about our children?" Ellen wailed. "Aren't you concerned about what's going to happen to them?"

"You wouldn't have had to worry about your children," Abby said with the superior air that Ellen just hated, "if you hadn't put Dwight Jr. and Elaine in that colored school."

"It is not as if we had a choice," Ellen replied with an air of resignation. Her oldest child, Elaine, was as beautiful or possibly even more beautiful than Abigail's Louise. Elaine had delicate skin and her auburn hair was as beautiful as any little white girl could possess. But her brother, Dwight Jr., could not be mistaken for anybody's white child. Though he was fair, possibly even fairer than his sister, Dwight, Jr.'s hair had a characteristic frizz, that in combination with his fullness of lips, marked him unmistakably as a descendant of Ham. But for all of that, Elaine adored her brother and would not have agreed to attend the separate white school without him. No less a personage than Charles Sumner had made several attempts, both legal as well as humanitarian, to get the Boston public schools to accept Negro children. But public education in Boston did not open to Negro children until after the Civil War. Dwight and Ellen sent both of their children, along with Ben and Phoebe Parks, to the Abiel Smith School of Boston. This school was established for black children in 1834. By enrolling their children in this school, Ellen and Dwight Ingraham declared the children's Negro ancestry to all of Boston. Louise Collins, on the other hand, attended the Boston public school along with Boston's other white children.

"Well, I think you're just going to have to stick it out, like everybody else," Joe said. "Now, if the two of you will excuse me, I think I'll take a nap, before I go back to my little sweatshop."

"Oh, Abby," Ellen wailed, "what are we to do?"

"What does Dwight say?" Abby asked her sister.

"Oh, he just thinks I'm being silly," Ellen replied. Sitting there wearing the frightened look of a fugitive slave, continually wringing her hands, Abby could see that Ellen was *not* being silly. Ellen had seen what the white folks of Mississippi did to runaway slaves. Or maybe it was because she remembered the terrible beating Joe himself had received after the whites caught Joe and Abby together. Ellen was frightened because she had been so happy. She loved her freedom, the freedom to be herself, the freedom to love Dwight and her children. Boston had given Ellen a life, a real life. And now the mere thought of losing it all to a slave catcher was just unbearable to Ellen.

Joe excused himself. No answer. Ellen couldn't take Joe's nonchalance and Abby's indifference. "I guess I'll go talk to Wes and Ruby," she said. With that she abruptly left.

It was funny how Ellen always felt closer to Wes Parks than her own twin brother. Wes and Ruby seemed more like her real family than Joe and Abby. Wes and Ruby helped her deal with the fact that she looked white but knew in her soul that she really was a Negro. Ellen's great fear was that if she were ever returned to Mississippi they would beat her senseless, not only for escaping but for her "passing" as white. She knew that neither the fact that she was a woman nor that she was Barton Collins' daughter would save her. Besides, her father was dead and she was just another piece of property that belonged to the owners of Collinswood Plantation. Ellen was not brave enough to undergo such terrible pain. Ellen was emotional, intuitive and imaginative…all of which now conspired to put her into a state of panic.

Wes and Ruby had always found ways to help Ellen. They loved her as if she were one of their children…which in a way she was. Ellen could rely upon them when she really needed help, as when both kids got sick at the same time during a bitter winter storm and needed constant attention. Or when Dwight broke his leg and needed Wes to help him back and forth. Or when one of Dwight's friends asked, "And who is the father of this one?" and Ellen had been so distraught that she left her home and stayed with Wes and Ruby. She did not return to Dwight for over a month. Of course, Dwight was affected by the incident as well, but he just took it in stride. Ellen was devastated because she had never been able to resolve the hypocrisy of passing for white in her own mind. But through it all, Wes and Ruby had always been there for Ellen. And often she wondered just how she would manage if she ever lost them.

"Wes, how are we going to deal with this situation?"

Wes looked up from his cluttered desk in the cramped room he called his study where he and Yerby were discussing current events.

This has certainly been a morning for interruptions, he thought to himself. But when he looked up and saw who it was, he smiled. Wes was used to Ellen disturbing him, and asking the most random questions as if he could read her mind. He gave her a friendly look. "Hi Ellen," he said cheerily. "I would like you to meet Frank Yerby. "He will be my house guest for awhile." The figure sitting across from Wes, though dressed in strange clothes and wearing framed spectacles unlike any she had seen before, seemed vaguely familiar.

"Have we met before, Mr. Yerby?" Ellen asked.

"Let's say that our paths have crossed in the past," Yerby said

Nodding in his direction, Ellen said, "Then I am happy to renew our aquaintance, Mr Yerby."

"Please," Yerby responded, "call me Frank."

"Very well, Frank," Ellen replied, and turning back to Wes, she continued, "You need to tell me what you think we should do."

"What the heck are you talking about?" Wes asked looking over at Frank, as if to say, "its always like this around here."

"What am I talking about?" Ellen exploded. "I am talking about the same thing everyone else is talking about...I am talking about the slave catchers, I'm talking about the Fugitive Slave Law!"

"Ah, yes," Wes Parks nodded. "The Fugitive Slave Law...but surely you don't have anything to fear."

"Maybe not me, but what about Elaine and Dwight, Jr.," Ellen replied. "They both attend the Abiel Smith School and Dwight, Jr. doesn't look white." Earlier, Wes had not been as concerned about the Fugitive Slave Law. He had allowed his own personal wealth and status to make him complacent. Even though he was as black as ebony and he himself was also a fugitive slave, Wes had originally believed that he and his family were immune from the Fugitive Slave Law. But as blacks began to be put on the federal slave ship for extradition to South Carolina, he began to realize he could not just ignore it. Even with his own wide circle of white friends and customers, this law had deprived him and his family of all civil rights and legal standing. So regardless of his own economic distance from the fray, Wes began to realize tht he should be concerned.

"Wes, I think Ellen's right to be afraid," Yerby said. "Ellen, her children and all that look like them are going to be special targets of slave catchers…for obvious reasons.

"Obvious reasons?" Ellen asked. "What would those obvious reasons be, Mr. Yerby?"

"The most obvious reason is that you are so beautiful," Yerby said with deadpan seriousness.

"Mr. Yerby!" Ellen exclaimed, "I'm a married woman. Your remarks are highly inappropriate and most unwelcome, sir."

"I meant no offense," Yerby replied without emotion. "However, it remains as I have said: the physical beauty, the physical attractiveness, of octoroons like you and even darker-skinned mulattos, made you vulnerable even when you had some legal rights. Now with the law saying that you have no rights that a white man must respect, you could be kidnapped off the street and sold before anyone knows you're missing."

Ellen considered Yerby's point and then said, "That's one reason…are there others?"

"Yes," Yerby replied. "Southern brutality towards blacks is based upon their absolute belief in the racial superiority of whites. The presence of octoroons who look white, but legally can be treated like any dark-skinned, kinky-headed African…no offense intended," Yerby said, looking at Wes….

"None taken," Wes replied.

"…makes certain white folks, especially those whites who actually believe in the Bible, cringe. If the brutalities whites have codified into the Fugitive Slave Law could happen to those who look white, they could also happen to those who are white."

"I still don't see how that is an obvious reason," Ellen persisted.

"Some whites might not want you around," Yerby said. "They might not want to be reminded of their own, ah, indiscretions...."

"Or they might be concerned that one of us might help people of color from the inside," Ellen interrupted.

"Little chance for that," Yerby scoffed. "Secret societies run this land. Nobody gets anywhere in America without being initiated."

"Which brings us back to the question I asked in the first place," Ellen said impatiently.

"I'm going to a meeting of the Boston Vigilance Committee tonight," Wes said. "Why don't you and Dwight join us? I know that Elaine and Dwight Jr. must have told you about it." Boston's octoroons, passing for white, and even those who were not consciously passing rarely, if ever, socialized with Negroes in public. As much as Ellen loved Wes and Ruby...even though her children, Dwight Jr. and Elaine, attended the Abiel Smith School, Ellen could never have recognized Wes, Ruby or their children, Ben and Phoebe, in public. Ellen rationalized that she abided by the social taboo against integration to save her white husband from embarrassment...though, in reality, Dwight Ingraham would never be embarrassed by anything his wife ever did, so much did he love Ellen. For his part, whenever Dwight Ingraham looked into other men's faces as they looked at his sultry, seductive wife, he became even more convinced that he was the luckiest man alive. But the reality of Boston forced Ellen to become a "white woman," even with the difficulties for her children. Ellen never wanted to go back to being a "nigger"...either in Mississippi or in Boston.

"Well, I don't know if tonight would be convenient," Ellen stammered, embarrassed by her own mixed reactions to Wes' invitation.

"I know what you're thinking, but there will be some of the most important white people in Boston joining us," Wes said, "including William Lloyd Garrison and Charles Sumner. Don't worry, it will be all right."

"I think Wes is right," Yerby added. "If you are fearful, the best thing you can do is become active and known. That way you increase your own personal security."

"Besides, it's time you began to learn to act like a free citizen, instead of a scared housewife!" Ruby barged in.

"If Dwight decides it's all right," Ellen replied hesitantly, "we will meet you in front of the hall at eight p.m." When Ellen returned home and mentioned the Boston Vigilance Committee meeting to Dwight, he could not restrain his enthusiasm. "Of course, we should go," he replied with that special smile reflecting what a good person he actually was. "But I don't think Elaine and Dwight Jr. need come."

"Oh, no," Ellen agreed. "They should stay here, at home." Then thinking to herself, she asked out loud, "Do you think they'll be all right?"

"Of course, they will, my dear," Dwight assured his wife. "We'll not be gone long."

• • •

Ellen and Dwight Ingraham awaited Wes and Ruby Parks outside Boston's African Meeting House as planned. The meeting-house was packed with people. Many people of color were gathered together for the meeting, but Ellen was surprised to see the number of whites in attendance. "It could not have been otherwise," Dwight whispered to her.

"Why is that?" Ellen asked.

"Because when David Walker, himself a fugitive slave who had settled in Boston, wrote his *Appeal To the Coloured Citizens of the World*, he stated that the wretchedness black people were forced to suffer was a consequence of the religion of Jesus Christ. Ever since then, Walker's charges stung the Christians around here. They had no defense. Christian authorities everywhere in the North have tried to distance themselves from their Southern neighbors and begin to practice, if nothing else, the acts of kindness and sympathy required of all Christians worthy of the name."

"I don't see why the accusation of a Negro would make any difference," Ellen said. "White people's religion is Christianity. Some white people hold slaves; others don't. It's just a matter of which way society should be run." Ellen had a way of simplifying things that sometimes drove her husband crazy."

"Walker argues that the practice of Christianity is really a practice in deception and hypocrisy," Dwight explained to his wife. "He says that Christians, in reality, practice the exact opposite of their stated beliefs in order to deceive and gain control of non-white people *and their lands* all over the world. Well, that really unnerved those around here who believed that their acts will be judged. These Christians up here in the North were not prepared to be judged by the actions of Southern slavers."

"I still don't understand why they should care what some black fugitive slave says," Ellen said.

"It's because the accusation was made by a black," Dwight said, "who then published the charges in writing which greatly alarmed those who are concerned with the moral standards for the community. One cannot claim moral authority over right and wrong as do the great prelates of the church and universities, and at the same time be accused of being a hypocrite." As a writer, Dwight had always understood that ambiguity was the essence of civilization. He had no illusions regarding the moral authority whites had in relation to black slaves. His was a more practical objection. The absurd social concepts required by the institution of slavery would deny him the love and happiness he had found with his wife and children. In addition, Dwight believed that the foundation of an institution so dependent upon force could only mean that a clash of terrible proportions would occur when an equal and opposite force, which is the rule of nature, suddenly emerged. As an Aristotelian, Dwight Ingraham held an intellectual commitment to the "mean" and believed "extremes" of any sort, but especially extremist social and political orders, merely sowed the seeds of future tumult. Fathers creating a heaven for themselves by preparing a hell for their sons. Dwight continued the discussion with his wife. "The Christians were concerned that coloreds everywhere, especially those who could read, would believe David Walker. I'll bet you believed that the prohibition against teaching slaves to read originated in the South."

Ellen looked at her husband. "Didn't it?"

"No, it didn't," Dwight smiled. "It was those who were so concerned by Walker's charges in the North who urged the prohibition against reading in the South...as well as the North. You remember me telling you that Charles Sumner said that the reason he has been unable to get the public schools in Boston to accept colored children was because all the pastors of Boston's Christian churches met, and decided that it was not a good idea to teach them to read. They were afraid of coloreds reading David Walker's *Appeal*.

"But what about the Abiel Smith School here; it educates colored children?" Ellen said.

"That's just the point," Dwight replied excitedly. "The fact that coloreds have their own school and are teaching colored children to read has almost destroyed the belief in the basic inferiority of the colored people. So once again the issue comes down to force, which vindicates Walker's accusation. Besides, his accusation galled church leaders, some of whom really are true believers. So ever since David Walker's *Appeal*, Bostonians, spurred by the Christian community have been engaged in restoring the colored people's God-given human rights...if not their civil and legal rights, which is the source of all the anti-slavery activity around here. But look, here are Wes and Ruby." The two couples nodded to each other cordially, but without speaking. Then together and accompanied by Frank Yerby, they entered the building.

Even in Boston's African Meeting House, strict rules of segregation applied, and whites and blacks were expected to sit in their assigned sections. So upon entering the auditorium, the couples separated. Dwight and Ellen found seats in the main section reserved for whites. The sitting areas reserved for colored people were on either side of the main area and in the balcony. Here, Wes, Ruby and Frank found seats. William Lloyd Garrison, the chairman of the Massachusetts Abolitionist Society, and other speakers involved with the abolitionist movement, sat on the raised platform. At the podium, Frederick Douglass was addressing the gathering:

"It is well and good that we gathered here are concerned about the hundreds of black slaves fleeing the terror of Southern slavery," Douglass declared. "No one here need be reminded that many good-hearted white people daily provide shelter, food and clothing for runaway slaves. These same people provide transportation and guides to their next 'station' to freedom. These are the good white people of the North."

A spontaneous cheer rose up first from the colored section and then found its way over to the white onlookers, who clapped in a dignified, controlled manner. When the cheering began to quiet down, Douglass continued. "That we need supplies and money to help these people and others in the effort to guide runaways along the path to freedom is evident. I sympathize with many of you well-intentioned whites who want to know: how will this all end? What will stop the ever increasing numbers of Negroes streaming North?" Frederick Douglass looked over the white section into the reserved, dignified faces of those good Christians whose very presence signified their commitment to the cause…and saw that he had their attention.

He continued. "But I ask you, my friends, what I consider a reasonable question. To what end do you do these things? Are you trying to return fugitive slaves back to their slave masters? Do you want to send them to the United States' Liberian possession in Africa? Do you believe it more practical to expand the Underground Railroad routes far into Canada? Are you here in this African Meeting House to learn ways of assisting Negroes to escape to anywhere as far away from Boston as possible?"

There was an uncomfortable murmur in the white section, and a somewhat subdued shuffling in the colored section as the colored people could feel white people thinking, "you black people ought to be damned glad for our kindness." But as if he were totally unaware of the hostile reaction to his remarks, Douglass continued his criticisms: "During my recent travels to Belfast, Ireland, no one there questioned my humanity or offered me insults. When I rode in a cab, I was seated beside white people. In my hotel accommodations, I entered the same door and was shown into the same parlor that white people used. At dinner I dined at the same table as whites and no one seemed offended. In Ireland, I found no difficulty in obtaining admission to any place of worship, of instruction or of amusement. I was accepted on equal terms with all people. I met nothing to remind me of my complexion. Everywhere I was treated with the kindness and deference paid to white people. In short, in Ireland I was not told: 'We don't allow niggers in here'."

Several white people, shaking their heads, got up and walked out. Undeterred, Frederick Douglass continued, "Here in Boston, when I approached the entrance of the menagerie, the doorkeeper, using a harsh and contemptuous tone said: 'We don't allow niggers in here.' When attempting to find a seat at a revival meeting in the Reverend Henry Jackson's meetinghouse, I was met by the good deacon, who told me in a pious tone, 'We don't allow niggers in here.' While traveling on the steamer *Massachusetts* from New York to Boston, chilled to the bone with cold, I went inside the cabin just to find a little warmth. But I was soon touched on the shoulder and told, 'We don't allow niggers in here'. And finally, arriving here in Boston, hungry and tired, I went into an eating-house near the home of my friend Mr. Campbell, but I was met by a lad in a white apron who said, 'We don't allow niggers in here.'

Frederick Douglass agitated the white citizens in attendance. They had come to hear what good Christians they were and how much the coloreds appreciated the efforts white Bostonians were making on behalf of the colored community. It had been over twenty years since another black man, David Walker, had hurled these same dreadful accusations against God's "elect" here in Massachusetts.

William Lloyd Garrison stepped up to the rostrum, and elbowing Frederick Douglass to the side, began to try to placate the white audience…many more of whom had stormed out of the hall in disgust. "Please, ladies and gentlemen," Garrison spoke out, "do not let the sentiments of this former slave cause you distress. He can hardly be expected to understand the differences between our need for an orderly society, where the separation of the races is in everyone's benefit, and the institution of slavery."

Garrison saw that some of the whites were mollified by his remarks and he continued. "We understand the great cause for which we fight. If, at times, we must deal with ingratitude, it is understandable, considering the state of ignorance in which the black race has been kept. Yet, we should not be discouraged as we lower our hand to assist those unfortunates that civilization has passed over."

Seeing that much of the white hostility incurred by Frederick Douglass had been dissipated, mostly because those offended by Douglass' remarks had left, Garrison introduced his next speaker, a rather tall and angular man who many would later say reminded them of Abraham Lincoln. Paschal Beverly Randolph, who often wore Lincoln's trademark stovepipe top hat, had a swarthy, olive complexion that identified him to many as a mulatto. Tonight Randolph was Garrison's secret weapon. A member of both the Liberty as well as Free Soil Parties, P.B. Randolph maintained a Dionysian hold over most women. He, too, was a grand master in a secret society. But rather than being committed to world domination his group was committed to overthrowing the Olympian reign of terror and re-initiating the world into the Dionysian rites of free love.

Before Garrison introduced P.B. Randolph, Ellen had been thinking, *What a terrible bore, this is…why did I let Wes talk me into coming here?* But as soon as Ellen saw him, listened to him, devoured him with her eyes, Ellen believed she was destined to make love to Paschal Beverly Randolph. Ellen hung on the mulatto's every word, but did not hear a thing. She was mesmerized by some mysterious force and remained that way until the end of the meeting.

The meeting continued. The speakers represented every aspect of abolitionist thought. They all agreed that the Fugitive Slave Law was a terrible thing, and that what was needed was more routes, more stations, more conductors and more financial support for the Underground Railroad.

This was the purpose for the meeting…the reason that the whites had attended the meeting. The whites wanted more people like Wes Parks and other prosperous coloreds in the Boston area to take up the cause by becoming active participants on the Underground Railroad. They wanted to establish more colored "stops" and "stations." Wes Parks volunteered to establish an Underground Railroad Station on his property, and also to shoulder some of the financial burden for maintaining the station, including providing transportation to the next station or stop. The white Bostonians all applauded him and the other blacks who committed themselves to the effort. The main reason that so many prominent white Bostonians had turned out for the meeting was to see for themselves that coloreds were participating in the effort to move these fugitive slaves along. Otherwise, they had no choice but to fully support the Fugitive Slave Law and return the black runaways to their masters. But now that they saw blacks like Wes Parks participating, they agreed to continue to provide substantial sums of money to the effort…money that was needed to purchase supplies for stationmasters and food and clothes for the passengers. When Garrison and his supporters were satisfied that the commitments they sought were in place, the meeting adjourned.

Wes Parks and Frederick Douglass closeted together in earnest conversation, carefully beyond earshot of Garrison or any of his informants. Dwight Ingraham sought out Charles Sumner, the Free Soil candidate for Massachusetts' seat in the United States Senate. Ingraham was writing an article for the *Atlantic Monthly* on the Free Soil Party's platform. They discussed how the Fugitive Slave Law was impacting Sumner's political aspirations and the future of the Free Soil Party. So while their husbands were occupied, Ellen and Ruby joined some of the other women who gathered about the fascinating and mysterious Paschal Beverly Randolph.

"Dr. Randolph," an elder Boston matron asked imperiously, "please tell us what type of medicine you practice." Randolph was just embarking on his career as a spy and intelligence agent. Later he was one of the only two men Abraham Lincoln trusted implicitly with the power of the Presidency. It was rumored that during the war, Lincoln and Randolph had exchanged identities on more than one occasion. The other man Lincoln twisted was General Ethan Allen Hitchcock. But for now, P.B. made his living off of women.

"Madam, I practice medicine where the complaint involves the affections," Randolph replied. "My patients are those who have resolved to cure their loveless, unhappy lives." His words electrified the prim and proper Boston matrons, who had been taught that a chaste religious woman could not enjoy the marital bliss associated with sexual pleasure. "I treat patients who are afflicted by passions that have long been unsatisfied," he continued. "I have found that where the nerves and the mind are in disarrangement with their sexual system, there is a need for the kind of intervention only I can provide."

"Dr. Randolph, how does your indulgence in free love assist the furtherance of spiritual enlightenment?" a stern-faced Boston matron asked.

"Without love, there is no spiritualism," Randolph replied.

"Without love, there is only materialism. But this world exists only because of the love that finds its truest and highest expression in humanity. And to understand spiritualism is to practice acts of love at the spiritual level."

"But how can we practice pure, spiritual love?" another matron asked.

"For some, the only way to learn how to love at the highest level is to practice love at the human level and try to raise it up," Randolph explained.

Some of the women were scandalized at what they considered public vulgarity. These left in a huff. However, Randolph's words gave others, including Ellen, a feeling of exhilaration, as if they had been liberated from some self-imposed obligation to get as little pleasure from life as possible. Ellen, however, was more than liberated; she fell in love. Ellen had known only her husband, Dwight, and until now she had never thought about sex in any other terms than as the process by which she had children. Now, since neither Ellen nor Dwight wanted additional children, there had been a minimal need to have sex. Randolph stirred in Ellen a different sensation, a sizzle racing through her body, like molten lava pulsing through her veins. Ellen was on fire. And she needed P.B. Randolph to quench the flame.

"Dr. Randolph," Ellen blurted out, "where is your practice located?"

Women had been infatuated with P.B. Randolph for as long as he could remember. Growing up a homeless orphan in New York City's Five Points slums, Randolph survived only with the help of women. Randolph took care of the old ones and made love to the young ones. Women who were sick or beaten or robbed or molested could depend upon him. Randolph loved women and took away their pain...not just the ordinary pains that masqueraded as life, but also the ultimate pain known by all women: the pain of rejection, the pain of being unwanted. *My dear*, Randolph thought to himself as he looked at Ellen's glowing face, *you have given these hens something to cluck about.* He knew that with that one honest, innocent question, Ellen had damaged not only her own reputation, but that of her husband's as well, in the eyes of these white matrons.

Ellen Ingraham was not unaware of how these custodians of Boston morality already felt about her. They knew she was not white. When she attended social functions to which Dwight had been invited, she was made to know that her presence was unwelcome. Ellen had been far too familiar with white people in public. They were offended by the way she took liberties after the exchange of pleasantries at some private affairs where she wasn't even welcome. This very evening, the Brahmin matrons would have expected Ellen to sit in the colored section, but instead she sat with Dwight in the white section. There was no doubt that Ellen sitting with the better class had egged that Frederick Douglass to say the vile things he did about the citizens of Boston. The city had every right to enact regulations to keep peace between the races. But Ellen was not thinking about the sensibilities of the Boston matrons when she asked P.B. Randolph that indiscreet question, though it might have been better if she had.

But Randolph was nothing if not gallant. He came to Ellen's aid. "I am so happy that my host, Mr. Garrison, asked one of you to remind me to announce that my practice is in upstate New York... though I am considering practicing here in Boston a couple of days a month." A murmur rose from the group of women. "And now, thank you, ladies, for your warm reception to your fair city. I hope to see all of you again. Now, I will say goodnight, ladies."

CHAPTER TWENTY-ONE

The next morning Freddie Douglass and Wes Parks discussed plans for the Underground Railroad station that Wes was putting on his property. They needed to decide where to hide the fugitives, how to construct secret entrances and exits, where to lay out the escape route away from the house, and most importantly, the location of the underground tunnel, or station, that Wes Parks committed to sponsor. That meant that he had to dig a tunnel that would not be visible at ground level. An underground tunnel gave fugitive slaves and the family assisting them some security. Some of the whites assisting fugitive slaves had underground tunnels, but most did not. The whites risked nothing; they were in no danger for assisting fugitive slaves...especially in Boston. The whites shared a common interest in getting rid of as many blacks as possible. A white could go into court and free any colored person accused of being a fugitive slave. But a black family assisting a slave to escape was a different matter. Coloreds whose home did not have an escape tunnel ran the serious risk of not only having the fugitive recaptured, but having their entire family, legally free or not, put back into slavery.

"I don't think you're going to have any problem, Wes," Freddie said. "You should be able to build your tunnel anywhere." Wes' property was situated on the north side of Beacon Hill and his many acres spilled down towards Roxbury. In the spring, Wes' land was suitable for cultivating the most delicious vegetables. His orchards of fruit and maple trees resembled a miniature forest. Ruby preserved apples, pears and peaches, which she distributed to many of Boston's black families all year around. But even with so much land under cultivation, Wes' property was large enough for the underground tunnel Freddie required.

"No problem digging it, just a problem keeping it a secret," Wes observed.

"You are right about that," Freddie agreed. "I'd suggest you have two. That way you…"

"Hold on there," Wes interrupted, "aren't you getting carried away? Digging one tunnel is going to be difficult enough. I know you don't think I'm going to dig two of them."

"I guess you're right," Freddie agreed.

How long do you think it should be?" Wes asked.

"It needs to be long enough to get your passengers away from the house and hidden until they can be on their way, that's all," Freddie replied. "Twenty, thirty yards at the most, ought to do it." Freddie and Wes continued surveying the property discussing whether to begin the tunnel from the apple cellar in the house or the barn in the back. But soon the conversation turned to Freddie's frustration with the whites. "These people up here say they want to help us, but they really don't," Freddie complained. "These whites up here just want to get rid of us."

Wes nodded his agreement.

"Colored folks can't even ride on a coach here in Boston," Frederick Douglass continued. "The only reason these people up here in the North are helping get slaves into Canada is because old David Walker really showed what hypocrites they are."

"And they killed him for it," Wes observed.

"But he really showed those Christians up. When did he write his book, almost thirty years ago? They still haven't got over it," Douglass laughed. "So now all these good Christian white folks are kindly helping as many blacks as they can get out of the country…like that American Colonization society sending blacks back to Africa. What do you think of that?"

"A lot of black people seem to want to go back," Wes observed. "What's the difference between sending them to Africa and taking them to Canada?"

"Now that's a good question, Wes!" Frederick Douglass said thoughtfully. "Too bad I don't have a good answer."

The two ex-slaves stared out over the land, each lost in his own thoughts. Wes was mentally estimating the materials he needed to build the tunnel. But Frederick Douglass brooded about vengeance.

"They act like they still own us," Freddie exploded.

"In a sense they do, Freddie," Wes replied with a shrug. "Isn't that why your line goes all the way to St. Catharine's in Canada? There is no life here in America for blacks other than one of servitude…either as a slave or as a debtor. And in many ways, it's hard to tell which is worse."

"Not even in Canada will blacks really be free," said a figure strolling toward them from the house. "Besides which, it is really cold in Canada."

"Hi, Frank," Wes said pleasantly. "Freddie, this is Frank Yerby. He's staying with us for awhile."

Wes was massively built, standing nearly six foot three inches and weighing two hundred and fifty pounds. Freddie lacked little in comparison, either in height or weight. Both men towered over Yerby. He and Douglass shook hands. "And why is that, Frank?" Wes asked.

"Because the whites, whether in the North or the South, whether in U.S.A. or Canada, all came for one thing," Yerby replied.

"And what's that?" Douglass asked impatiently.

"Land!" Yerby explained patiently. "Free land! Their religion; all their hopes and dreams and all their aspirations, goals and desires are wrapped up in controlling the land. And whites have no intention of sharing the land with anyone, let alone ex-slaves. The Northern whites just want to get rid of blacks…into Canada, back to Africa, anywhere. Just as long as they don't interfere with their plans to grab as much land as possible." Wesley Parks and Frederick Douglass thought about Yerby's remarks. Yerby continued.

"Thousands of Europeans are streaming across the Atlantic every month with but one purpose: to own land and get wealthy. Many of them will succeed; many more will fail; but all of them know that here in America the land is reserved exclusively for the white man. The only controversy is whether the white men with black slaves will be allowed to deprive white men without slaves access to all this free land."

Frederick Douglass manfully struggled to refute this arrogant stranger. "You apparently have never been a slave," Douglass began, trying to be as condescending as possible, the way William Lloyd Garrison behaved with him. "You have no way of knowing the level of cruelty and evil to which the slave masters descend," Douglass continued. "These Northern whites are different because of their religion. They are God-fearing people and for that reason they cannot treat us like animals and must defend black slaves against Southerners."

Yerby stared at Douglass with a look of pity. The great gulf in understanding made further comment futile. "Well, that is one way to look at it," Yerby replied diplomatically. "But, I fear there it must rest for the time being. Ruby asked me to tell Wes that Ellen is here and I am afraid that I have been remiss in delivering the message." But even before the men could return to the house, out came Ellen Ingraham to intercept them.

"Mr. Douglass, " Ellen said immediately, "I am so happy I found you."

"And why is that, Miss...?" Freddie asked, his face lighting up at the sight of the beautiful octoroon from Mississippi.

"I had hoped that you could put me in contact with Dr. Randolph," Ellen replied earnestly.

"Oh, I see," Freddie replied somewhat dejectedly, "I was hoping that I, myself, could be of some service to you."

"Oh, but you can," Ellen replied quickly. "You see, I wish to contact Dr. Randolph on a professional matter. He told me last night that he was planning to open an office here in Boston. I wanted to know how soon we might expect his Boston office to open."

"Dr. Randolph?" Freddie said in a tone that indicated to Ellen as well as Wes that Frederick Douglass was no great admirer of Paschal Beverly Randolph. But Freddie, despite his humble origins and previous status as a slave, could be a gentleman. Of course, much of Freddie's cultural pretension, as well as his anger at being segregated, was the result of his having a white father; being half-white was Freddie's greatest advantage...as well as his greatest burden. The problem was that Freddie didn't look half-white. He couldn't go around with a sign that said, HALF-WHITE NEGRO. However, he did always wear formal attire in public as a way of saying, I'm a half-white Negro. Freddie just never understood that to a white man a half-white Negro is still called a nigger.

Freddie believed Ellen Ingraham was the loveliest woman he had ever laid eyes on. He also believed, from what his acquaintances said and from what Freddie himself had observed, that P.B. Randolph was a first class charlatan. *Why not me?* Freddie asked himself. But even though Freddie had secret thoughts about Ellen, never would he reveal his secret thoughts nor would he disparage any other suitor— even if that suitor was someone like P.B. Randolph.

"Dr. Randolph?" Douglass repeated. "Are you referring to P.B. Randolph with whom I shared the podium at the Vigilance Committee Meeting, last night?"

"Yes, the same," Ellen replied, barely able to contain her excitement. "Do you know how to contact him in his New York office?"

"I believe he can be contacted in Stockbridge. That's in upstate New York, just south of Syracuse, in Madison County."

"Oh, thank you, Mr. Douglass," Ellen said gratefully and flew down the street before anyone in the Parks household realized she was gone. Ruby came out and stared after her friend in utter shock. "Well, I never…"she exclaimed. "What has gotten into Ellen and who is this Dr. Randolph she's talking about?"

"You know this doctor?" Wes asked.

"Yes…"

"Then tell us about him," Ruby demanded.

"Doctor!" Freddie scoffed, "P.B. Randolph's no doctor. The last time I heard, he was cutting hair and claiming to be able to communicate with the dead."

"What?" Ruby exclaimed.

"Yes," Freddie continued, "he is associated with those spiritualists. Some say he has been able to contact departed family members. Some say he is also associated with the growing free love movement in New York."

"Free love movement?" Ruby exclaimed. "What is that?"

"Women are beginning to believe that marriage is just another form of slavery," Yerby said. "They are concerned with women's rights, and free love is one of the ways they are protesting their frustration at being dominated by men. The spiritualist movement and the free love movement and the anti-slavery movement all overlap in certain women's circles."

"You don't think that Ellen…?" Ruby exclaimed. "You can't think…!"

"I don't know about your friend," Freddie said, "but I have heard that many white women are infatuated with Paschal Beverly Randolph."

"Ellen's not white!" Ruby said abruptly. Then after a short pause, Ruby looked over to Freddie. "Why does he call himself, doctor?" she asked.

"He sells these concoctions and love potions," Freddie replied. "Many of his customers, men as well as women, swear by them." Wes thought back to the days of his childhood in Da's Belly. His childhood friend, Kpadunu, belonged to the guild that knew the most about roots and herbs and their use in casting spells. Here they most certainly would be calling you a doctor as well, my friend, Wes thought to himself, a witch doctor!

Freddie did not stray far from the truth in his characterization of Paschal Beverly Randolph. Randolph saw himself as a champion of women's rights, and in his feminist pursuits Randolph preached the magic of eroticism. He believed that human beings could not experience joy or happiness in its truest or most genuine sense without having that exquisite experience of love…pure, strong, earnest, spontaneous and reciprocal. Randolph taught that true sexual love required a non-repressive society. "Love is a magnetic force," Randolph would say, "A person's will can be projected just as effectively through love as through hate. But love is a far better method of communication because it is so pleasurable when wills share the ecstasy of love. Hate needs fear to project the will, love needs nothing except will."

. . .

Ellen Ingraham lost no time making contact with P.B. Randolph. Without subtlety or guile, she sought out the man she believed could open up her soul and peer into its depths. Ellen wrote to Randolph, asking him when he planned to return to open his Boston office. "I wish to consult with you, immediately," she wrote. The days she spent waiting for his reply seemed like an eternity. She was distracted to the point of ignoring the simplest of her household duties. Dwight knew something was wrong; the children knew as well. And then after two weeks Ellen received a reply, she was disappointed.

"My dear lady," Randolph wrote, "although my circumstances will not permit me to return to Boston at this time, you are most welcome to come to Stockbridge for a consultation. Please inform me of the time of your arrival and I will make suitable accommodations." Even before she had finished reading his letter, Ellen knew what she would...what she must do.

"Oh, Abby," Ellen cried, "you've just gotta go with me. I can't go by myself. What would people say?"

"They'd say the same thing about you whether I went or not," Abby said. Ellen and Abby were sisters. Accidents of birth, paternity and race notwithstanding the bond between Ellen and Abby was there forever. They were sisters; they loved each other like sisters; they fought like sisters and they were the only family they had. Even if they weren't sisters by blood, they certainly were by marriage. I need Ellen far more than Ellen needs me, Abby reflected. If anything ever happens to Ellen, I will truly be alone. So Abby thought and she decided that she would go with Ellen. I'm probably more in need of a consultation with this Dr. Randolph than Ellen is, anyway, Abby thought to herself, sort of looking forward to her encounter with this fine love doctor.

"But Abby, two sisters traveling together will not cause any concern," Ellen was pleading, unaware that her sister had already decided to go with her.. "We can continue on to New York City, if you like...I will even pay for the trip. "

"Since when have I needed some uppity nigger to pay for me!" Abby reacted flashing a venomous look.

"Oh, Abby, I didn't mean..." Ellen said, wringing her hands together in despair. Her beautiful green eyes began to swell and a great flood of tears tumbled down her cheeks. "It's just that I had not realized how really lonely I have felt, and Dr. Randolph seems to know exactly what I feel and how to help me. Oh, Abby, what am I going to do if you don't help me?" With that the flood of tears became a torrent. The sobbing figure of Ellen Ingraham was enough to melt the hardest, most insensitive heart, and Abigail Collins was far from that.

It was just that Abby had been bitterly disappointed with her life, with her husband and mostly with herself. The circumstances of her birth had begun to weigh her down. At first, it was a lark for Abby to find out that her real father was not Barton Collins, but Wilks Thomas. Abby's mother, Suzanna Collins, certainly got even with Bart for having all those yard children, including Joe and Ellen Collins, by his mulatto slave, Candy. Abby loved Ellen and Joe Collins, and when she learned that they were not her brother and sister, it was like a message from heaven blessing her love. When she came to Boston with Joe, Abby had been the happiest woman alive.

Now, everything had changed. Her economic situation was precarious. No longer was she the daughter of one of the wealthiest planters in Mississippi. She no longer lived on a plantation where her every whim was satisfied. Now she was nobody, an outcast in white society and forever banned from returning home. She was the white woman who married a nigger. Joe chased women, gambled and spent their modest income on every vice imaginable. Abby really needed Ellen. Ellen was her only family and her closest friend. She loved Ellen. To Abby, Ellen meant home. Ellen made Abby feel like what it meant to live in Mississippi, to be white, to be somebody, to be one of God's chosen. Ellen *looked* white, had beauty, talent and strength of character in much greater measure than Abby. She was married to a successful white Bostonian who had given her two loving and beautiful children. Still, around Abby, Ellen knew her place. In all things, Ellen was deferential. Ellen kept Abby's world from completely collapsing in on her. Abby would never be completely mean to Ellen or be insensitive to her. Well-bred Southerners did not treat their "good niggers" that way.

"Oh, Ellen," Abby said, hugging Ellen as she convulsed in tears, "don't cry, honey, don't cry. Of course, I'll go with you to see Dr.

Whateverhisnameis."

"You will?" Ellen cried happily. "Oh, thank you, thank you ever so much. I knew I could depend on you. I love you so much...."

"Now, now, honey chile," Abby comforted her. "Don't I always look after you, don't I always take care of you? Dry those tears and let's start planning our trip."

Joe Collins had no objections to Abby leaving; as a matter of fact, it was the best news he had heard in weeks. However, Dwight Ingraham positively refused to allow his wife to leave without him. For several weeks, Ellen begged and pleaded to no avail. Abby's attempts to convince Dwight failed as well. Dwight believed a trip to New York to visit this "quack" was absolutely unnecessary and possibly dangerous. Dwight had made some private inquiries about Dr. Paschal Beverly Randolph and was not pleased by what he heard. Dwight was no prude; the fact that he had married a Negro and brought her to Boston, estranging himself from many of his family and friends, testified to his liberality. Yet, Randolph's reputation as a spiritualist and a libertine disturbed him. Dwight was not completely convinced that his wife's medical emergency was genuine and could hardly escape his Bostonian roots where the strict control over all women's behavior was taken as a husband's God-given responsibility. Besides, he had observed that this strange malady did not even manifest itself until after Ellen had met this svengali. But Ellen continued her pleadings.

"Dwight," she begged one evening, "I know that he can help me."

"But why can't you see one of the doctors here in Boston?" her husband reasoned. Dwight believed she was just trying to wear him down, but he would not give in. He believed...rather he *hoped* that his wife's problem, whatever it was, would soon pass.

"If you loved me, you would let me go," Ellen said in desperation.

"It's only been a couple of weeks since you were afraid to leave the house. You were afraid of slave catchers," he replied. "Now you want to go traipsing about the country unescorted because you've met some Voodoo witch doctor."

"Maybe that's why I've got to see him," Ellen replied, "because he does know magic and is the only one who can help me." It was the kind of argument that even better men than Dwight Ingraham failed to comprehend. But in the end Dwight Ingraham could not hold out against his wife; he loved her too much. She asked so little of him and gave him so much happiness that he could not claim he loved her and deny her this wish. When Dwight saw that he was only risking further deterioration in their relationship by his objection, he made travel arrangements for Ellen and Abby to journey to Stockbridge, New York, to consult with Dr. P.B. Randolph.

"Guess what!" Ellen cried bursting into Dwight's study. She had just returned from visiting Ruby.

"What?" he smiled. Their relationship had been great since his decision.

"Freddie Douglass is here now," Ellen told him. "Freddie and Wes are going up to Canada with their friend Frank Yerby. They'll escort Abby and me to New York. Wes will meet us in Stockbridge on his return trip and escort us back to Boston."

"Sounds great," Dwight said trying to sound enthusiastic. Freddie had returned to Boston to inspect Wes' Underground Railroad station.

"Freddie's returning to New York soon," Ellen continued. "He and Wes are taking a fugitive slave to Canada. Freddie is showing Wes the Underground Railroad route from Boston to Canada. And Frank Yerby has decided to tag along."

It was a fair day when the strange party arrived at Boston's railroad terminal: a white woman, a colored woman who passed for white, a fugitive slave, a former fugitive slave, an African and an alien all boarding the three car B&W passenger railroad train for Worcester, Massachusetts with connections, regular and underground, to St. Catharines, Ontario, Canada. Ellen and Abby boarded. The conductor, a middle-aged professional railroad man, was boarding the passengers. He looked at Abby and Ellen, and beamed, "Good day, ladies! Traveling to Worcester with us today?"

"We're going to New York, "Abby replied.

"Well, then, you're planning to catch the Western in Worcester," the conductor replied. "It takes you right into Albany, New York. Your fare will be $1.67 for each of you ladies."

"I hope you will help us to our next train," Abby said…exuding Southern charm. The conductor was tickled. But Abby always acted this way around Ellen. How else could Abby keep the men from staring at Ellen…overlooking her completely. Abby knew how to keep the train conductor's attention on her.

"You can depend on me, madam, I'll make certain to see you safe on board. Now," he said, glancing at the others, "do any of these colored boys here belong to you? Because we don't allow no coloreds to ride in the coach with the white folks. But I can make special allowances if any of these belong to you."

The conductor was having his own private joke. He recognized Freddie from a previous trip. Douglass had refused to ride in the baggage car with the other blacks. And the conductor, eyeing his frock coat, white shirt and silk cravat, was deliberately baiting him. As a matter of fact, only Shields Green, the fugitive that Freddie and Wes were escorting to Canada, had the look of a slave.

Ellen tried her best to put on a brave front, but passing for white had always been difficult for her. Dwight had always been there to take care of things. Now she realized that this was her first time away from his protection. She began to experience a sickening fear. It started in the pit of her stomach, began to crawl up into her breast, making her heart pump just a little faster and her breathing just a little more difficult, until she desperately needed more air.

FRANK YERBY:

"This one here," Abby said smoothly, indicating Shields Green, "…this one is with us." And turning to the fugitive slave, "Now Shields, you take care of our trunks, you heah"…emphasizing her Southern drawl.

"Yes'm," Green replied, keeping his head low and his eyes glued to the platform.

"Well," the conductor said, "for you ladies he can ride for half fare…but he's gotta go up front and ride in the baggage car." The conductor motioned Green to the next car. And with that Shields Green hefted Abby and Ellen's luggage and lurched forward.

After seating Abby and Ellen in the Overton passenger carriage, the conductor returned to the platform and seated the remaining white passengers, including three shady-looking characters whose evil glares and sardonic grins immediately suggested that they might be slave catchers. And like the bloodhounds used in their fiendish trade, the three slave catchers had caught the scent of fear, not from any of the four black men, but from the white one, Ellen, herself.

"That'n's an octoroon as sure as I'm born," whispered the one whose grimy fingers most matched the blackness of his jagged teeth. "Some rich feller's yard chile."

"And I'll be damned to glory," one of his accomplices murmured in reply, "if that nigger with them ain't a runaway, too." The other two nodded in agreement.

"Yes siree," the third one said, "we done got us some runaways for sure. And even if they not, that little white abolitionist lady ain't gonna do nothing about us cashin' in."

"After riding this train car for the past month with nuthin' to show for it 'cept a sore behind," the leader said, "this here trip is going to pay off, right fine. Yes indeed, that one there is gonna fetch us a handsome price."

"Oh, Abby, do you see them?" Ellen whispered hoarsely as she peeked at the three slave catchers leering at her.

"Don't pay any attention to them." Abby replied. "They just poor white trash." But both of them knew better. Abby and Ellen both grew up on slave plantations in Mississippi. They immediately recognized the "poor white trash" on the train as slave catchers. And now Abby and Ellen found themselves in a grave situation.

Why did I want to see this Dr. Randolph? Ellen asked herself. The B&W railroad train had been meandering over the New England countryside for the past two hours. Why had she been so taken with this colored man? Ellen allowed her thoughts to distract her from the real danger posed by the three slave catchers.

And as all too often happens, Ellen had a clear realization of what she had done. What a fool I've been, she berated herself. But it was too late for that. In times of crisis, some superior individuals are able to pull themselves back from their own peculiar madness. Ellen tried to do just that. I've jeopardized not only my marriage, she thought to herself, but possibly my own life and that of Abby's, as well. And these others…especially Shields Green, who could be returned to slavery even before he had ever tasted freedom. *I may not have made the smartest move*, she thought to herself, *but at least I can try not to make the situation worse. Wes will take care of us; I just need to be patient.*

CHAPTER TWENTY-TWO

Now madam," the grinning B&W conductor said, addressing Abby, "the Western arrives on that track over there, later this afternoon, and it leaves from there tomorrow morning at 8:00 a.m. sharp. So you tell your boy, here, to get your bags down on the platform in plenty of time."

During the nearly four hours that it took the B&W to travel thirty-five miles from Boston to Worcester, Ellen and Abby bumped, rattled and twisted so badly that both of them were heartily thankful for the stopover. They could still feel the imprint of the B&W's wooden seats, even as they stood there on the platform. Ellen felt the eyes of the three slave catchers watching and mocking her. She was caught and she knew it. Abby knew it too, but Abby knew there would be no problem. Even if Ellen were arrested, Abby could get her released straight away. After all, Abby was white. The three bounty hunters continued to lurk about the B&W platform while Abby and Ellen continued to chat with the conductor, watching, waiting but trying to appear inconspicuous.

"That little ride was nothing," the conductor said responding to Abby's complaint's about her sore "rumble seat," "tomorrow you're traveling over a hundred miles and it's gonna take more than eight hours."

"Then we had better try to get some rest," Ellen interjected. *She is putting on a brave front,* Abby noted. *I know I'd be scared out of my mind by now.*

Actually Ellen wanted to do nothing more than get back on the B&W and return with it to Boston. But her body ached so from the Boston train ride, that even the thought of getting back on that railroad car made Ellen cringe in pain. It was not only that. What little pride Ellen had remaining would not allow her to abandon the trip, even if this entire idea was stupid and that she had been a silly fool for proposing it. *How can I look so white and behave just like a little colored pickaninny?* she asked herself. So rather than following her instincts, Ellen decided to see her ill-fated journey through to the end. Turning to Abby, she said, "Possibly this gentleman can direct us to someplace where we can rest for the evening. Lord, I'm tired."

"I agree, honey, I'm tired and hungry, too," Abby replied.

"You two ladies can go down the street there," the conductor said pointing across the tracks in the direction of Worcester's main street, "Mrs. Sumner has a nice comfortable boarding house. And she has a right decent cook, so I've been told. All the young ladies stay there on their way to New York. It's not far from here. Anyone can direct you. Your boy here can stay in her barn out back." With that, Shields picked up their bags and followed Abby and Ellen up the street to Mrs. Sumner's Boardinghouse.

Watching the two retreating figures, one of the slave catchers said, "Let's get 'em now."

"Now, boy," the leader of the group said, "don't you go gettin' ahead of yourself, you heah?"

"What you mean, Claude?"

"We got the law on our side. All we've got to do is get to New York. We won't have no problem getting warrants. Besides, if we grab them now, how we gonna get them back down South?"

The one who made the suggestion, named Jake, had a sheepish look on his face. "I guess I don't know, Claude," he admitted.

"That's right. Now you let me do the thinkin'. Once we get to Albany and get our warrant, we can take a steamer pretty near all the way down to Charleston with nobody sayin' nothing to us."

"That's a good idea," the other slave catcher, Jake's brother, said.

"Of course there is one problem," Claude mused.

"What's that?"

"Can't have no white woman nay sayin' us before the judge," Claude observed.

"Then I guess we just going to have to get rid of that little white abolitionist," Jake's brother said. "By the sound of her voice she a Southerner who's turned on her own people. I say whatever happens to her, she deserves."

The three all nodded their heads in agreement. Claude fingered his Bowie knife with a loving caress. He had kept it with him since his days in the Mexican War; it had defended him and given him lots of pleasure. An evil smile played at the corner of his mouth, around which bristled his tobacco-stained whiskers. *Soon, very soon,* the slave catcher thought to himself.

Freddie had spotted the three slave catchers even before they spotted Ellen. Spotting his enemies came second nature to Freddie Douglass. He knew his enemies by their smell…a rat-like odor, a cross between a skunk and an outhouse . He knew them by their dirty fingernails and rotten teeth. He knew them by the tobacco running down their scraggily faces. Not only could Freddie always spot slave catchers, but he also always understood how dangerous they actually were.

"Do you think they'll do anything at that boardinghouse?" Wes asked Freddie.

"I don't think so…but I don't think we should take any chances," Freddie counseled. "Some one should keep watch."

"I think someone should get in touch with Shields," Yerby said. "Shields can tell the ladies that we're watching over them."

"Do we tell them about the slave catchers?" Wes asked.

"If we tell them," Freddie said, "they might give us away. Our only real advantage is surprise. And that's no real advantage since they have the law. If they bring her before the judge and accuse her of being a fugitive, Ellen will not be able to testify on her own behalf. Only a white person can testify in court! So I don't think we should tell them. We just need to protect them."

"It's all well and good to talk about *protecting* them," Wes frowned, "but did you see their weapons? They've got six-shot revolvers, rifles, Bowie knives and whips. Not one of us has a weapon of any kind. Being unarmed makes protecting damsels in distress very difficult."

"Even if we had weapons," Yerby piped in, "I'm not certain that we could beat these killers." Yerby had not gotten over his travels in Mississippi; nor had he erased his memories of Pedro and Bessie hanging from a tree, victims of an ill-planned and ill-fated revolt. "I think in the long run," he continued, "we need a good plan. That'll be better than trying to shoot it out with these "good ole boys.""

"You're right, of course," Wes agreed, "but I still think we need weapons. "In this country a man's not a man unless he can protect himself and his women. There is also the fear factor. These boys don't fear nothing but the whip, the knife and the gun. They're not afraid of smart niggers, they're afraid of smart niggers who will fight." After pausing, Wes continued, "But of course, if it ever comes to using them, I agree, we'd be lost. Them boys have probably killed more men before they were grown old enough to shave then all of us put together." Wes' last remark certainly was not true. The Dahomean warrior, Nyasanu Hwesu Kesu, son of Gbenu, now known as Wesley Parks, had presented the heads of many enemies to his king. If ever Wes got his hands on any weapons, it was certain he would make good use of them.

"All this is well and good," Yerby announced, "but shouldn't somebody get down to Shields and let him know what's going on?"

"I'll watch over them for sure," Shields vowed to Freddie after being told about the slave catchers. And so the New England night passed in relative security. The four black men took turns watching the slave catchers as well as Mrs. Sumner's boardinghouse.

The next morning, Abby and Ellen arrived at the Western Railroad platform, escorted by Shields who carried their luggage. The two sisters were happy that they had taken the conductor's advice and stayed at Mrs. Sumner's boardinghouse. The food was appetizing and the beds were comfortable. By 8:15 a.m., Abby and Ellen were once again chugging through the Massachusetts landscape towards Albany, New York. In the baggage car, Freddie began laying out his plan. "As soon as we get to Albany, we need to get them away from the train station as quickly as possible," he told Wes, Frank and Shields. "I have friends in Albany who operate an Underground Railroad station. Shields, you'll continue to act as Ellen and Abby's servant, and you'll follow me there."

Shields Green had run away from South Carolina over three weeks ago. His master had trusted Green to go into Charleston and sell his services as a laborer. Green had been holding back some of his wages for over two years. When he thought he had enough money, Shields caught a ship out of Charleston bound for New Bedford. From New Bedford, he booked passage on the Underground Railroad. Sad of eye and calm in demeanor, Green did everything he was told. Everyone with whom he came in contact marveled at his patience. Shields seemed a perfect slave, one who readily obeyed commands without question and without delay. However, Shields Green was in total control of himself. In his heart Shields Green had never been a slave; he had always been a free man. Freddie liked Shields. He liked his patience; he liked his steadfastness. *An army with men such as he,* Freddie thought to himself, *would be invincible.* Freddie said aloud, "When we get to Albany, we must move quickly. I hope that you gentlemen understand that I am motivated only by the need to get Abby and Ellen to safety. They are both in extreme danger...as are we all."

"So this is what it's like being a conductor on the Underground Railroad," Wes said in a half joking manner. "I can't imagine how someone could go through this on a daily basis."

Freddie gave Wes a long look. "If someone wasn't going through this very thing every day, far fewer black people would be able to escape from slavery," he said with a grimace. "So from now until we reach Canada, which is the only really safe place for any colored person these days, I must insist that you trust me and do exactly as I say."

"Absolutely," Yerby replied.

"Yessir," Green joined in.

"Yes, I will follow your directions," Wes said, though less enthusiastically. He still was concerned about their lack of weapons. Wes did not like to think about the likelihood of their surviving any confrontation with those slave catchers, without weapons and without any legal protections.

"Rensselaer is a town that lies directly across the Hudson River from Albany," Freddie said. "That's where the free coloreds mostly live, since the only coloreds allowed in Albany proper are servants or slaves living with white families. The first place those slave catchers gonna go looking for Ellen and Abby as soon as they get their warrant is in Rensselaer."

"Why will they think Ellen and Abby would go over there?" Wes asked.

"Because that's where Stephen Meyers runs his Underground Railroad station," Freddie replied. "Slave catchers always think that a fugitive slave will seek help among his own people first. So here's the plan. At Albany, I'll get off first. Shields, you take Ms. Abby's and Ms. Ellen's bags and make certain that they follow me, no matter what. You understand?"

"Yessir," Green replied.

Then turning to Wes and Frank, Freddie said, ""I want you two fellas to take the ferry across the river to Rensselaer. Over past the docks, you should find Pete's Porterhouse. Anyone should be able to tell you where it is. You should be safe enough there until I come for you. Okay?"

Wes and Frank nodded their agreement.

"When I'm certain the ladies are safe, I'll meet you at Pete's. Then we'll go over to Stephen Meyers' place. He'll get us out of there with no problem."

"We should be able to find Pete's alright," Wes agreed. "Do they serve food? "

"Oh, yes," Freddie chuckled. "You'll be able to eat all you want over at Pete's."

Each of them fell back into his own thoughts about how this adventure would end. Not one of them doubted that they could protect the women whose fate had been put in their charge. Frederick Douglass had conducted many fugitive slaves to safety; he was certain of success.

When the Western Railroad reached Albany, it was early evening and the setting sun began to cast its long shadows over the bustling capital of New York. The passengers disembarked from the train, each bustling off to reach their destinations before nightfall draped its gloom over the city. Shields unloaded the ladies' bags and directed both of them to follow the retreating figure of Frederick Douglass. For his part, looking neither to the right nor left, Freddie marched directly towards Albany's downtown area.

The three slave catchers gathered below the railroad platform. From their vantage point they had a clear view of the two women and their black boy. They watched as Abby and Ellen alighted from the train, and Claude gave Jake his final instructions. "Don't crowd them. Just follow them so we know where we can get a hold of them when we need to. I'm gonna get the warrants and some help from the police. When you find out where they're at, Jake, you meet me down across the river where them free niggers live. Right across the river there! You hear me, boy?"

"Yes, Claude," Jake replied.

"All right, you two get on now…and don't lose them, you heah?"

Claude watched as Jake and his brother tagged after Abby, Ellen and Shields Green. "Guess I'm gonna have to disturb the old fugitive slave commissioner this evening," he thought to himself. "But I'm certain he won't mind a bit, seeing as how I'm bringing him a tidy little sum just for signing some papers." And off Claude went.

A block past the train station, Freddie allowed Shields and the women to catch up to him. As they approached, Freddie whispered to the group, "Follow me! I'm gonna lead you up the street to a livery stable." All three of them nodded in agreement.

Any attentive passerby walking the Albany streets on this particular evening might have noticed this strange parade. First came a distinguished Negro strolling up the main street, smartly dressed in his cutaway coat, white shirt and cravat, behaving as if he were a person of means and importance. On a couple of occasions, the Negro gave a silent greeting to white passersby, each of whom returned a sign of recognition. Once the Negro paused to shake hands with another well-dressed gentleman. After the Negro and the man exchanged a few brief words, the gentleman shot the briefest glance in the direction of Abby and Ellen. Then he hurriedly changed directions and headed back from where he had come. Several paces behind the Negro trudged two white women, with their man carrying their bags. The women gave the impression that they were bound for the nearest boarding house. Behind them, keeping to the shadows at a discreet distance, crept two seedily dressed white men. Armed to the teeth, the men stalked their prey with the instincts of seasoned hunters. Following them, if only with their eyes, from the windows of dozens of vantage points, were white citizens concerned with keeping Albany free of fugitive slaves…and of slave catchers.

Not more than one and a half blocks from the railroad terminal, Freddie walked into a livery stable. As soon as Abby and Ellen followed him through the entrance, the doors of the livery stable were quickly shut and bolted so that when Jake and his brother attempted to enter they could not. Jake banged on the door. No answer. He banged again and continued to bang until he tired of slamming his fist against the door.

"You'd better get back across the river and meet Claude," Jake said to his brother. "Tell him where I am." Then Jake took up a spot where he could observe all the comings and goings at the livery stable while he awaited Claude.

Inside the livery stable, Freddie went up to the two women. "I am so happy you are safe, "he said. "I was quite worried. But you both behaved wonderfully. And now, let's get you out of here."

"Where are we?" Abby asked.

"This livery stable belongs to friends who will assist you to safety," Freddie replied. "This gentleman," indicating a black coachman, "will take you there now."

The liveryman directed the women through a tunnel that connected the livery stable to another one directly across an open paddock area between the two buildings. Both of the stables, as well as the exercise yard in between, belonged to the Mott sisters. They earned a considerable income providing transportation for the many visitors to New York's state capital. The Mott sisters also operated an Underground Railroad station. Inside the second stable Abby and Ellen were assisted into a handsome carriage hitched to a team of beautiful chestnut brown horses. Shields wanted to accompany the women, but neither the liveryman nor Freddie would permit him to do so. "They've gotten hundreds of runaways out of Albany," Freddie told Shields. "They know what they're doing." The liveryman loaded the women's bags and then took off toward the outskirts of the city. A mile or so from the main section of town, he turned into a long entrance. A high wall guarded the path and a great arched stone gateway led to the Mott sisters' spacious English-styled manor house. As long-time members of the Albany abolitionist society and operators of an Underground Railroad station, the Mott sisters had assisted hundreds of fugitive slaves each month. But that evening they made certain that Abby and Ellen were well fed while they chatted about the activities of the abolitionist groups around Albany. Then Abby and Ellen were each escorted to their bedrooms where they slept safely and securely. The next morning, the Mott sisters hugged Abby and Ellen as though they were their own dear relatives and sent them on their way. And as the sun's morning rays began streaking across an azure sky, Abby and Ellen found themselves in a well-appointed coach, speeding toward Syracuse along a secret road known to but a few... or so it was thought. And once they were on the road trailing away from Albany, the two women began to feel safe and secure...happy that their brief adventure with the slave catchers would soon be over.

. . .

Freddie didn't think it was wise for Ellen or Abby to continue to Stockbridge. "Them slave catchers are certain to get warrants that can be served anywhere in New York...or in the United States for that matter," he told them. "My friends will take you to Syracuse where the Reverend May will see you safely to his home. I will meet you there and we will return to Boston." Only the better-educated, better-dressed and better-connected Negroes such as a Freddie or a P.B. Randolph were ever allowed into Albany proper and only during the day. Even the acceptable free Negroes were required to be out of Albany by curfew. The Albany highlands, with its rolling hills and

FRANK YERBY:

scenic vistas, was restricted to whites only. So, after escorting Abby and Ellen to the safety of the Underground Railroad station, Freddie and Shields retraced their steps across the railroad tracks and down to the Albany Basin, where they took a ferry across the Hudson River to Rensselaer. Upon reaching the other side, Freddie quickly led the way to Pete's Porterhouse where they found Wes and Frank waiting for them.

A century earlier, Rensselaer's shanties and cabins had served as slave quarters. Now the same shanties and cabins had served as housing for the free Negroes, as well as the many of the newly arriving Irish immigrants. Tensions between these two racial groups were an ongoing problem. Both competed for the same low paying day jobs that for generations had belonged to Negroes. Now few if any of the free black laborers were fortunate enough to get work. But everyday they had to pay the fare across the Hudson just to look for work. And if no work was found, they had to pay to take the ferry back to Rensselaer. Irish immigrants, on the other hand, found permanent employment doing the jobs that once belonged to Negroes. Some of them even moved across the river and lived in Albany permanently. No Negro day laborer got a permanent position in Albany unless it was as a house servant. But the final insult was that Albany even began to hire Irish immigrants as policemen. The Irish cops lost no time cooperating with the slave catchers.

Jake and his brother found Claude at one of Rensselaer's waterfront bars. "I've got the warrants," Claude announced to Jake. "Them niggers what was on the railroad is over here right now." "What about the women?" Claude asked.

"Well, I don't rightly know," Jake drawled out, hesitantly. "They sorta disappeared in the livery stable."

"Well, that's all right," Claude replied. The glimmer in his eye told Jake that Claude had put one over on somebody. "The Albany police...."

"Yeah, where are the police?" Jake's brother blurted out. "I thought that they were gonna be in on the pickup."

"No, no," said Claude, "the Albany police want to stay away from this one. Besides, they have no authority over here in Rensselaer…and we don't need them."

"Don't need them?" Jake's brother repeated. "Why don't we need them?"

"Because they told me how the abolitionists get them slaves outta Albany." Claude replied proudly. "There's a road out of Albany over to Syracuse that all them abolitionists take. If we're there about dawn, we should catch them in a carriage with a nigger coachman. The police sergeant who gave me the information said we shouldn't have any problem getting them on a downstream steamer because there's a river landing just north of Albany that we can use.

"But we can't have that white woman get them released as soon as they're arrested," Jake complained.

"Don't worry," Claude replied. "With these warrants, the law's on our side and I'm only taking two of them back down to Charleston. That'll give us plenty of time with that Southern abolitionist lady."

"What about those other niggers who've been watching us?" Jake asked.

"They don't got no idea what we up to. They probably think we just a bunch of dumb crackers. But we gonna fool them boys, all right."

Jake slapped Claude on the back. "That's why I always say, 'Ole Claude is one of the smartest fellas I know'."

The next morning, in time to greet the new day, the three wily slave catchers chose a remote spot not far from the Motts' estate on the "secret" road that led to Syracuse. There they waited until a handsome coach driven by a dark-skinned Negro appeared. The three slave catchers pulled the coach over. The Negro coachman protested, "I am sorry, but you gentlemens has the wrong party. I'se Sam, Miss

Motts driver, and I'se taking these here ladies to Syracuse."

"Well, Sam, you just turn this here rig around and head for the closest landing going south before I take this whip to your black hide," Claude barked out. And then addressing Abby and Ellen, Claude said, "You nigger wenches stay where you are and there won't be no trouble."

"I ain't no nigger! I'm white." Abby screamed at the slave catchers.

"Effen you ain't no nigger," Jake asked, "How comes you'all been given us such a merry chase all over the lord's creation?"

"Because you were chasing us," Abby said.

"Well, we chasing you because you're runaway niggers, and we got the papers to prove it," Jake's brother declared. "And now we gonna take you back home and git our reward."

Claude and his men knew they would get no reward other than a beating if they tried to sell Abby down South; she was white. Plantation masters resented mistakes like that. If Claude and Jake had kidnapped a white woman, even an abolitionist white woman, the lords of the lash would make them pay dearly. They were very particular about those things. They could not take the white one with them.

"How soon will that next southbound steamer get to the landing, nigger?" Claude asked Sam.

"It comes along about 10:00 in the morning," Sam replied.

"And how long is it going to take to git to that landing?"

"It not far from here," Sam explained, "it's just around the next bend."

"Well, that's it, then," Claude announced. "We have plenty of time. It's only about 7:00 a.m."

The slave catchers pulled the coach off the road into a secluded gully where they tied Sam to a tree. Each of them took turns in the coach with Abby…forcing Ellen to watch. Once, when Jake's brother made a menacing move towards Ellen, Claude said, "You know we can't do anything to her right now. Let's get her back to her people first…and git our money." So Jake's brother was forced to turn his attentions to Abby once again…although she had long since passed out from the brutality of their repeated sexual assaults.

Sometime later, Claude asked the two brothers, "Are you boys about through with her?" Nodding, they prepared to leave the coach to Claude. "You know I can't cut her in here," Claude told them impatiently. "Tie her up and take her down over there by those rocks." And there in the dirt and grime, Claude performed gruesome ritual murder upon the broken and abused body of Abigail Collins as Ellen sat motionless, frozen into a catatonic state of sheer horror. Afterward Claude put Sam in the coach and said, "Now get us down to that river landing before I lay your black nigger hide wide open with this whip."

"Yessir," Sam replied as he turned the mules pulling the coach back up onto the road and down toward the river landing.

· · ·

In the meantime, since all men stand defenseless before the mocking contempt of fate, Freddie believed Abby and Ellen were safely on their way to Syracuse. Freddie decided to have Stephen Meyers drive them to the ferry landing a couple of miles above Albany. There they could catch a westbound steamer to Syracuse, which would get them to Syracuse long before Abby and Ellen arrived. They would be there to welcome the women. Meyers took them to the very landing where the slave catchers held their victims.

As Freddie and Wes, Shields and Frank approached the landing, Freddie immediately recognized the Mott family coach. Often when Syracuse's abolitionist society failed to provide transportation for fugitives arriving from Albany, Sam would bring fugitives from Albany not just to Syracuse but all the way to Douglass' home in Rochester.

The distinctive red patch on the side of the coach told all associated with the Underground Railroad that the occupants were fugitives and in need of assistance.

"What's that coach doing here?" Freddie wondered. *Possibly the women decided to take the steamer to Syracuse,* he thought. *If they did, it was a damned stupid decision. Those slave catchers have got their warrant from Albany by now. What is Sam thinking about? He should know better.* Freddie was getting worked up and apprehensive. He would never forgive himself if anything happened to those ladies.

Wes spotted Ellen and Sam, shackled together with leg irons and manacled at the wrists. Sam stood bent over and downcast, but Ellen, with a crazed, wild look on her face, stood rigidly erect, like a marble statue, giving some grace to the otherwise drab steamer platform.

"They've got Ellen chained to another black man," Parks said, "I don't see Abby."

"What's the plan now?" Wes Parks glared, as Douglass went deadly pale. He couldn't move; he couldn't think clearly; his eyes were riveted on Ellen. He had never lost a passenger before. This was a first. Like so many others who successfully face dangers, Frederick Douglass was unprepared to handle this turnabout.

"Do you want that I should mosey on down to where they are?" Shields asked.

"I, for one," Yerby stated emphatically, "think we need a plan before we do anything."

"The plan is to try to get as close as possible to them," Douglass said, trying to pull himself together, "and outmuscle them. Maybe we can throw them in the river before they realize what's happening."

"We need weapons," Wes said matter of factly.

"No time for that now," Douglass said, pulling himself together. Turning to Shields Green, he said, "All right, you try to get down there without them noticing you. Get as close as you can to the one over by Ellen and Sam." And then to Wes, "You take that one, and

I'll take the other. Don't bother with their guns, just pitch them in the river so that we can get the women and get outa here."

Whether Wes Parks had a secret call to his Tau Vudun for protection, or Yerby's belief in the guilt of the victim had a corollary that rewarded bold deeds, is not certain. Just let it be said that the Negroes were able to sneak down to the landing and surprise the three slave catchers. Shields approached Jake who had been guarding Ellen and Sam. Shields Green was over six feet tall, as were both Freddie Douglass and Wes Parks. His servant's garb and his shuffling gait made Shields appear smaller and less powerful than he actually was. Before Jake realized what was happening, Shields caught Jake full on the chin with a powerful blow. He was unconscious before he hit the wooden landing. Lifting him bodily into the air, Shields tossed Jake into the Hudson.

"What the heck!" Claude shouted, as he and Jake's brother reached for their revolvers. But Wes and Freddie were on them immediately. The fury pent up in Freddie drove him through to Jake's brother before he could fire a shot, and grabbing him by the throat, he nearly squeezed the life out of him. Wes, who had not forgotten how to disarm an opponent, easily overpowered Claude. Wes was even successful in taking Claude's revolver before pitching him into the Hudson River. Freddie threw Jake's brother into the river. He fell awkwardly against a river piling, causing his spine to twist and pinching a nerve. The pinched nerve was not serious. With prompt attention and rest, he could have recovered the full use of his legs within a couple of days. But the need for his legs was more immediate, since the Hudson River's strong, swift current kept pulling him underwater. The pinched nerve kept him from using his legs and kicking up to the surface. Jake's brother remained underwater until he drowned. His body floated nearly ten miles downstream before it was discovered.

They took Ellen back to the Mott estate. Ellen's recovery took a long time. The shock, the grief, the guilt over Abby's rape and murder thoroughly traumatized Ellen, leaving her with only minimal control over her body and mind. Only after several months could Ellen walk even a few steps without assistance. Even after her physical recovery began, Ellen continued to fall into states of depression and disorientation. The doctors advised Dwight that Ellen's condition could worsen if he attempted to take her back to Boston, so Dwight and the children came to Albany to visit her. At first she refused to see them. But gradually, she permitted them short visits that became awkward and difficult. Sometimes Ellen did not even recognize them…or at least so she would pretend. Gradually, Dwight realized that there was nothing he could do for his wife, and his visits became less frequent until he stopped coming altogether. Under the gentle and loving care of the Mott sisters, Ellen's recovery took over a year. Even then it was another six months before she could take complete responsibility for herself.

Abby's body was found in the bushes a half-mile off the road. They brought Abby back to Albany, and Joe Collins came with their daughter, Louise, to claim his wife's body. From that time on, Louise's hatred for anything colored was surpassed only by her absolute hatred for Ellen Ingraham. Ellen had taken her mother away. "That woman caused my mother's death," Louise would say. "Instead of being home with me, my mother was out helping this blubber-lipped, burr-headed nigger, and she got murdered for it."

That was the story Louise told whenever she was asked about her mother's death. More than one listener concluded from Louise's story that fugitive slaves had killed Abigail Collins. The slave catchers, Claude and Jake survived escaping down to Charleston, South Carolina. Shields Green took his sorrow onto the Underground Railroad and all the way to St. Catharines in Ontario, Canada. After her slow recovery and return to Boston, Ellen forsook her family and also migrated to St. Catharines in search of she knew not what.

CHAPTER TWENTY-THREE

*W*hen a civilization becomes so at odds with the very reason for its existence and the barbarian howls at the gates, often there appears as if by divine inspiration a warrior who battles with a single-minded purpose in defense of the civilization. Such a warrior was General Ethan Allen Hitchcock. However, General Hitchcock carried within himself what could truly be called the "victim's guilt." He was responsible for the deaths of thousands; when he looked into the mirror he saw a murderer. Ethan Allen Hitchcock had persuaded General Zachary Taylor, head of the American army, that the United States must attack Mexico.

"You have to do it," Hitchcock told Taylor, "otherwise Quitman will take California and bring it into the union as a slave state."

"Quitman!" Taylor shouted. "Always Quitman. There's no way out of this?"

"Sir, it is simple. California is closer to Houston, Texas, than it is to Washington, D.C. Neither we, nor the president, have any choice, if California is to be a free state."

"Mr. President," Zachary Taylor had told President Polk, "put any responsibility for failure squarely on my shoulders." Polk realized he had no choice. He left the Mexican War to Zachary Taylor. Taylor neither asked for nor received any direct presidential orders regarding the Mexican War. The United States attacked Mexico, and paying a ghastly toll in human pain, suffering and blood, won the war. Taylor and Hitchcock vowed to bottle Quitman up in his slaveholding South.

When Zachary Taylor cashed in his popularity as a war hero to become elected the twelfth President of the United States, Hitchcock was confident that he could redeem himself for having initiated such a terrible war. Taylor's term started well enough. They achieved their goal of admitting California as a free state. But then disaster struck when they decided to go after John Quitman.

Hitchcock brooded over it. John Quitman had outsmarted him at every turn. It was absolutely unbelievable how Quitman had gotten his head out of the noose that they created. That damned Mexican War, Hitchcock thought to himself, we're still paying…and now Zach's gone. I knew it! I knew it was going to happen…and there was nothing I could do to stop it, Hitchcock brooded. And he knew that Quitman was behind Zach's death. I should have anticipated it, he would say to himself. After all John Quitman was Supreme Sovereign Grand Inspector General of Scottish Rite Freemasonry and Zachary Taylor was a Mason.

It all happened so quickly. In February, 1850, Zach flew off the handle and told a delegation of Southern congressmen and senators that he would hang any secessionist daring to lead any state out of the union. In June, Quitman retaliated by convening his Nashville Secessionist Convention. Nine days later, Zachary Taylor directed a federal grand jury to indict John Quitman for his role in Narciso Lopez's invasion of Cuba. Then on July 4, 1850, Zach took ill. He died three days later, retching up a mysterious black slime. And so, Hitchcock knew, Quitman would be unstoppable. It was Quitman in Texas, Quitman in Mexico, Quitman in Cuba. Quitman had just about ended Hitchcock's career in San Francisco when Hitchcock had confiscated the ships bound for the *planned invasion of the Mexican State of Sonora by Quitman's Knights of the Golden Circle. When Jefferson Davis, Secretary of War and Hitchcock's superior, learned that Hitchcock had disrupted the Sonora invasion, he had him transferred to an isolated post in Pennsylvania. His absence had not been missed.*

. . .

It had been confusing to Ellen. They were heading south, but everyone referred to the direction as heading upriver. Ellen didn't mind the trip; in fact, the rocking of the riverboat as it butted its way against the current seemed to have a therapeutic effect. From the very beginning of this trip, Ellen stopped having her recurring nightmares. Now, for the first time in years, she had been able to get a full nights sleep.

"This is a roundabout way to get to Kansas," Yerby observed. He had joined Ellen and General Hitchcock on the lower deck of the riverboat *River Maiden* steaming "up" the Missouri River towards Leavenworth, and ultimately to Lawrence, Kansas.

"This is not a roundabout way to Kansas," General Hitchcock replied. "This is the *only* way into Kansas. We have heard that no one with our sympathies gets across Missouri unmolested. Fortune will have smiled on us, indeed, if we can get into Kansas this way."

"Howdy, folks," Shields said good-naturedly. The one positive thing about booking third class passage was that rarely was there a problem with whites and blacks interacting. Shields felt no apprehension about ambling over to the little party of General Hitchcock, Frank Yerby and Ellen Ingraham. From the time Ellen had joined the St. Catharines' community of escaped slaves, Shields was rarely far from her side. When she first arrived in the Canadian province of Ontario, Shields gave Ellen his own well-built cabin, adequately stocked with provisions to last through the long Canadian winter.

Shields slept in a tent while he built another cabin for himself. Ellen had announced to the entire St. Catharines' community that she was colored and an escaped fugitive slave from a plantation in Mississippi. "For the past many years," she told the colored community of St. Catharines, "I have lived in Boston and passed for white. Now I feel like I've come home. We are all fugitive slaves." The colored community of St. Catharines loved Ellen and quickly accepted her. In the loving, giving environment, Ellen began to find something inside her; something she hadn't known even existed. It was a personality...and something more. It was a will. Certainly not a very strong will nor very certain...but nonetheless she began to feel inside. It was some force that prompted her to say *I will...*

The colored community in St. Catharines settled around Harriett Tubman's sprawling log structure. Her home in reality was a series of several log cabins connected together...some directly, others by interconnecting covered walkways. Four of the main cabins opened directly upon a large common that included a kitchen and dining area. Harriett had personally conducted over three hundred fugitive slaves to St. Catharines. Many more found their way there along other Underground Railroad routes with other conductors like Freddie. So the log cabins belonging to St. Catharines' colored community clustered about Harriett Tubman's home in the same way that all the activities in this colored community centered upon Harriett Tubman. Everyone called her Mother Harriett and she thought of them all as her children. St. Catharines' colored community was a model of loving cooperation, for in reality the bitter Canadian climate demanded that everyone cooperate to survive.

"Tell me about Ellen Ingraham, Freddie," Harriett had asked her old friend during one of his trips. Freddie did. During the narration, all Harriett Tubman could say was, "That poor child! That poor thing!" And from then on, Ellen had a second mother in Harriett Tubman. For a while they were constant companions. Harriett introduced Ellen to an elder in the Cathar community for whom St. Catharines was named. They too welcomed Ellen into their community as one of their own. The Cathars willingly assisted the fugitive slaves, giving them land on which each could build a home. The Cathars also taught the former slaves survival skills, including the most basic: reading and writing. They taught them farming, building, clothes making, metallurgy and animal husbandry. Ellen found that she could help others learn while she was learning herself. She liked being a teacher and helping her people in the St. Catharines' colored community learn to read and write.

. . .

"Who is that white woman living with the coloreds?" Hitchcock asked the elder. He had come to St. Catharines to recruit volunteers for the free state cause in Kansas. He had spent several days observing some prospective recruits, and he was generally looking for young, unattached males. Hitchcock knew he could depend upon the Cathars; they'd been involved in this kind of struggle for centuries. His initiations gave Hitchcock status with the Cathars. He had been initiated into England's Order of the Rose, France's Order of the Lily and Austria's Order of the Double Eagle, in formal ceremonies taking place in each of three countries. In the United States, Hitchcock was a member of the Council of Three of the *Fraternitas Rosae Crucis*. Every once in awhile Hitchcock spotted the rare individual that he knew would make a perfect spy. This was Hitchcock's specialty; he had organized the Spy Company credited with winning the Mexican War. Hitchcock was certain that Kansas was the next critical battlefield and he intended to recruit as many spies and agents as he could for the struggle.

"You're probably talking about Ellen Collins," the elder replied. "But she's not white; she's colored and a fugitive slave."

A number of the fugitive slaves, as well as members of the Cathar community, were swayed by the general's simple call to help in the struggle to keep Kansas from becoming a slave state. Two of these were Ellen Collins and Shields Green, and this was why they and others from St. Catharines were riding upriver with the spy master.

. . .

So when Shields ambled over to the party, Ellen smiled at him, "Hello, Shields."

"Been talkin' to some of the boys down in the boilers," Shields said. "They say that on the last several trips when this here boat stops at Leavenworth, some of the passengers are taken off the boat."

"That doesn't sound good," Hitchcock murmured to no one in particular.

"Why is that?" Ellen asked.

"Because it means that the pro-slavery group is not only blocking access to free state homesteaders from St. Louis to Lawrence but from Leavenworth to Lawrence as well," Hitchcock said, concern knotting his eyebrows. "This might be a problem."

It was more than a problem. The South was tightening the blockade on the Kansas borders. They were effectively denying homesteaders from the non-slave states of the North access to the territory and access to free government land. The Democrats were populating Kansas with Southern sympathizers. The pro-slavery strategy to bring Kansas into the Union as a slave state was to deny all free state sympathizers entry into Kansas. Enraged over the admission of California as a free state in 1850, the first act of the pro-slavery Democratic Party when it swept into power and took control of Congress, was to enact provisions in the Fugitive Slave Law preempting the Missouri Compromise and opening up Kansas land to homesteaders. Hundreds of thousands of acres of land were up for grabs. The Democratic Party, whose platform was to serve the interests of Southern slaveholders, intended to grab as much as it could.

But the law was still the law. The federal land grant office offered any American citizen access to hundreds of thousands of acres of valuable Kansas land under the rules of "squatter sovereignty." The Democrat-controlled Congress had initiated the greatest land giveaway in the history of the United States. Homesteaders could obtain clear title to forty-, eighty- or one hundred and twenty-acre parcels of Kansas land by meeting minimum claim filing and homesteading requirements. These requirements included measuring and providing a legal description to identify the parcel to the federal land office, laying the foundation for a residence, digging a well and clearing one-tenth of the land claimed for cultivation. Less than twenty years later even some of the forty-acre parcels would be worth millions.

Gamblers, mercenaries and slave catchers poured into Kansas from Missouri and all over the South. The Knights of the Golden Circle and the local vigilance committees described themselves as thoroughly sound on the goose to describe their rabidly pro-slavery sympathies, and in staking their claims to the free land made their pro-slavery sympathies known. These gangs filed numerous land claims on behalf of large plantation owners as well as for themselves. Agents of eastern banking interests, including Caleb Cushing and his Brahmins, also connived to control large parcels of Kansas land. But even facing such competition, thousands of free state homesteaders poured into Kansas. They also sought free land; land for themselves to be passed down to their children. It was a rare opportunity for which free state homesteaders, Mexican War veterans and second generation immigrants would fight...and die. The pro-slavery vigilantes used every means available to keep homesteading free staters out of Kansas...including robbery and murder. At first, the homesteaders came into Kansas across the Missouri River. The Fugitive Slave Law closed that route. Then the homesteaders began going into Kansas from Iowa through Nebraska. This was the route that Hitchcock had hoped was still open, but once again he had misjudged. If the riverboat were stopped at Leavenworth, Hitchcock thought, if he were recognized, Jefferson Davis would see the spy master court-martialed and dismissed from the army.

"See that battery across the river?" Hitchcock said to Yerby, motioning to the shore opposite Leavenworth. "That's to remind any riverboat captain what will happen if he decides not to stop."

"You mean that we are going to be boarded?" Yerby asked.

"That's what I mean," Hitchcock said.

The pounding paddlewheel slowed and the triple-decker began angling over toward the docks on the Leavenworth side of the river. "I'm on my way up to the first class section. You must explain to the others that my presence must be kept strictly confidential. Is that understood?" Hitchcock asked Yerby.

"I will pass your message along," Yerby agreed. And with that Hitchcock skipped—which was something to see for a man of his age and girth—up the gangway to the first class section, where he joined a group of army officers reporting to duty stations outside St. Louis. "Hitchcock wants his presence to be kept secret," Yerby whispered to Ellen just as the *River Maiden's* captain pulled his vessel into a space that served as Leavenworth's wharf and gangway. "Please pass the word to the others." The riverboat had not even fully docked before armed men, dressed in every imaginable type of costume, including Indian feathers and vests, swarmed aboard. "Do not to mention the General under any circumstances," Ellen passed the word to Shields Green as well as other St. Catharines recruits. Most of the members of their band got word just as the vigilantes came crashing aboard.

"All the second class and steerage passengers on deck!" shouted the officer in charge of the boarding party, a dark-visaged man. Once everyone was assembled, the armed boarding party proceeded to the passengers' cabins where they opened and searched every bag. The boarders seemed to know which bags belonged to the homesteaders. These they pitched unceremoniously off the riverboat onto the wharf to be hauled away by a slave gang.

"Ladies and gentlemen, we regret the interruption in your journey to St. Louis," Davy Atchison drawled at the forty or so passengers huddled on the second-class deck. The speaker accentuated his Southern drawl to mimic the manner of a Southern aristocrat. Slapping a short riding quirt to his side, Davy Atchison continued. "We understand that a group of troublemakers sent by abolitionists in Boston are on this boat. As representatives of the Vigilance Committee for Leavenworth, we don't rightly intend to let them continue." He looked over the free state homesteaders. "I have a list of names. If you would please disembark this boat when I call your name, it will be a lot easier on all of us. Please remember that we have your names and we can identify all of you...." As their names were called, one by one, most of Hitchcock's recruits were identified and marched down the gangway with other Northerners coming to Kansas for the land. But not all of the agents Hitchcock had recruited for the struggle in Kansas were on that list.

"...Ellen Collins...Shields Green...," drawled Atchison. Shields and Ellen followed the others down the gangplank. Yerby just stared at Ellen. Her tragedies and sorrows had taken away none of her beauty. She needed neither fancy clothes nor jewelry to make her beautiful. Her long auburn hair began taking on such a look as to remind one of the plumage of some great beautiful bird. No jewelry could enhance the golden texture of her skin or the mysterious brilliance of her blue-green eyes. In St. Catharines, Ellen lived a frontier existence. Her body had developed and matured with the many hours of physical work she put into her vegetable garden and her cabin. Yerby decided that Ellen's beauty was not merely physical; it was something more; something that came from within.

All of the free state homesteaders were taken down the gangway and marched towards the middle of town where they were interned in a large square area. Leavenworth's internment area was nothing more than a great muddy pit sectioned off by empty packing crates forming a rectangle, with armed men patrolling the perimeter at regular intervals. A coarse group of men crawling out of Leavenworth's tents, hovels and shanties gathered to leer at this latest crop of free state homesteaders being denied entrance into Kansas. These grimy, lice-ridden ruffians were eyeing their prey, trying to decide just which one of these free staters would be most likely have anything of value. They were looking for anything they could trade for their rotgut whiskey, anything they could use to pay off gambling debts, or anything they could sell for a bowl of beans or a piece of meat. They laughed and jabbed at each other as they looked over their intended victims.

As soon as Davy Atchison and his vigilantes had rifled through all the homesteaders baggage, seized all their weapons and stolen all their money, the free state homesteaders would be released from the internment area and told where they could pick up their remaining belongings. "Don't come back this way or try to get into Kansas or we'll skin you," Atchison told them with a glare that indicated that they should take his threat seriously. Now without weapons or money, each homesteader had to decide whether to risk continuing his trek into Kansas or to return home, penniless.

Across the muddy way from the internment area was a row of buildings representing Leavenworth's gambler's paradise, where alcohol and cards controlled the lives of its patrons. But these huddled about a well-built two-story building boasting a big sign in front of its swinging doors: A. B. MILLER. The most prominent building in Leavenworth, Miller's place catered to all the vices, with rooms upstairs where patrons could avail themselves of the town's only ladies of the evening. Miller's boasted the best stocked bar in Leavenworth, as well as the town's most active gambling parlor. Day and night, the ruffians and bushwhackers gambled at Miller's roulette, faro and poker tables, squandering the loot they had lifted from homesteaders, emigrants…or each other. Leavenworth was a den of thieves, cut throats and murderers. Lots of money was won and lost. Fights kept Tiny, Miller's bouncer, always tossing someone out, either by breaking someone's head with his club or, on rare occasions, a couple of times a week, by shooting someone too drunk or too stupid to continue to live. In Leavenworth, the only law was the vigilance committee that was run out of A.B. Miller's saloon.

Leavenworth's members of the sporting fraternity were well armed, sound on the goose and ran Leavenworth without any challenge. Miller and his cronies were tied directly into the ruling Democratic Party through Caleb Cushing. The Boston Brahmins owned Leavenworth. They provided the alcohol and gambling tables. They also provided the weapons, including the artillery battery guarding the Missouri river. A modern telegraph office tied Cushing's private offices directly to Leavenworth.

Inside her private office at A.B. Miller's saloon, Louise Collins, Caleb Cushing's personal agent in Leavenworth, was looking over the newest group of free state homesteaders from the *River Maiden*. And then she saw Ellen Collins Ingraham, standing knee deep in mud among the group of detainees. At first she could not believe her eyes, but her heart beat just a little quicker. *That can't be her,* Louise told herself, as she stared at her aunt through her new-fangled binoculars.

"Tell Davy Atchison to come here," Louise told one of the messengers she kept at her disposal.

The dark-visaged bearded man who was responsible for removing the free state homesteaders from the *River Maiden* pushed into Miller's and knocked at the little office at the front of Miller's with the sign PRIVATE.

"Did you call for me?" Davy Atchison asked.

"Yes, come in," Louise replied. "What's that woman's name?" she asked Atchison. Davy Atchison had been selected by Jefferson Davis as captain of Leavenworth's vigilance committee. Atchison and Davis had served together in the Mexican War. Atchison became wealthy by preventing free state homesteaders from getting into Kansas by riverboat.

Looking over his lists, Atchison said, "Ellen Collins."

"Thank you," Louise dismissed Atchison. She looked over at the man slouched on the overstuffed sofa. "I'll be right back," she said, and slipped next door to the telegraph office. "Send the following message priority and secret to Mr. Cushing's office," Louise told the telegraph operator. The operator took the message and read the following: Ellen Ingraham here. Please advise. Louise.

"Bring me the reply as soon as you receive it," Louise told the telegraph operator.

"Yes ma'm," the operator replied.

Back in the well-appointed office she shared with William Quantrell, Louise said, "Well, Billy boy, my prayers have been answered. I've finally got her."

"Got who, hon?" Billy Quantrell asked.

"Ellen Collins Ingraham," Louise said simply. "She's in that party of nigger lovin' free-staters, Davy took off the *River Maiden.*

"Ellen Ingraham?" Billy asked thinking out loud. Then after a few seconds, he whistled, "You mean your aunt, the one who had your mother killed by those abolitionists?"

"The very one," Louise hissed. "Now I've got her and she's going to pay."

"Are you going to tell Caleb?"

"Course, doll-baby," Louise replied. "Sent the telegraph just now. We should hear from him soon." The young man seated at the table was another of Caleb Cushing's special agents. But in this operation, Louise was the senior member. Quantrell took his orders from her, for Louise reported directly to the Attorney General. Cushing built A.B. Miller's specifically to serve as headquarters for the Kansas territory.

Louise installed everything to her specifications, with handcrafted furniture and customized brass finishings shipped from Europe. Quantrell did not even know Caleb Cushing. All he really knew was that Cushing was the Attorney General of the United States.

Caleb was Louise's mentor; he shared with Louise a close personal bond. Actually, they had been introduced by a mutual acquaintance, Chief Justice Roger Taney. Upon leaving pubic school, Louise wrote to the Chief Justice praising his Dred Scott decision. In his reply, Judge Taney recommended that Louise call upon Caleb Cushing. Cushing offered to mentor Louise as his agent; Louise accepted. Caleb taught Louise everything about the business of politics as he and his business partners understood it. First, Louise became his mistress. He taught her the Machiavellian arts of seduction, deception and betrayal. Then he taught her how to acquire and pass along important information. She learned how to use petty vices, gambling, drinking and sex to secure intelligence and pursue high-level government activities. Cushing tested Louise in many situations against free staters and abolitionists, as well as against her own fellow trainees. Caleb trained her to be absolutely merciless, and Louise passed every test. After Cushing was satisfied with her training, he sent Louise to Leavenworth as his personal representative. Her job was to prevent free state homesteaders from entering into Kansas. She was to destroy any support for free state or abolitionist ideas.

John Quitman had recruited Billy Quantrell. Quitman knew the Quantrells of Kentucky well.

As federal agents of the Attorney General, Louise and Billy were implementing the will of the Congress of the United States to create an American confederation of slaveholders that would control all the land and the wealth of the Americas. In order to get a little extra leverage, Cushing suggested that Louise seduce Billy Quantrell. Cushing had very little leverage over his grand master...not that he would ever attempt to use it. What Cushing did want was to control his two agents. The fact that the nation's top spymaster directed his mistress to seduce the agent of his superior, Grand Master Quitman, was natural and not unexpected. What was unexpected was that the two agents actually fell in love. Maybe it was because they were young and retained a residue of innocence from their childhood. Possibly it was the fact that they both believed in the natural order of things: Planters should rule. Or maybe they reasoned that, despite all of the bloodshed and misery they had already brought to innocent white homesteaders and their families, somehow the end justified the means.

It did not matter that they loved each other. The responsibility for every parcel of land stolen, every homesteader driven off the land, every well poisoned and every crop ruined, lay ultimately with Louise Collins and William Quantrell. They gave the orders and rewarded the results. But in spite of the foulness of their deeds and the hurt it brought so many, Louise and Billy desperately loved each other. And, in a way, their love made them seem worse monsters then they actually were.

How such an occurrence could take place between two souls as corrupted and evil as these undoubtedly were, is hard to say. One generally associates true love with compassion and truth, not ruthlessness and lies. But therein lies the mystery of life, because undoubtedly Louise loved Quantrell as much as she had made Quantrell believe he loved her. It has always been believed that true love cannot exist between practitioners of the black arts. Louise Collins and Billy Quantrell were intelligence agents using evil means to attain equally evil ends for their evil masters. Their lives revolved around deceit and treachery. Their plans were contrived in the parlors that served gambling, alcoholism and prostitution. Love requires compassion and honesty. The one who loves you is the one you trust. The one who loves you wants only what is good for the person you love. So it was hard to believe that love existed between Billy Quantrell and Louise Collins, but it did.

"It's hard to say how Caleb is going to react," Louise mused as if to answer Billy's thoughts. "If he turns her over to me, I'm gonna let our boys have some fun with her awhile. Then I'm gonna work her upstairs, until nobody wants any more. Then I'm going to throw her out into the street." The thought of Ellen's being raped by Leavenworth's collection of human scum and then made to work in Miller's upstairs brothel seemed to give Louise a great deal of satisfaction. "Caleb is very smart. His plan to stop all them nigger lovin' homesteaders here in Leavenworth was pure genius. Not only are we turning the nigger lovers around and heading them back to where they came from, but our boys are able to take enough loot off these clodhoppers to make it worth their while. And we're making a profit."

"A profit!" Quantrell laughed. "I'll say it's a profit, especially since these good ole boys never get tired of bringing everything they've got right back here to Miller's gaming tables and to us." Quantrell laughed and he motioned. "Let's go upstairs."

Louise shook her head. "I told you, Caleb will be sending a reply soon. You don't want Jimmy comin' upstairs and disturbing us, do you?"

Billy was not happy but the shrugg of his shoulders let Louise know she was still in charge. He continued the conversation. Quitman always pestered him about Louise and Cushing's plans. Usually Billy didn't feel right reporting on Louise, but this was important.

"Why is Caleb sending the Sharp's rifles and cannon with those nigger lovers going to Lawrence?" Billy asked. "These homesteaders, especially those from Massachusetts, are coming into Kansas carrying Sharp's repeating rifles. That's the best rifle in the territory." Not only was the Sharp's repeating rifle the best rifle in the United States, it was the best in the world, or so many of the vigilantes thought. The Sharp's repeating rifle could do something no other rifle could do; it could fire as rapidly as its holder could cock, insert a bullet into the breech and pull the trigger. A man armed with a Sharp's rifle could hold off twenty men or more. Davy Atchison had taken quite a few Sharp's rifles from freestaters recently. In Massachusetts, the Reverend Henry Ward Beecher presented Sharp's repeating rifles to many homesteaders recruited by the Massachusetts Emigrant Society to come to Kansas. The law and order vigilance party referred to the Sharp's repeating rifles in the hands of free state homesteaders as Beecher's Bibles.

"You said it yourself, doll," Louise said, "it's like he is sending the weapons directly to us, but they cannot be traced to us. If the government wants to know where the Sharp's rifles went, the records say they went to Lawrence while in reality, they are right here in Leavenworth."

"Besides," Quantrell quipped, but watching Louise's reaction, "you can't have a war if only one side is doing the shooting, now can you?"

"You men," Louise sniped back, "all you ever think about is war. Assassinations are so much more interesting." Just then the telegraph messenger came through the door. Hurrying over, he delivered a note into Louise's hand. She opened the envelope and slowly read the message. "Interesting…" she mused more to herself than to her lover across from her.

"Well…" Quantrell asked impatiently.

"He wants me to let Ellen continue on to Lawrence," Louise said.

"I don't think that's so smart," Billy said. "He wants them to go to Lawrence! Lawrence is the abolitionist capital of Kansas and headquarters of every free stater and homesteader…"

She interrupted him. "He wants me to follow her to Lawrence and report on all free state activity from there. This means that we are not going to be able to see each other for a while." Motioning the messenger over to her table, Louise said, "Tell Davy Atchison to put all the passengers back on the boat and let them go their way."

"What about their belongings?" Quantrell asked. "The boys are going to be very unhappy about losing their share of the loot."

"Jim," Louise said, "tell Davy to give the passengers back their belongings. I will pay their shares." Jim ran off to give Louise's orders to Davy Atchison. "Besides which, we'll win it all back tonight," she laughed after Jim had left. "Now, Billy-boy, you come upstairs with me, we've got a lot to do before I leave for Lawrence."

CHAPTER TWENTY-FOUR

There are a heck of a lot of men out there, Ms. Ellen," Shields said, coming through the side door of the large one-story clapboard building that served as Lawrence's schoolhouse. "I believes we'd better head back towards the center of town." As proud as he was of the schoolhouse that he had erected, Shields knew that the schoolhouse offered little protection against the thousand or more men bearing down on Lawrence. These men did not look as if they had any respect for either schools or teachers. Shields believed that if the town were attacked, the only line of escape would be across the Kansas River. And to get to the river, they had to go through the middle of Lawrence.

"Don't be silly, Shields," Louise Collins retorted, "those men aren't going to attack this schoolhouse. Today's Election Day, silly, and we white folks are going to vote." Louise had followed Ellen to Lawrence, and had actually been quite helpful in recruiting students during the short time she had been at the schoolhouse.

"But that is an awful lot of men out there, just to vote," Ellen said quietly. Once again, Ellen felt Louise's cold stare as if Louise were stalking her, waiting for the opportunity to…. *To what?* Ellen asked herself. *She has to resent me somewhat. That is why I have tried to be patient and understanding though she acts so strange and distant.*

Louise had arrived in Lawrence a week after Ellen. She joined another homestead party who also was delayed in Leavenworth. Louise and her young man promised to show them a different route around the blockade if they could join their party as far as Lawrence.

Ellen was overjoyed to have family near. A niece was a blessing after so many years of being "a stranger in a strange land." Ellen showered Louise with the love that had been stored away for the past four years. Ellen looked to Louise to fill a great void in her life. But she didn't. Nothing Ellen did or could do would make any difference in the hatred Louise felt for the woman she blamed for her mother's death. If Ellen could not understand the cold, distant demeanor with which Louise maintained their relationship, it was because Ellen did not want to understand. When Ellen attempted to hug her niece, Louise would withdraw with an involuntary shudder from all but the briefest physical contact. Louise did not try to be cordial, since she thoroughly enjoyed her game of cat and mouse with Ellen. Against Louise, Ellen really had no defenses. All Ellen could do was wonder whether Louise's attitude was actually something Ellen was imagining.

Yet even though she hated Ellen with every fiber in hre body, Louise was very helpful in organizing Lawrence's first school. As soon as she arrived she began making suggestions and organizing details that began to make things happen. Instead of waiting for people to come and inquire about a school, Louise surveyed the town to see how many school-aged children were in Lawrence and the surrounding area. She visited homesteaders outside Lawrence and was often gone for days at a time. Louise suggested that the adults of Lawrence had learning needs as well. She held political education classes in the evening for adults. Louise's ideas generated interest among many of the citizens of Lawrence. In a very short time, homesteaders and their children within a ten mile radius of Lawrence began trekking to Ellen's one room schoolhouse. Yet, the more successful the school became, the more her relationship with Louise deteriorated.

"I don't know what to do about her," Ellen had finally confessed to Frank Yerby.

Ellen and Frank enjoyed a special kind of intellectual relationship. Ellen liked the mysterious author who, for whatever reason, had linked his fate with hers. Yerby, himself, seemed uncertain about exactly how he felt about her. "All I know," he confided to her, "is that I am on some sort of quest that involves unlocking the mystery of my own immortality...as well as yours."

"What do you mean by that?" Ellen asked him.

"I really don't know," he replied shaking his head. "I am hoping you will tell me. But I think it has to do something with beliefs."

"Beliefs?"

"Yeah," Yerby said. "There is the idea that what one believes forms the reality of the believer." Yerby stared off into space attempting to grasp the meaning of his own thoughts, "It's the idea that the world is a thought, a mental concept...a belief. For example, before this glass ever existed"—he indicated the thick glass mug that was used to drink water—"there had to be a mental conception of this glass...somewhere in someone's mind."

Ellen thought about it awhile and finally, shaking her head, said, "Okay, but what does that have to do with beliefs?" she asked. "I don't have to believe in this glass, it's real."

Yerby looked at Ellen and frowned. He tried to think of a way to explain it to her. "Think of it like this. Our beliefs are guides to the way we think and behave. For the most part, our beliefs direct us to behave properly for our own benefit as well as for those around us. For some time, I have proclaimed the 'victim's guilt'. And now I have learned that this is a false belief which I must correct."

"Why must you correct it?"

"Because false beliefs are like ghosts: they haunt you!"

"Haunt you?" Ellen asked wide-eyed.

"Yes, haunt you," Yerby replied softly, "they make your life unbearable." Yerby gazed at Ellen to see whether or not she had gotten his meaning, but all he got was a blank look in return. "I have been given an opportunity to redeem myself for imposing this false belief of the victim's guilt."

Ellen stared at Frank, the blankness on her face reflecting the void in her mind. Ellen reached over and touched Yerby's hand sympathetically. There was a kinship between them. "I'm sorry, Frank, I simply cannot understand what you are about." Then Ellen looked deeply into his eyes and said, "But I am certain that you will work it out for me. After all, you are a brilliant man."

Meanwhile Shields paced nervously about, pausing only to occasionally peek out the door at the hundreds of riders swarming into Lawrence. "These men are not going to hurt you," Louise scolded him. "Why don't you just sit down and relax...or else go to your cabin. You're bothering me with your silly fears. All you niggers are so afraid of the least thing, it's no wonder you need white people to take care of you and a white God to look over you."

"Then why are these men here?" Yerby asked, his steady brown eyes penetrating through Louise's pretensions, as if to say: "You don't fool me, Miss Thing. I know your daddy's half black and his momma, your grandmamma were all black! The same blood running through Shields is running through you, only its been diluted some."

"How should I know," she snapped at Ellen, ignoring Yerby's very existence. "But if you're so scared, you should take your two darkies and go. As for me, I'll stay right here, thank you." And with that she skipped out the door while tying a great bow in the white ribbon she had placed in her hair.

Outside, dust and dirt swirled about, darkening the sky and blotting out the sun, as wave after wave of fierce, heavily armed Missourian ruffians and bushwhackers continued their steady flow into

Lawrence that election day, March 30th 1855. But now it was too late for Ellen, Frank and Shields to leave the schoolhouse. Even Louise was forced back. Riders were everywhere, trampling on garden plots, crashing through fences, toppling huts and shanties…displaying the arrogance of an invading army. They challenged Lawrence's residents' attempts at opposition with pitiless eyes and menacing weapons, warning them what the price of any protest would be. Shields now could see that no longer was it even possible for them to get into town. They all withdrew back into the schoolhouse. And now they faced a new fear; with the continual bumping from the horses, the schoolhouse building itself threatened to give way. Ellen, Louise, Shields and Frank found it impossible to breathe without choking. Dust and dirt filled the air. They had to resort to tying kerchiefs over their mouths and noses. The kerchiefs also filtered out the pungent odor of droppings from over a thousand horses.

"Do you think the schoolhouse will hold up?" Ellen shouted nervously at Shields, trying to be heard above the din of snorting, neighing horses and shouting, yelling men.

"Don't know," Shields shouted back, "But I reckon we gonna find out, that's for sure." He looked around the room, searching for a way to prop up the walls against the continual pounding. It was hard to see through the dust now clouding the air. And still more riders continued the pounding. Shields got an idea. He grabbed the long wooden benches used by students during class. "We can use these benches to brace the walls," he shouted at Frank, who raced over to help. They wedged the benches against the corners of the room, adding much needed support to the tottering structure. "Put your weight against the wall," Shields yelled out. Ellen and Frank quickly leaned against one of the buckling walls. After a while even Louise joined the effort to hold the walls in place. Just as it seemed that nothing they did would keep the walls from collapsing on top of them, the stream of horses began to slow and the trots slowed to a walk. Then gradually and finally, the crush of riders came to a complete stop. Men began dismounting and milling about, displaying no clear purpose or intent. But very quickly, their officers efficiently organized the mass of men and animals into ranks and companies, displaying a discipline quite surprising for this seemingly unruly lot.

But it should not have been surprising; these were fighting men and familiar with military discipline. Most were veterans of the Mexican War, some had participated in the campaigns to grab Canadian lands and all had engaged in the numerous Indian Wars, whether in the swamps of Florida, in the backwoods of Georgia or on the Kansas plains. As a matter of fact, Leavenworth stood on land that still belonged to the Indians. But vigilantes never recognized any Indian rights. Any Indian land they wanted, they took. Any Indian remaining on the land that the whites took was murdered. The whites not only retaliated against any Indian who attempted to resist, but against his family and any nearby Indian village, tribe or clan. The attacks were continuous and merciless. The vigilance committee riders reflected the discipline of an invading army that had done it all and knew that the best way to be successful was to follow orders. So even though the men riding into Lawrence were ruffians and bushwhackers, who murdered homesteaders and jumped land claims, they rode in packs like wolves and understood how to take orders from their leaders, A.B. Miller, Davy Atchison and William Quantrell.

As soon as she could, Louise slipped out to meet Quantrell at their pre-arranged meeting place near the Kansas River. "Billy," she squealed and flew into his arms. Their lips sought each other's greedily and they held each other, hungrily, desperately. It was a while before they could separate from each other's embrace and gaze into each other's eyes. "You boys sure make an entrance," Louise murmured, finally catching her breath as she clung tightly to him. "There is no doubt that after a show like that, we'll soon control Kansas and get rid of every nigger-loving free stater in the territory."

"The vigilance committee has taken over the polling place in Lawrence." Quantrell kissed Louise's quivering lips. "We are organizing the vote by companies. After each company votes, they will ride back to Missouri. My company will take the ballots to Lecompton where all the votes will be counted. Nothing has been left to chance." Once more they embraced each other. This time their embrace lasted a long time.

Afterwards Louise laughed gaily. But then a frown clouded her face as often happened when she tried to think of what could go wrong. "What if the free staters do the same thing in another town?"

"Don't worry," Quantrell replied with a pleased look as he retrieved a small cigar from his vest pocket, "we've taken over every polling place in Kansas."

. . .

And so they did. After the election was over and all the votes were tallied, the law and order vigilance party won a clean sweep. A vigilante associated with the law and order vigilance party controlled every seat in the newly formed Kansas territorial legislature except one. Taking over Lecompton, the territorial capital of Kansas, the law and order vigilance party lost no time in adopting Missouri's entire constitution as the model for Kansas' new constitution. The law and order vigilance party enacted a tougher slave code. Death was the punishment for anyone enticing, decoying or carrying any slave belonging to another out of Kansas. Death was the penalty for aiding or helping a slave escape to freedom. A five-year jail sentence was given anyone convicted of publishing, circulating, printing or writing anything that argued against the right of a person to hold slaves. The new laws of Kansas made it a crime punishable by imprisonment for anyone to hold any opinion contrary to one that upheld the right of whites to own slaves. Caleb Cushing, Jefferson Davis and, above all,

John Quitman, were overjoyed with the successes they were enjoying in Kansas. They began thinking of Kansas as already safely under their control and soon to be admitted to the Union as a slave state.

Meanwhile, as the law and order vigilance party consolidated its power in Lecompton, the citizens of Lawrence as well as freestate homesteaders all over Kansas were still reeling from the law and order vigilance party's Election Day *blitzkrieg*. Lawrence was still trying to recover from the physical devastation. It took Shields and Frank almost two weeks to repair all the damage to the schoolhouse that tottered so badly that they almost decided to pull it down and rebuild from the foundation up. The cabins in the rear had been completely demolished. All four of them were forced to sleep in tents; the schoolhouse served as their common living area. The entire spring crop had been ruined. What the horses had not trampled, they had eaten. There was an immediate need to plant for the summer, but the supply of seed in Lawrence was low. Louise "volunteered" to go to Kansas City to get garden seed, as well as the other supplies they needed just so that they could survive until the fall. Ellen was very unhappy about her niece traveling alone.

"At least let Shields go with you," Ellen pleaded.

"I don't need your darkie," Louise retorted sharply. "White men out here know how to look out after a lady." With that she ordered Shields to bring her a wagon and a mule from Lawrence's livery stable. Louise took off the next morning and did not return for two weeks. Yerby noticed that Louise still wore the white ribbon in her hair; it was the same type of ribbon that the border ruffians wore when they invaded Lawrence. But Yerby decided not to mention it to Ellen; he just couldn't bear seeing any more hurt in Ellen's eyes.

Tom Boone, one of the free state homesteaders from St. Catharines, came out to the school to see how Ellen had faired. Looking about, he surveyed the damage. "Don't look like they left you much, did they?" It was more of a statement than a question.

"They destroyed the cabins in the back," Ellen replied. "Shields braced the schoolhouse walls and prevented it from collapsing. But the cabins in the rear were crushed and everything inside them was destroyed. Our vegetable garden was ruined. Louise went to Kansas City to get some seed and supplies."

"So we heard," Tom observed. "Not one vegetable plot in the whole town survived. Those vigilantes plan to starve us for certain. " Tom nodded to Frank as he walked up. Yerby nodded back. "By the way, have you heard about the outcome of the election?"

"No," Ellen replied. "I've been too busy around, here."

"Look's like the vigilantes took control of the entire territory. They elected the entire legislature. Those bushwhackers call themselves the Law and Order Party. The mayor is calling for a meeting tonight. Hope to see you this evening." With that Tom Boone turned around and headed back towards the center of town.

That evening not only were most of Lawrence's townfolk in attendance at the mayor's meeting, but many of the free state homesteaders from the surrounding area attended as well. "The entire process was a fraud," Stoddard Hoyt, mayor of Lawrence was saying. "There are only 369 registered voters in Lawrence, but 1,034 votes were cast. There are only 2,905 registered voters in the entire state of Kansas, but 6,307 votes were cast." Stoddard Hoyt had migrated to Lawrence just prior to the great land rush. Stoddard was a Quaker. He and his party originally came to assist the Indians whose land was being stolen despite the numerous government treaties giving them title. Quakers and many other Christian denominations coming to Kansas made Lawrence the center of free thought and homesteaders' rights. Once Kansas land became available to settlers, the various religious groups in Lawrence decided that Stoddard Hoyt's even disposition and sensitive nature would make him the ideal mayor for Lawrence. The mayor called this evening's meeting to discuss exactly how the Christian community of Lawrence should react to the new order imposed by the law and order vigilance party.

"What can we do?" one of the homesteaders asked. "Governor Reeder doesn't intend to support us. He sides with the border ruffians and the bushwhackers that put him in power." A 'bogus legislature' was elected from which there is no appeal. The free staters all agreed.

"Governor Reeder has promised to order new elections wherever a case of fraud is indicated," Mayor Hoyt responded, "I believe we have enough evidence to prove that the election here in Lawrence was fraudulent."

"If there was another election here in Lawrence," a free stater shouted out, "what's to prevent the same thing from happening again…or worse?"

There was a pause in the discussion; everyone knew the answer to that question.

"I came to Kansas," one stern-faced homesteader announced, "to raise my family on my own land, free to enjoy all the benefits of this great country. I will not run away. I will stay and fight. Who's with me?"

A great cheer went up. The people needed to release their emotions, and they cheered and clapped and allowed themselves the pure joy of believing that despite the overwhelming odds against them, they would win. The meeting broke up without any other decision than to invite free staters from all over Kansas to participate in a free state convention.

And indeed a free state convention was held in Topeka several months later. The only free stater elected to the Kansas legislature resigned, calling the legislature "bogus." "This is not a legislature representing the citizens of Kansas," he shouted out at the free state convention. "I utterly repudiate it! It degrades the respectability of popular government and insults the virtue and intelligence of the people."

It took several meetings and conventions, but on the Fourth of July, 1855, free staters from all over Kansas joined together to support an official free state policy of repudiation. Dr. Charles Robinson was nominated to become the first governor of the free state of Kansas. In his acceptance speech, Robinson said: "Let every man stand in his place, and acquit himself like a man who knows his rights, and knowing them, dares to maintain them. Let us repudiate all laws enacted by foreign legislative bodies. Tyrants are tyrants, and tyranny is tyranny, whether under the garb of law or in opposition to it. Our ancestors thought so and let us think and act that way as well. We are not alone in this struggle. The whole nation wants us to have the rights entitled to every free American citizen. I hear millions of freemen and bondsmen, patriots and philanthropists and revolutionary heroes everywhere, speaking in the voice of God, saying to the people of Kansas, 'Do your duty!'"

"Repudiate the law," laughed Louise. "You can't repudiate the law."

"Why not, dear?" Ellen asked sweetly.

"Because the law is the law," Louise sputtered. "It must be obeyed."

"Our people are fully determined to repudiate the political takeover by the slave owners," Ellen said. "But you are right, dear, we must not violate them. "

"It sounds like you people are confused," Louise laughed. "How can you not violate the laws if you intend to repudiate them?"

"There is nothing they can do to us if we do not violate their laws," Ellen replied. "We will keep as far away from the legal machinery set up by the 'bogus legislature' as possible."

And that was what the free staters of Lawrence tried to do. None of the laws passed by the Kansas territorial legislature guided the conduct of Lawrence's citizens. They brought no suits to court; no probates to judges; they brought no complaints before the justice of the peace; nor did they pay any taxes levied by the "bogus leg-islature." Citizens settled disputes by appealing to Mayor Hoyt or someone the mayor designated. Local town regulations were passed and enforced by the town's committee of safety. Conflicting squatter claims between free state homesteaders were brought before a special town commission of which Ellen was a member. This commission settled all claims peaceably.

The only way the "policy of repudiation" could succeed in Law-rence was that everyone attempted to be guided by rules of civilized behavior. Mayor Hoyt met with the pastors of Lawrence's Presbyteri-an, Episcopal and Congregational Churches and discussed how they could influence their congregations to support the policy of repudia-tion. More than three quarters of the citizens of Lawrence attended one of these three congregations. Hoyt made a special plea to each of the pastors that they work together to resolve disputes between and among members of their congregations.

"You are aware," Hoyt told each pastor, "that this decision to repudiate the laws of the bogus legislature, will make every free state homesteader in Kansas, a target for assassination. Furthermore," he continued, "the Law and Order Party intends to use the bushwhack-ers and ruffians to destroy Lawrence."

"Perhaps it would be wiser to counsel our flocks to leave before it is too late," Reverend Bishop, pastor of the Presbyterian Church, suggested.

"The consequences of our leaving this land to those people and slavery might end civilization as we know it in America, altogether," Reverend Cordley of the Episcopal congregation responded. "We already bear the guilt for the millions of slaughtered Indians, and Africans and Mexicans…but now they are turning on *white home-steaders*. It has to end somewhere.

"We have no choice here," the Congregationalist pastor agreed, "this evil is never satisfied; it feeds on weakness and thrives on ignorance. We must stay and fight."

So the religious leaders consented to Mayor Hoyt's proposal. Furthermore they recommended that each of them provide financial support for Ellen's school, both to educate the children and support the adult population. They agreed that the welcome committee would assist all newcomers to Lawrence. The welcome committee would also be responsible for making certain that vigilance committee members were not slipping into Lawrence.

"The days before us will be very hard," Ellen told the mayor and the pastors when they called upon her to discuss their plans for making Ellen chairman of the welcome committee. "I don't know if I am able to do what you ask."

"But of course you are, Auntie," Louise broke in. "And I will be here to give you all the help you need."

Mayor Hoyt beamed. "You see, gentlemen, I knew we could rely on these two young ladies."

Looking first to her niece and then to the religious caucus, Ellen sensed that the decision had already been made. Bowing her head she said softly, " Well, I guess you can count on me to help these people in whatever way I can."

Ellen's reluctance to enter into an alliance with Lawrence's religious leaders was not based only on her own inexperience. Her religious conversion in St. Catharines changed the way she thought and behaved. The Cathars differed greatly from mainstream Christians. If one were to go to St. Catharines seeking a wondrous church whose architecture spiraled to the sky, touching the very heavens with the prideful creations of man, you wouldn't find it. The Cathars believed that no matter how grand and extravagant the temple, the soul of man is more wondrous by far. They taught Ellen that the absolute beauty and wonder of life is in the hands of the living. And the sole purpose of living was to experience and share love. The Cathars believed that by bringing more and more love into your life, you brought yourself joy and pleasure without measure. "If a single flower can turn its face to the light of the morning sun and experience the exquisite joy of living," the Cathars taught Ellen, "then what ecstasy can a human create for itself and others around them." And Ellen accepted their teachings as the motivation of her new life. She now sought to bring joy and share love with all she met. This new direction was reflected in every one of her lessons to the children as well as the adults. Ellen would begin with the Cathar's Prophecy:

The Church of Love is proclaimed...

It has no structure, only understanding.

It has not rivals; it does not compete.

It has no ambition since it seeks to serve.

It has no membership, save those who belong.

It acknowledges all great teachers who have shown the truth of Love.

Its members practice the truth of Love in their daily being.

It recognizes the mission as a conscious transmutation of the ego into that which is capable of giving as well as receiving great amounts of Love.

Its members recognize each other by their deeds and the loving embrace.

They are dedicated to the silent loving of neighbor and environment and to the supremacy of the great idea that the purpose of Life is to Love without fear, without reserve and without reward.

It has no secrets, no Arcanum, no initiation save that ALL THAT BELONG, BELONG.

On the other hand, Louise was given a golden opportunity to express her quite different philosophy. "If our policy of repudiation is to work," Louise told a group of younger free state men, "we've gotta be able to defend ourselves.

"That's right," one of the free staters shouted back.

"We need guns and cannon," Louise said. "We need to organize companies of militia that can be counted on when the time comes."

Louise and her followers were able to force Stoddard Hoyt to order several hundred Sharp's rifles and several howitzer cannon from Lawrence's New England friends. Through his contacts with Amos Lawrence, for whom the town was named, large orders were placed on behalf of the free staters with weapons manufacturers. Quantrell was alerted of the shipment dates and times. Many of these weapons found their way into the vigilantes' arsenal at Leavenworth, Hitchcock's double agents in Leavenworth were able to divert some of these back to Lawrence's free staters. In this way, Lawrence's free staters came into possession of several hundred Sharp's rifles. They even obtained a howitzer cannon.

And so haphazardly or fatefully, the battle lines between these two opposing forces were drawn, and an inexorable conflict between good and evil began to take shape in Kansas. This conflict would take the full measure of Frank Yerby and his so-called victim's guilt.

CHAPTER TWENTY-FIVE

Well, Josh," the tall black captive said to his companion, "today's the day I'm gonna leave y'all. I'm gonna go back to Iowa, get my family and head north to Canada."

Hank and Josh were two of the twenty-five fugitive slaves Claude Coombs was taking back to St. Louis. Claude figured that each one of this bunch of hardy bucks was worth five hundred dollars at one of St. Louis' slave auction houses. Claude had become quite good at his work. The Albany affair had taught Claude a lesson. "In this business you've gotta be close to your own kind," Claude explained to Jake. "You can't expect those abolitionists in the North to help us."

"I don't know about that," Jake replied, "but them niggers whopped us pretty good. I just can't believe niggers attacking white men like that. I'll tell you, Claude, times is changing and things are not going to be the same."

"Hank, I think you should think about it awhile," Josh said. "Even if you get away, they just gonna catch you again…what with the scars across your back, half your ear gone and those brands they put on you."

"You ain't lying about that," Hank replied. "Them white folks have scarred me up something fierce. Don't see how my wife can stand to touch me, but she does. And I can't leave them without any way to survive the winter. I've got to get back to them." Hank was a blacksmith and there wasn't a lock that Hank couldn't open. The manacles and shackles were no obstacle to Hank's running away. He only needed the right time, when no one was watching, to make his getaway.

Until his capture several weeks earlier, Hank had lived on a small plot outside Sioux City with his wife and three children. He had escaped from a Carolina plantation nearly five years earlier. Hank blacksmithed for local farmers, repairing their tools, shoeing their horses and mules and making wheels for their wagons and buggies. Claude spotted Hank walking down a lonely stretch of Iowa road. He was returning from a job on a neighboring farm. Claude and his men swooped down on the unsuspecting black man, easily subduing and manacling him, and led him away to a pen where they kept the other captives. Now here they were in Leavenworth, awaiting a riverboat to transport the fugitive slaves to the auction houses of St. Louis.

"I don't see how you expect to make it during the day," Josh said.

"Oh, yes," Hank replied, "the day is better. There's pattyrollers at night… and dogs. Can't outrun those dogs. But during the day, once you get away, you can just disappear. 'Specially if you can get into Kansas." What Hank failed to understand was that night or day, it didn't make any difference. There was nowhere Hank could hide. He bore the marks of a runaway slave, and nothing and no one would interfere with Hank's being captured and forced back into slavery under the Fugitive Slave Law.

Claude's gang of black captives squatted down by the side of the wharf in a docking area where cargo was loaded and unloaded. Here there were bales of cotton and tobacco as well as crates of every size marked for many destinations. Away from the river and surrounding the town was the timberline. The woods were a little more than a hundred yards away from the docking area. Claude was going to herd his twenty-five blacks into the hold of the next riverboat heading for St. Louis. The fugitives were going to be quite cramped, chained in the bilge of the river boat, but the trip would last only five days.

While Claude was chatting with Jake and the other members of his gang, Hank thought to himself that this was his chance. He loosed himself from the manacles and shackles on his ankles and wrists. Then he began sneaking away from the other fugitives toward the woods. Slipping between the crates and bales of tobacco, Hank crept as low as he could. Not far to go now, he thought to himself, pushing along as quickly as he dared. Hank rested behind the last crate between himself and the woods. One hundred yards away the tree-line bekoned. Hank got to his feet and, keeping low, started running towards the trees. Halfway there, he turned and saw that no one had noticed his escape. So he stood up and began running for his life. But that was Hank's fatal mistake. Shouts raised the alarm and shots erupted. Summoning up all the energy and speed he could muster, Hank willed himself into the cover of the trees. He was almost there when from a great distance in the rear, Hank heard the crack of a Kentucky rifle. A fraction of a second later, Hank felt an explosion in his head. The blue sky faded into blackness and as his body tumbled down, his sightless eyes peered into the portals of death. Instantly the air was filled with yells and shouts. Grizzled frontiersmen who had been waiting for the riverboat came running to where Hank lay, the wet ground soaking up the blood trickling from an ugly head wound. "That was the best gol'darn shot that I have ever seen in my entire life!" one of men cried out.

"Claude shot half that nigger's head off from over one hundred and fifty yards away," another exclaimed.

"If that shot went ten yards, it went over two hundred yards," another shouted. Soon well wishers, patting him on the back, surrounded Claude, declaring Claude's head shot the best one Leavenworth had ever seen. Claude was picked up and pitched high upon the shoulders of the enthusiastic ruffians and deposited in the nearest saloon. They celebrated Claude's remarkable head shot with stories and drinking long into the night. The celebration resulted in Claude and his boys missing the riverboat heading for St. Louis. The next day, Hank's body was displayed in front of the saloon with a sign that read: "This nigger was shot in the head from 250 yards by Claude Coombs, September 11, 1855." The final distance was only exaggerated by one hundred yards, but no one in Leavenworth minded. With little else to amuse or entertain, these rough men made Claude Coombs their hero. Border ruffians and bushwhackers prowling all over Kansas and Missouri alike regaled each other with Claude's celebrated "head shot."

But Lawrence's two newspapers, the *Herald of Freedom* and the *Free Stater*, carried stories of the event as if it were an atrocity. A newspaper artist drew a picture of the dead man's corpse displayed outside the Leavenworth saloon. But true to her Southern roots, Louise Collins found the event exhilarating. "Have you heard about them shooting that nigger in Leavenworth?" she asked Ellen, maliciously. "I heard it was Claude Coombs who did the shooting. They say it was just about the best shot anyone did see in these parts. Claude Coombs...wasn't he the one who tried to take you back home?"

Ellen's face went white as she struggled to subdue the terrible memories his very name summoned to her mind's eye. Ellen looked at her niece with a dawning appreciation for the depth of Louise's malice. "He was the man who tried to kidnap me...and also the man who murdered your mother."

Louise stared at her aunt with unblinking eyes. "My mother was murdered by a burr-headed, blubber-lipped nigger running away from his lawful master," Louise said. "All you escaped niggers need to be in a cage where you belong." Soon, Louise thought to herself, *Billy is going to destroy Lawrence and every nigger lover here.* Claude Coombs would join in the attack. Whether or not Claude Coombs was her mother's murderer was not going to get in the way of her revenge.

Ellen felt as if she had been slapped across the face. For the first time she was beginning to see Louise as she really was: the orphaned child whose grief had turned into hate. Confused about herself, living in a society with extreme racial views, Louise did not understand that she displayed the very infantile behavior of the sambo that whites wanted all black people to exhibit. But in her niece's eyes Ellen saw pure malice.

"You blame me?" Ellen cried out, "you blame me for your mother's death?" Even as the pain clutched at her heart, Ellen could see Louise's face twisted into an evil grin of triumph. With that, Ellen turned and left the schoolhouse and returned to her clapboard cabin. Ellen's grief forced her physically into her rough-made bed which she refused to leave for the next three days.

"You must get up," Frank called. But Ellen could face neither her own guilt nor Louise's accusations...or the terror of knowing that Claude Coombs was less than fifty miles away. And no law existed in Lawrence, in the Kansas territory, or anywhere in the United States that could prevent Claude from coming to the schoolhouse, seizing Ellen and doing anything he pleased with her. And one day, Ellen knew, he *would* come for her. It was this final acceptance of the inevitability of her fate that forced her to realize that she was not in control. So she just remained on her cot buried under her blankets and waited. Each day, Frank pleaded with her to come out. But Ellen did not want to come out. She had never been able to face her own guilt. She had wanted love; she had needed love. She was so attracted to P.B. Randolph. She intended to betray her husband to make love to a man that she did not even know. She herself could not understand it. It was just that she wanted to know just for a short while what it was like to be free. Ellen wanted to be herself and forget the pretense that she was white. She had desires and longings that needed to be fulfilled that had nothing to do with race. Ellen had never been white, nor had she ever felt white. What she always felt was illegitimate. She felt that she had always lived a lie. She had wanted to find the truth in the arms of another mixed-breed like herself. This need in Ellen cost Abby her life… and had made Louise an orphan.

The longer Ellen lay on her cot the more she became aware of another emotional irritation. It wasn't very strong at first. But she felt angry at being physically intimidated by someone as foul as Claude Coombs. The longer she laid on her cot, the longer her anger lingered. The longer it lingered in Ellen's consciousness, the more her anger turned into rage. *How dare this hateful, foul man have so much power over my life?* Ellen's inner self shouted out all at once. *I will not let him destroy me.* With that Ellen rose up. She felt light-headed and dizzy from her self-imposed withdrawal. She wobbled to the door, opened it and stared into the concerned face of Frank Yerby.

"Decided to come out, did you?" Yerby smiled.

"Let's just say that I've had enough guilt. Now I want some getting even."

Ellen walked over to the schoolhouse, opened the door and stepped inside. Louise had conducted the classes during Ellen's absence. Her students welcomed her back. They all ran up to Ellen, shouting, "Mrs. Collins! Mrs. Collins!" Her children gave her a new confidence. She was very pleased to see them and all at once her anxieties over Claude Coombs faded.

"The children seem happy to have you back," Louise observed. It was the end of the class day. They were alone. Both Frank Yerby and Shields Green were busy replanting the ten acre vegetable gardens that they hoped would provide food during Kansas' harsh, artic-driven winter. Louise was relieved that Ellen had returned. In teaching children, Louise learned a valuable lesson: She did not like children. I'm letting Billy Quantrell know right off that I'm not raising no bunch of nasty, yelling brats, Louise thought to herself. "I'm getting bored with this place," Louise told Ellen. "Now that you're back, I think I'd like to visit St. Louis for awhile."

"St. Louis," Ellen said. "Why St. Louis, Louise? Do you have friends there?" St. Louis was the slave market of the West. With several slave auction houses that kept black slaves in pens, St. Louis vied with New Orleans as the prime dealer in human flesh. It was where Kansas free staters believed all the plots and conspiracies against them emanated. The very sound of St. Louis made homesteaders shudder. If Louise was going to St. Louis, she was far more sympathetic to the pro-slavery cause than Ellen had suspected.

"If you must know, I have a friend in St. Louis who has come to see me from Boston, " Louise said truthfully.

"From Boston!" Ellen's voice had an edge of emotion in it. "Who is he? Is it someone I know?"

"His name is Caleb Cushing," Louise smiled pleased with her own self-importance. "But, I don't believe you know him." A week later, Louise boarded the first river boat to have reached Lawrence in months, carrying her down the Kansas River to the Missouri River that took her east to St. Louis.

Caleb had booked reservations for Louise at St. Louis' finest and most elegant hotel. She occupied a suite of rooms with a number of servants who brought her champagne, drew her bath and massaged her body. Caleb Cushing occupied the entire top floor. For the next two weeks, Louise and Caleb discussed their plans for Kansas. Actually, Caleb and Louise only discussed Kansas when Cushing was too exhausted from their other, more intimate, discussions. Caleb Cushing was by no means young nor athletic… and without the personal feelings of young lovers that fuel their passions and bring ardor to their lovemaking. This meant that during that two-week period, Caleb and Louise had a lot of time to spend discussing Kansas.

"We know that we can wipe out Lawrence, Topeka and all the other free state settlements in Kansas," Caleb explained patiently. Louise had asked him the question that Billy Quantrell continued to ask:

"Why don't we just go into Lawrence and kill every abolitionist and burn the town to the ground?" Men like Quantrell had but one prescription for everything: violence. They did not understand that even violence had its limits. "In this case, my dear Louise," Caleb explained, "further violence against the homesteaders will work against us."

"How will getting rid of all those nigger-loving abolitionists work against us?" Louise wanted to know.

"We're trying to bring Kansas into the Union as a slave state and control all the land in the territory. Northern free states are not likely to support our petition for statehood if all the homesteaders from the Northern states have been murdered."

Louise thought about it awhile and finally admitted that what he said was true. Caleb and Louise were having lunch in the hotel's elegant dining room. Looking up, Cushing was distressed to see Ethan Allen Hitchcock sitting at a nearby table with a couple of his army buddies. Cushing had hired Hitchcock as the agent for the Massachusetts Emigrant Aid Society. Cushing had given Hitchcock specific instructions for organizing free state resistance to the law and order vigilance party takeover. Using Massachusetts Emigrant Aid Society monies, Cushing had paid for the purchase of all the weapons bound for Lawrence.

And as luck would have it, Hitchcock spied Cushing at the same instant. Hitchcock did not recognize Louise. *Why would Cushing come all the way to St. Louis to have lunch with that intriguing young woman?* Hitchcock wondered, and he resolved to learn more about Cushing's beautiful female companion.

Cushing knew that he had revealed himself to a dangerous adversary. *Well,* he thought to himself, *when the time comes, I'll just have to take care of General Ethan Allen Hitchcock, personally.*

Three days later, Louise re-boarded a riverboat steaming west and five days later was in the arms of her Billy, in their own little slice of heaven above A.B. Miller's saloon in Leavenworth. And Louise knew she was in love because she was far happier in the squalor of Leavenworth with Billy Quantrell, a no good bushwhacker, than she was in the luxurious St. Louis hotel with the Attorney General of the United States.

After awhile the lovers' attention turned to Lawrence and the need for the vigilantes to do their work. "Claude's shooting that nigger has rallied free staters from all over Kansas," Louise told Billy. "Some of their churches even held memorial services for him. Caleb's concerned that this kind of abolitionist sentiment will spread."

"What's happening in Lawrence?" Quantrell mumbled distractedly.

"They are calling it a 'repudiation movement'," Louise explained.

"I've been saying that we just go down there and kill every abolitionist we can find." Billy snorted. "When will somebody listen to me?"

"Caleb says that we need to prepare first."

"Prepare what?"

"Caleb wants them to form a militia," Louise said. "He knows just the person to put in charge. They can use those rifles you've helped to smuggle to them." Louise spoke of older weapons...muskets, rifles, along with some older Navy Colts and single shot pistols. Louise was unaware of the other Sharp's rifles being smuggled into Lawrence under the false bottoms of shipping crates marked "Books." The militia that Louise was helping to form in Lawrence was being armed with Sharp's rifles.

The Sharp's repeating rifle revolutionized fighting. Instead of having to reload the rifle after every shot, the Sharp's rifle could fire multiple rounds without having to reload. A few men armed with Sharp's rifles could hold off a much larger force armed with conventional, single-shot rifles or muskets. The only drawback was that the Sharp's rifle required a newly developed cartridge combining the bullet with the gunpowder. Lawrence's militia had no ammunition for their Sharps rifles. Neither did they have cannon balls or cannon shot for their howitzer cannon. In fact, very little gunpowder and shot for the standard muskets and pistols could be found in Lawrence. "They're not organized yet. We need to smuggle gunpowder and shot into Lawrence," Louise told Billy. "You can't just go in and shoot a whole town that can't shoot back."

"Why not?" Quantrell asked. "We just need to get it over with."

"For one reason," Louise replied, "Caleb doesn't want you to. He didn't go to all the trouble of getting them those rifles and not have them used. You can't start a war with only one side. It takes two sides to start a war. It will take Northern votes to bring Kansas into the Union as a slave state. We won't get their votes if you go into Lawrence and murder all the free staters and they're not fighting back. How are we going to blame them for starting it?"

"If their policy of repudiation catches on," Quantrell said, "there will be no war and Kansas will be lost. Does Caleb know that?"

"All you men ever think about is your little wars," Louise smiled demurely. "Of course, Caleb has thought about it. He organized the Jayhawkers under Jim Lane, didn't he?"

"Caleb didn't organize them, you did!" Quantrell said with only a touch of jealousy. "You have planned your war well. You twisted that Jim Lane around your finger. When the time comes, Caleb can thank you when he is forced to send in the army to restore order here in Kansas."

"Yes!" Louise smiled. *And you and I will see a petition for admitting Kansas into the union as a slave state pass Congress.* "But right now, Lawrence needs ammunition for their weapons so that they can fight back when you attack them." Billy Quantrell did the only thing he could; he sulked. *If I wasn't so much in love with this woman,* he thought to himself, *I don't think I could take her bossing me around.* But as if she could hear his thoughts, Louise said, "But Caleb didn't say nothing about letting more nigger-lovers into Lawrence or letting them continue to get their supplies."

Billy Quantrell looked at Louise and let out a yell. He did not wait; he ordered his vigilante band of border ruffians into Kansas and blockaded anyone or anything from reaching Lawrence. By mid-October, vigilantes from Missouri, South Carolina and Texas poured into Leavenworth and signed on to patrol all around Lawrence. They stopped and robbed every free state homesteader who fell into their hands. They ambushed supply wagons sneaking supplies into Lawrence. The bodies of homesteaders or free state emigrants the vigilantes shot or lynched were left unburied, as a warning to others.

• • •

As the blockade around Lawrence grew tighter, the homesteaders began to feel shortages in food and supplies. After awhile, even the best efforts of the churches failed to prevent their parishioners, especially the children, from going hungry. Ellen began to notice a steady decline in school attendance. The children who did come to school were listless and inattentive. Citizens complained to the committee of safety and Mayor Hoyt.

Jim Lane addressed the members of Lawrence's committee of safety. "The problem is simple," Lane said. "There is not enough food and supplies getting through the blockade. My militia could go out and escort the supply trains through, but we do not have ammunition for our weapons."

"Is there no way to bring in more supplies without resorting to violence?" Hoyt asked.

"We are not resorting to violence," Louise retorted. "We are protecting what is ours. But if Colonel Lane is to protect us, he needs ammunition for his rifles."

So the mayor, a good-hearted, God-fearing man, finally capitulated and permitted the committee of safety to choose someone to pick up the gunpowder and ammunition. Mayor Hoyt had hoped that by keeping the gunpowder and ammunition out of Lawrence, he would avert bloodshed. Louise reported that the ammunition had been brought to a roadhouse on the Santa Fe Road outside the vigilantes' blockade. "The vigilante pickets are far too gallant to molest women," Louise stated. "Ellen and I can bring the powder and ammunition back to Lawrence without any problem." The committee of safety voted to give Louise permission to ride out and secure the ammunition.

When Ellen and Louise returned from the committee meeting, Frank could sense the bad news. "Louise and I are going out on Santa Fe Road to pick up gunpowder and ammunition," Ellen informed Shields and Frank. Yerby held back his impulse to ask Ellen whether or not she had lost her mind. It was too late for him to point out the obvious. Yerby realized that someone had to go. His personal interest in Ellen's safety could not override the fact that if the bushwhacking vigilantes from Missouri attacked, Lawrence would need ammunition and gunpowder to defend itself. But Yerby could not resist the more subtle argument that he hoped might catch Ellen off guard. "How compatible with your Cathar beliefs is getting gunpowder and bullets that will be used to harm and even kill?"

Ellen's look bore the perplexity of someone who did not know whether to feel hurt or amused. Then she just smiled and said, "I know that you worry about me, Frank, and you don't want me to go. But it's something I have to do. I owe it to Louise."

"You don't owe Louise anything."

"I owe Louise her mother's life." Ellen said, without emotion, merely as fact.

"Have you stopped to consider that Louise may be working with the law and order vigilance party?" Frank asked Ellen, giving her a direct look.

Ellen hesitated in her reply. "Yes, I have considered it. But I can't believe it's possible. Louise has colored blood. She wouldn't betray her

FRANK YERBY:

own people or protect the people guilty of murdering her own mother. I refuse to believe that of Louise. She may be a little confused."

"You!" Yerby said very sharply. "You are the only one who is confused. Louise knows very well what she is about."

"And what is that, Frank?" Ellen asked.

"She is about satisfying that need inside her for vengeance."

"All I have ever done was try to love her," Ellen sighed.

"Ellen, love always enrages those who hate," Yerby said. "Louise just might be reacting in an opposite way than you had intended."

"But why shouldn't I love her?" Ellen sighed. "I am her aunt. Her mother was my sister. I loved her mother so much…and I would not have harmed her for the world." The tears gathering unbidden in the corners of Ellen's eyes now began their gentle descent down her cheeks. And then great heaves of emotion seized her and Ellen's entire body convulsed into uncontrollable sobs. All Yerby could do was sit there and hold her close as the flood of tears washed away the pain. After awhile, Yerby said, "Your pain drives you to seek forgiveness, but I don't think Louise is ready to forgive you." Even though his words were meant to be comforting, Yerby saw the terrible hurt in Ellen's eyes. So he added. "But if anything can reach her, your love can."

Later on in the evening, Frank and Shields discussed what they should do. "The reason Hoyt and the committee are sending women is so that they won't be molested by the ruffians. If we ride with them, the chances of their being stopped will increase."

"On the other hand, they might just think we the white women's servants," Shields replied.

"The vigilantes know that there are no slaves in Lawrence," Yerby said. "No, I think we need to stay away from them but keep them in sight, which means we need horses."

"Well, that may be what you think, but I intend to be right in that wagon with Ms. Ellen all the way to the Santa Fe Roadhouse and back." Shields' decision was final. Yerby got a horse and the next day just before dawn rode out southwest toward the Santa Fe Roadhouse ahead of Shields and the two women. Shields secured a wagon and a team of six good trace horses. In the early morning light, Louise and Ellen boarded the wagon and Shields Green drove off at a good pace towards the Sante Fe Roadhouse. As Yerby rode across the plains keeping the wagon with the two white women and their black driver in sight, he watched for any horsemen riding the Santa Fe Road approaching from either direction. But *mirabile dictu*, they met no one. Of course, Louise had arranged that none of the vigilantes interfere with their journey to the roadhouse. Louise planned that this would be a pleasant journey for Ellen…since it was to be her last.

Without any incident on the road, Shields pulled the wagon up to the entrance of the Santa Fe Roadhouse just as the evening stars began making their twinkling appearance in the purpling sky. The Santa Fe roadhouse was in reality a compound of log cabins clustered near a solid two-story log structure surrounded by a high wooden fence, gated front and rear. The roadhouse was far sturdier and more solidly constructed than most of the buildings in Lawrence. This was a surprise to Yerby, who wrote about the lack of wood to build in Kansas in his novel, *Western*. The roadhouse had a big barn for the horses and wagon. The main roadhouse building opened into a great hall with a huge stone fireplace raised above the floor. To the right lay a large dining room with two long tables facing each other. At the end of the dining room was the entry to the kitchen. To the left of the entrance into the roadhouse, stairs led to the guestrooms on the second floor. Louise and Ellen approached a great desk behind which an elderly gentleman beamed at his guests.

"Welcome, welcome," the proprietor of the Santa Fe Roadhouse greeted the ladies. "How long will you be staying with us?" The hostler squinted through round spectacles that did little to improve his failing eyesight.

"Just until tomorrow morning," Louise replied. "We have come to take delivery of books for the school."

"Yes, of course, Madam," the proprietor responded. "We have a very nice room for you upstairs. Your boys can stay out in one of the cabins."

"Do you have separate rooms for me and my aunt?" Louise asked.

"Of course," the proprietor replied.

The women went upstairs and washed some of the Kansas plains off their hands and faces, Frank helped Shields remove the traces and led the horses into the barn where they were watered and fed. Frank and Shields came back into the roadhouse just as Ellen and Louise came downstairs.

"You two boys can go out to the cabin in the rear," the smiling roadhouse manager said. "Suzie back in the kitchen will ring the bell when she has your food buckets ready."

"Yessir," Shields said almost automatically. He and Frank retreated back out the door and found the empty cabin in the rear.

Louise and Ellen discovered that the Santa Fe Roadhouse was hosting a number of guests that evening. Several men lounged about the room with the great fireplace. One, in particular, was very familiar to Louise... a face she would have known anywhere. Claude Coombs lounged in front of the great fireplace with his running dog, Jake, and Billy Quantrell.

Louise watched Ellen with a devilish gleam in her eyes. For nearly five years, Louise had waited for this moment. She had Ellen completely under her control and she intended to enjoy every moment. Four other men slouching about belonged to Quantrell's group. One of them was an agent that Hitchcock had sent into Leavenworth to join Quantrell's vigilance committee. But there were other men lounging about as well, not members of Quantrell's vigilante group of border ruffians and bushwhackers. As a matter of fact, the roadhouse keeper could not remember when so many guests had arrived all at the same time. The others lounging in the dining area, totaling seven altogether, were agents of Ethan Allen Hitchcock. He had sent them to the Santa Fe Roadhouse to protect Ellen as soon as he learned about Louise's plot. They had been here most of the day.

"Didn't think you'd see us again, did you, little lady?" Jake grinned as he got up to intercept Ellen and Louise.

"I don't believe she is particularly interested in your company," a voice boomed from the stairs. General Hitchcock slowly descended. "Ellen, please step over here. Gentlemen…" At his command all seven of his men stood with drawn pistols facing the surprised vigilantes. "If you gentlemen will drop your weapons," Hitchcock continued, "you will be searched. Please cooperate and you will soon be on your way."

Louise was livid. She and Quantrell exchanged looks. *How can this be happening?* Billy read the question in Louise's eyes. She had planned this trap so carefully. Louise looked at the bulldog-like man descending the stairs. Though his stern face and icy stare gave no indication of weakness or lack of resolve, that was exactly what Louise must have read there, because suddenly she leapt for the revolvers lying on the floor and shouted, "Here, Billy, kill her! Kill her!" But neither Billy Quantrell nor Claude Coombs were fools. Both took advantage of the momentary diversion to race for the door and make good their escape. Both had killed so many homesteaders, that neither expected any mercy if captured. But Jake, who was always more apt to do something stupid, took the gun from Louise. Hitchcock's men were all army veterans, clear headed and deadly under fire. Jake got as far as cocking the trigger before the guns in the hands of all seven men barked out at the same time. Jake's body convulsed violently under the impact of the forty-four caliber lead balls slamming into him. The slave catcher was dead even before his body hit the floor. But not all of Hitchcock's agents' bullets hit Jake; others found another target. Louise's body lay crumpled on the floor next to Jake's, her face twisted into a hateful

FRANK YERBY:

grimace as a trickle of blood crept from two wounds in her chest.

"You must leave at once," the proprietor said excitedly. "This will look bad for me...very bad."

"Come on, Ellen, your 'books' are loaded in our wagon," Hitchcock said. Ellen was sitting on the floor cradling Louise's head in her lap and gently rocking to and fro just as she had with Dwight Jr. and Elaine when they were babies. "Come, Ellen," Hitchcock repeated. "Those others are on foot, but we still need all the time we have to get away." Ellen acted as if she had not heard him. Finally, Hitchcock thundered, "Ellen, snap out of it. We must go *now!*"

Ellen looked up and said, "She had so much hate in her." But she got up and looked at Hitchcock. "We can't just leave her here."

"What are you suggesting?" Hitchcock said. He intended to leave the fallen where they lay.

But Ellen insisted. "We must bring her back to Lawrence with us so she can be given a proper burial." Frank and Shields hitched the wagon to a fresh set of horses, then wrapped and loaded Louise's body. Hitchcock's men drove the wagon loaded with the boxes of ammunition for the Sharp's rifles and crates of gunpowder and shot. A full moon bathed the Kansas prairie in a bright light that guided Hitchcock's party and Ellen back to Lawrence. On a couple of occasions, riders—or rather the shadows of riders—were spotted, but just before dawn the group descended upon the familiar plain. And, without further incident they rode into Lawrence.

CHAPTER TWENTY-SIX

W hy are we wasting time?" Billy Quantrell exploded. "We have enough men here to wipe out every nigger-loving abolitionist in Kansas, starting with Lawrence."

Davy Atchison listened to Quantrell's ranting with his usual patience. But he gave the orders now. Most of his land in Missouri as well as in Kansas, was actually Indian land that he claimed after driving off the Indian population. In aquiring his land, Atchison learned patience. With patience, Atchison had raised himself to become an important person in the Democratic Party, and he was now a member of the party's inner circle. Quantrell knew that Atchison, was Jefferson Davis' protégé. He couldn't bypass Atchison, even though with Louise's death Quantrell now was Cushing's top Kansas agent. Quantrell needed Atchison's permission for any attack against Lawrence.

Quantrell led a company of three hundred vigilantes out of A.B. Millers' saloon. Atchison controlled another eight hundred ruffians who worked for him on one of his three plantations. They camped at Salt Creek about three miles from Leavenworth. Quantrell wanted Atchison to allow him to lead this combined force in a direct attack on Lawrence. Atchison counseled patience.

"We know how you feel about Lawrence," Atchison said. "Miss Collins was a fine woman and a patriot. All of us mourn her loss and vow to avenge her death at the hands of those damned abolitionists, but we have to wait until the time is right. Everything must be done legal." Actually, Atchison was more concerned with the free staters' Sharp's rifles. He feared that any showdown might be a bloody affair, and thus urged caution. He didn't want his men slaughtered in a senseless attack on Lawrence. But Quantrell had other ideas. When he rode off from Atchison's plantation he knew exactly what he intended to do.

"You know Wilson Shannon, don't you, Lyle?" Quantrell asked the balding, middle-aged editor of Leavenworth's newspaper, *The Herald*. Billy had invited Lyle Eastin to join him for a drink at Miller's. They were sitting in A.B. Miller's saloon discussing the sad state of affairs that the Kansas territory had fallen into. Like everyone else in Leavenworth, the editor of Leavenworth's newspaper was a drunk. As he sat across the table from Quantrell, Lyle Eastin greedily eyed the whiskey bottle sitting on the table between them. Quantrell poured a glassful of the particularly well-aged whiskey that the editor slurped down in a single gulp.

"You mean Governor Shannon?" the inebriated little man replied to his host.

"The very same," said Quantrell, pouring Lyle Eastin another glass of whiskey.

"Certainly, my boy," Lyle Eastin beamed as he downed another glass. "I was wondering why you invited me over to your table. You need a favor, eh? Need me to put in a word with my friend the Governor?"

"Don't you think that the governor should know about the lawlessness in Lawrence?" Quantrell asked, slyly.

"Lawlessness?" Eastin gasped in mock concern.

"Actually, it's more like outright anarchy," Quantrell asserted. "I believe that it is your responsibility to apprise Governor Shannon of the situation in Lawrence, don't you?"

"Certainly, my boy," the inebriated editor replied, "certainly." Stumbling to his feet, the editor downed his final glass of whiskey and lurched out. And true to his word, after sobering up somewhat, Lyle Eastin sent his friend, Wilson Shannon, a telegraph message regarding the alarming conditions in Lawrence, where heavily armed outlaws were entrenched inside the city limits. Furthermore, Eastin warned Shannon that over a thousand of these outlaws, armed with cannon and Sharp's rifles, were resisting legal authority and were threatening the lives of innocent families who came to Kansas from Missouri seeking free land. Eastin recommended that a militia be called up to engage and disband this rebel force.

Quantrell followed Caleb Cushing's instructions to the letter. Cushing's agent in Lecompton was Daniel Woodson, who served as Governor Shannon's secretary. As head of Kansas' Law and Order Party, Woodson was the second most powerful man in the Kansas territory. Woodson had been warning the governor that the situation in Lawrence was deteriorating and urged immediate action against the repudiation movement. Once Shannon Wilson received Eastin's telegram he signed a proclamation drafted by Woodson calling for a state militia to enforce the law in Lawrence. Immediately, some 1500 vigilantes answered the governor's call, most from Missouri. Overrunning the area, the vigilantes lost no time attacking isolated homesteads all around Lawrence, driving free staters from their homes. Only their fear of the Sharp's rifles prevented the vigilantes from directing an assault on Lawrence itself.

Although thoroughly 'sound the goose,' Wilson Shannon was not a murderer. Alarmed at how quickly he situation deteriorated, Governor Shannon wired the President of the United States, describing the situation. Homesteaders were being attacked and driven out of Kansas. Shannon repeated what his friend Lyle Eastin told him. A militia of vigilantes armed with Sharp's repeating rifles and howitzer cannon were planning to attack Leavenworth. Shannon requested authority to use federal troops to restore order. The governor also notified Colonel E. V. Sumner, Fort Leavenworth's commander, that he was to march immediately upon receipt of orders from Washington. Finally, the governor telegraphed Atchison, Quantrell and the other militia commanders and directed them to cease their activities and desist from attacking Lawrence until he heard from Washington. Replying from the militia camp at Wakarusa, only three miles away from Lawrence, Quantrell replied to the governor that his vigilante forces grew weary of waiting and inaction. They would not remain in camp but a few days longer, Quantrell said. They were prepared to march on Lawrence.

Governor Shannon received word from the president that orders putting the United States troops bivouacked at Fort Leavenworth at his disposal were being forwarded. However, in Washington, pro-slavery leaders were anxious to bring about a conflict in Kansas. With the law and power on their side, they could crush the free-state movement once and for all. Jefferson Davis made certain that federal troops were never put under Governor Shannon's control, but the governor decided not to let the vigilantes carry out their attack against Lawrence.

• • •

"The Committee of Safety will come to order," Mayor Hoyt announced. "Governor Shannon desires to address us about this most urgent situation that we find ourselves in." The committee had but twenty members. Lawrence's other citizens waited outside to learn of the governor's proposal. To most of the free state homesteaders, Shannon was the enemy. Shannon was a pro-slavery advocate who served the interests of those determined to bring Kansas into the Union as a slave state. He had authorized the use of vigilantes. They assaulted homesteaders and had now encircled Lawrence. But the governor was unwilling to permit the final bloody assault upon Lawrence; he didn't want innocent blood on his hands. And so even without federal troops to enforce his commands, Shannon intended to stop this war, separate the opposing forces and avoid bloodshed. That was why he had decided to come to Lawrence and offer a peace proposal. "We will give Governor Shannon our attention," Mayor Hoyt commanded.

"As your territorial governor," Shannon began, "I have come to resolve what has become a serious misunderstanding between the citizens of Lawrence and myself. Regardless of the rumors, I did not request those vigilantes from Missouri to represent the government of Kansas in a war against the town of Lawrence or any other town here in Kansas."

"Then what are you proposing, Governor?" asked one member of Lawrence's committee of safety. It was the question that was on everyone's minds.

"In return for the commitment of the citizens of Lawrence not to resist the execution of any laws enacted by legal authority, I will withdraw all legal authority from any force not made up of Kansans."

"But what if they come anyway, Governor?"

"I will commission a militia from Lawrence under the command of General Jim Lane, here, to take any action he believes appropriate to resist the invaders. In addition, I will secure remuneration for any damages or loses suffered at the hands of an illegal invasion."

With that the committee wasted no time in approving Wilson Shannon' proposed peace treaty. Next Governor Shannon met with Quantrell and the other militia leaders. There were thirteen separate militias representing vigilance committees from the law and order vigilance party in Kansas, as well as groups from all over Missouri and other pro-slavery states. Governor Shannon explained that he had not authorized their invasion. "The citizens of Lawrence have agreed to allow all legal writs and warrants to be served by the sheriff," Governor Shannon announced. "There is no need for this militia or this action." The governor's announcement caused quite a bit of grumbling among the vigilante leaders. Their militias had been assembled outside Lawrence for some time and their men already anticipated what they were going to do with their share of plunder.

"We can't back out now," Quantrell shouted, "our men won't follow us."

"If you attack," Shannon replied, "you'll be branded as outlaws. And when I get authorization from the President, I will order the federal troops to arrest every one of you militia captains." Shannon knew he had them. Most, if not all the militia captains, as well as many of the vigilantes themselves, held multiple land claims in Kansas. These claims were valuable. But if the governor branded them as outlaws, they would lose all rights to their claims. Some of the larger gangs had hundreds of acres that they intended to work with slave labor. Davy Atchison already owned several sizable plantations. So while plunder was what the ruffians were after, their leaders were after a lot more. One by one the militia captains agreed to quit the field and return to their homes. Everyone except Quantrell, whose vow to revenge himself on Lawrence for Louise's death remained uppermost in his mind. But other forces intervened.

Throughout the invasion beginning on December 1, 1855, the weather had been moderate. However, on December 9th an arctic wind began to blow. The icy wind froze what it touched and by evening an arctic storm of sleet and snow plunged temperatures to below zero degrees. This blizzard froze Quantrell's men who wore little more than a shirt and saddle pants, forcing the ruffians to beat a hasty retreat back to Leavenworth. The abrupt weather change saved Lawrence from destruction that day. Quantrell would not allow Lawrence to be so fortunate in the future.

However, for the time being, all around Lawrence free state homesteaders celebrated the peaceful settlement negotiated by Governor Shannon. Everyone was happy. Everyone except a tall, raw-boned man with a bearded face and piercing, unsmiling eyes. John Brown railed against the treaty. Only recently had John Brown joined his sons at the free state settlement at Osawatomie. When news of the attack on Lawrence reached his settlement, John Brown and his four sons rushed to the town's defense. Brown and his sons arrived in Lawrence the day the treaty was announced to the townspeople. At the meeting, Brown argued that the only satisfactory way of concluding the issue was by soundly thrashing the law and order vigilance party. "We've gotta send those border ruffians and bushwhackers back to Missouri with their tails between their legs," John Brown thundered. But the citizens of Lawrence, who had suffered through not only the invasion but also through a protracted blockade, were only too happy to avoid further violence. They had no intention in engaging in the serious battle urged by John Brown; the citizens of Lawrence intended to avoid such a conflict at all costs.

Only Ellen Collins paid any attention to John Brown at all. And though she shuddered at his words, Ellen had a premonition that this stern-faced prophet was correct. If John Brown's vision of the future was accurate, the free staters of Lawrence had not seen the last of those bushwhackers and border ruffians who were bent on their destruction. And even though the arctic winds blew harsh winter storms over the plains of Kansas with such ferocity that few Missourians harbored any ideas of attacking Lawrence that winter, it was just a matter of time before Lawrence would come under attack once again. Even the most naïve free stater, such as Lawrence's kindly mayor, Stoddard Hoyt, knew there would be no peace.

"You can't just wait," Yerby said to Ellen, "the town's gotta do something."

"Like what?" Ellen asked.

"I don't know what," Yerby replied. "But I know those 'bush-whackers' will be back to continue their blockade." The committee of safety had been meeting continually. Ellen had been elected to join the committee and had attended all the meetings. She did not need Frank Yerby to tell her about the situation. But a restatement of the obvious was not Yerby's primary intention. Rather he was employing one of the subjects he knew would divert Ellen's attention. In the dreariness of winter and the stillness of the evening, Yerby used all his imagination and skill to prevent Ellen from being drawn into the black hole of self-accusation and guilt. Yerby was using every device he could think of to keep Ellen's attention focused on the present and not on the past...not on Louise's death. The harsh winter prevented Ellen from holding classes. Her enforced idleness caused her to be assaulted by more frequent bouts of depression.

"If you don't know what can be done," Ellen asked, "why do you keep talking?" Ellen was getting frustrated with Frank. She needed some space. If she were to be saved, she would have to save herself; Frank couldn't do it.

Ellen needed time to get in touch with her own feelings. Louise's death drove her perilously close to insanity. *Louise wanted me at that roadhouse,* Ellen thought to herself. *But did she mean to kill me?* Ellen turned the entire incident over and over in her mind. *It looked that way,* she told herself. But then Ellen could not decide what affected her more, Louise's attempt on her life or Louise's conspiring with her own mother's killer. It might have occurred to Ellen that whatever Louise's intent, Ellen had nothing to do with it. Louise had been destroyed by her own hate. Ellen had tried to love her. And in the end, Ellen finally realized that Louise had hated her and would have killed her at the roadhouse had it not been for Hitchcock. This realization saved her and helped her fight back her own demons and her feelings of guilt.

Nonetheless Frank kept at her "Try this out," Frank said. "If you can get the free state settlements all over Kansas to join together, the

Law and Order Party could not concentrate just on Lawrence. You could change the course of what seems inevitable." Ellen looked at Frank with such a lovely smile that he could have been happy to remain on the desolate Kansas plains forever.

"Why that's a wonderful idea, Frank," she said, giving him a look that warmed away the arctic chill that invaded the Kansas plain. "I'll bring it up at the next committee of safety meeting."

. . .

Though neither of them realized it then, that was the birth of the Topeka Movement. In the spring of 1856, a constitutional convention of all the free staters was held in Topeka. A petition for admittance was drafted and sent to Congress, and a body of state constitutional officers was elected. Charles Robinson was elected Governor of the free state of Kansas. Throughout Kansas, the Topeka Movement lifted the spirits of those homesteaders and those working for a free state. But, though the free staters were unaware of it, they had become the architects of their own doom. The Topeka Movement also gave the pro-slavery forces reason to celebrate.

"We've got them, Davy!" Billy Quantrell exclaimed excitedly to Davy Atchison. Both were sitting in A.B. Miller's saloon in Leavenworth when the boy brought the telegraph message from Lecompton: "That entire gang's been indicted."

A Lecompton grand jury appointed by a law and order vigilance party judge handed down indictments against every officer elected by the Topeka Convention on the charge of treason. The charges were based upon their several statements repudiating the legislature and its laws, as well as their submission of a petition for statehood in the Union. The petition for statehood included a prohibition against slavery, in violation of Kansas territorial laws.

"That's what we've been waiting for," Atkinson beamed.

"Not only that," Quantrell said. "They indicted the Free State Hotel as well as the *Herald of Freedom* and *Free State* newspapers in Lawrence. We'll burn them all to the ground."

"Call out the boys," Davy Atkinson said. "Now we'll show those nigger-loving abolitionists." So once again, on May 21, 1856, the earth rumbled and the air was thick with dirt and dust as hundreds of riders thundered across the Kansas plains and into Lawrence. This time they didn't wear white ribbons; they were loaded down with weapons of war.

When the vigilantes came swarming into town this time, Ellen and the other members of the committee of safety were meeting with the mayor, discussing the crisis in the great meeting room in Lawrence's Free State Hotel. The committee had only just learned of the indictments handed down against the leaders of the Topeka Movement in the past several days. "What should we do?" was what people wanted to know. Gaius Jenkins, an original free state homesteader in Lawrence, owned a forty acre parcel. He wanted to defend the town and proposed that the free state leadership be defended. The majority of the committee voted not to resist. Jim Lane, commander of Lawrence's militia, and most of his lieutenants, left Lawrence when they heard about the indictments, days before Quantrell arrived.

Many months later, after the Lecompton government released Gaius Jenkins along with other leaders of the Topeka Movement, Jim Lane snuck back into Lawrence and shot Jenkins dead in the street. Some say that it was over a land claim. But Lane was one of Cushing's agents. Louise Collins had recruited him.

"Bring all your weapons to the Free State Hotel within one half hour," boomed Atchison. "If you do not surrender all your weapons, we will bombard the town."

"What weapons are you referring to?" Mayor Hoyt asked politely.

"You know what weapons that we want, your cannon, all your

Sharp's rifles and all your ammunition," Quantrell demanded. Members of the committee of safety went over to the wooden shanty that served as Lawrence's armory. They brought out five boxes of Sharp's rifles…one hundred altogether. But they also took extra precautions to hide several other boxes of rifles. A shipment of Beecher's "bibles," two hundred Sharp's rifles, remained hidden from Quantrell. Quantrell expected to find the hundred rifles listed on the shipping manifest, and he was aware of their six pound howitzer cannon and forced the committee to surrender it. "And now to business," Quantrell said to the militia leaders. "Get those weapons back to camp," he ordered one of his lieutenants.

Then Quantrell looked around; there was such a stark difference between Lawrence and Leavenworth. Here in Lawrence, the streets were clean. The neat little wooden houses boasted modest flower gardens in the front and large vegetable gardens in the rear. The spires of several Christian churches of remarkably stable and aesthetic design pierced the sky. Commerce within Lawrence reflected its commitment to the wellbeing of its citizens. Lawrence's businesses included general and hardware stores, an apothecary, a post and telegraph office, a land claim legal office, livery stables, doctors, dentists, shipping firms, warehouses and two newspapers. In contrast, Leavenworth was a squalid and filthy pesthole; a dirty little dunghill whose only commercial activities, gambling, drinking and prostitution, were indulged in by those whose business was murder, land grabbing and war. Quantrell hated Lawrence. "Search the town," Quantrell shouted to his men. "Seize any contraband and arrest any Topeka leader. If anyone resists, shoot them and burn their house down."

Then the outrages began. Gaius Jenkins and other free state party leaders who remained in Lawrence were arrested. The vigilantes raided every home. They took money, valuables, clothes and livestock. A few who attempted to prevent the vigilantes from entering were shot and their wooden cabins burned to the ground. No one was spared. Women pleaded with the invaders, but to no avail. One of the unfortunate victims was the brother-in-law of the Reverend Ephraim Nute, pastor of Lawrence's Unitarian Church. The victim was shot dead by one of the bushwhackers and his scalp was taken back to Leavenworth as a trophy.

Then the vigilantes turned their attention to the Free State Hotel and the two newspapers. Quantrell ordered his men to destroy each of the structures with cannon fire. After inflicting as much damage as possible with the bombardment, he ordered what remained to be burned to the ground. The orgy of violence on the citizens of Lawrence, as well the surrounding area, continued until the border ruffians, burdened with loot, turned and headed back to Leavenworth.

Even before the first building was burned or the first citizen shot, Quantrell began searching for Ellen Collins. He had a score to settle. But throughout the day and even as the fires from many burning buildings lit the night, Quantrell searched in vain. All anti-slavery people understood the need for an escape route and the value of an underground tunnel. One of the first tasks Shields Green had set for himself was to plan and build an escape route from the school. He and Frank dug and reinforced an escape tunnel that led to a secret trail across the plains to a secure cave on the side of Mount Oread. There Shields and Frank led Ellen to outwait her pursuers. Finally only Quantrell and a few men remained. So after making one final search without success, he ordered his men to burn down the schoolhouse.

Once again, upon hearing of the attack on Lawrence, John Brown and his sons rushed to its defense. And once more he was too late. But as he and his sons rode to assist Lawrence, Quantrell and his men invaded, looted and burned down John Brown's home and those of his neighbors living in the free state settlement at Osawatomie. When John Brown returned to find his home destroyed and his belongings gone, he and his sons rode to a pro-slavery settlement on the Pottawatomie Creek. Sneaking up on individual cabins, Brown captured five sleeping pro-slavery men. In front of their wives and children, Brown ordered his sons to kill the five men. Four were hacked to death with swords; the fifth was shot in the back when he attempted to escape. Free staters were to pay many times over for those foul murders committed by John Brown and his sons.

During the next several months, the law and order vigilance party continued its embargo against Lawrence. Not a sack of flour or bushel of meal was available for miles around. Over two thousand men, women and children in Lawrence slowly starved. The spirits and hopes of the *free staters* all over Kansas sank to a very low level in the face of this fearsome pro-slavery power of the Democratic Party.

CHAPTER TWENTY-SEVEN

No season is more beautiful in Washington than springtime. And there is no journey more pleasant in the nation's capital than the one taken by Congressman Preston Brooks up Pennsylvania Avenue to the Capital building. But a pleasant drive on a springtime day was the last thing on the mind of this grim-faced congressman from South Carolina. At the Capitol steps, Brooks leapt from his carriage and grasping his heavy metal-tipped walking stick, dashed inside. Looking neither to the right nor to the left, Brooks strode over to the Senate chambers and pushed through the heavy doors right onto the Senate floor. The Senate was in recess; several senators milled about and others sat at their desks. Brooks paused briefly and looked around the Senate floor until he spotted Lawrence Keitt, the junior senator from South Carolina. They nodded to each other. The two legislators were closely acquainted; they even boasted of distant family ties.

Today these two close friends of South Carolina intended to give a demonstration of Southern pride and will. The South had willed that Kansas be brought into the Union as a slave state, and now they intended to show the entire country what would happen to anyone who opposed this will. Such a person was Charles Sumner, the junior senator from Massachusetts. Preston Brooks approached the Massachusetts senator as he sat at his desk busily replying to a stack of correspondence.

"I have read your speech *"Crime Against Kansas"* twice, sir," Preston Brooks shouted at Sumner. You have libeled South Carolina and the good name of my uncle, Judge Butler." Sumner turned to see who it was that had spoken. But without waiting for any reply, Brooks raised his heavy metal-tipped cane and struck a vicious blow to Sumner's head. The force of the blow lifted the surprised senator half out of his seat, leaving a gaping four-inch head wound gushing blood. Sumner was unconscious before his body even fell to the floor. Not satisfied, Brooks then leapt upon Sumner's prostrate body and began laying so many blows that his cane at last broke upon the senator's bleeding back.

While Brooks administered the beating, Keitt drew his cane and threatened any senator who might be bold enough to interfere. Finally, Senator John Crittenden of Kentucky decided to intervene, pushing Keitt out of the way. He seized Brooks, bodily preventing the South Carolina congressman from inflicting further injury on the unconscious junior senator from Massachusetts.

Preston Brooks and Lawrence Keitt had been offended by Charles Sumner's remarks about the assaults against free state homesteaders in Kansas. It was no secret that the Democratic Party was behind the campaign of terror and intimidation against the northern homesteaders trying to get free Kansas acreage. But that Charles Sumner would charge them for their crimes in the Senate of the United States was unacceptable. The lesson that Brook and Keitt taught American society was that in the end the issue could be decided only by force and violence, because the South respected neithr law nor order. Charles Sumner lingered between life and death for three months, and a year would pass before he could leave his hospital bed. More than three years would pass before he returned to the Senate floor.

The assault on Senator Sumner occurred on May 22, 1856, the day after Quantrell's vigilantes sacked Lawrence. And it reverberated all over the United States, North and South. Americans were given a glimpse of the vision the Democratic Party and its pro-slavery leadership held for the country. More importantly, Americans saw that the issue of slavery had very little to do with race, but everything to do with power. More importantly, it had to do with who was going to benefit from the bounty that was America.

Abolitionists and free staters were as indignant as pro-slavery vigilantes were jubilant. Northerners who willingly tolerated daily assaults on blacks, both slave and free, now understood that their white skins afforded them no protection where the issue of slavery was involved. Even with the complete power of the federal government in their hands, Southerners preferred to resolve their issues through acts of violence. They were unprepared and unwilling to resolve differences through civilized discussion. For these people, slavery was not only an institution compatible with America's democratic ideals, it was an institution that was compatible with their fundamental religious beliefs, as well.

The bloody beating of a United States Senator, peaceably conducting his business at his desk in the chamber of the United States Senate, dramatized the issues at stake for American freedoms. Americans glory in slaughter and have no pity for any other race of man save their own kind. Devoid of intelligence, corrupt with power, the ferocious Southern spirit that masqueraded as "chivalry" showed all Americans that it was capable of using violence even against other white men. On May 22, 1856 one day after the sacking of Lawrence, the Democratic Party demonstrated that it has prepared not only to murder defenseless homesteaders on the lonely Kansas frontier, but also attack defenseless senators in the very halls of congress.

The *Albany Evening-Herald* reflected the opinion of Northern abolitionists when it wrote:

"This attack carries home a more vivid understanding of what the Free States have consented for years to live under. The degradation was as real years ago, but never so much as now. But the North has always lacked manly self-assertion, especially in the Senate, where a majority of the representatives voted, only a few weeks ago, to reject the petition of Free Kansas for admission and surrender her citizens to the unchecked brutalities and inflamed indignation of the Border Ruffians."

The sacking of Lawrence and beating of Charles Sumner galvanized anti-slavery opinion in the North. Good people from every religious faith and civic affiliation came to a common understanding of the seriousness of the threat to a free America for themselves and their children. These incidents left no doubt that the Democratic Party intended to rule the American society by repression, terrorism and intimidation. They did not mean to strip personal liberties, and the right to life, only from the wild Indian, the savage African and the lazy Mexican, but also from freethinking whites and ambitious settlers.

Decent citizens everywhere began to answer the call for a free and open society and for the right of God-fearing Americans to live in peace. Americans started to come to Kansas with a commitment to civilization and freedom. Hundreds of young, idealistic men and women responded to the challenge. They came from colleges, from professional occupations, from churches, from secure and comfortable families. They came determined to join the fight on the cold, dreary Kansas plains and to win the struggle for a free America. Many more Americans were now determined that Kansas would be free.

• • •

But in the meantime, the citizens of Lawrence were starving. After the sacking, the vigilantes kept up the blockade. There was hardly a grain of cereal or a drop of milk within twenty miles. Lawrence with its burned-out buildings and rubble-strewn streets looked like the war zone that it was. Here and there people could be seen sifting through the debris and the garbage heaps…looking for lost memories or past dreams…or for something to eat.

An amiable soft-spoken man made his way through Lawrence's rubble to a single story office building sitting in the middle of Lawrence's town square. It was one of the few edifices left undamaged by the vigilantes' attack. The Reverend Cordley knew that, as of yet, no supplies had gotten through the law and order vigilance party blockade, yet he had promised his elders that he would inquire. So he was off to see the mayor. *That blessed man*, Reverend Cordley thought. *I just don't see how he manages it. I am certain that I couldn't.* So now to avoid looking into the listless, hungry eyes of the children and the parents looking for a miracle, Richard Cordley was going to add to the burdens of Mayor Stoddard Hoyt. Stepping up to the door, the pastor of Lawrence's Congregational Church pushed it open to the rather drab frontier office occupied by the mayor of Lawrence. Reverend Cordley spied the little round man hunched over his desk in the corner, busily at work.

"Reverend Cordley," the mayor said with the genuine warmth he displayed for all of his visitors, "please have a seat. How can I help you, my friend?" Stoddard Hoyt asked one of his favorite ministers.

"Mayor Hoyt," the minister said timidly, "my people want to know if you have any news."

"Yes, Reverend, we have had some word," Stoddard Hoyt told his visitor. "You know Ellen Collins and her two boys are organizing the collection effort. They have sent word from Topeka that free staters from all over are coming to help."

"But we need food," the pastor said.

"Yes, we know," Mayor Hoyt replied. "They sent out wagons twice. Neither of them got through. They are trying to organize a large wagon train and get some support from local homesteaders to bring the supplies in."

"But my people want to know when." Reverend Cordley pushed Hoyt even though he knew it served no purpose. It was out of his hands now.

"Well, Reverend," Lawrence's mayor replied sadly, "we are doing all we can." Stoddard Hoyt stared out his office window. He had prayed that supplies from Topeka would have arrived by now. But the vigilantes' blockade had been effective and was reducing Lawrence's population to starvation. Jim Lane's militia and Ellen Collins and her "boys" Frank and Shields had left Lawrence in hopes of bringing some supplies back to the beleaguered town. Nowhere else were free state settlements under the pressures that were being applied to Lawrence. Recruits and supplies were being collected in Topeka. It was just a matter of time before some supplies were smuggled into Lawrence—at least that was what Mayor Stoddard Hoyt prayed for. *God bless these people,* the mayor thought to himself. *Neither starvation nor desperation has turned the people of Lawrence from their faith or commitment.*

The pastors of each of the various Christian denominations continuously minded their flocks. Each of the churches had organized and shared its meager resources. The pastors made every attempt to assist their parishioners. Many of them had actually performed the miracle of the loaves and fishes. However, the miracle was no longer working. It had been over two months since Ellen Collins and her men had volunteered to try to bring provisions to Lawrence through an Underground Railroad route. A town without a school didn't need a schoolteacher. Some attempts to bring provisions through the blockade had been successful, but many more had failed, and Lawrence's provisions were down to a minimal level. Choices were being made as to who would eat and who would not. Mayor Hoyt stared out at the ramshackle, burned-out buildings that were once a great hotel and two bustling newspaper offices. He stared out at the broken, violated, burned homes of Lawrence's citizens. But looking at the destruction was easier for Mayor Hoyt than facing this good man.

Hoyt noticed a cloud of dust rising up in the west. "Oh, my God, here they come again," was the mayor's first thought, and panic seized this devout man whose piety had been severely tested. But then he saw the beaming face of Reverend Cordley and took a second look. He saw why the minister smiled. Through the dust rolled covered wagons pulled by lumbering oxen. A long train of them rolled up the street and into the center of town. The mayor and the minister raced out the door to join the gathering crowd of cheering townspeople. Ellen Collins, Frank Yerby, Shields Green and many other citizens from Lawrence had gone foraging for food and were now bringing in a huge wagon train of settlers and supplies into Lawrence. Jim Lane's militia even seemed to be providing an escort, though in reality the militia had met the wagon train barely a mile outside town.

"We are so happy that you made it back safely," Mayor Hoyt said to Ellen. She noticed that the good-natured soul's rotund figure was beginning to look thin and drawn. "Where did you find all these settlers and all these provisions?" Hoyt asked. "It's like manna from heaven."

"Our many friends promised to help," Ellen replied, "and more help is on the way." While Mayor Hoyt and the ministers took charge of the food and supplies, Ellen, Frank and Shields dragged themselves back to their mud huts. Many grateful townspeople came up to Ellen, and grabbing her hands, thanked her for the food. Some even kissed her on both cheeks. When Ellen, Frank and Shields left the townsfolk, they and the newcomers alike were in high spirits.

"There are hundreds of free state people pouring across the border into Kansas," Ellen told the Committee of Safety the following day. The bushwhackers are attacking them but many of them are getting through. Some are fighting back and winning."

"Then why aren't they coming into Lawrence?" asked Brett

Falks, one of the committee members. Falks had invested a considerable fortune in borrowed money in his dry goods store. The vigilantes were not content with robbing him, they burned down his building as well. Falks had all but decided to pack up the few belongings remaining to him and return home to New York. But to do so meant that he would not only be penniless but overwhelmed by a mountain of debt he could not hope to repay.

"It's those forts," announced Jim Lane, the commander of Lawrence's militia. "They're riding patrols out of Franklin, Saunders and Titus, attacking everyone headed towards Lawrence. Most of the newcomers getting through are coming through routes west of Topeka."

"Possibly we should all go to Topeka," Mayor Hoyt suggested. Some members of the committee agreed with the idea.

"After all we have suffered and all the lives that have been lost, how could we consider giving up?" Ellen Collins spoke up. "Besides, the only reason they have not attacked Topeka is because they want Lawrence first. Once they have driven us out of Lawrence, they will concentrate on Topeka. After that, there will be no place in Kansas where free state homesteaders will be safe."

"They certainly are not safe here," another committee person countered.

"No, they are not," Ellen replied. "But because we have remained firm, Topeka has grown and thrived. We are helping hundreds of good men and women to find their way here and build a free Kansas."

"That's very noble but we are evading the problem," Jim Lane said. "The problem is that as long as those bushwhackers are safe behind their stockades, they are free to attack anyone coming to Lawrence. The forts must be destroyed."

No one spoke. The idea of attacking anyone was not only morally disagreeable to most of the committee, but rather awkward. Such a course could drive a wedge between the various religious groups, especially the Quakers, of which Mayor Hoyt was one. Yet, the choice was clear. Parents could watch their children starve; homesteaders could be driven off of their land; righteous, God-fearing people could allow themselves to be murdered—or they could drive the vigilantes out of their lairs. "Many of the young men coming into Kansas are more than willing to fight," Lane continued. "They have joined our militia here and others militias formed in different parts of Kansas. We have the Sharp's rifles. All we need is the will…the will to defend our loved ones and ourselves. My men are ready."

The debate went on far into the night; but in the end the citizens of Lawrence found that they had no choice. If they were to survive, the forts that blockaded the town had to be destroyed. The only other choice was to abandon Lawrence to the law and order vigilantes. In the end the decision was unanimous. Lawrence's committee of safety authorized Jim Lane to prepare for the assault. However, Mayor Hoyt requested that he first be allowed to attempt a settlement with the vigilantes. Hoyt was commtted to avoiding any unnecessary bloodshed, and he wanted to give the bushwhackers every opportunity to vacate the forts voluntarily. Certainly the mayor understood love; he probably knew a lot less about hate; but about necessity Stoddard Hoyt knew nothing at all.

"If you announce that we are coming," Lane argued, "you take away the advantage of surprise."

"I absolutely refuse to condone any attack against those forts before giving those men an opportunity to surrender beforehand," Hoyt said adamantly. And in the end Lane knew there was no way he could prevent Hoyt from making his peace overture. Since Lane would not be prepared to march for several days, that gave Hoyt more than enough time to resolve the issue with the vigilantes.

"What?" Yerby yelled at Ellen after she announced her intentions to join Mayor Hoyt on his peace mission to the ruffians' stockade. "If you want to commit suicide why not get it over with? Why are you dragging it out?" Yerby had lost all of his detachment and objectivity where Ellen was concerned. Since Louise's death, Ellen had become withdrawn and less communicative with him. They had taken a trip to Boston. The Massachusetts Emigrant Aid Society asked her to speak to a group at Fanueil Hall. Her simple description of the harsh, brutal conditions in Kansas and the courage of the free state homesteaders in the face of the vigilante attempts to drive them out did more to recruit emigrants than all the lurid newspaper accounts and headlines on "Bleeding Kansas". Her own bravery inspired men, young and old, to take up the cause of freedom, decency and civilization.

Ellen still had not the courage to face either her husband or their children, both of whom were now well into adulthood. Instead, after her speech Ellen went up to St. Catharines where the fugitive slave community welcomed her back into the Cathar fellowship as one of their own. But towards Yerby, Ellen became more distant, more aloof. Now Yerby no longer was an objective observer of the human condition; he had become a despondent, nervous suitor whose affections were not merely spurned but went unrecognized. Ellen did not purposely try to hurt Yerby's feelings; she had merley become insensitive. But her insensitivity only inflamed Yerby's love and blinded him to everything but his own emotional attachment and his petty jealousies.

The more Ellen distanced herself from him, the more Yerby began to fantasize an imaginary romance between Ellen and Shields. Yerby noticed that Ellen often laughed when she and Shields were together, something she seldom did with him now. *How could she reject me for that old, country black whose only intelligence comes from his hands and feet?* Yerby asked himself. Ellen and Shields had no emotional relationship. Shields was devoted to Ellen and, in turn, she trusted and relied upon him. Neither of them wanted or expected anything more from the other. But Yerby, on the other hand, wanted and even expected Ellen to return his affections. He knew that such a love was impossible. How could the creation fall in love with the creator? Yerby was a silly old fool for falling in love with his own creation. But that was Frank Yerby's problem and not Ellen's. In his life, Yerby had known many loves and had caused a lot of pain. Now it was his turn to feel pain. Nonetheless Yerby continued to behave like a love-sick schoolboy. He was annoyed and it showed, but Ellen neither understood Yerby's emotional state nor cared. Toward Yerby, Ellen was a classic study of both ignorance and indifference.

"This is important, Frank," Ellen said to him in a tired, resigned voice. "I am a Cathar and I am bound to support Stoddard. If you don't want to join us, I'll understand."

"It's not that and you know it," Yerby protested.

"Know what?" Ellen's emerald green eyes flashed with emotion. She was tired of Yerby acting as if he controlled her. She intended to see this thing through to the end. So much was at stake she had no time for Yerby's sophomoric hysterics. "We leave tomorrow," she said matter of factly. "So, if you don't mind, I would like to get some rest." With that Ellen turned on her heel and went out to her hut.

All the while, Shields observed them both without saying a word. *Them folks sure do have a time with each other,* he laughed to himself.

The next morning the group of peacemakers led by Stoddard Hoyt rode forth from Lawrence under of flag of truce. They headed southwest towards Washington Creek where Fort Saunders sat some twelve miles away. Quantrell now maintained his headquarters there. Since Louise's death he had avoided Leavenworth and its memories. He and his band roved between Saunders and Fort Titus, which sat nearest the law and order vigilance party's capital at Lecompton and Franklin, which sat only four miles east of Lawrence. These so-called "forts" were actually big log houses with port-holes from which the defenders could shoot. They were amply stocked with provisions and weapons, giving the bushwhackers safe havens. The vigilantes could raid homesteaders or rob supply trains bound for Lawrence and afterwards retreat to the closest of the three forts. As long as these forts provided a secure refuge for Quantrell's men and the other gangs of bushwhackers roaming the Kansas plains, neither Lawrence nor any of the free state homesteaders living in the vicinity were safe.

"Major," the lookout shouted, "Major Quantrell."

"What is it, Jimmy?" Billy Quantrell answered in a surly voice. He was in the middle of a poker hand and did not take kindly to being disturbed.

"I think you'd better come see this, sir," Jimmy replied. The sentry was the youngster who had done all of Louise's bidding in Leavenworth. When barely seventeen, Jimmy had left his family in Missouri to join one of the vigilance committees in Leavenworth. When Quantrell gave him the opportunity to join him in Kansas and get into the action, Jimmy jumped at the opportunity. His family was poor and the loot Jimmy was able to get from raids on the homesteaders was more than his pa made in a year doing plantation work.

"This had better be important," Quantrell said angrily, "or I'll...." But he stopped in mid-sentence and swore out loud. "Well, I'll be goddamn, if this don't beat all." Standing in front of his stronghold was a short, round man; in a wagon sat a woman and a darkie carrying a white flag. And it was not just any woman; it was her! "What you all want up here?" Quantrell asked his unexpected guests, as he looked about for other free staters.

"We have come to discuss a matter of some importance," Mayor Hoyt replied.

"Which is?" Quantrell asked, his voice dripping with sarcasm.

"We have come to discuss terms for a peace settlement," Mayor Hoyt announced.

"A peace settlement," Quantrell exclaimed. "Well I'll be...you nigger-lovers planning to leave Lawrence, are you? Well I can't guarantee your safety, but maybe something can be worked out. When are you all planning on leaving?" Billy Quantrell thought about Louise and the outline of a treacherous plan began to form in his mind. Now he was going to have his revenge on Lawrence. *I'll make any promise they want to hear to get them out of Lawrence,* Quantrell thought gleefully, *I'll only keep my promise to burn that abolitionist town to the ground with every one of those nigger-lovin' abolitionists in it.*

Stoddard Hoyt thought to himself, *I haven't made myself clear.* He decided to start all over. So he looked up at Quantrell and said, "You must understand our position. You are forcing this violence on us."

"What are you talking about?" Quantrell asked, genuinely failing to comprehend exactly what this short little man was talking about.

Looking up at the almost six foot frame of the leader of the vigilantes, who by now was standing directly in front of him, Mayor Hoyt gave his brave reply. "Sir, I am afraid I have given you the wrong impression. We are not leaving Lawrence; we are offering you and your men the opportunity to vacate this property as well as those blockhouses located at Titus and Franklin."

Had Major William Quantrell of the Kansas militia, acting under the authority of General Davy Atchison and the Kansas territorial governor, Wilson Shannon, been told that his parents were black and that he was being returned to slavery, he could not have been more amazed or confounded by Mayor Hoyt's words.

"You see, sir," Hoyt continued, "you and your men are doing the people of Lawrence great harm. Many innocent people have suffered because of your attacks and the people of Lawrence are determined to remove you from this area … by force if it should become necessary. However, it is our desire to avoid bloodshed, so I am appealing to your sense of decency, if not for our sakes, then for the sake of your own men, for whose lives you bear some responsibility."

At first, Quantrell was amused. *This pathetic little man, hiding behind that woman, Louise's aunt, must be kidding,* he laughed to himself. But then he became concerned. There were not that many of them here at Saunders and less than a hundred men manned all three forts. "Jimmy," he called out, "tell Claude to scout around and see if we have any other visitors." And then, turning to Hoyt, Quantrell gave an evil sneer. "We've been in that miserable abolitionists haven of yours twice now," Quantrell shouted. "You cowards let us take control without firing a shot in your defense. What gives you the nerve to come up here, hiding behind the skirts of a woman to threaten us. Did Jim Lane put you up to this?"

Even though Lane worked for Cushing, Quantrell hated Lane with a passion that few could understand. Some said that it was just an act; the two men had to make everyone believe that they were on opposite sides. But it was no act. There was a story that Lane was responsible for the murder of Quantrell's brother. Others said that Quantrell hated Lane because Lane and Louise had been lovers. Quantrell could not stand knowing it; nor could he bear the thought that Jim Lane knew Billy Quantrell knew. Whatever the reason, the two conspirators working for Cushing genuinely hated each other.

Ellen watched the mayor's peace proposal with growing concern. She could see that it was not going well at all and once again she wondered how she had gotten herself into this situation. But she was committed to her Catharine teachings and would not abandon Stoddard Hoyt, the elder of Lawrence's Quaker community, as well as the mayor of the town. His faith and strength had sustained them this far. Hoyt had a vision of a flourishing civilization in Kansas. It was his mission to make that vision a reality. And this was the mission of the others who had left St. Catharines and followed him here. And if it was Ellen's fate to die here, then so be it, her life would have had meaning.

Stoddard stood firm paling under the angry glare of the murderous vigilante with whom he had come to negotiate. "I have come to make no threats, sir," the mayor replied. "I have merely come to offer you the opportunity to avoid the inevitable bloodshed that must follow from your actions here."

"I don't make war on women," Quantrell sneered, "even if lily-livered cowards like you hide behind them. And that darkie there will bring a good price at the market in St. Louis. But you, sir, are going to pay for your insolence." With that, Quantrell pulled out his Colt revolver and calmly shot Stoddard through the head.

Instantly, Shields dropped the white flag he held and turning the wagon in which he and Ellen rode, made a mad dash away from Fort Saunders with the bushwhackers laughing and filling the air with ear-piercing yells. Several of Quantrell's men began firing their pistols in the air just over the heads of the fleeing horses, which made them run all the faster.

"Shall we go get 'em, Major?" Jimmy asked.

Quantrell thought about going after them, but decided against it. "No, let them go," he said with a smile. "When they tell them nigger-loving abolitionists what happened here, they'll be leaving Lawrence like rats off one of them sinking riverboats."

Quantrell might have reported the incident to Lecompton or to Davy Atchison in Leavenworth, and he might have saved himself a lot of trouble and considerable embarrassment, but he didn't. And as always happens, this slight oversight by an arrogant man flush with power put Quantrell and the vigilantes in a vulnerable position.

News of Stoddard Hoyt's murder spread like wildfire. It spread through Lawrence and it spread throughout all of Kansas' free state settlements. Women openly mourned in the street. All the churches held memorial services in his honor. The Quaker community was devastated with grief. Stoddard Hoyt had been such a pillar of strength for that dedicated group during their time of troubles that it was difficult for any of them to envision how they could continue without him.

Jim Lane prepared his one hundred and fifty man militia to attack the forts, and many others rushed to join up when news of Mayor Hoyt's murder spread. Several Quakers, preferring a fall from grace, renounced membership in their community and enlisted in Lane's militia, as well. They were fully prepared to sacrifice their souls to free Lawrence from the state-sponsored terrorism imposed by Kansas' law and order vigilance party. Everyone in Lawrence understood that each man had to make peace with his own conscience, whether to go and fight or to remain at home. But the time the militia rode out, over three hundred free state men joined in the attack.

"What do you think it will be like?" one of the former Quakers asked Yerby. The militia marched in an orderly column two abreast while all the other volunteers straggled afterwards in a disorderly, haphazard fashion. It couldn't be helped; there was no time for drill.

"What do you mean, son?" Yerby replied knowing all along what the youngster, who could not have been more than eighteen, meant. Yerby could smell it. He could smell fear oozing from the youngster's brow and down from his underarms. Nor was he the only one who smelled of fear. This was the first battle most of these free staters would see. They did not know what to expect. Some of the volunteers pulled off the road their trembling legs unable to get them any closer to fort Franklin and the upcoming battle between the free staters and vigilantes.

"Do you think we can lick them?" the young man quavered, trying to keep his voice from betraying his terror.

"Don't worry," Yerby reassured him, "we're gong to lick them all right."

"I sure hope so," the boy said, the doubt sounding in his voice, "I sure hope so."

Lane decided to attack the fort closest to Lawrence in hopes that Quantrell had not sounded the alert. Franklin was only four miles away and an easy march for the militia. When they arrived at Franklin, no alarm had been raised and all was peaceful at the log blockhouse and adjoining corral, stable and smaller cabins. Months of complete freedom of movement had made the vigilantes complaisant. But unfortunately, Lane's men could not curb their enthusiasm and lost the element of surprise. They raced down upon the settlement, yelling and shouting. Before the militia could attack with effect, the defenders all made it safely inside the log house and prepared to do battle.

Lane surrounded the fort with free staters. His men poured volley after volley onto the thick log structures, but their attack had little effect. The bullets bounced harmlessly off the thick oak logs. The bushwhackers, inside, returned the militia's fire with volleys of their own from the gun ports built into the side of the log stronghold. But their shots were equally ineffective. Lane was able to get his men concealed behind fences, mounds of dirt, and anything else that would afford them some protection. And for awhile the issue between the two warring parties remained stalemated, neither side being able to inflict any harm on the other.

"Let's smoke them out," one of Lane's lieutenants called out.

Lane agreed. Looking around, he found a wagon and they loaded it with hay from the corral. Then Lane motioned to one of his men. "Roll it against the blockhouse," he shouted. Dousing the hay with kerosene, militiamen hurled fiery torches into the wagonload of hay. Very quickly the blazing hay began to burn the fort's log supports and structures. The militiamen raised cries of triumph as the wooden structures began to burn and smoke began to envelop the settlement. Soon the defenders inside Fort Franklin began choking on the thick gray smoke.

"We surrender," the vigilantes yelled, begging for mercy. Lane permitted the fifteen gasping, choking vigilantes to escape the smoldering log structure unharmed, to the jeers and cheers of Lawrence's victorious free staters.

"Put out that fire," Lane ordered, directing his men to retrieve water from a nearby creek to put out the flames. "Lieutenant Holmes, check on casualties and report back."

"Yessir," his eager subordinate replied.

When the report came back, Lane discovered that neither a uniformed militiaman nor any other man had suffered any harm in the attack. Once the fire was out, the militia seized a goodly amount of provisions and weapons, including a cannon. "We'll be able to use this against Fort Saunders, eh Bickerton?" Lane asked a lieutenant who had artillery experience. Bickerton had served as a gunnery sergeant in the Mexican War before bringing his family out to Kansas to settle his own land.

"Well, sir," Bickerton replied, "she's a fine artillery piece, there's no doubt, but there is not an ounce of powder or any shot for it."

"I guess that was fortunate for us," Lane said wryly, "else our casualty figures might have been far different and the outcome might have been in doubt, considering how green most of these men are."

"No doubt, laddie," Bickerton replied. "But since we'll be needing this piece against Saunders and Titus, we'll have to go back to Lawrence so I can salvage some shot and powder."

Lane thought about it and said, "I can't go back to Lawrence. Every minute we delay, they'll be able to use to get ready. Look at these boys here; they were scared to death. If Quantrell is able to get more men from Lecompton and make a fight of it, we won't stand a chance."

"So what do you want to do, leave this fine weapon here?" Bickerton asked.

"No," Lane replied. "I'm sending you back to Lawrence with these provisions and the prisoners. I want you to take the cannon and do what you have to do to make it functional."

"Okay, Major," Bickerton replied in his thick Irish brogue.

"Meet me at Saunders no later than noon tomorrow, do you understand, Lieutenant?" Lane glared at him. "That is an order."

"I will do my best, sir," Bickerton snapped back with military precision.

"I don't want your best," Lane snapped, "I want you there! Is that understood."

"Yessir!" came the immediate response.

Bickerton left for Lawrence with the prisoners, the cannon and the provisions. The vigilantes were forced to walk, while their horses were used to transport the captured supplies and the prized cannon.

Lane ordered the captured rifles and handguns distributed to the volunteers who carried knives and hoes as their only weapons. He then directed that all the buildings that made up Fort Franklin be burned to the ground. Then he headed toward Washington Creek and Fort Saunders.

"Bradley," Lane shouted at one of his other officers, "you and Cline get those stragglers organized into two units. I want them marching two abreast and pretending they're soldiers by the time we get there, do you understand?"

"Yessir," came the instant reply.

But Quantrell was not to be caught napping. As soon as his scouts reported the movement of Lane's militia, he and the twenty-five men garrisoned at Fort Saunders fled to Fort Titus, where they could expect support from Lecompton. In the meantime, when Lane's men came within rifle range of Fort Saunders, Lane called for a halt and rested his men. But at dawn, while preparing for the attack, the free staters found the second stronghold vacated and stripped of weapons and provisions. What the vigilantes did leave on crossbars erected in front of the log house was the mutilated body of Stoddard Hoyt.

"Lower his body," Lane ordered. Quickly the men, including Yerby as well as the young ex-Quaker, carefully untied Hoyt's shot-riddled corpse and laid it on the ground. A suitable burial plot was found for the Quaker's body and the entire company of free staters offered their final respects to the brave man.

"On to Titus," shouted Henry Shombre, the young ex-Quaker, who before the attack on Franklin was bathing in his own sweat, terrified at the thought of battle.

"Wait," Lane and his other officers shouted. But nothing could stop a large contingent of men, mostly the volunteers and former Quakers, from immediately riding out for Fort Titus, the last of the bushwhacker strongholds.

Fort Titus would not be as easy a target as Franklin. It was a far larger settlement with more men...now considerably reinforced by Quantrell's garrison from Saunders. Titus was located only two miles from Lecompton, the territorial capital and headquarters of the pro-slavery law and order vigilance party. Any attack on Fort Titus would certainly bring assistance from their friends at Lecompton. Titus was only a mile from the camp where all free state homesteaders captured by federal soldiers were being interned. The commandant of this camp, Major John Sedgewick, took his orders directly from the territorial governor, Wilson Shannon. Sedgewick's orders were not to interfere with the vigilance committee activities, even if they involved attacks on the free state homesteaders. However, Sedgewick was to preserve order if free state homesteaders retaliated.

The bushwhackers at Fort Titus, backed by a company of federal troops, had every reason to feel confident in their ability to repel any attack that Lawrence could launch. At Titus, the free staters should have found themselves out-manned and out-gunned. Sometimes, however, what should be is not what actually is.

The free stater vanguard, the young men eager to avenge Stoddard Hoyt's murder, attacked Fort Titus before dawn the next morning. And, without realizing it, took away all of the advantages Titus' defenders should have enjoyed. Since the attack was so sudden and ferocious, the ruffians had little time to send out for help. Once they had encircled the fort, the free staters prevented anyone from warning Lecompton. However, in the initial attack, Henry Shombre, the young ex-Quaker, was shot and killed.

Once Lane's more disciplined militia arrived at Fort Titus, the attack became more systematic. Lane deployed his men and poured volley after volley upon the stronghold. On their part the vigilantes returned shot for shot, and the matter remained undecided for a couple of hours. Then a roar from the free staters went up as a horse-drawn wagon with several men and a cannon thundered up to Lane's command post.

"Glad to see you made it, Lieutenant," Lane shouted.

"Glad to have made it, sir," Lieutenant Bickerton replied. "I would have arrived sooner had the major remained where he ordered me to meet him."

Lane gave his subordinate a wry look. "Well, now that you're here, let's put that cannon to work."

"Yessir, Colonel darling," the Irishman mischievously replied.

Bickerton was quite ingenious. In addition to putting together the proper gunpowder charge necessary for the field piece, he had rummaged through the rubble of Lawrence's newspaper buildings and salvaged the printing presses and type and had molded the metal from the *Herald of Freedom* and *Free Stater* newspapers into cannon balls. Bickerton quickly began pouring round after round into the walls of Fort Titus. As his men loaded each cannon ball and prepared to fire, Bickerton's men would shout, "All right you, bushwhackers, here comes another issue of the *Herald of Freedom!*" Under the unexpected bombardment, resistance crumpled. Quantrell's garrison waved a white flag in surrender. Before anyone either at Lecompton or the federal internment camp were aware of what had happened, the Lawrence militia had captured Fort Titus and its entire garrison, burned the settlement to the ground, and marched their prisoners back to Lawrence. The prisoners included Billy Quantrell, and Claude Combs.

• • •

"He's a murderer!" Ellen screamed. "He should be put on trial! What's wrong with you people?" Wilson Shannon had come to Lawrence to discuss a prisoner exchange. Shannon sought the release of all prisoners captured by the Lawrence militia in their raids against the law and order vigilante strongholds in exchange for all homesteaders held in federal internment camps, as well as the Topeka Convention officers arrested for treason.

"I am here not to decide which side is right or wrong," Shannon announced, "I'm here seeking a truce." It was true. The Kansas War had taken its toll on the territorial governor. He came not to further the pro-slavery cause. His prisoner exchange was Shannon's last effort to further the cause of peace. Wilson Shannon was fundamentally a decent person who found himself on the wrong side of the Kansas war. "I have announced my resignation both to the legislature in Lecompton as well as to the president," the sad-eyed territorial governor announced to Lawrence's committee of safety. "My only interest here is to see that all the prisoners are returned safely before I leave office."

"You weren't interested in releasing innocent homesteaders captured by federal troops who have had them interned in Lecompton for months," Ellen shouted defiantly.

"That is true," Wilson Shannon admitted. "But what is done is done. And I am here now offering to release them."

There was still some grumbling among other members of the committee of safety. They wanted to try William Quantrell and his accomplices for Stoddard Hoyt's murder and, if found guilty, hang them. Of course, Shannon had been given instructions to obtain their release at all costs.

"You see that Major Sedgewick has accompanied me," the governor continued. "We make no threats and will take no action against you for your attacks against the settlements at Franklin and Titus. Our only purpose is to obtain the release of your prisoners in exchange for those we now hold in Lecompton." As he looked around the room at each committee member, Shannon continued, "But I must have every one of those men you are holding no matter what they have done…including William Quantrell."

"Ellen," one of the members of the committee finally said, "no one here can ever forget what you have done during these terrible times. You have risked your life numerous times for our children and us. If we have anything to eat, if we have any prospects of surviving another winter, it is because of you. We all loved Stoddard. We know you witnessed his brutal murder at Quantrell's hands. If we could bring him back, we would. Stoddard acted upon the dictates of his conscience and so must we."

"But if his murderer is freed," Ellen argued, "how can we excuse our own guilt…our own complicity?"

"This is a war, Ellen," another committee person said. "We are now engaged in negotiations for a prisoner exchange. The governor is offering to free all of those captured and interned for merely crossing into Kansas, and all of our friends who were arrested on charges of treason. He is even willing to return all of the Sharp's rifles and cannon confiscated by Quantrell. Certainly you must agree that we must meet him halfway. When he resigns, we will need all the help and weapons we can get."

Rising from her seat, Ellen said quietly, "I do not agree with you, but I will yield to your decision." And she walked out of the meeting.

CHAPTER TWENTY-EIGHT

A s he promised, once he arranged for the prisoner exchange, Wilson Shannon resigned as territorial governor of Kansas. Daniel Woodson became acting governor. Woodson was chairman of the Kansas law and order vigilance party and no one in Lecompton was sounder on the goose. Woodson took his orders directly from Jefferson Davis, so it came as no surprise to anyone that only four days after taking office, Woodson issued the following proclamation:

> *For some time now the Kansas territory has been infected with large bodies of men, many of whom have come from states hostile to the property rights of honest plantation owners. These men have combined and confederated together, and amply supplied with munitions of war, have been engaged in murdering the law-abiding citizens of the territory of Kansas and driving others from their homes. These armed men have held law-abiding citizens as prisoners of war, plundered property, burned down houses and even robbed United States post offices. All of this has been done for the purpose of subverting by force and violence the government of the territory established by the*

congress of the United States.

Now therefore, I, Daniel Woodson, acting governor of the territory of Kansas, so hereby issue my proclamation declaring the said territory of Kansas to be in an open state of insurrection and rebellion; and I do hereby call upon all law-abiding citizens of the territory to rally to the support of the territory and its laws, and require and command all officers, civil and military, and call all other citizens of the territory to aid and assist, by all means in their power, putting down the insurrectionists, and bringing to punishment all persons engaged with them, to the end of insuring immunity from violence and full protection to the persons, property and civil rights of all peaceable and law-abiding inhabitants of the territory.

For weeks prior to this announcement, Quantrell had been holed up at A.B. Miller's bar, sulking about, drunk most of the time. He could not get over being captured by the free-staters and locked up in their jail. The more he thought about it, the more he drank and the fouler his mood became. Few could approach him, he even killed a man.

"Where's that nice looking filly I used to see around here with you, Billy?" the Missourian inquired good-naturedly, trying to make small talk. Quantrell eyed the young adventurer with bloodshot eyes. It was during one of his regular bouts of drinking and gambling. Without saying a word, Quantrell pulled out his navy Colt and shot a forty-four caliber lead bullet into the young man's liver. With a look of surprise and pain etched upon his face, the twenty-three year old slumped to the filthy floor, his life fading away with the blackish-red mixture of blood and bile oozing from the gaping wound in his side.

But now this good news in the form of a proclamation from Lecompton woke Quantrell from his drunken stupor. "Tell the boys," Quantrell said to Claude Coombs, now Quantrell's closest companion. Billy Quantrell went upstairs to prepare for his much anticipated final assault on Lawrence and the revenge he so sorely desired. "Now we ride on Lawrence!" Quantrell shouted jubilantly.

However, the political winds were shifting in Washington, bringing about changes that affected Kansas. A presidential election was coming up in November, and bleeding Kansas was certainly an issue. The deteriorating Kansas situation was eroding the electorate's confidence in the Democratic Party's ability to govern at the national level. Daily, Christians outside the South read about new atrocities in Kansas. Denunciations rang out from the pulpits of most Protestant denominations as ministers lectured their congregations on how black slavery today could become white slavery tomorrow. From the sacking of Lawrence and the beating of Charles Sumner, it became apparent that the slave owners who controlled the Democratic Party meant that neither blacks nor whites should remain free. "Bleeding Kansas," the symbol of the emerging despotism, might soon become a bleeding America. Because of its obsession with slavery, Democratic Party members in the North and West deserted in droves. Only the party's control over the corrupt big city political machines like Tammany Hall and the Pendergrass Machine, appealing primarily to the newly arriving immigrants, prevented the party's complete collapse outside the South.

So Daniel Woodson's proclamation could not have come at a worse time either for the Democratic Party's plans to put their candidate James Buchanan into the White House, or for John Quitman, the Supreme Grand Master of the Western Hemisphere. Quitman was extremely displeased with events. Neither Jefferson Davis nor Caleb Cushing seemed to understand the gravity of the situation. So the supreme grand master, now Congressman John Quitman, decided to clarify the situation for his two minions.

"Gentlemen, I assume you have read the proclamation issued by that fool Woodson," Quitman said, coming directly to the point. They supped in the type of private chambers befitting the three most powerful men in Washington and, therefore, the three most powerful men in America, and possibly, the three most powerful men in the world. Certainly they were powerful enough to plunge millions of Americans into a bloody war and institute a new low in civilized behavior. Quitman maintained as his personal residence the top three floors of the National, Washington D.C.'s finest hotel. A staff of over a hundred slaves and overseers saw to every whim of his or his guests, but today the mood was definitely not whimsical. He continued: "That idiot out there is going to ruin us!"

"But your supreme worship," Cushing replied feebly, "it was your plan to take over Kansas by running those abolitionists off. We only did what you instructed us to do."

"Did I tell you to have that young pup, Brooks, beat up Sumner on the floor of the United States Senate?" Quitman thundered, fixing his steely-eyed stare on both Davis and Cushing.

"But General," Cushing said throwing up his hands in protest, "we had no way of knowing what he and Keitt were planning. Had we known…"

"And you call yourself the Attorney General!" Quitman screamed. "How many times have I told you that it is your *business* to know everything that could possibly affect our plans."

Both men sat silent before Quitman's rage. They knew that the slightest word from him and their political careers would be over… and that would not be the worst that could happen. As the supreme grand master of the most powerful brotherhood in the world, his reach extended anywhere, even to the highest levels of power, as Zachary Taylor had learned.

"I want this business in Kansas to be quieted," Quitman said sharply.

"Yes, your most worshipful master," came the instant reply.

"We have to settle the situation in Kansas," Quitman told Davis and Cushing. "Take it off of the front pages. This means putting the vigilantes out of business for a while."

"How are you going to do that without giving up everything we have won?" Davis asked respectfully.

"Get rid of Woodson, immediately," Quitman continued, as he glowered at his two subordinates.

"Who, most worshipful grand master, should we put in his place?" Cushing asked.

"Who shall we select?" Quitman repeated the question, "Who should we select?" Then, looking away, he said, "I know just the man to solve all of our problems in Kansas."

• • •

"The decision of the Lawrence committee of safety is unanimous," intoned Clifford Foote, Lawrence's new mayor. "The Wabaunsee Rifles are duly commissioned as a unit of the Free State militia and will be given arms and supplies. If there is no other business, this meeting is over."

Ellen and others, including Quakers, had tried to prevent the formation of another military unit in Lawrence. Once again, her arguments went unheeded. Since Woodson's proclamation, thousands of vigilantes had poured across the border into Kansas. Once more, Lawrence found itself cut off and beleaguered. This blockade was more savage than the one imposed by the ruffians holed up in the three forts. Lane's militia had ridden out and had not been heard from since, so the Wabaunsee Militia was called up to protect Lawrence. The whole town expected an all-out attack at any time. Many townspeople loaded the few belongings they could carry and escaped west to Topeka. The vigilantes continued to systematically attack the isolated settlements and individual homesteaders. It was just a matter of time before all the individual gangs of bushwhackers would join up for their final raid on Lawrence. But one of the homesteaders, Joseph Cracklin, came to Kansas determined to fight for his land

and his rights. Cracklin persuaded a number of homesteaders to join him in the fight. Fifty-eight of them formed Cracklin's Wabaunsee Rifles, the militia Ellen tried to prevent from receiving a commission from Lawrence. Ellen's group argued that the new territorial governor, John Geary, had promised to protect the free-staters from another attack. "Why don't we give Governor Geary a chance?" Ellen complained at the committee of safety meeting. "He has said that he would use federal troops to enforce his proclamation."

· · ·

Indeed, it was during the American occupation of Mexico after the Mexican War that General Quitman promoted Lt. Colonel John White Geary to full Colonel and appointed him commandant of Mexico City. During the heaviest fighting of the war, Geary's regiment, the second Pennsylvania, stormed Chapultepe Castle, forcing its way into Mexico City. After the war, Quitman selected Geary to become San Francisco's first judicial officer. Geary sat on the State Constitutional Convention that brought California into the Union as a free state. He sat as a Democrat but without the pro-slavery sympathies held by many of his fellow party members. Geary even expressed his anti-slavery views to Quitman after Geary was elected San Francisco's first mayor. But Quitman knew he could depend upon his former subordinate. Quitman selected John Geary to become Kansas' new territorial governor because Geary was as tough as they come. Geary was given complete control over all federal troops stationed in Kansas and a presidential mandate to establish peace in Kansas whatever the costs.

Even before he arrived at the territorial capital in Lecompton, Geary rescinded Woodson's proclamation and issued one of his own:

The employment of militia is not authorized by the territorial governor except upon request by the commander of the federal troops

*stationed in Kansas; Federal troops have been placed at the disposal
of the territorial governor to insure prompt compliance with the law;
Therefore, the services of such volunteer militia are no longer required
and are ordered to immediately disband; Furthermore, all bodies of
men, armed and equipped with munitions of war, which do not immediately disband or quit the territory will answer to their peril.*

Dispatching his proclamation to every town, hamlet and
settlement in Kansas, Geary hastened to Lecompton. He wanted
to prevent any further violence. This was why Ellen and Frank had
hoped that the committee of safety would delay the establishment of
another militia. They believed establishing the Wabaunsees so soon
after the new governor issued his proclamation was a deliberate insult. "The new governor should be given a chance," Ellen had told
the Committee of Safety.

"You know those ruffians are not going to abide by that proclamation," Yerby said after the meeting. "The pro-slavery people
bushwhacked the free staters and federal troops arrested them when
they fought back. Maybe it's not such a bad thing that we have some
protection."

"But we have to have faith," Ellen pleaded, "or the violence will
never end." Ellen looked at Yerby. *He seems very sad,* she thought. *He
seems to be getting tired.*

But Yerby was thinking, *This woman has bewitched me, I have
fallen in love with my own creation. But this is impossible,* he screamed,
but no one heard since it was only in his mind. *It is not possible that I
could have these feelings for her.* Yerby tried to understand this complete
infatuation he had for Ellen. It could not be mere physical beauty, he
had made love to many beautiful women. He had married beautiful
women. He had been pondering his feelings for Ellen ever since they
arrived in Lawrence. He wondered about his unreasonable jealousy
directed at Shields and the precious little time remaining to them.

Remaining to them…that was a joke. There was no them. With that thought, Frank would have agreed with Ellen; he was a little sad.

What was even sadder was that their brief time together was to end in frustration and loneliness. His love for this woman would not be fulfilled. *Love?* He asked himself. Was that just a feeling below his belt…or did it start a little higher? He envied Shields his ability to love Ellen without the expectation of love in return. Yerby was becoming a victim of his own need to be fulfilled, his own vanity, his own belief that somehow he, Frank Yerby, was entitled to Ellen's love. He wanted her and often he believed he would go mad if he could not have her. But this road led to insanity. So Yerby's only salvation by necessity was a continued participation in the drama, the plot of a tale that he had had absolutely no hand in writing.

"These new homesteaders do not have the faith that you Quakers have," Yerby remarked to Ellen. "They came here not for ideals but for land. They came not to establish the values of civilization in this godforsaken wilderness, but to stake their claims and establish their patrimony for themselves and their families. And to them this is worth fighting and dying for."

"Then Frank," Ellen asked, "why did Abby and Louise die? And why am I still alive?"

"You are alive because I love you." Yerby said abruptly, without thinking, giving full vent to his feelings and allowing himself the full range of his own emotions. "And I believe that love is the only thing that matters."

But at that moment fate intervened to prevent either Ellen or Frank from exploring this confession of the heart.

"They're comin'," Shields Green shouted, as he broke into their narrow shack. "Come on, they're putting up barricades in the town square." Then he dashed back out, not waiting either for Ellen or Frank to catch up.

In the town square, at the corner of Henry and Massachusetts

Streets, barricades completely blocking the street had been erected. The people had overturned wagons and piled everything on top including furniture, doors and metal plate. Behind the barricades, women and children were digging trenches. At the opposite end of town, at Rhode Island Street, another group of women and children were similarly engaged setting up a barricade. Ellen joined the women at the Massachusetts Street barricade and immediately began helping.

"All able-bodied man capable of shooting a gun follow me," Joseph Cracklin, the newly-appointed commander of the Wabaunsee Rifles, began shouting. Leaving Ellen at the barricades with the other women and without saying a word, Frank and Shields joined the other men standing in line to receive weapons.

The vigilantes' ranks around Lawrence swelled to thousands...all of them were well-equipped and well-organized. Mayor Foote telegraphed an urgent message to Governor Geary, but none of the committee of safety believed that it would do any good. This time they knew Lawrence was doomed.

Yerby, Green and the others were given Sharp's rifles and ammunition. Then each of them received brief instructions on how to load and fire their weapons. The Sharp's was easily and quickly loaded. The Sharp's breech-loader allowed a man to shoot as quickly as he could eject a shell and insert another bullet. Furthermore, the Sharp's rifle was so accurate that even someone who had never fired a gun before could boast of hitting something, if only the man next to the one he was aiming at.

While the men were getting their instructions, Cracklin raced to the edge of town toward a log cabin situated at the top of a ridge. From here, with his spyglass, Cracklin could see hundreds of men grimly riding towards Lawrence, and knew Billy Quantrell was on his way, leading that vanguard. *He'll take the most direct route over the timberline and down into a ravine,* Cracklin thought to himself. *That way he'll come up directly in front of Lawrence.*

Cracklin positioned his men along the top of the ravine that ran almost three quarters of a mile around the hilly area in front of Lawrence. "If he comes this way, I'll have a special surprise for him." Cracklin's men had a cross fire on every part of the ravine…and all his men had Sharp's repeating rifles. "You men," Cracklin shouted to the group of volunteers he had just recruited, "fill in the gaps between those men there." Cracklin pointed to gaps. The young commander of the Wabaunsee Rifles had carefully chosen the site for his ambush, for he remembered his lessons from his days at the military academy. Cracklin planned to catch Quantrell's men exposed as they climbed up the hill from the ravine, while his own men were well concealed and under cover. He put his men in position to cover the entire ravine with rifle fire, no one could come up that hill without being exposed to the rapid firing Sharp's rifles from several directions. Had Cracklin a battery of cannon, his firepower would have been devastating; as it was, it would still be pretty damned effective.

Of course, the ambush would only work if Quantrell's men dismounted and climbed up the hill on foot. If they decided to charge the hill, they would punch right through the line and clear out the fewer than one hundred defenders with little difficulty. But Lieutenant Cracklin, the military academy graduate, did not allow himself to think about that. Once he was satisfied that his men were deployed to the best of his ability, he ordered them to take cover and remain out of sight.

Before long the vigilantes emerged out of the trees and assembled at the bottom of the ravine. Shields Green looked over at Frank Yerby, who was at least ten yards away. Fortune smiled on Shields, and on them all. Quantrell's vanguard began to dismount and lead their horses up the hill on foot. They were completely unaware that anyone waited at the top.

And now our rapid firing Sharp's should make all the difference, Cracklin thought, as he waited until the ruffians got half way up

FRANK YERBY:

the hill before ordering his men to open fire. The Wabaunsee Rifles blazed away, catching the border ruffians completely by surprise. But these were professionals; they returned fire instantly. The Wabaunsees continued their rapid fire giving the vigilantes no opportunity to reload. The firepower of the Sharp's rifles blasted Quantrell's advanced group right off the hill and back down into the ravine. Under the blistering Wabaunsee fire power, Quantrell's advance party was forced to withdraw helter-skelter and break off his attack. He returned to report Cracklin's ambush to the other company commanders and Davy Atchison, who were with the main body of vigilantes. They needed a plan of attack. When the Wabaunsees saw Quantrell's men withdrawing, they let out a war hoop that could be heard all the way back in Lawrence.

Though the skirmish ended in the late afternoon, Cracklin's men lay upon the ridge the remainder of the day and for the entire night. "Do you think they'll attack again?" Shields asked Frank.

"I don't think so," Frank replied. "They'll probably wait for reinforcements. Once they find out how thin our line is, they'll just ride right through us."

"I hope nothin' happens to Miss Ellen," Shields remarked and then fell silent.

So do I, Yerby thought silently to himself.

Early the next morning, to the surprise and wonderment of every citizen in Lawrence, Governor Geary arrived at the head of a column of federal troops. And even more amazing, there was a federal artillery unit now posted on Mount Oread with a commanding view of all the approaches to Lawrence. Geary had sent the unit to take the position the night before. So not only did Lawrence's citizens meet the new day with the welcome sight of federal troops riding to their defense, but for the first time, they saw the Stars and Stripes fluttering on the summit of Mount Oread. Townsfolk from Lawrence ran out to tell the Wabaunsee Rifles about the arrival of the federal troops. Ellen was one of the first to reach Lawrence's heroes still manning their posts at the ravine. "Oh, Frank," Ellen wailed, as she threw herself into his arms, "I was so worried about you."

More women joined Ellen in giving the Wabaunsee Rifles praise and thanks, for their heroic defense of the town. Trudging back to town with the others, Yerby didn't feel like a hero, but if that was what it took to hold Ellen in his arms he would gladly play the part. Joyous townsfolk and happy militiamen, most barely in their twenties, danced and yelled and embraced each other, as once again Providence seemed to have saved the free state community of Lawrence. Frank and Ellen just stood there holding onto each other…knowing this minute of love for them would have to last an eternity.

. . .

Governor Geary sat with Lawrence's committee of safety. He listened to the committee's detailed discussion of the looting and burning of the town, as well as the blockade that reduced the citizens to starvation. "I promise you that as long as I am governor," Geary said in response, "Lawrence, Kansas, will have the full protection of the United States Army." Geary continued discussing with the mayor and committee of safety members his plans for bringing peace to Kansas. After concluding his inquiry with representatives of Lawrence, Geary, accompanied by his secretary and a military escort, made his way to Franklin, where the law and order vigilance party militia was headquartered. Geary called all the company commanders together and asked, "Who are you and what is your business in Kansas?"

Replying for the group, Quantrell spoke out. "We're a territorial militia called together by the governor of Kansas. We intend to wipe Lawrence, the nigger-loving capital of Kansas, off the map and kill every nigger-loving abolitionist in the Kansas territory."

"I'm the territorial governor of Kansas," Geary responded. "I called up no militia. So I now order you to disband immediately and return to Missouri or wherever you came from."

"Don't look to me like you brought enough troops here with you for that kind of talk, Governor," Quantrell said boldly.

"Hold on there, Billy," Davy Atchison spoke up. And then directing his comments to Governor Geary, he said, "First let me say, sir, that we respect your authority, Governor. Could I talk to these here boys for a spell?"

"Yes, I'll wait outside," Geary responded.

"Now, boys," Atchison said to the twenty or more assembled, vigilance committee leaders as soon as Geary left, "we can't afford to fight against the army. Billy Quantrell, you ought to know that!"

"Know what?" Quantrell exploded. "All I know is that every time we get ready to go down there and kill every nigger-loving one of them free staters, somebody comes up with some rule as to why we can't do it. The only time we went down there and got everything we wanted was when we took over the vote. What kind of a world would it be if we could only get what we wanted through the vote?"

"It might be efficient, but it wouldn't be much fun," one of the other gang leaders shouted out. And the others started to laugh.

Governor Geary rejoined the group and asked, "Have you decided what you will do?"

"Governor," Atchison replied, "we are law-abiding citizens and we will do as you ask. Ain't that right, boys?" All the other ruffian leaders murmured their agreement. But Quantrell just stood there glaring, first at Geary and then at Atchison.

Then, stomping off, he shouted, "This ain't over, not by a long shot. There's gonna be a time when no rules will prevent me from destroying Lawrence!" Going back to where his men were gathered, he gave them the news and told they had to head back to Leavenworth. But to Claude and Jimmy, he said, "I've been thinking about how I can make certain them nigger lovers don't forget me."

"How's that?" Claude asked.

"By stealing their prize nigger," Quantrell laughed. "You two follow me. We've some unfinished business with that abolitionist lady, back there in Lawrence."

. . .

Later that afternoon, while the citizens of Lawrence were still celebrating. Frank Yerby gave the normally imperturbable Shields Green a scare. Shields decided to give them some privacy and for once allow Ellen out of his sight. So Shields was very surprised when Frank came up to him with a worried frown. "Have you seen Ellen?" Frank asked.

"Nossir," Shields replied, with a deadpan look that belied his concern, "I thought you all was together."

"No, some of the members of the committee of safety sent for her," Frank said, concern trembling in his words, "and I have not seen her since."

Nor would he. At that very moment, with Claude and Jimmy leading the way, Ellen was tied across the back of a horse led by William Quantrell, streaking towards the Missouri border.

CHAPTER TWENTY-NINE

"Mr. Frank, they've found her!" Shields Green burst into the cabin that he and Frank Yerby had called home for the past year. Rather, it was their home when they were not roaming all over Kansas, Missouri, and into Texas on their continual search for Ellen Ingraham. And not a day, not even an hour had passed during the past year without Yerby feeling gut wrenching, mind numbing pangs of guilt. *How could I have let them take her?* he asked himself over and over again. *Why didn't I protect her when she needed me most?*

Yerby replayed the scene in his mind. Ellen had come to him, clinging and crying, letting him know how much she loved him and yet…in that instant, in that all too brief a moment she was gone. *The boy… his name was Jimmy…was sent by the committee of safety,* Yerby recalled. *They needed her at a meeting.* But there was no meeting. That was the last time he saw her. Even after a year, Yerby could feel the pain, feel the guilt, cry the tears as if it were only yesterday. How he longed to hold her just once more, feel her breath on his face, wipe away the sadness from her eyes…be the man he had always wanted and hoped to be, just for her.

"Mr. Frank, did you hear me?" the fugitive slave said again, "they've found her. Miss Ellen, she's alive."

Frank Yerby sank to his knees as he had done many times recently, but this time instead of begging for her life, he offered a prayer of thanks to whatever merciful power had seen fit to safeguard Ellen. Recovering, he stood up, and embracing Shields Green, he asked, "Where is she? Is she safe?"

"I can't say for sure," Shields replied, "but Mr. Foote says that she's on a plantation just over the Missouri border in Clinton County. She's doing poorly."

"Clinton County!" Yerby exclaimed, "That's not more than fifty miles from here. How did he find her?"

"That general friend of your'n," Green replied, "General Hitchcock done told Mr. Foote of Miss Ellen's whereabouts." And with that, Yerby was out of his cabin and down the street leading to the mayor's office.

"I understand that they have located Ellen Collins," Yerby exclaimed breathlessly as he burst into Mayor Foote's office. The austere, scholarly-looking lawyer who had replaced Stoddard Hoyt as Lawrence's mayor looked up from his paper-strewn desk. One look told Yerby that he was unhappy with this interruption. Clifford Foote was a no-nonsense kind of person who, for all his free state background, was as insensitive as any of the pro-slavery adherents to anything having to do with colored people. Foote was of the opinion that it was a great misfortune that Africans were ever imported into America and he looked forward to the time when all the darkies were shipped back to Africa...or to Canada...to anywhere away from here.

"Yes, that is correct," the mayor replied dryly as he looked up from his desk. "We just received a dispatch from General Hitchcock concerning her whereabouts. I assume that your 'boy' delivered my message. I thought you should be informed immediately."

"Yes," Yerby stammered, "you were absolutely right. What plans are you making for her rescue?"

"Her rescue?" The mayor frowned and began fumbling with some papers. "Yes, her rescue," he repeated to himself now more as a statement than as a question. "Well, you see that might be somewhat difficult considering her status, you see."

"Her status!" Yerby tried to control his outburst, but it gave the cold-eyed attorney a start. "What do you mean her status?"

"Well, I understand that she was a fugitive slave. And, well," the lawyer stammered, "there is the law, not that I agree with it personally, you understand." Foote turned his attention back to the papers on his desk for a moment in order to collect his thoughts. "But as you well know, being an educated Negro, as much as we all regret this terrible law, we still must obey it. After all, it is the law."

"Do you know what she has done in defense of this town?" Yerby stormed. "If it had not been for Ellen Collins, there might not be a Lawrence, Kansas, today."

"I am certain that is true," Mayor Foote replied, nodding his head in agreement, "but you must understand that the issue of Kansas and statehood is still far from resolved. And the Buchanan administration is still very sound on the goose, if you get my meaning. We certainly do not want another attack from the vigilantes, do we? Especially now that John Geary has resigned as territorial governor. Who knows how long federal troops will remain here to defend us? So you see, there is really nothing more we can do." The mayor began once again to fumble with his papers, hoping that this "colored boy" would just take the hint and leave.

Yerby understood Foote's meaning. The mayor had made himself very clear. Ellen *was* a fugitive slave. No matter that her looks betrayed no inkling of black blood; no matter how great the sacrifices she had made in defending the citizens of Lawrence; no matter that she was a victim in the struggle to make Kansas free. To this white man, Ellen Collins was a nigger. No matter what, this white man believed that no nigger was worth fighting for. So Yerby abruptly left Foote's office and decided to seek out the one white man he knew who would not fail to see Ellen's rescue.

"Can you get us some horses and supplies?" Yerby asked Shields.

"Where are we going and for how long?" Green replied.

"We're gonna need some help to rescue Ellen," Yerby said. "We need to find John Brown."

"Marse Brown will help," Green agreed. "I'll see what I can do. I've done enough work for these folks 'round here that they surely owe me that."

Not long afterward Frank and Shields rode out in search of Captain John Brown. It was rumored that Brown and his band were raiding pro-slavery settlements on the other side of Franklin. When Frank and Shields got there, a homesteader told them that John Brown had taken off towards the Missouri border a couple of days earlier, after Charles Hamelton, the Georgia bushwhacker, and his gang.

News of Hamelton's treachery had spread throughout the free state settlements of Kansas like wildfire. Hamelton lived on a homestead in a free state settlement near Ottawa. Believing Hamelton to be a free stater, all the homesteaders in the area befriended him and helped him through a bitter Kansas winter. But a week ago, a gang of bushwhackers had arrived at Hamelton's homestead and Hamelton led them on an attack against his free state neighbors. One by one, he pillaged and burned their cabins, taking eleven men captive.

When word reached John Brown of Hamelton's attack, Brown took after him. Once Hamelton spotted John Brown on his tail, Hamelton herded his free state captives into a ravine by the Marais des Cyr River and his men shot them all. Five died, five were wounded, and by pulling one of the dead bodies over him, one homesteader escaped injury altogether. Hamelton and his gang then took off for the Missouri border. Unable to follow, Brown and his sons camped at the Indian trading post located where the Marais des Cyr River

FRANK YERBY:

crossed the Kansas border into Missouri, and there, Yerby and Green caught up with him.

"We found Ellen Collins," Frank told the war captain after greeting him and the members of his band, including his three remaining sons. Their camp was by the river's edge, considerably downstream from the trading post. "We need your help to rescue her."

"If we want to get her out alive, we'd need some kind of plan," Brown said simply. "And right now my only plan on this battlefield is keeping myself and my boys alive for another day."

Yerby could see the strain on John Brown's face. He, too, was tired and needed rest.

"You say that General Hitchcock sent word of Ellen's whereabouts?" Brown asked.

"Yessir," Green responded.

"Why don't we contact the general? If anyone has a plan to rescue that lady, the general does."

There was no telegraph station at the Indian trading post. There were only wretched Indians trying to get the Indian agent to accept their paltry trade goods for clothing, utensils, and especially for food. The Indian agent usually looked away from the feathers, beads and other useless symbols of this once proud people, now fallen into a state of degeneracy and helplessness. Once in a while an Indian did bring something of value that the agent wanted. Then the agent would offer the Indian a drink of rotgut whiskey. It usually took only one drink to get the Indian to trade his valuables for a whole bottle of whiskey. What the Indian children almost never got was the food they needed to keep from starving. So the only thing one found on this miserable acre of man-made hell were a bunch of drunken Indian men and starving, sickly Indian women and children.

Yerby returned to Lawrence to send a telegraph message to Hitchcock and to await his reply. Green decided to remain with John Brown, who did the same thing he always did when he passed the trading post. He tried to keep the agent from cheating the Indians and tried to teach the Indians how not to be cheated. But it was like trying to teach a shark not to bite and an infant not to cry. Hitchcock's response to Yerby's message came the next day. The terse message read: *"Meet me in St. Catharines."*

• • •

It was early summer, so the trip to St. Catharines was not as arduous as it might have been, and in many ways it was quite pleasant. Riverboat and rail travel, even in the steerage section and baggage car, was an enjoyable relief from the dangers and hardships of frontier life.

The gathering, if it had not been for the seriousness of their purpose, might have been taken for a family reunion. "Well, gentlemen, and ladies," Ethan Allen opened, "some of you well know it is far easier for a slave to escape on his or her own than to be rescued by others. My suggestion is that we provide Ellen with all the information and support necessary and let her make a run for it." Ethan Allen Hitchcock sat outside on the porch of Harriett Tubman's St. Catharines home, enjoying his pipe. As with most of the construction in this Ontario community, Harriett's home boasted hardwood floors and windows. Large and well-insulated against the bitter Canadian winters, Harriett Tubman's home was the center of St. Catharines colored community. Lots of love and good times were always found there. Tubman's home was not so much log cabin as it was a collection of cabins all joined to a common area...and it was huge. At any one time Harriett lodged four or five families with her while they built cabins of their own elsewhere. However, with the group planning to rescue Ellen assembling in St. Catharines, Harriett had cleared her home of everyone to make room for the rescue party.

The group had grown considerably larger since Yerby set out to rescue Ellen. As soon as John Brown had arrived at St. Catharines, he told Harriett Tubman about their mission. She offered her home as a meeting place—little wonder since Harriett belonged to Hitchcock's spy network as well. Hitchcock not only built his network upon vigilance committees and postal agents, his spies were part of the Underground Railroad. Freddie Douglas and Harriett Tubman were very familiar with Hitchcock's intrigues. For some time now John Brown had taken his orders directly from Hitchcock. Since Harriett had trained Ellen while she lived in the Quaker sanctuary, Harriett had more than a passing interest in her safety. So when Yerby told Harriett of Ellen's adventures in Kansas, Harriett decided to go to Rochester and talk to Freddie. After that the party began to grow.

"Ellen's being held as a slave on a plantation in Missouri," Harriett told Freddie. "The general is organizing a rescue."

"Count me in," Freddie said. "I'll meet you back at St. Catharines. But I've gotta go to Boston."

"You can count on us," Wes Parks told Freddie as soon as he learned about Ellen. "Ruby and I'll meet you in St. Catharines. But I've gotta get the kids. Ben is over at Harvard. I have no idea where Phoebe is. And I've gotta tell Joe, though it'll be just a waste of time."

"Why is that?" Freddie asked.

"Joe Collins has become a low life pimp. He lives off women… and drugs," Wes replied. Though they had been friends, Wes could not understand why Joe Collins had turned out the way he did. The path Joe took could not have been more different than Ellen's, his twin. Joe became a major distributor for the shipping interests who brought drugs into Boston harbor from the Orient. The members of Boston's elite willingly overlooked Joe Collins' Negro ancestry, as long as he was able to develop their opium markets. Right now Wes knew that Joe would have nothing to do with anything not directly related to pushing drugs or selling flesh…not even the rescue of his own sister, enslaved or not.

"Dwight, Ellen has been captured by slave catchers, and she's on a plantation in Missouri."

"Ellen's a slave!" was all that Dwight Ingraham could say.

"Ruby and I are going up to St. Catharines. Freddie here, Harriett Tubman and some others are planning a rescue. Do you want to join us?"

Dwight often thought of Ellen. He remembered their love and how much she had meant to him once…and still did. "Of course I'll go," Dwight Ingraham replied without hesitation. "But I'll have to meet you there. I have to tell Dwight Jr. and Elaine. Just don't leave St. Catharines without us."

"We won't," Freddie assured him. On the way, Freddie sent P.B. Randolph a telegraph message about Ellen. For years, Randolph had felt guilty over his role in Abby's death and Ellen's suffering. When he got Freddie's message, Randolph's reply was immediate: "I will join you there."

So when Ethan Allen Hitchcock suggested that Ellen be allowed to escape on her own, none of the rescue party, now having doubled from the original Kansas band, liked the idea.

"With all due respect to your experience, General," Yerby said, "if Ellen had wanted to escape on her own, don't you think she would have done it by now?" Dwight Ingraham looked over at the general, interested in his reply.

"It was just a suggestion," Hitchcock said. "Possibly you have a better one?"

"I don't think she has it in her to make any attempt at escape," Yerby offered, "else she would have done so long ago. For Ellen to escape her slavery she must escape from herself … that she cannot do." The others nodded their heads in agreement. "We have no choice," Yerby reiterated. "We have to rescue her."

"If she hasn't tried to escape in over a year," Harriett agreed with Yerby, "she certainly is not going to try to escape now."

"I'd like to know why Mr. Yerby says she can't escape by herself," the general asked. "Why must we go in to get her?"

"Ellen blames herself for Abby's and Louise's deaths," Yerby explained. "She probably believes that she deserves what happened to her."

Hitchcock thought about it for a while. "You could be right," he conceded. "But let me say this. The chances of our succeeding are not good and some of us may not survive the attempt. Is the chance of sacrificing several lives worth saving one?" He looked over the group. He could see that none of them had actually considered the costs of this nearly impossible mission. But he saw no weakness in their faces; they remained firm in their resolve. "Okay," the military tactician said, "I see this is going to be a three-pipe problem. Let's get down to work."

Ethan Hitchcock had detailed information on the plantation where Ellen was being held. The Clinton plantation was located outside the town of Plattsburg in Clinton County, Missouri. As Yerby had observed, it was barely more than fifty miles from Lawrence and only about thirty miles from the Kansas border. Even so, the Clintons boasted that none of their slaves had ever escaped. They employed over one hundred patty rollers to patrol every possible escape route day and night. These patrols used dogs specifically bred for tracking and attacking runaway slaves. In addition, the Clintons had devised an ingenious intelligence system using the slaves themselves to inform on one another. None of the slaves could be trusted. The slightest infraction and the most innocuous remark were reported to the overseers and punished. The overseers, both black and white, were chosen for their bulk and their brutality. The punishment for any attempted escape was death. They often beat the slave to death; but on occasion they let the dogs have them. The slaves on the Clinton plantation were as servile and degraded as any in Missouri. Only the bravest or most desperate slave ever even attempted escape, but none had ever made it out alive *and come back to tell the tale.*

"I can get her out," John Brown said confidently. "These people are not invincible. My sons and I have been fighting and beating them for the past five years. Just give me information about the plantation, and we and whoever joins us will get her out." One look at the steely-eyed fighter left no doubt in anyone's mind that if Ellen were to be rescued, John Brown could do it.

And so, they all agreed on a plan of attack. It was decided that the women should remain in St. Catharines. All agreed but Harriett Tubman.

"I know more about helping slaves escape plantations than any of you will ever know," she declared. "I'm coming with you. Besides, they are less likely to suspect a woman." John Brown would lead the rescue party into Missouri. He, his sons, and Dwight Ingraham would masquerade as slave catchers, while Wes, his son, Ben, Freddie, Dwight Jr., Shields, Randolph, and Yerby would be a gang of fugitive slaves. Once they assembled outside the Clinton plantation, someone had to get onto the plantation, locate Ellen and bring her out.

"Don't you agree, *Mr.* Yerby?" the general said with a smirk. "You don't expect us to ride onto the plantation and seize her by force, do you?" Yerby kept silent, disregarding Hitchcock's sarcasm. "This means that someone has to go onto the plantation, find Ellen, and bring her out to rendezvous with the rest of us. Who will that be?"

"That will be my job," Harriett stated matter-of-factly. "I won't have no trouble locating Ellen."

"Well, that settles it," Hitchcock said. "We'll…"

"Hold on." Shields Green spoke up. "I should be the one to go onto the plantation and find Miz Ellen. If there's any trouble, I'll be able to handle it, better'n she can," he said referring to Harriett. Shields' proposal set off a controversy that took several days to settle. Who should go onto the Clinton plantation, Shields Green or Harriett Tubman? Shields was adamant. He, too, had borne a heavy burden of guilt. First, Abby's death; he knew that he should have gone with them that day. And then there was Ellen's abduction. This time, Shields decided, he would not be denied. The group became embroiled in such a discussion about who should go, that it threatened to disrupt the entire mission.

In the end both Freddie and Brown supported Harriett. She was the best person for the job, they decided between themselves. Together they convinced the other members of the band. Seeing that the group was decided against him, Shields relented and accepted the group decision. And it was a tribute to his own strength and character that while he felt personally offended by this rejection, the ex-slave never allowed his feelings to affect his relationship with the others or interfere with carrying out the rescue mission.

● ● ●

The capital of Missouri considered itself the New Orleans of the west. It bustled with economic activity…its wharves and warehouses bursting to the limits with produce and commodities, including wheat, tobacco and cotton destined for the East Coast as well as European markets. Within its commercial district, St. Louis had everything required to keep a plantation operating at peak efficiency. In its stockyards, one could find the finest farm animals and the highest quality horses. And in the middle of St. Louis, auction houses offered a wide assortment of slaves for any purpose imaginable. And it was here in St. Louis that Ellen Collins' little band of rescuers was able to purchase their supplies, weapons, wagons, horses and mules.

"Why do we need this keg of nails and this barrel of scrap iron?" Dwight asked, as they loaded their supplies into the wagon.

"You'd be surprised how handy nails and iron are out west," Hitchcock replied. "I'll bet if you asked Captain Brown, he'd tell you that a keg of nails at the Indian trading post would be worth their weight in gold. Isn't that right, Captain?"

One of John Brown's sons piped up, "You're right about that, general!"

In St. Louis, as planned, Ethan and Harriett separated from the others and continued by river to Kansas City. In Kansas City, they hired a buggy and two fine horses and drove the fifteen miles to the Clinton plantation. On the way, Hitchcock and Tubman discussed the best way for her to get onto the plantation. Hitchcock favored a direct approach. "Why don't I just take you up to the house and sell you to the Clintons?" he said. "That way you won't be a stranger and you'll have more freedom of movement."

"That won't work," Harriett replied, "The first thing they'll want to do with some old and leathery nigger like me is put me out in the fields. And I'll never get near Ellen. And that's even if they'll buy me at all. They've probably got all the field slaves they need, especially if harvesting is over. It would be easier for me if I sneaked onto the plantation. That way I can make contact with Ellen without too much trouble. Nobody will be watching me."

"But what if someone sees that you don't belong on the plantation?" Hitchcock asked. "You'll be in a lot of trouble."

"Nobody has ever heard of a black woman sneaking onto a plantation for any other reason than to be with her man," Harriett chuckled. "And the plantation masters don't mind that a bit. They know that even someone like me wants a little lovin' sometimes. You just give me some information about the other plantations in the area and I'll be all right."

On the road, they passed many riders, but none of them paid much attention to the white gentleman and his black slave. They merely tipped their hats and continued on their way. When they got near the plantation Hitchcock let Harriett out. "You've gotta make all the arrangements in three days' time," he told her. "If you want, you can leave me a message under that big rock by that grove of poplars over there. But no matter what, you have her here in three days.

Do you understand? Three days."

During the past eight years, Harriett Tubman had conducted over three hundred slaves to freedom. So when she stared at Hitchcock, it was with a decided fit of pique. *This white man don't know nothing, but thinks he does,* she thought to herself. But Harriett decided that to say anything to him would just be a waste of breath. And, in an instant, she disappeared, right before his eyes. With a shake of his head, Hitchcock wheeled his carriage around and returned to Kansas City, where he would spend the next couple of days before meeting the rest of the rescue party.

• • •

"Harriett!" the surprised Ellen whispered. She could rightly say by now that very little surprised her any more, but the slightly built, exceedingly strong and sinewy black woman, appearing sprite-like in her cabin, certainly did. "How did you get here? Where did you come from?" Ellen asked.

Harriett noticed immediately that this was not the beautiful yet sad-faced woman she had met in St. Catharines seven years ago. Gone was the full-figured, soft look of a young ingénue. Here was a withered, thin middle-aged woman with leathery skin and washed-out hair that told a story of past hardships. It was not that Ellen had lost her beauty. Ellen would always be beautiful, even by those rather ephemeral standards that most people used to judge beauty. But now, Harriett decided, Ellen had gained some other look, some indefinable internal glow born of indomitable will and essential goodness. Ellen's beauty seemed to emerge from what those holding religious beliefs would call a great soul.

"I've come to rescue you," Harriett said simply.

"Rescue me!" Ellen exclaimed with a degree of understandable skepticism. "All by yourself?"

"No," she explained, "there is a group of your friends coming here to take you away. John Brown's leading the way and they'll be here in three days."

"Oh, the people from Lawrence are finally coming for me," Ellen said.

"No, honey chile," Harriett explained patiently, "not the people of Lawrence—your family…your friends. They're the ones coming for you."

"Oh dear," Ellen replied, with a look of concern.

"What's the matter?" Harriett asked, "don't you want to be rescued?"

"Yes, of course I do," Ellen stammered, "but…"

"But what?" Harriett asked.

"Well, you see," Ellen blurted out. "I am the only teacher here and there is so much more for me to do," which, of course, was not her real concern. *How am I going to face them?* she asked herself

Harriett looked at Ellen awhile. A wave of sympathy passed between them. Harriett wanted Ellen to know that she understood. And after a long silence, Harriett told Ellen softly, "There are many more to be taught back home."

"If I leave, some others, including children, will have to be taken along as well," Ellen said in resignation.

"If it were up to me, I'd rescue the whole plantation," Harriett replied, "but there are others who need to know." The next night Harriett sneaked back to the poplar grove and left a message for Ethan, telling him that Ellen insisted on bringing out an additional ten slaves from the Clinton plantation. She concluded her message with, "All twelve of us will meet you here as planned," leaving Hitchcock no option other than to accept the additional fugitives. And so Ellen consented to the rescue, despite the fact that her fear of facing her rescuers outweighed the fact of her actual bondage.

Harriet Tubman was right not to give the rescue party any choice in bringing the additional slaves. Hitchcock, in particular, was very disturbed. But since he had no choice, he passed the message along to John Brown and the others when he met with them at the agreed upon site, outside Plattsburg on the Platte River. "I know we didn't plan on this, but I don't think we really have a choice," Yerby said. "We've come this far, we can't turn around now."

"I don't see what difference it makes," John Brown said, "one or eleven, we've still gotta get back over the border into Kansas without getting caught by the patrollers."

"It makes a big difference," Hitchcock said. "If we're pursued, we could put Ellen on a horse and abandon the wagons. Then it would be a race to the border. With all those other pickaninnies, we would have to keep the wagons and there is no way we could outrun any of the patty rollers. That means that we'd have to stand and fight. And I don't have to tell you what our chances in a fight would be."

"Then we'll just have to stand and fight," Freddie said grimly. Wes Parks and Frank Yerby agreed and Shield Green merely sat back and listened. Throughout the trip, Shields had studied Dwight Ingraham. Shields wondered why he had married Ellen in the first place. And once he married her, how could he have let her leave him just like that. *Must be a lot more about white folks that I just won't ever understand,* he decided.

Likewise did Dwight study P.B. Randolph. He wondered what his wife had seen in this foppish, rather delicate mulatto with fiercely burning eyes. During the journey, Shields was able to strike up a conversation with Dwight. Actually the discussion was by mutual consent. Dwight, who knew that Shields had been with his wife from the very beginning, was eager to learn every detail of their adventures together. Dwight's easy-going manner and lack of racial animus made it easy for he and Shields to get along. They talked often and shared a lot of personal information. Shields shared stories with the white man about the cold Canadian winters and the equally cold Kansas plains.

He told how his wife braved the bushwhackers to bring ammunition and shot for the Sharp's rifles back to Lawrence. He also narrated the events that led to Louise's death.

Both the younger Ingraham and Wes' son Ben listened to Shields' stories with fascination. The two twenty year olds became as intrigued with Shields as they were by John Brown and his sons. The two young Bostonians never tired of asking Shields to recount some of his Lawrence adventures…or getting the Brown brothers to talk about their skirmishes with the border ruffians. "Tell us the real story behind the Pottawattamie massacre," Dwight Jr. asked one evening. He and Ben loved to hear every one of their stories. But on this occasion, John Brown's sons each went silent. After a while they left the two young men, driven by guilt, to face their own demons not to be exorcised until Harper's Ferry.

On the other hand, P.B. Randolph kept mainly to himself. He opened up only to Hitchcock, with whom he shared a passion for esoteric philosophy. Both of them had been initiated into the ancient mysteries of the *fama frateritatis*. This gave them close fraternal bonds. It was rumored that John Brown, too, had been an initiate into the same brotherhood, but his more practical bent did not permit him to take pleasure in the flights of intellectualism that both Randolph and Hitchcock enjoyed so much.

Freddie and Wes entertained themselves by indulging in their interminable political debates. Neither quite agreed with the other's viewpoint, but each allowed good manners and mutual respect to get them around those issues over which they simply could never agree. How could it be otherwise? Wes had been an African ruler and the master of many slaves. His own brother had sold him into slavery. Wes had had many wives. Wes Parks had few illusions about life. Freddie had been born a slave. He had earned his status as a leader of black people only by virtue of the white man's good graces. He proved his worth by serving the abolitionist cause and being a conductor on the

Underground Railroad. Freddie actually believed his position was both earned and deserved. He actually believed that somehow he was "different from the other blacks." Possibly, Freddie believed that his having a white father raised his status. The fact that he never met his father, who may have been some wandering plantation worker who one day took his mother by force, did not seem to play any role in Freddie's thinking. Many years later, when Frederick Douglass married Helen Pitts, a white woman twenty years his junior, it was thought that Freddie finally received the reward he thought he deserved. Between Wes and Freddie, all the complexities of being African and American played themselves out. But through it all the two of them remained good friends. In his daily conversations with his Tau Vudun, Wes Parks asked his ancestors to take special care of Frederick Douglass.

"How many men is she bringing?" John Brown asked.

"Harriett didn't say," Hitchcock replied. "We'll just have to see."

"Well, the plan, as I see it," John Brown said, "is to divide the women and children into each of the two wagons with the general in one and Frank in the other. The rest of us will divide into two groups flanking either side of the wagons but out of sight of the road. We will have a picket a mile or so in front and another in the rear. We've got ten men armed and on horseback; we should be able to surprise any bushwhacker patrol. The biggest danger remains the mules' slow pace."

"What'll we do if we're attacked?" Douglass asked.

"We'll have to beat off the attack, hitch the wagons to horses and pray that we get across the border before those ruffians can bring reinforcements," John Brown replied. He looked each of the men in the eyes and said, "If we are attacked, there won't be more than eight or ten in their group. But we can't let a one of them escape to sound the alarm. Is that understood?"

The group murmured and shook their heads in agreement. None of them, not even Ben and Dwight Jr., was under any illusion about the danger of this undertaking. No one in Missouri was hated more than "nigger stealing" Yankees. Even cattle rustlers and horse thieves got more respect. Rustlers were still hung as soon as they were caught, but to the Missourians, hanging was too good for anyone caught stealing niggers.

. . .

"I'm glad it's a moonless night." Ethan thought to himself, "but for the life of me, I can't find that poplar grove." It was the night when the rescuers planned to meet Harriett, Ellen and her group. But in the dark, Ethan Allen was having a difficult time locating the meeting place. *I'm getting old,* he thought to himself. *Never was much good at field work. This kind of thing is for younger men.* Hitchcock wandered around for quite a while before he located the meeting place.

Huddled about Ellen and Harriett were five women, three children and two men. Harriett had assigned each of the children to an adult and spread them about just far enough to minimize the sounds children can make, even those as well behaved as these children were, Hitchcock remarked to himself. Their eyes as big as saucers, each of them clung to an adult but no sound escaped their little mouths.

"We were beginning to get anxious," Harriett said as Ethan approached them.

"I got kind of lost," the spymaster replied sheepishly. "But I'm here now, so get your group moving. We'll meet the others just over that rise there," he said pointing westward. Harriett signaled the group of fugitives and, to Hitchcock's amazement, the group lined up, quickly, efficiently and noiselessly, into single file as though they were an Indian war party. Then Harriett moved the fugitives forward toward the waiting wagons and horses.

At the sight of her husband and son, Ellen was overcome with emotion. But unlike the time after Abby's death when she was so laden with guilt that she could not face them, Ellen hugged Dwight and Dwight Jr. Tears of joy and happiness flooded down her face. Dwight Ingraham wept as well and soon, not a dry eye remained in the group, except, of course, for the grizzled old veteran, Pottawattamie Brown. One by one, Ellen embraced all who joined in the rescue...all except P.B. Randolph, at whom she could stare only in a state of total bewilderment. Randolph, recognizing Ellen's embarrassment, gave a deep bow...which relieved whatever tension anyone in the party might have felt.

John Brown's stern demeanor helped the band regain its composure. He reminded everyone that they remained in a great deal of danger. "It will be dawn soon," the captain said, "and you all will be surely missed. Let us be on our way."

Brown quickly realized how impractical it was to ride parallel to the wagons. It was too dark and the horses stumbled about. He decided to divide the party into a vanguard in the front and a rear guard behind with individual scouts front and rear. Even so, the mules were slow and by morning they had barely gone five miles. But they continued to plod on and by midday, the little band had covered quite a distance. And still there was no sign of any pursuit. John Brown rode back to the wagon where Ethan Allen rode with Ellen and Harriett. "We should have seen someone by now," he said. "Do you think we ought to send scouts out to make contact?"

The general frowned. "If you do, you risk having the scout captured and then they'd know for sure what we're up to. I think they're playing cat and mouse with us. How far is it to the border?"

"About thirty miles," one of John Brown's sons who had just ridden up from the rear replied. The young veteran reported that no one was following them yet.

"When are we gonna stop, anyway?" Yerby asked, joining the discussion. "I'm not used to all this riding and I need a break! And I know the women and children are tired." He glanced into the rear of the wagon where he could see that the women and children were totally exhausted.

"Stop!" John Brown shouted. "We can't stop...until we cross that border. And we won't be safe even then...not until we get to Lawrence."

"But the children," Ellen protested, "they need a comfort break if nothing else."

"Just because we haven't seen them, doesn't mean they haven't seen us." John Brown insisted over the noise of the wagon wheels and trotting horses. Surveying the horizon, he said "If they haven't attacked yet, it's only because either they haven't enough men or they plan to hit us once we stop. They know time is on their side." Then, looking into the wagon at the children's scared faces, he softened a bit. "All right," he said, "we'll keep going until it's dark, then we can stop."

John Brown was correct on both points. There weren't enough patrollers to attack the band of fugitives. The Clinton plantation had begun transporting its crop of tobacco to the Missouri River. The entire crop was due at the auction houses in St. Louis. The owner of the plantation, as well as the smaller growers, needed every white man available to watch and control the slaves transporting the crop. So right now, there weren't enough patrollers available to attack a group of armed men the size of John Brown's party.

But everyone on the Clinton plantation was well aware of the escape. One of the black informants had reported the escape to his master early the very next day. The Clintons sent a rider to Leavenworth with a promise to pay one hundred dollars to any man helping to round up the band of fugitive slaves. The rider was told to make certain that Claude Coombs got the message. If the most famous slave catcher in Missouri were involved in the chase, the Clintons knew these fugitives wouldn't get far. "Claude Coombs will chase them to hell and back," the elder Clinton laughed. "I'm glad these niggers tried to escape; these other darkies need to see what will happen if they try it." Claude Coombs was happy to retrieve Clinton's slaves. And when the rider let it be known that Pottawatomie Brown was leading the escape, Billy Quantrell signed up as well. Getting their provisions at the expense of the Clintons and organizing themselves under Quantrell's leadership, close to seventy slave catchers rode out of Leavenworth. "We'll catch them nigger stealers by noon tomorrow, 'less I miss my guess," Claude exalted, rubbing his Bowie knife lovingly.

Of course, John Brown didn't know any of this. All he knew was that they had to get to the Kansas border as fast as they could. By nightfall his group was exhausted, still uncertain whether they had been seen, and with some ten miles to go. "We can't run the risk of fires even though we'll have sentries out all night," Brown told the others. "You'll have to make do with the bread, dried fruit and nuts we brought." Brown divided the men into three watches. He put each watch under the supervision of one of his sons. Then Brown took the better part of an hour to explain to each man his sentry duties. "Primarily your job is to stay alert, identify everything you see and hear around you. If you notice any change in what you see or what you hear, that is a signal that someone or something is out there. If you spot someone out there, get back here as quickly and as quietly as you can and report what you saw or heard."

"What if you can't get back because you think they'll catch you?" Ben asked. He had taken a leave from his studies at Harvard to join this group, and standing guard over the lives of others was a new experience. Even though he felt the question might imply cowardice on his part, he was intelligent enough to know that his question needed to be asked.

"If you can't get back here safely, hide yourself as best you can," John Brown replied. "That many men would certainly be spotted by another sentry, unless they come single file Indian-style, which is not very likely." After the first watch had been posted and the women had served what food was available, Brown, Hitchcock and the others began to discuss plans for the next day.

Wes Parks stripped himself to the waist and strode out into the darkness, evading Brown's sentries with ease. Almost laughing out loud, he slipped within a yard of Freddie without his knowing it. A half mile past the perimeter of their camp, Wes sank to his knees and dug a small pit in the soft Missouri soil. Inside the pit he lit a small fire. Reaching into the pouch he wore around his neck, Wes withdrew some gnarled roots, gummy leaves and a sachet of white powder. The former African chieftain threw the contents of his pouch into the smoldering fire, producing a great misty cloud that drifted towards the fugitives' camp and enveloped it in its secret inner sanctum. Chanting in an ancient tongue, Wes sat cross-legged until once more out of the dark appeared his father, grandfather and great grandfather, his Tau Vudun. Quietly he began to speak with them, asking for their assistance in tomorrow's trials.

"Mighty ones," Wes intoned, "great were your deeds when you walked the land of Da's belly. Now your son is in much need of your help."

One of the spirits, the eldest of them all, moved over and flashed a ghostly smile at his great-grandson. "Hwesu, my son," the elder replied, "you have always enjoyed our favor. Why would you doubt us now?"

"Maybe this land has weakened the boy," his father's ghost remarked in mock anger. "His warrior's blood is cool and his body has grown soft like a woman's."

"No, father," Wes cried out, prostrating himself and heaping the soil from his native land that he kept in another pouch upon his head, "the strength of our land still flows through my veins."

"Then why do you wish to save this woman who has the color of a fishes' belly?" asked his grandfather with gravity.

"Because in this land of the Furtoos, there is no love of honor...these white people love only beauty. This woman must be saved because her beauty puts them to shame," Hwesu replied.

"That is enough," Hwesu's great-grandfather commanded. "There is no need to put the boy to a test, now." And directing his words to Hwesu, "Yes, my son, we are quite pleased with you. Now run quickly and get some whiskey. We have brought a great visitor. You must present him with an offering."

Without hesitation, Wes leapt up and retraced his steps to the camp. Creeping past the sentries was no problem, since now they all, including Freddie, were sound asleep at their posts. "Sleep well, my friends," Wes whispered, "my Tau Vudun will protect us all." Slipping into camp, Wes took the bottle of Hitchcock's special Scotch whisky from the general's valise. One of the spymaster's few pleasures was his Scotch whisky; he was seldom without it.

Wes returned with his stolen prize to where his Tau Vudun waited. With great solemnity and reverence, Wes offered up the Scotch whisky to his ancestors. But to his surprise, instead of accepting the offering, they all rushed upon him and rudely forced him onto his knees. Suddenly a knobby-kneed, old black man with darting eyes and a mischievous grin appeared among them. Reaching for the Scotch whisky, the old man drank greedily, smacking his lips until very little of the whisky remained. Then casting away the bottle, the old man nimbly leapt over to where Wes knelt and touched the African on his head. Then as quickly as he had appeared, the ancient one disappeared again.

"Was that Papa Legba himself?" Wes asked in wonder and surprise.

"Very good, my son," Wes' great grandfather said proudly in the ancient language of Dahomey. "Very good, indeed."

• • •

Back in camp, John Brown was talking. "They're almost certain to hit us tomorrow. And they're gonna have a pretty big group with them."

"If they're gonna hit us, we'd better be ready," Hitchcock said grimly.

"But that's the problem," one of John Brown's sons said. "We can't get ready until we know *where* they're gonna hit us."

"Then," Brown said, "someone has to ride out and make contact with them and get back in time to warn us."

"Warn us to do what?" Dwight Ingraham ventured to say.

"I have a little plan that might work," Hitchcock smiled. "Tomorrow all the women and children will ride in one wagon. That wagon will stay far in the rear. We'll load the other wagon with the dynamite, gunpowder and that keg of nails and scrap iron. As soon as we get word that they are coming, we'll stop and turn around. The wagon with the women and children has to get as far away as it can. The rest of us will wait until they have overtaken our surprise wagon, we set it off, and BANG, no more slave catchers."

"That sounds like a great plan," Wes stepped up and said. No one had seemed to notice him leaving, nor did they hear him come back…nor were they aware of the guardian mist. "But…"

"But what?" John Brown asked.

"But there seems to be one or two problems." Wes answered.

"Such as…?"

"First of all, how do you know they will be coming from in front of us? They could be coming from the plantation."

"No," Brown offered, "if they were coming from the plantation they would have hit us by now. They'll be coming from in front of us, from Leavenworth, most likely."

"Even if that is true," Wes continued, "how are you going to release the mules and set off the dynamite in time to blow up the entire ruffian group of a hundred or more men?"

"I might be able to help you, sir." It was Ben, Wes' son, who spoke. "I study physics and engineering and during the summer, I worked on a railroad gang. We were always blowing things up." General Hitchcock and Captain Brown gave Ben a look that said they were impressed. Even the normally impassive Wes Parks gave his son a brief smile of pride. "I can estimate the size of the blast from the amount of explosives we use, I can even arrange for the force of the blast to go in any direction you choose, back, front or to either side, it doesn't matter. All I need is a bearing and a marker."

The band of rescuers spent the rest of the night perfecting their plan. Brown decided to send Shields Green with his oldest son on the scouting mission. Without knowing exactly where the patrollers were, Hitchcock's plan had no chance of success. Shields and the younger Brown left two hours before sunrise.

At dawn, everyone else broke camp. One wagon was filled with all the explosives; the other with Ellen, Harriett and the other women and children. Brown decided to put Yerby in charge of the wagon with the women. Then the party began the last leg of their dash towards the Kansas border.

The sun had passed its noontime height, and they were within five miles of the border, when the two familiar riders who had left camp before dawn appeared on the horizon. They were racing towards the group as if their lives depended on it...which they did. Waving and shouting, John Brown's son and Shields Green came to a stop in front of the wagons. "They're on their way!" Brown's son said excitedly. "And there's a lot of them."

Brown called the group to a stop. Getting off his horse, Yerby turned the wagon with the women and children around, and urged the mules back the way they had come...back, he hoped, to safety. Hardly had Yerby gotten the wagon back down the trail, when a great cloud of dust appeared on the trail behind them. Soon, horsemen began to emerge from the dustcloud pounding down the trail toward the waiting men. "Here they come!" Freddie shouted.

"That's good," Hitchcock smiled. "That's very good. If they think we're running, they may overlook this wagon until its too late."

Wes and Freddie unhitched the mules while Ben set the fuses for the dynamite, positioning the barrels of gunpowder and kegs of nails and scrap iron to explode with maximum effect on either side and to the rear of the wagon. The riders grew closer, bandanas pulled up over mouths and noses to keep out the dust. But their grim faces and evil eyes leered out at their prey, leaving no doubt as to their murderous intent. Few if any slaves witnessed such a sight, even without bedsheets and hoods, without feeling absolute terror. "All right," Brown shouted, "everyone mount up, and as soon as young Ben lights those fuses, slowly move back...on the count of ten. After that make a break for it. Wes! Get those mules going." Each of them turned around slowly and walked their horses slowly. Then all together they began their wild retreat.

When Quantrell saw their quarry trying to escape, he urged his vigilantes to ride faster. "We've got those nigger-stealers, boys," Billy Quantrell shouted. And he and Claude Coombs jumped into the lead, with the rest of the gang not far behind, riding like demons from hell.

So intent were they on their victims that they paid scant attention to the wagon that the fugitives had left behind. No sooner had Quantrell, Coombs and a few others passed it by when three sickening explosions, rolling one after the other in rapid succession, belched out among the riders. Caught completely by surprise, the hapless would-be slave catchers let out collective groans of pain and agony and, for most of whom, it was the last sound they would ever make. White-hot metal and gigantic tongues of flame lashed into their ranks with murderous fury, as if all the evil they had perpetrated had suddenly taken on an independent existence and turned on them with the fury of hell. Where only moments earlier, over seventy men sat on their horses and chased their prey, now there was only a hellish scene of dead and dying men and horses sprawled haphazardly all over the road, clumped in ditches, splattered against rocks, pitched into trees and sprayed into bushes for a hundred yards in every direction.

Only the ruffians in the far lead and at the very rear escaped injury...and these numbered not more than ten, including Claude Coombs. Billy Quantrell was knocked unconscious. John Brown directed his band to dismount and use their Sharp's rifles to pour a savage volley at the surviving ruffians. Dazed and leaderless, they fled off the road into the thicket in all directions.

Once they had fled and only the dead and the dying remained, Brown signaled Yerby to return with the women and children. When the wagon reached the scene of the carnage, Brown ordered everyone to remount. "Now let's make a run for the Kansas border and not stop," he shouted. "We've got no more surprises left."

Claude lay crouching on the side of the road beside the unconscious form of Billy Quantrell. He saw Ellen in the wagon as it approached. In a fit of uncontrollable rage, he pulled out his Colt revolver, leaped out on the road and, taking dead aim at Ellen, fired. At that very instant, Yerby saw Coombs and threw himself in the path of the bullet. The forty-four-caliber slug slammed into Yerby's back and exploded out of his chest, lodging deep into the wagon's wooden paneling. The force of his body threw both Harriett and Ellen backwards into the wagon, but neither one of them was injured. Yerby's wound was mortal.

Instantly, Sharp's rifles rang out. So many forty-five-caliber bullets tore into Coombs' body from so many directions that he twisted around like a corkscrew before slamming into the ground. The most famous slave catcher in the territory entered the torments of hell that had been waiting for him for some time.

Without pausing either to consider his victory or to care for his wounded comrade, John Brown pushed the party towards the Kansas border at a breakneck pace. However, the band was to have no more run-ins with slave catchers and they were able to get to the border without further incident. They crossed the Kansas border onto the Kickapoo Indian reservation. From there they made their way down to Lawrence. Sometime that evening, just as the reddish rays of the setting sun turned into a deep purple night, Frank Yerby died. Ellen Ingraham continued to cradle him in her arms all the way into Lawrence.

John Brown and his party remained in Lawrence only long enough to pick up supplies, to the relief of the mayor and many of the town's citizens. The next day John Brown led the rescue party and the eleven freed slaves out of Lawrence and back to St. Catharines.

EPILOGUE

In January of 1861, one of the first acts of the new Congress under the presidency of Abraham Lincoln was to admit Kansas into the union as a free state. This single act so enraged the South that one by one, led by South Carolina, the Southern states seceded from the union...initiating the bloodiest war in American history. In 1863, William Quantrell, now an officer in the Confederate army, led a raid on Lawrence, Kansas. For three hours Quantrell's men engaged in a orgy of murder, arson and robbery. Quantrell ordered every man in Lawrence shot. Billy Quantrell finally enjoyed the revenge he had sought for over ten years.

• • •

In Pride's Castle, there was a great celebration of Frank Yerby's gallantry and heroism in the ballroom.

• • •

When Frank finally returned to his bed in the stark white hospital room in Madrid, he barely heard his wife say to his nurse, "Do not announce his death until next week."

LIST OF YERBY'S CHARACTERS

Alaric Teudisson/ Aizun ibn al-Qutiyya	*An Odor of Sanctity*	Sumayla's lover and Kamil's father
Prince al-Kamil ibn Karim	*An Odor of Sanctity*	Sumayla's son by Alaric Teudisson
Abu L'Fath Nasr	*An Odor of Sanctity*	Grand Vizier/ Arian agent of Asturias King
Abu Kitab al-Mitar	*An Odor of Sanctity*	Vizier of Correspondence
Al-Mugira	*An Odor of Sanctity*	Emir's brother
Al-Mundhir	*An Odor of Sanctity*	Emir's son
Abd al-Karim ibn al-Hixim	*An Odor of Sanctity*	Sumayla's husband and Kamil's stepfather.
al-Harrani	*An Odor of Sanctity*	Royal Court physician
Al-Wallid	*An Odor of Sanctity*	Emir's brother
Adin	*An Odor of Sanctity*	Royal taster
Alvaro	*An Odor of Sanctity*	Ex-Jew and leader of the "Exalted Ones"
Ariston	*The Goat Song*	
Pamela Ingraham Bibbs	*A Darkness at Ingraham's Crest*	Cousin of Dwight Ingraham

Lance Brittany	*Floodtide*	Finiterre Plantation Owner
Morgan Brittany	*Floodtide*	Bessie's mistress
Bessie	*Floodtide*	Pedro's lover
Duncan Childers	*The Serpent and the Staff*	
Abigail Collins	*A Darkness at Ingraham's Crest*	Daughter of Wilks Thomas and Susanna Collins
Barton Collins	*A Darkness at Ingraham's Crest*	Owner of Collinswood/ father of Joe, Ellen Collins
Joe Collins	*A Darkness at Ingraham's Crest*	Escaped slave/ Ellen Ingraham's twin brother/ Abigail Collins' Husband
Suzanna Collins	*A Darkness at Ingraham's Crest*	Barton Collins' wife and Wilks Thomas' lover
Pride Dawson	*Pride's Castle*	
Dangbevi	*Dahomean*	Wes Parks' wife, killed by his brother
Victor Drury	*Pride's Castle*	
Murielle Duclos	*Devilseed*	
Fakhr	*An Odor of Sanctity*	Emir's wife
Harry Forbes	*Speak Now*	
Stephen Fox	*Foxes of Harrow*	
Garcia	*An Odor of Sanctity*	Kamil's Brother in Law/ Leader of the "Exalted Ones"
Gbenu	*Dahomean/ A Darkness at Ingraham's Crest*	Wesley Parks' father
Gbochi	*The Dahomean*	Brother who sold Wes Parks into slavery
Walad Goissuintha	*An Odor of Sanctity*	Alaric's Sister/Al-Wallid's wife
Horeth ibn al-Jatib	*An Odor of Sanctity*	Sumayla's former master
Ellen Collins Ingraham	*A Darkness at Ingraham's Crest*	Escaped slave/ daughter of owner of Collinswood plantation
Dwight Ingraham	*A Darkness at Ingraham's Crest*	Ellen Collins Ingraham's Husband

FRANK YERBY:

Iolanthe	*The Saracen Blade*	
Conchita Izquierdo	*Floodtide*	Ross Pary's fiancée
Eduardo Izquierdo	*Floodtide*	Conchita's father
Father Juan	*An Odor of Sanctity*	Arian priest
Kpadunu	*Dahomean*	Wes Parks' childhood friend
	A Darkness at Ingraham's Crest	
Cathy Linton	*Floodtide*	Harry Linton's niece
Henry Linton	*Floodtide*	Owner of a tobacco plantation on Key West
George and Henry Metcalf	*Floodtide*	Friends of Ross Pary
Muneca	*The Old Gods Laugh*	
Natalia	*An Odor of Sanctity*	Daughter of al-Wallid
Nyasanu Hwesu Kesu	*Dahomean/ A Darkness at Ingraham's Crest*	Wesley Parks' African name
Sharon O'Neill	*Pride's Castle*	
Wesley Parks	*Dahomean/A Darkness at Ingraham's Crest*	Escaped slave; former African prince
Ross Pary	*Floodtide*	Plantation owner/architect to planter elite
Pedro	*Floodtide*	Fisherman's nephew
Father Prefectus	*An Odor of Sanctity*	Pastor of San Acisclo's Church
Bruce Randolph	*Griffin's Way*	Sent by Lovegood Fund to build black school
Ruby	*A Darkness at Ingraham's Crest*	Wesley Parks' last wife
Father Shannon	*Pride's Castle*	
Enzio Siniscola	*The Saracen Blade*	
Abbot Spera	*An Odor of Sanctity*	Catholic apologist
Lady Sumayla	*An Odor of Sanctity*	Nasr's co-conspirator and Abulafia's protogé
Walad Tarub	*An Odor of Sanctity*	Emir's favorite wife
Theodora	*An Odor of Sanctity*	Alaric's daughter and

		Emir's daughter-in-law
Teudis Lord of Tarrabella	*An Odor of Sanctity*	Alaric's father
Wilks Thomas	*A Darkness at Ingraham's Crest*	Father of Abigail Collins
Tolomeo	*Floodtide*	Fisherman
Fanny Turner	*The Girl From Storyville*	
Wallace	*Floodtide*	Ross Pary's personal slave
Nathan ben Yehudah	*Judas, My Brother*	

LIST OF HISTORICAL PERSONAGES

Abraham Abulafia	Author of the Zohar
Abd al-Rahman II	Ninth-century emir of Spain
Abu'l Asi al-Hakam	father of Abu al-Rahman II
Ayagunda	A manifestation of Obatala
Alfonso II	Ninth-century King of Asturias
Akhenaton	Pharaoh of the Eighteenth Egyptian Dynasty 1350-1334 BC
Joaquin Aguero	Leader of the Cuban Revolt on July 4, 1851
Davy Atchison	United States Senator
Bickerton	Lawrence militia gunnery sergeant
Reverend Bishop	Pastor of Lawrence's Presyterian Church
Preston Brooks	South Carolina Congressman
John Brown	Militant Free Stater
James Buchanan	15th President of the United States
Judge Butler	South Carolina U.S. Senator
Carlos Casteneda	Twentieth-Century Author
Chango	Voodoo's Angry War God
Clintons	Plantation owners in Clinton County, Missouri

Reverend Cordley	Pastor of Lawrence's Episcopal Church
John Crittenden	U.S. Senator from Kentucky
William Crittenden	Lieutenant in militia/american mercenary
Caleb Cushing	U.S. Senator/ Attorney General of the United States
John J. Crittenden	President Millard Fillmore's Attorney General
Damballah	African Great Sky Father/ Rainbow Serpent
Frederick Douglass	Black crusader
Arthur Conan Doyle	Nineteenth-century author/spiritualist
Lyle Eastin	Editor Leavenworth's newspaper, *The Herald*
Colonel Angel Elizalde	Cuban military commander
General Manual Enna	Cuban military commander
Baldomero Espartero	Caudillo who overturned Spanish monarchy; Narciso Lopez's patron
Eulogius	Bishop of Toledo and martyr
Brett Falks	Owner Lawrence dry goods store
William Lloyd Garrison	Abolitionist
John Geary	Kansas territorial governor 1856-1857
Ambrosio Jose Gonzales	Havana Club agent
Shields Green	Participant in John Brown's Raid on Harper's Ferry
Jose Guiterrez de la Concha	Captain-General of Cuba/ Spanish Crown's personal Cuban representative
Charles Hamelton	Missouri bushwhacker
Hattie Hamilton	Madam of sporting establishment in Storyville
Ethan Allen Hitchcock	U.S. Army General/member, Council of Three of the Fraternitas Rosae Crucis
Lucy Holcombe	William Crittenden's fiancée
Gaius Jenkins	Free State leader
Lawrence Keitt	South Carolina U.S. Senator
General Jim Lane	Commander of the 1st Lawrence Militia
Amos Lawrence	Abolitionist/ Namesake of Lawrence, Kansas
Papa Legba	African Trickster God

Abraham Lincoln	Sixteenth President of the United States
Narciso Lopez	General who led two unsuccessful attempts to overthrow Spanish rule in Cuba
James Russell Lowell	Publisher of the *Atlantic Monthly*
Reverend May	Operator of an Underground Railroad station in Syracuse, New York
Stephen Meyers	Operator of an Underground Railroad station in Rensselaer, New York
A.B. Miller	Owner A.B. Miller's Saloon/ Leader of Leavenworth's Vigilance Committee
Colonel Joaquin de Rada Morales	Cuban military commander
Reverend Ephraim Nute	Pastor of Lawrence's Unitarian Church
Obatala	Voodoo God of Reason and Justice
Theodore O'Hara	Poet, "Bivouac of the Dead"
Oshun	Voodoo goddess/wife of Chango
Edgar Allen Poe	Writer
William Quantrell	Irregular Confederate Officer responsible for the Civil War Massacre in Lawrence, Kansas
John Quitman	General United States Army/Governor of Mississippi/ Sovereign Grand Inspector General of Scottish Rite Freemasonry
Governor Reeder	Kansas territorial governor
Dr. Charles Robinson	Kansas Free State governor
Major John Sedgewick	Commander U.S. internment camp
Wilson Shannon	Kansas territorial governor 1855-1856
Henry Shombre	Former Quaker/ Lawrence militiaman
Mott Sister	Operators of an Underground Railroad station in Albany, New York
Colonel E. V. Sumner	Fort Leavenworth's army commander
Charles Sumner	Massachusetts U.S. Senator
Charles Sumner	United States Senator
Harriett Tubman	Underground Railroad conductor

Cirilo Villaverde	Narciso Lopez's personal friend
David Walker	Author *David Walker's Appeal To the Coloured Citizens of the World*
Daniel Woodson	Acting Kansas territorial governor

LIST OF AUTHOR'S CHARACTERS

Moses Abulafia	Lady Sumayla's mentor
Judith Abulafia	Wife of Moses Abulafia
Babaluaye/Tolomeo	Voodoo high priest of the Lukumi
Boone, Tom	Hitchcock's Cathar recruit
Carlos	Ben Parks' friend
Carlota	Pedro's wife
Cobb	Judge Smith's slave
Louise Collins	Joe and Abigail's daughter
Claude Coombs	Slave catcher
Clifford Foote	Mayor of Lawrence
Hank	Slave shot in the head by Claude
Stoddard Hoyt	Mayor of Lawrence, Kansas
Dwight Ingraham Jr.	Dwight and Ellen's son
Elaine Ingraham	Dwight and Ellen's daughter
Jake	Slave catcher
Jim	Telegraph messenger
Josh	One of Claude's captives
Khalid	Lady Sumayla's servant

Lengvold	Abu L'Fath Nasr's Gothic name
Lucinda	Abby's black serving maid
Squire & Dame Matthews	Boston Property owners
Oma	Playmate of Conchita Izquierdo
Pete	The Matthews' dog
Gbenu/Ben Parks	Wesley and Ruby's son
Phoebe Parks	Wesley and Ruby's daughter
Quissan	Lady Sumayla's agent
Sam	Driver for Mott sisters
Scipio	Quitman's Slave
Judge Smith	Judge in Natchez court
Suzie	Cook for the Santa Fe roadhouse
Tommie	Ben Parks' friend
Yazmin	Lady Sumayla's maid

OVERVIEW OF YERBY' NOVELS

The Foxes of Harrow (1946)

When Stephen Fox arrived in New Orleans in 1825 on a pig boat, with a ten-dollar gold piece, a pearl stick pin, he pitted himself against the indolent, slave-ridden, castebound planters, with the skill and daring of the card-sharp he was. He gambled, won and built "Harrow", the greatest mansion house and plantation in Louisiana. He also took the love of three women: Odalie Orceneaux, his wife; her sister, Aurore; and Desiree, his Black mistress. Fox had a child by each of them. This story is charged with blood and passion and strife between the races.

The Vixens (1947)

America's latter-day secret societies are born in this sequel to The Foxes of Harrow: Defeated feudal lords of the South attempting to set back the clock of history. White Leaguers and Klansmen swoop down to terrorize recently liberated Blacks. Brawling, thieving northern carpetbaggers display no conscience other than the dollar sign. Mulatto half-breeds wander about with confused identities fall victim to there own confused behaviors. As creeping swamps and forests reclaim the once luxurious Southern mansions, scalawags, men of Southern birth and breeding, and carpetbaggers reach out and feed on the decay of a wounded, bitter South.

The Golden Hawk (1948)

This is the story of desperate men, escaping the harsh rule of European aristocrats whose voracious appetites for treasure outweighs all other considerations. Piracy became their only option and all of Europe felt their wrath.

Pride's Castle (1949)

Pride Dawson joined those "Robber Barons" whose brazen contempt for human decency or moral restraint left a legacy of the "public be damned" that is the cornerstone of American public policy ... even today. Ethically bankrupt and corrupt beyond comprehension, the robber barons perverted economic and political processes, converting the public good to their own personal ends and acquiring untold riches from the misery and work of poor workers. Dawson built an empire and destroyed all who opposed him. With plunder as a goal and power as an instrument, Pride's Castle depicts a man with an unbounded appetite for ruthlessness. And it also tells of his boundless love for Sharon O'Neill, a woman with as much goodness in her soul as he had evil.

Floodtide (1950)

Born in a shack on Natchez-Under-the-Hill, the abode of cutthroats, thieves, brawling river men and ladies of easy virtue, Ross Pary had but one goal: to reach Natchez-on-the Hill, where gentlemen planters lived a life of graciousness and ease in porticoed mansions. In physical distance, there was less than a mile between the two worlds, but in social distance, the residents of Natchez-on-the-Hill flourished a half-world away. Yet, there is more to Floodtide than Ross Pary's struggle for social acceptance through the passions and conflicts of his tangled loves. It is the very chivalrous world of the old South which reached the floodtide of its fortunes in the lush decade of the 1850s.

A Woman Called Fancy (1951)

Fancy fled an incestuous marriage arranged by a drunken father, with little education and no money. But with the priceless gifts of courage, honor and high personal integrity, she won out against all odds and wrenched from life a position of respect and security.

The Saracen Blade (1952)

The teeming world of the 13th century witnessed bright colors, banners fluttering against the sky above the lists at a tourney. Fair damsels with their long hair caught in cunning nets of gold thread, clad in silk and samite, velvet and ermine waved at bejeweled noblemen flaunting the arrogant insignias of their proud houses. A corps of sober monks clad in brown and black habits served the lordly bishops. And above all, the clean, bright gleam of a crusader's chain mail worn by nobles and knaves alike proclaiming that this society valued war above everything. This is a story of crusaders ... turning their savagery on Christian and heathen alike. A war against miserable serfs, wearing coarse jerkins smelling of dumb sweat, bound to their lord's service forever forced to labor on lands, which can never belong to them. This was a time when nobles, secure in their castles and armor felt secure enough to commit any barbarity no matter how ghastly upon the peasant. This is also the time when conspiracies, assassinations and proscriptions from Pope and King alike maintained the Holy Roman Empire in continual chaos and ceaseless war. These despised masses were beaten at their masters' whim, always hungry, old and toothless at forty, dying in the nobles' and priests' wars by the thousands and knowing not why. The European world held in a state of the mindless barbarism from which only nobles might escape. And heredity, rank and privilege were the rewards bestowed only upon the most evil and ruthless men. It was from these oppressed masses that Pietro di Donati, the son of a murdered blackmith sprang, to become a wealthy knight and to marry into one of the powerful families of Europe.

The Devil's Laughter (1953)

Down the street came a parade of children; they were beating a small keg for a drum and playing homemade flutes. And on the ends of improvised pikes, they bore the heads of three cats, still dripping blood. Even the French children who witnessing the spectacle of human heads daily paraded through Parisian streets had become inhuman monsters. Paris had become so paralyzed with hatred for everyone and everything associated with the noble class that reason, itself, stood decapitated. And during the French Revolution, French society and the French people sank into depravity. This was the society that Jean Paul Marin, who at the age of twenty, was beaten and imprisoned helped to create.

Bride of Liberty (1954)

Polly Knowles loved her sister's fiancé, Ethan Page. And even knowing, Ethan loved her sister still, Polly followed Ethan from bloody Bunker Hill to the bitterly cold campground of Valley Forge... and to the final victory at Yorktown winning his gratitude...and his love. This is the story of the birth of a nation and the forging of destiny.

Benton's Row (1954)

From the day in 1842 when Tom Benton arrives in the Red River Valley, one jump ahead of a Texas posse bent on hanging him, to the day in 1920 when his wife Sarah, aged ninety-seven, dies peacefully in her rocker on the veranda of the plantation house at Broad Acres, the history of one pioneering Southern family unfolds in a story of triumphs and tragedies. Set in the exotic and mysterious Louisiana river country, the spellbinding story of four brawling generations of Bentons and how it is brought to a violent end by its illicit black branch of the family is told.

The Treasure of Pleasant Valley (1955)

Handsome, aristocratic Bruce Harkness came to California in 1849 determined to erase the scars of the past. Behind him lay his family's ruined plantation, and the mocking memory of a beautiful woman who loved him but married another. Amid the feverish greed and brutality of a world gone mad, Harkness tasted a vengeance sweeter than love in the arms of his best friend's Mexican wife and in his insatiable lust for gold. This story tells how the life of a Mexican in California became forfeit.

Captain Rebel (1955)

This is the story of the little-known exploits of the Confederate blockade-runners who supplied the Confederacy with guns and supplies. Tyler Meredith, not only rebels against the United States, but he betrays his own kind by romancing a Negro beauty, Lauriel, in a strange, illicit affair. Lauriel's father, the slave-owning Rene Doumier who hates every drop of Negro blood in his own veins and Ben Butler, the Yankee General who occupied New Orleans earning the title, 'the Beast' make this a never to be forgotten story.

Fairoaks (1956)

Guy Falks, a Southern aristocrat, who, without knowing it, lived a lie about his heritage. He earns a fortune in the African slave trade by forming a partnership with a chieftain whose desire for white women makes him willing to sell his own people in order to feed his lusts. Fairoaks tells the story of a vast Southern plantation and of four generations of angry men and loyal women willing to make any sacrifice for its possession. Driven by the twin furies of ambition and revenge, Guy Falks immerses himself and others for eighteen long years in the evils of selling human flesh even as he indulges his own passions with women from the despised and despoiled African race.

The Serpent and the Staff (1958)

Duncan Childers was born to be a physician, but is driven by a rendezvous with fate and the passionate love of two women. Childers emerges from the crushing poverty of New Orleans' Irish Channel only through the support of the social prominence and connections of one woman but experiences self-sacrifice and dedication of another. Great were the forces arrayed against him: the hate of a woman who was his wife and the love of the woman who was his nurse. Also this is the tale of how a former slave struggled to bring the blessing of modern medicine to his own people despite the wrath of the Ku Klux Klan who vowed to keep all 'niggers' in their place.

Jarrett's Jade (1959)

James Jarrett arrived in Savannah in 1736, clad in kilt and tartan, the first of the Georgia Jarretts, a Highland aristocrat, Laird of Clan Jarrett's. He meant to reestablish Clan Jarrett as a great Southern dynasty in the New World. But his love for Simone Duclos whom he purchased at a slave auction, forced Jarrett to live a double life, eventually driving the son on the eve of the War for Independence in 1776 to hate own his father.

Gillian (1960)

Gillian, the heiress of an Alabama fortune, is capable of great loving kindness and an appetite for corrupting and ruining lives.

The Garfield Honor (1961)

Roak Garfield loves a woman and leaves for the Civil War. But a cruel fate causes the woman to kill herself and her unborn child. Vowing vengeance, the woman's brother searches for Roak across the Texas panhandle where he learns that Roark has married the daughter of a wealthy rancher. Escaping to Mexico, Garfield becomes involved with a beautiful Mexican woman whose brother also vows to kill the American for his sister's honor. This is a story terrible game of cat-and-mouse played by desperate men across half a nation. It also is a story of women who find themselves helplessly trapped in schemes of vengeance and power.

Griffin's Way (1962)

Di Cadwallader, head of the Ku Klux Klan, has determined that in post-war Mississippi there will be no equality between the races even if he must murder women and children and whites and blacks, alike. Even Laurie Griffin, the wife of another man, who Cadwallader claims to love those is not safe from his murderous intent. The climate of evil is so compelling that the black man, sent to educate the children of ex-slaves, embezzles the funds he is given and amasses a personal fortune with which he intends to flee North. This is a story about what actually happened in the South after the Civil War.

The Old Gods Laugh (1964)

Almost immediately on his arrival in Costa Verde, a fictitious Central American republic, the American correspondent, Peter Reynolds, is plunged into the violent revolution against the dictator, Miguel Villalonga. The key to the revolution lies with Padre Pio, the Catholic priest held hostage in the mountains by a band of guerrillas. This man of god wields power over the Indian peons and is sought both by the dictator as well as the guerrillas dedicated to his overthrow. Yet, the conflict is determined by the "old gods" residing in the great volcano of Zopocomapetl which erupts, pouring their fury upon rulers and rebels alike.

An Odor of Sanctity (1965)

In the tumultuous battleground between East and West that was Spain, Alaric, the Christian Goth, wades through the raging sea of religious passion and hate. Raised as a Christian, admired by the Moors and employed by the Jews, Alaric is a feared swordsman as well as a scholar and prophet. Some claimed that he was a saint, others a devil and in the end he could have been the messiah. It might have been better had the Emir, al-Rahman II followed the advice of his counselors and put Alaric to death. But in the end, he, too, fell under Alaric's spell ... preparing the fall of Islamic Spain to arian Christianity.

Goat Song (1967)

Ancient Greece is where Ariston, a young heroic Spartan, is cursed and blessed by a the Hellenic ideal of male beauty. This is the time of the Peloponnesian War, a period of dynamic energy, of burgeoning culture and festering decadence, of excessive cruelty and ... male sexuality. Here on battlefield and slave market, temple and brothel, is found the discourses of Socrates and the Dionysian revel of Alcibiades, the brutalizing code of Sparta and the brilliant sophistication of Athens. Ariston enslaved and brought to Athens is fated to see how these competing philosophies force Sparta to engineer her own defeat.

Judas, My Brother (1968)

Frank Yerby writes in Judas, My Brother: "This novel touches on only two issues which, in a certain sense, might be called controversial: whether any man truly has the right to believe fanciful and childish nonsense; and whether any organization has the right to impose, by almost imperial fiat, belief in things that simply are not so. To me, irrationality is dangerous; perhaps the most dangerous force stalking through the world today. This novel, then, is one man's plea for an ecumenicism broad enough to include reasonable men; and his effort to defend his modest intellect from intolerable insult."

Speak Now (1969)

Harry Forbes didn't give a damn about Paris. It was a city, a place where he could earn good money as a jazz musician, a place to forget his blackness. There was no room in his life for a white girl like Kathy Nichols. She was too young, too much the daughter of a wealthy Southern tobacco planter. But Harry found himself giving his name to another man's child and marrying this white woman that he dared not love.

The Dahomean (1971)

Nyasanu Dosu Agausu Hwesu Gbokau Kesu, was son of Gbenu, a great chief. Hwesu, himself, was governor of the province of Alladah in Dahomey, husband to six wives one of whom was daughter of the king. Hwesu was a young lion. He was unconquerable in the battles waged over a vast empire ravaged by tribal wars. But Hwesu was betrayed by his own brother and sold to the white men who came in tall ships to tie black slaves in chains and to a strange land across the sea.

The Girl from Storyville (1972)

From the very beginning fate drove Fannie Turner in a most terrible way. Her life circumstances, family, evil her own desires conspired to drive her not only to make the wrong choices, but have not the slightest inkling of what it would take to slow or even halt her descent into hell. Fannie Turner is driven by the idea of her own evil nature and this idea drives her into believing that she must behave as if she were evil. Deserted by her own prostitute mother, Fanny confuses her need to find love and respectability with behavior which invites only betrayal and humiliation. She is fated to work in Storyville, the notorious New Orleans red light district at her own mother's house of prostitution. Even Phillippe Sompayac, who offers Fanny a way out and a respectable life is damned for even knowing her.

The Voyage Unplanned (1974)

Life in WWII France and the titanic struggle against the Nazi holocaust is described in this passionate story of a Jewish woman willing to fight and die for freedom. It is also the story of John Farrow, a man in love with the lovely Jewess and the story of their war-torn past. She had vanished in Nazi-occupied France and he believed her dead. But now her ghost haunts him and he has reason to believe she survived the holocaust and his betrayal. So he must find her. It is also a story of the founding of the OSS (which would be rechristened as the CIA), and how it adopted the Gestapo's methods of population control and terror.

Tobias and the Angel (1975)

Tobias and the Angel is a wild, extravagant and erotic comedy describing the sexual revolution of the sixties.

A Rose for Ana Maria (1976)

Diego, a young Spanish revolutionary living in Paris, has killed the Spanish Consul to France. It was a revolutionary act ordered by his superiors in Spain. He intends to return to Spain and continue the fight against fascism that had been being waged since the beginning of the Spanish Civil War in 1935. But in exchange for help to flee France, Diego must team up with another revolutionary, Ana Maria, the foul-mouthed, provocative daughter of aristocracy for another assignment: another assassination. Their story is one of how youthful idealism can lead not only to love... but also tragedy.

Hail the Conquering Hero (1978)

In this sequel to The Old Gods Laugh, Manuel Garcia Herredia, another dictator, controls Costa Verde. Herredia uses bribery, blackmail and murder to protect a vast heroin empire known only to the United States State Department. Costa Verde is a virtual concentration camp.

Herredia believes the new United States ambassador, James Randolf Rush, to be a potential threat and attempts to ensnares Rush in a sex scandal leading to disgrace... and recall. But when the voluptuous teenaged courtesan, Herredia delivers to Rush's living quarters divulges Herredia's plan, Rush threatens to go public with his dicription of the atrocities committed against the women of Costa Verde. After that not only is Rush's reputation ... but his very life is in danger.

A Darkness at Ingraham's Crest (1979)

In this sequel to the The Dahomean, Hwesu, has lost his land and people and even his name. No longer Nyasanu Dosu Agausu Hwesu Gbokau Kesu, was son of Gbenu, he is simply Wes Parks, black slave. Yet, Hwesu has lost neither his physical power nor his metalworking and healing skills... nor the magic left to him by his Dahomean ancestors. And through the magic of his ancestors, his own intelligence and will and devotion to the spirits, Hwesu wages a relentless struggle against his white masters, Confounding their assertion of intellectual superiority at every turn ... until he demostrates all with the intelligence to understand,,, whites as well his own people the basic inferiority of the plantation master. And how he will eventually be defeated. But if there is a white person who can see how Wes intends to use his power, it is the Northern-born, liberal-minded, Pamela Bibbs, owner of the Ingraham's Crest plantation. And despite the twisted feelings and emotional ties Pamela has for this Black slave, Pamela, too, becomes swept up into the evil consciousness of being a slave owner whose use of the whip on her hapless victims is a brutal and savage as any of the other white plantation masters. And Wes realizes that if he is to make good his plans for escape and revenge, he must decide how to handle Pamela Bibbs.

Western (1982)

This tale of love, honor and revenge is set in the post-civil war period of Kansas. The settling of these American grasslands and how the life of a Civil War veteran, Ethan Lovejoy, who is haunted by the fact that he murdered his own brother was determined by the inexorable economic forces which smiled upon Abilene and rejected Marthasville. And it is the story of the transition of Kansas from a territory to a state.

Devilseed (1984)

In the 1850s, gold lures thousands to California. Miners dug it, Bankers stacked it... and the glittering bordellos of the Barbary Coast was where Murielle Duclos who sailed into San Francisco at the age of fifteen years old was sent to get it. Abused and controlled by her mother's lover, Murielle was forced into a life of prostitution. But even there, the political struggle between the Mexicanos and the Americans for ultimate control of California, gave Murielle the opportunity to become wealthier than all her rivals. Murielle realized her ambitions by understanding a simple fact: in the Golden State, power is more important than gold.

McKensie's Hundred (1985)

Rambling Rose McKensie is caught up in the Civil War in a way no self-respecting daughter of one of Virginia First Families should have been. Under the spell of Count Sisimond Kurt Radetsky, a member of the Austrian Death's Head Secret Service Rose serves the confederacy as a spy. Rose believes in the South's aristocratic pretensions of chivalry and honor. She hopes that her sacrifices will make the cavalier aware of how equally endowed with feelings of honor, courage and patriotism are Southern women who want but the opportunity to be respected by their men. It takes Radetsky's murder of innocent black children during the New York Draft riots to make Rose realize what an absolutely monster she has married and the evil basis of the entire southern way of life.